Praise for THE NAMING OF THE DEAD

'Masterly . . . Ian Rankin's finest novel. It is more than a crime novel, or rather, Rankin's achievement is to show, convincingly, how crime permeates society'   *Scotsman*

'His richest and most complex work to date, it comes close to transcending genre fiction'   *Scotland on Sunday*

'Rebus may seem to be running on something very near empty, but there is no sign that Rankin has lost any of the energy to continue this consistently impressive series'
Sunday Times

'Combines the page-turning appeal of a modern police procedural with the moral complexity of a political novel'
Irish Times

'Politics crashes head on into Inspector Rebus's usual interests (solving grisly murders and supping pints) in the latest of this award-winning series. *The Naming of the Dead* set against the 2005 G8 Summit is yet another irresistible page-turner from the UK's best crime novelist'
Mail on Sunday

'Not only an intriguing murder-mystery but an excellent piece of reportage. Ian Rankin, despite his dodgy musical tastes, has produced yet another class act'
Evening Standard

'This one, with its heady mix of crime and current affairs, is staggering. He is now at the top of his game and has almost catapulted himself out of the more limited crime genre altogether'   *Daily Mail*

'Rankin is on top form here, with a suitably scornful attitude to Bob Geldof and the wishy-washy Live 8 endeavour. Excellent stuff'   *Dublin Evening Herald*

Born in the Kingdom of Fife in 1960, Ian Rankin graduated from the University of Edinburgh and has since been employed as grape-picker, swineherd, taxman, alcohol researcher, hi-fi journalist and punk musician. His first Rebus novel, *Knots & Crosses*, was published in 1987 and the Rebus books have now been translated into 26 languages. Ian Rankin has been elected a Hawthornden Fellow, and is a past winner of the prestigious Chandler-Fulbright Award, as well as two CWA short-story 'Daggers' and the 1997 CWA Macallan Gold Dagger for Fiction for *Black & Blue*, which was also shortlisted for the Mystery Writers of America Edgar Award for Best Novel. Several Rebus novels have been televised on ITV, starring John Hannah and, most recently, Ken Stott as Inspector Rebus. *Dead Souls*, the tenth novel in the series, was shortlisted for the CWA Gold Dagger Award in 1999. An Alumnus of the Year at Edinburgh University, he has also been awarded four honorary doctorates, from the University of Abertay Dundee in 1999, from the University of St Andrews in 2001, in 2003 from the University of Edinburgh and in 2005 from the Open University. In 2002 Ian Rankin was awarded an OBE for services to literature. In 2004 *Resurrection Men* won the Edgar Award for Best Novel. In 2005 *Fleshmarket Close* won the Crime Thriller of the Year award at the British Book Awards. Ian is the winner of the Crime Writers' Association Diamond Dagger 2005. In 2005 he was also awarded the Grand Prix de Littérature Policière (France), the Deutsche Krimi Prize (Germany) and the Icons of Scotland award. He lives in Edinburgh with his wife and two sons. Visit his website at www.ianrankin. net.

By Ian Rankin

The Inspector Rebus series
Knots & Crosses
Hide & Seek
Tooth & Nail
(previously published as Wolfman)
Strip Jack
The Black Book
Mortal Causes
Let It Bleed
Black & Blue
The Hanging Garden
Death Is Not The End (*novella*)
Dead Souls
Set in Darkness
The Falls
Resurrection Men
A Question of Blood
Fleshmarket Close
The Naming of the Dead
Exit Music

Other novels
The Flood
Watchman
Westwind

Writing as Jack Harvey
Witch Hunt
Bleeding Hearts
Blood Hunt

Short stories
A Good Hanging and Other Stories
Beggars Banquet

Omnibus editions
Rebus: The Early Years (Knots & Crosses, Hide & Seek, Tooth & Nail)
Rebus: The St Leonard Years (Strip Jack, The Black Book, Mortal Causes)
Rebus: The Lost Years (Let It Bleed, Black & Blue, The Hanging Garden)
Rebus: Capital Crimes (Dead Souls, Set in Darkness, The Falls)

All Ian Rankin's titles are available on audio. Also available: *Jackie Leven Said* by Ian Rankin and Jackie Leven.

Ian Rankin

The Naming
of the Dead

An Orion paperback

First published in Great Britain in 2006
by Orion
This paperback edition published in 2007
by Orion Books Ltd,
Orion House, 5 Upper St Martin's Lane,
London WC2H 9EA

An Hachette Livre UK company

Typeset by Deltatype Ltd, Birkenhead, Merseyside

Printed and bound in Great Britain by Clays Ltd, St Ives plc

The Orion Publishing Group's policy is to use papers that
are natural, renewable and recyclable products and
made from wood grown in sustainable forests. The logging
and manufacturing processes are expected to conform to
the environmental regulations of the country of origin

www.orionbooks.co.uk

To everyone who was in Edinburgh on 2 July 2005

We have the choice to try for a new world every day, to tell what we know of the truth every day, to take small actions every day.

A. L. Kennedy, writing about the march on Gleneagles

Write us a chapter to be proud of.

Bono, in a message to the G8

SIDE ONE
The Task of Blood

Friday 1 July 2005

1

In place of a closing hymn, there was music. The Who, 'Love Reign O'er Me'. Rebus recognised it the moment it started, thunderclaps and teeming rain filling the chapel. He was in the front pew; Chrissie had insisted. He'd rather have been further back: his usual place at funerals. Chrissie's son and daughter sat next to her. Lesley was comforting her mother, an arm around her as the tears fell. Kenny stared straight ahead, storing up emotion for later. Earlier that morning, back at the house, Rebus had asked him his age. He would be thirty next month. Lesley was two years younger. Brother and sister looked like their mother, reminding Rebus that people had said the same about Michael and him: *The pair of you, the spit of your mum.* Michael ... Mickey if you preferred. Rebus's younger brother, dead in a shiny-handled box at the age of fifty-four, Scotland's mortality rate that of a Third World nation. Lifestyle, diet, genes – plenty of theories. The full post-mortem hadn't come through yet. Massive stroke was what Chrissie had told Rebus on the phone, assuring him that it was 'sudden' – as if that made a difference.

Sudden meant Rebus hadn't been able to say goodbye. It meant his last words to Michael had been a joke about his beloved Raith Rovers in a phone call three months back. A Raith scarf, navy and white, had been draped over the coffin alongside the wreaths. Kenny was wearing a tie that had been his dad's, Raith's shield on it – some kind of animal holding a belt-buckle. Rebus had asked the significance, but Kenny had just shrugged. Looking along the pew, Rebus saw the usher make a gesture. Everyone rose to their feet. Chrissie started walking up the aisle, flanked by her children. The usher looked to Rebus, but he stayed where he was. Sat down again so the others would know they didn't have to wait for him. The song was only a little over halfway through. It was the closing track on *Quadrophenia*. Michael had been the big Who fan, Rebus himself preferring the Stones. Had to admit, though, albums like *Tommy* and *Quadrophenia* did things the Stones never could. Daltrey was whooping that he could use a drink. Rebus had to agree, but there was the drive back to Edinburgh to consider.

The function room of a local hotel had been booked. All were welcome, as the minister had reminded them from the pulpit. Whisky and tea would be poured, sandwiches served. There would be anecdotes and reminiscences, smiles, dabs at the eyes, hushed tones. The staff would move quietly, out of respect. Rebus was trying to form sentences in his head, words which would act as his apology.

I need to get back, Chrissie. Pressure of work.

He could lie and blame the G8. That morning in the house, Lesley had said he must be busy with the build-up. He could have told her, *I'm the only cop they don't seem to need.* Officers were being drafted in from all over. Fifteen hundred were coming from London alone. Yet Detective Inspector John Rebus seemed surplus to requirements. Someone had to man the ship – the very words DCI James Macrae had used, with his acolyte smirking by his shoulder. DI Derek Starr reckoned himself the heir apparent to Macrae's throne. One day he'd be running Gayfield Square police station. John Rebus posed no threat whatsoever, not much more than a year away from retirement. Starr himself had said as much: *Nobody'd blame you for coasting, John. It's what anyone your age would do.* Maybe so, but the Stones were older than Rebus; Daltrey and Townshend were older than him too. Still playing, still touring.

The song was ending now, and Rebus rose to his feet again. He was alone in the chapel. Took a final look at the purple velvet screen. Maybe the coffin was still behind it; maybe it had already been moved to another part of the crematorium. He thought back to adolescence, two brothers in their shared bedroom, playing 45s bought down Kirkcaldy High Street. 'My Generation' and 'Substitute', Mickey asking about Daltrey's stutter on the former, Rebus saying he'd read somewhere that it was to do with drugs. The only drug the brothers had indulged in was alcohol, mouthfuls stolen from the bottles in the pantry, a can of sickly stout broken open and shared after lights-out. Standing on Kirkcaldy promenade, staring out to sea, and Mickey singing the words to 'I Can See For Miles'. But could that really have happened? The record came out in '66 or '67, by which time Rebus was in the army. Must have been on a trip back. Yes, Mickey with his shoulder-length hair, trying to copy Daltrey's look, and Rebus with his forces crop, inventing stories to make army life seem exciting, Northern Ireland still ahead of him …

They'd been close back then, Rebus always sending letters and postcards, his father proud of him, proud of both the boys.

The spit of your mum.

He stepped outside. The cigarette packet was already open in his hand. There were other smokers around him. They offered nods, shuffling their feet. The various wreaths and cards had been lined up next to the door, and were being studied by the mourners. The usual words would crop up: 'condolence' and 'loss' and 'sorrow'. The family would be 'in our thoughts'. Michael wouldn't be mentioned by name. Death brought its own set of protocols. The younger mourners were checking for text messages on their phones. Rebus dug his own out of his pocket and switched it on. Five missed calls, all from the same number. Rebus knew it from memory, pushed the

7

buttons and raised the phone to his ear. Detective Sergeant Siobhan Clarke was quick to answer.

'I've been trying you all morning,' she complained.

'I had it switched off.'

'Where are you anyway?'

'Still in Kirkcaldy.'

There was an intake of breath. 'Hell, John, I completely forgot.'

'Don't worry about it.' He watched Kenny open the car door for Chrissie. Lesley was motioning to Rebus, letting him know they were headed for the hotel. The car was a BMW, Kenny doing all right for himself as a mechanical engineer. He wasn't married; had a girlfriend but she hadn't been able to make it to the funeral. Lesley was divorced, her own son and daughter off on holiday with their dad. Rebus nodded at her as she got into the back of the car.

'I thought it was next week,' Siobhan was saying.

'I take it you're phoning for a gloat?' Rebus started walking towards his Saab. Siobhan had been in Perthshire the past two days, accompanying Macrae on a recce of G8 security. Macrae was old pals with Tayside's Assistant Chief Constable. All Macrae wanted was a nosy, his friend happy to oblige. The G8 leaders would meet at Gleneagles Hotel, on the outskirts of Auchterarder, nothing around them but acres of wilderness and miles of ring-fenced security. There had been plenty of scare stories in the media. Reports of three thousand US Marines landing in Scotland to protect their president. Anarchist plots to block roads and bridges with hijacked trucks. Bob Geldof had demanded that a million demonstrators besiege Edinburgh. They would be housed, he said, in people's spare rooms, garages and gardens. Boats would be sent to France to pick up protesters. Groups with names like Ya Basta and the Black Bloc would aim for chaos, while the People's Golfing Association wanted to break the cordon to play a few holes of Gleneagles' renowned course.

'I'm spending two days with DCI Macrae,' Siobhan was saying. 'What's to gloat about?'

Rebus unlocked his car, and leaned in to slide the key into the ignition. He straightened again, took a last drag on his cigarette and flicked the butt on to the roadway. Siobhan was saying something about a Scene of Crime team.

'Hold on,' Rebus told her. 'I didn't catch that.'

'Look, you've got enough on your plate without this.'

'Without what?'

'Remember Cyril Colliar?'

'Despite my advancing years, the memory's not quite packed in.'

'Something really strange has happened.'

'What?'

'I think I've found the missing piece.'

'Of what?'

'The jacket.'

Rebus found that he'd lowered himself on to the driver's seat. 'I don't understand.'

Siobhan gave a nervous laugh. 'Me neither.'

'So where are you now?'

'Auchterarder.'

'And that's where the jacket's turned up?'

'Sort of.'

Rebus swung his legs into the car and pulled the door shut. 'Then I'm coming to take a look. Is Macrae with you?'

'He went to Glenrothes. That's where the G8 control centre is.' She paused. 'Are you sure you should be doing this?'

Rebus had started the engine. 'I need to make my apologies first, but I can be there inside the hour. Will I have any trouble getting into Auchterarder?'

'It's the calm before the storm. When you're driving through town, look for the sign to the Clootie Well.'

'The what?'

'Easier if you just come and see for yourself.'

'Then that's what I'll do. Scene of Crime on their way?'

'Yes.'

'Which means word will get around.'

'Should I tell the DCI?'

'I'll let you decide.' Rebus had wedged the phone between his shoulder and his cheek, so he could steer the mazy course to the gates of the crematorium.

'You're breaking up,' Siobhan said.

Not if I can help it, Rebus thought to himself.

Cyril Colliar had been murdered six weeks before. Aged twenty, he'd been locked away on a fixed ten-year stretch for a vicious rape. At the end of the sentence, he'd been released, despite the reservations of prison warders, police and social services. They reckoned he was as big a threat as ever, having shown no remorse, denying his guilt despite DNA evidence. Colliar had returned to his native Edinburgh. All the body-building he'd done in prison paid off. He worked as a nighttime bouncer and daytime muscle. His employer on both counts was Morris Gerald Cafferty. 'Big Ger' was a villain of long standing. It had been Rebus's job to confront him about his latest employee.

'What do I care?' had been the retort.

'He's dangerous.'

'Way you're hassling him would try the patience of a saint.' Cafferty swinging from side to side on his leather swivel chair, behind his desk at MGC Lettings. Anyone was slow with the weekly rent on one of Cafferty's flats, Rebus reckoned that was where Colliar would take over. Cafferty ran minicabs too, and owned at least three rau-cous bars in the less salubrious parts of town. Plenty of work for Cyril Colliar.

Right up until the night he'd turned up dead. Skull caved in, the blow coming from behind. Pathologist reckoned he'd have died from that alone, but just to make sure, someone had added a syringe of very pure heroin. No indication that the deceased had been a user. 'Deceased' was the word most of the cops on the case had used – and grudgingly at that. Nobody bothered with the term 'victim'. Nobody could say the words out loud – *bastard got what he deserved* – that wasn't the done thing these days.

Didn't stop them thinking it, sharing it through eye contact and slow nods. Rebus and Siobhan had worked the case, but it had been one amongst many. Few leads and too many suspects. The rape victim had been interviewed, along with her family and her boyfriend from the time. One word kept coming up in discussing Colliar's fate.

'Good.'

His body had been found near his car, down a side street next to the bar he'd been working. No witnesses, no scene-of-crime evidence. Just the one curiosity: a sharp blade had been used to slice away part of his distinctive jacket. It was a black nylon bomber, emblazoned with the phrase *CC Rider* on the back. This was what had been removed, so that the white inner lining was revealed. Theories were in short supply. It was either a clumsy attempt to disguise the deceased's identity, or there had been something hidden in the lining. Tests had proved negative for traces of drugs, leaving the police to shrug and scratch their heads.

To Rebus, it looked like a hit. Either Colliar had made an enemy, or a message was being sent to Cafferty. Not that their several interviews with Colliar's employer had been enlightening.

'Bad for my reputation,' was Cafferty's main reaction. 'Means either you catch whoever did it ...'

'Or?'

But Cafferty hadn't needed to answer. And if Cafferty

got to the culprit first, it would be the last that was ever heard of them.

None of which had helped. The inquiry had hit a wall, around the same time G8 preparations started focusing minds – most of them driven by images of overtime pay – elsewhere. Other cases had intruded, too, with victims – *real* victims. The Colliar murder team had been wound down.

Rebus lowered his driver's-side window, welcoming the cool breeze. He didn't know the quickest route to Auchterarder; knew Gleneagles could be reached from Kinross, so had headed that way. A couple of months back, he'd bought satnav for the car, but hadn't got round to reading the instructions yet. It lay on the passenger seat, screen blank. One of these days he'd take it to the garage which had installed the car's CD player. An inspection of the back seat, floors and boot had failed to turn up anything by The Who, so Rebus was listening to Elbow instead – Siobhan's recommendation. He liked the title track, 'Leaders of the Free World'. Stuck it on repeat. The singer seemed to think something had gone wrong since the sixties. Rebus tended to agree, even coming at it from a different direction. He reckoned the singer would have liked more change, a world run by Greenpeace and CND, poverty made history. Rebus had been on a few marches himself in the sixties, before and after joining the army. It was a way to meet girls, if nothing else. Usually there was a party somewhere afterwards. These days, though, he saw the sixties as the end of something. A fan had been stabbed to death at a Stones concert in 1969, and the decade had petered out. The 1960s had given youth a taste for revolt. They didn't trust the old order, certainly didn't respect it. He wondered about the thousands who would descend on Gleneagles, confrontation a racing certainty. Hard to imagine it in this landscape of farms and hillsides, rivers and glens. He knew that Gleneagles' very isolation would have been a factor in its choice as venue. The leaders of the free world would be safe there, safe to sign their names to decisions which had already been taken elsewhere. On the stereo, the band were singing about climbing a landslide. The image stuck with Rebus all the way to the outskirts of Auchterarder.

He didn't think he'd been there before. All the same, he seemed to know the place. Typical small Scottish town: a single, well-defined main street with narrow side roads leading off, built to a notion that people would walk to their local shops. Small, independently owned shops at that: he didn't see much that would inflame the anti-globalisation campaigners. The baker was even selling limited edition G8 pies.

The good folk of Auchterarder, Rebus seemed to recall, had been vetted, under guise of providing them with ID badges. These would be necessary so they could cross the eventual barricades. Yet as Siobhan had pointed out, there was an eerie tranquillity to the place. Only a few shoppers, and one joiner who seemed to be measuring up windows for protective boards. The cars were muddy 4x4s, which had probably spent more time on farm tracks than motorways. One woman driver was even wearing a headscarf, something Rebus hadn't seen in a while. Within a couple of minutes he was at the far end of town and heading towards the A9. He did a three-point turn and this time kept his eyes open for signposts. The one he wanted was next to a pub, pointing down a lane. He signalled, following the road past hedges and driveways, then a newer housing estate. The landscape opened before him, showing distant hills. In moments he was out of town again, flanked by neat hedgerows which would leave their mark on his car if he had to make way for a tractor or delivery van. There were some woods to his left, and another pointer told him this was home to the Clootie Well. He knew the word from clootie dumpling: a sticky steamed dessert his mother had sometimes made. He remembered the taste and texture as being similar to Christmas pudding. Dark and cloying and sugary. His stomach gave a small protest, reminding him that he hadn't eaten in hours. His stop at the hotel had been brief, a few quiet words with Chrissie. She'd hugged him, just as she had done back at the house earlier that morning. All the years he'd known her, there hadn't been many hugs. In the early days, he'd actually fancied her; awkward under the circumstances. She'd seemed to sense this. Then he'd been best man at the wedding, and, during one dance, she'd blown mischievously in his ear. Later, on the few occasions when she and Mickey had been separated, Rebus had taken his brother's side. He supposed he could have called her, said something, but he hadn't. And when Mickey had got into that spot of bother, ended up in jail, Rebus hadn't visited Chrissie and the kids. Mind you, he hadn't visited Mickey that often either, in jail or since.

There was more history: when Rebus and his own wife had separated, Chrissie had blamed him entirely. She'd always got on well with Rhona; kept in touch with her after the divorce. That was family for you. Tactics, campaigning and diplomacy: the politicians had it easy by comparison.

Back at the hotel, Lesley had mimicked her mother, giving him a hug too. Kenny had thought for a second before Rebus put the lad out of his misery by extending a hand to be squeezed. He wondered if there would be any fallings-out; there usually were at funerals. With grief came blame and resentment. Just as well he hadn't stayed. When it came to the potential for confrontation, John Rebus punched well above his already substantial weight.

There was a parking area just off the road. It looked like new-build, trees having been cleared, chippings of bark strewn across the ground. Room enough for four cars, but only one was waiting. Siobhan Clarke was leaning against it, arms folded. Rebus pulled on the brake and got out.

'Nice spot,' he said.

14

'Been here over a hundred years,' she told him.

'Didn't think I drove that slowly.'

She offered only a twist of the mouth, leading him into the woods, arms still folded. She was dressed more formally than usual: knee-length black skirt and black tights. Her shoes were smudged, having walked this same trail earlier.

'I saw the sign yesterday,' she was saying. 'The one leading off the main drag. Decided I'd take a look.'

'Well, if the choice was that or Glenrothes ...'

'There's a noticeboard back at the clearing, tells you a bit about the place. All sorts of witchy goings-on down the years.' They were ascending a slope, rounding a thick, twisted oak. 'The townspeople decided there must be sprites living here: shrieks in the dark, that sort of thing.'

'Local farmhands more like,' Rebus offered.

She nodded agreement. 'All the same, they started leaving little offerings. Hence the name.' She glanced around at him. 'You'll know what clootie means, you being the only native Scot around here?'

He had a sudden image of his mother lifting the pudding out of its pan. The pudding wrapped in ...

'Cloth,' he told her.

'And clothing,' she added as they entered another clearing. They stopped and Rebus breathed deeply. Damp cloth ... damp, rotting cloth. He'd been smelling it for the past half-minute. The smell clothes gave off in his old house, the one he'd grown up in, when they weren't aired, when the damp and the mildew got to them. The trees around him were strung with rags and remnants. Pieces had fallen to the ground, where they were decomposing to a mulch.

'Tradition has it,' Siobhan said quietly, 'they were left here for good luck. Keep the sprites warm, and they'd see no harm came to you. Another theory: when kids died young, their parents left something here, by way

15

of remembrance.' Her voice caught, and she cleared her throat.

'I'm not made of glass,' Rebus assured her. 'You can use words like "remembrance" – I'm not going to start blubbing.'

She nodded again. Rebus was walking around the clearing. Leaves and soft moss underfoot, and the sound of a stream, just a thin trickle of water pushing up from the ground. Candles and coins had been left by its edges.

'Not much of a well,' he commented.

She just shrugged. 'I was here a few minutes ... didn't really warm to the atmosphere. But then I noticed some of the newer clothing.' Rebus saw it too. Strung from the branches. A shawl, a boilersuit, a red polka-dot handkerchief. A nearly-new training shoe, its laces dangling. Even underwear and what looked like children's tights.

'Christ, Siobhan,' Rebus muttered, not really knowing what else to say. The smell seemed to be growing stronger. He had another flashback: to a ten-day bender many years before ... coming out of it to find that a load of washing had been sitting in the machine, waiting to be hung. When he'd opened the door, this same smell had hit him. He'd washed everything again, but still had to throw it all away afterwards. 'And the jacket?'

All she did was point. Rebus walked slowly towards the tree in question. The piece of nylon had been pierced by a short branch. It swayed just a little in the breeze. Threads straggling from it, but no mistaking the logo.

'*CC Rider*,' Rebus said in confirmation. Siobhan was running her hands through her hair. He knew she had questions, knew she would have been turning them over in her mind all the time she'd been waiting for him. 'So what do we do?' he prompted.

'It's a crime scene,' she began. 'A team are on their way from Stirling. We need to secure the locus, comb the area for evidence. We need to reassemble the original murder squad, start doorstepping locally ...'

'Including Gleneagles?' Rebus interrupted. 'You're the expert, so you tell me: how many times have the hotel staff been vetted? And how do we go about doorstepping in the middle of a week-long demo? Securing the locus won't be a problem, mind you, not with all the secret service teams we're about to welcome ...'

Naturally she had considered all these points. He knew as much and his voice trailed off.

'We keep it quiet till the summit's over,' she suggested.

'Tempting,' he admitted.

She smiled. 'Only because it gives *you* a head start.'

He admitted as much with a wink.

She sighed. 'Macrae needs to be told. Which means he'll tell Tayside Police.'

'But the SOCOs are coming from Stirling,' Rebus added, 'and Stirling belongs to Central Region.'

'So that's just the three police forces who need to know ... Shouldn't have any trouble keeping it under wraps.'

Rebus was looking around. 'If we can at least get the scene checked and photographed ... take the cloth back to the lab ...'

'Before the fun and games start?'

Rebus puffed out his cheeks. 'Kicks off on Wednesday, right?'

'The G8 does, yes. But there's the Poverty March tomorrow and another planned for Monday.'

'In Edinburgh, though, not Auchterarder ...' Then he saw what she was getting at. Even with the evidence at the lab, the whole place could be under siege. Getting from Gayfield Square to the lab at Howdenhall meant crossing the city ... always supposing the technicians had managed to force their way into work.

'Why leave it here?' Siobhan asked, studying the patch again. 'Some sort of trophy?'

'If so, why here specifically?'

'Could be local. Any family connections with the area?'

'I think Colliar's solid Edinburgh.'

She looked at him. 'I meant the rape victim.'

Rebus formed his mouth into an O.

'Something to consider,' she added. Then she paused. 'What's that sound?'

Rebus patted his stomach. 'While since I've eaten. Don't suppose Gleneagles is open for afternoon tea?'

'Depends on your overdraft. There are places in town. One of us should stay for the SOCOs.'

'Better be you then; don't want accusations that I'm hogging the limelight. In fact, you probably deserve a complimentary beaker of Auchterarder's finest tea.' He turned to go, but she stopped him.

'Why me? Why now?' Her arms stretching from her sides.

'Why not?' he answered. 'Just call it kismet.'

'That's not what I mean ...'

He turned towards her again.

'What I mean,' she said quietly, 'is that I'm not sure I want them caught. If they are, and it's been down to me ...'

'If they are, Shiv, it'll be down to their cock-up.' He stabbed a finger in the direction of the patch. 'That, and maybe even a bit of teamwork ...'

The Scene of Crime unit hadn't been thrilled by the news that Rebus and Siobhan had entered the locus. Prints of their shoes had been taken, for purposes of elimination, along with hair samples.

'Go easy,' Rebus had warned. 'I can't afford to be generous.'

The SOCO had apologised. 'Got to get the root, else we can't get the DNA.' On the third try with the tweezers, he'd been successful. One of his colleagues had almost finished videoing the scene. Another was still taking photographs, and yet another was in conversation with Siobhan about how much of the other clothing they should remove to the lab.

'Just the most recent,' she told him, her eyes on Rebus. He nodded his agreement, sharing her train of thought. Even if Colliar was a message to Cafferty, didn't mean there weren't other messages here.

'Sports shirt seems to have a company logo on it,' the SOCO commented.

'Your job could hardly be easier,' Siobhan said with a smile.

'My job's collection. The rest is down to you.'

'Speaking of which,' Rebus interrupted, 'any chance this could all go to Edinburgh rather than Stirling?'

The SOCO stiffened his shoulders. Rebus didn't know him but he knew the type: late-forties, half a lifetime's experience. There was plenty of rivalry between the various police regions as it was. Rebus held up his hands in mock surrender.

'All I mean is, it's an Edinburgh case. Makes sense if they don't have to keep traipsing through to Stirling every time there's something you need to show them.'

Siobhan was smiling again, amused by his use of 'they' and 'them'. But she gave a slight nod too, recognising a useful ploy when she saw one.

'Especially now,' Rebus was arguing, 'with the demos and everything.' He looked up to where a helicopter was circling. Gleneagles surveillance, had to be. Someone up there wondering at the sudden appearance of two cars and two unmarked white vans at the Clootie Well. Returning his gaze to the SOCO, Rebus realised the chopper had sealed the deal. A time like this, cooperation was paramount. It had been hammered home in memorandum after memorandum. Macrae himself had said as much at the past dozen or so briefings at Gayfield Square.

Be nice. Work together. Help each other. Because, for these few short days, the world would be watching.

Maybe the SOCO had been at similar briefings. He was nodding slowly, turning away to continue his work. Rebus and Siobhan shared another look. Then Rebus reached into his pocket for his cigarettes.

'No traces, please,' one of the other SOCOs warned him, so Rebus moved away, back towards the car park. He was just lighting up when another car appeared. The more the merrier, he thought to himself as DCI Macrae leapt out. He was dressed in what looked like a new suit. New tie, too, and a crisp white shirt. His hair was grey and sparse, face saggy, nose bulbous and red-veined.

He's the same age as me, Rebus thought. Why does he seem so much older?

'Afternoon, sir,' Rebus said.

'Thought you were supposed to be at a funeral.' The tone was accusatory, as though Rebus might have fabricated a death in the family to secure a Friday lie-in.

'DS Clarke interrupted proceedings,' Rebus explained. 'Thought I'd show willing.' Making it sound like a sacrifice. The words worked, too, Macrae's tightened jaw relaxing a little.

I'm on a roll, Rebus thought. First the SOCO, now the boss. Macrae had been pretty good actually, green-lighting a day off for Rebus as soon as news broke of Mickey's death. He'd told Rebus to go get slaughtered, and Rebus had obliged – the Scotsman's way of dealing with death. He'd found himself in a part of town he didn't know, no idea how he got there ... walked into a chemist's and asked where he was. Answer: Colinton Village Pharmacy. He'd thanked them by making the purchase of some aspirin ...

'Sorry, John.' Macrae said now, taking a deep breath. 'How did it go?' Trying to sound concerned.

'It went,' was all Rebus said. He watched the helicopter bank steeply as it turned for home.

'Hope to Christ that wasn't TV,' Macrae commented.

'Not much to see, even supposing it was. Shame to tear you away from Glenrothes, sir. How's Sorbus looking?'

Operation Sorbus: the policing plan for G8 week. To Rebus, it had sounded like something a slimmer would use in their tea instead of sugar. Siobhan had put him right, told him it was a kind of tree.

'We're prepared for any eventuality,' Macrae stated briskly.

'Except maybe one,' Rebus felt it his duty to add.

'Back-burner till next week, John,' his boss muttered.

Rebus nodded his agreement. 'Always assuming *they* agree.'

Macrae followed Rebus's eye-line and saw the car approaching. It was a silver Merc with tinted rear windows.

'Probably means the chopper wasn't TV,' Rebus added for Macrae's benefit. He reached into his own car's passenger seat and brought out what remained of a filled roll. Ham salad: the first had slipped down without touching the sides.

'The hell's this?' Macrae was asking through gritted teeth. The Merc had pulled to an abrupt stop beside one of the Scene of Crime vans. The driver's door opened and a man got out. He walked around the car and tugged open the rear passenger-side door. It took several moments for the man inside to emerge. He was tall and narrow, eyes hidden behind sunglasses. As he secured all three buttons of his suit jacket, he seemed to be studying the two white vans, the three unmarked police cars. Eventually he peered up at the sky, mouthed something to his driver, and stepped away from the vehicle. Instead of approaching Rebus and Macrae, he walked over to the signpost, the one informing tourists of the Clootie Well's history. The driver was back behind his steering wheel, eyes on Rebus and Macrae. Rebus blew him a little kiss, content to stand there until the new arrival consented to make introductions. Again, he thought he knew the type: cold and calculating, making show of being the real power. Had to be security of some kind, following up the chopper's call.

Macrae took only seconds to crack. Strode over to the man and asked him who he was.

'I'm SO12, who the hell are you?' the man replied in a measured voice. Maybe he'd missed the briefings on friendly cooperation. English accent, Rebus noted. Stood to reason. SO12 was Special Branch, based in London. One step away from the spooks. 'I mean,' the man went on, his interest still apparently concentrated on the signpost, 'I know *what* you are. You're CID. And those are Scene of Crime vans. And in a clearing just ahead of us there are men in white protective overalls making a detailed examination of the trees and ground.' Finally he turned towards Macrae, and reached a slow hand to his own face to remove the sunglasses. 'How am I doing so far?'

Macrae's face had reddened in anger. All day he'd been treated with the dignity which was his due. Now this.

'Care to show some ID?' Macrae snapped. The man stared at him, then gave a wry smile. *Is that all you've got?* the smile seemed to say. As he reached into his jacket, not bothering to unbutton it, his eyes shifted from Macrae to Rebus. The smile stayed, inviting Rebus to share its message. A small black leather wallet was held open for Macrae's inspection.

'There,' the man said, snapping it shut again. 'Now you know all there is to know about me.'

'You're Steelforth,' Macrae said, clearing his throat between words. Rebus could see his boss had been thrown. Macrae turned towards him. 'Commander Steelforth is in charge of G8 security,' he explained. But Rebus had already guessed as much. Macrae turned back to Steelforth. 'I was in Glenrothes this morning, being given a tour courtesy of ACC Finnigan. And Gleneagles yesterday ...' Macrae's voice faltered. Steelforth was already moving away from him, towards Rebus.

'Not interrupting your coronary, am I?' he asked, glancing at the roll. Rebus gave the belch he felt the query demanded. Steelforth's eyes narrowed.

'We can't all be dining courtesy of the taxpayer,' Rebus said. 'How is the food at Gleneagles, by the way?'

'I doubt you'll get the chance to find out, Detective Sergeant.'

'Not a bad guess, sir, but your eyes deceive you.'

'This is DI Rebus,' Macrae was explaining. 'I'm DCI Macrae, Lothian and Borders.'

'Based where?' Steelforth asked.

'Gayfield Square,' Macrae answered.

'In Edinburgh,' Rebus added.

'You're a long way from home, gentlemen.' Steelforth was heading down the path.

'A man was murdered in Edinburgh,' Rebus explained. 'Some of his clothing has turned up here.'

'Do we know why?'

'I intend keeping a lid on it, Commander,' Macrae stated. 'Once the SOCOs are finished, that's us done and dusted.' Macrae was at Steelforth's heels, Rebus bringing up the rear.

'No plans for any premiers or presidents to come leave a wee offering?' Rebus asked.

Instead of answering, Steelforth marched into the clearing. The senior SOCO stuck a hand against the Commander's chest. 'More fucking footprints,' he growled.

Steelforth glared at the hand. 'Do you know who I am?'

'Don't give a bollocks, pal. Fuck up my crime scene, you'll answer for it.'

The Special Branch man considered for a moment, then relented, retracing his steps to the edge of the clearing, content to watch the operation. His mobile sounded, and he answered it, moving further away to prevent being overheard. Siobhan gave a questioning look. Rebus mouthed, 'Later,' and dug into his pocket, bringing out a ten-pound note.

'Here,' he said, offering it to the SOCO.

'What's that for?'

Rebus just winked, and the man pocketed the money, adding the word 'Cheers.'

'I always tip for service beyond the norm,' Rebus told Macrae. Nodding, Macrae dug into his own pocket and found a fiver for Rebus.

'Halfers,' the DCI said.

Steelforth was returning to the clearing. 'I need to get back to more important matters. When will you be finished here?'

'Half an hour,' one of the other SOCOs answered.

'Longer if need be,' Steelforth's nemesis added. 'A crime scene's a crime scene, no matter what other wee sideshows there are.' Like Rebus before him, he hadn't been slow to work out Steelforth's role.

The Special Branch man turned to Macrae. 'I'll inform ACC Finnigan, shall I? Let him know we have your full understanding and cooperation?'

'As you wish, sir.'

Steelforth's face softened a little. His hand made contact with Macrae's arm. 'I'm willing to bet you didn't see everything there is to see. When you're finished here, come back to Gleneagles. I'll give you the *proper* tour.'

Macrae melted; a kid on Christmas morning. But he recovered well, stiffening his spine.

'Thank you, Commander.'

'Call me David.'

Crouched as if for evidence-gathering some way behind Steelforth's back, the senior SOCO made a show of sticking a finger down his throat.

*

Three cars would be making their way separately to Edinburgh. Rebus shuddered to think what the ecologists would say to that. Macrae peeled off first, heading for Gleneagles. Rebus had driven past the hotel earlier. When you approached Auchterarder from Kinross, you saw the hotel and its grounds a long time before you reached the town. Thousands of acres, but few signs of security. He had caught just the one glimpse of fencing, alerted by a temporary structure which he took to be a watch-tower. Rebus shadowed Macrae on the way back, his boss sounding the horn as he turned into the hotel's driveway. Siobhan had guessed Perth as the quickest road, Rebus opting to retrace his cross-country route, pick up the M90 eventually. Still plenty of blue in the sky. Scottish summers were a blessing, a reward for the long winter's twilight. Rebus turned down the music and called Siobhan's mobile.

'Hands-free, I hope,' she told him.

'Don't be smart.'

'Otherwise you're setting a bad example.'

'First time for everything. What did you make of our friend from London?'

'Unlike you, I don't have those hang-ups.'

'What hang-ups?'

'With authority ... with the English ... with ...' She paused. 'Want me to go on?'

'Last time I looked, I still outrank you.'

'So?'

'So I could cite you for insubordination.'

'And give the chiefs a good laugh?'

His silence conceded the point. Either she'd got lippier down the years, or he was getting rusty. Both, probably. 'Think we can talk the lab boffins into a Saturday shift?' he asked.

'Depends.'

'What about Ray Duff? One word from you and he'd do it.'

'And all I'd have to do in return is spend a whole day with him, touring in that smelly old car.'

'It's a design classic.'

'Something he won't begin to tire of telling me.'

'Rebuilt it from scratch ...'

Her sigh was audible. 'What is it with Forensics? They all have these *hobbies*.'

'So you'll ask him?'

'I'll ask him. Are you carousing this evening?'

'Night shift.'

'Same day as a funeral?'

'Someone's got to do it.'

'I'm betting you insisted.'

He didn't answer, asked instead what her own plans were.

'Getting my head down. Want to be up bright and early for the march.'

'What have they got you doing?'

She laughed. 'I'm not working, John – I'm going because I want to.'

'Bloody hell.'

'You should come too.'

'Aye, right. That's going to make all the difference in the world. I'd rather stay at home to make my protest.'

'What protest?'

'Against Bob bloody Geldof.' She was laughing in his ear again. 'Because if as many turn up as he wants, it'll look like it's all down to him. Can't have that, Siobhan. Think about it before you sign your name to the cause.'

'I'm going, John. If nothing else, I need to look out for my mum and dad.'

'Your ...?'

'They're up from London – and not because of anything Geldof said.'

'They're going on the march?'

'Yes.'

'Do I get to meet them?'

'No.'

'Why not?'

'Because you're just the sort of cop they're afraid I'll grow into.'

He was supposed to laugh at this, but knew she was only half joking.

'Fair point,' was all he said.

'Have you shaken off the boss?' A conscious change of subject.

'Left him at valet parking.'

'Don't joke – they actually have that at Gleneagles. Did he toot the horn at you?'

'What do you think?'

'I knew he would. This whole trip, it's shaken years off him.'

'Kept him out of the station, too.'

'So everybody wins.' She paused. 'You think you've got a crack at this, don't you?'

'What do you mean?'

'Cyril Colliar. The next week or so, nobody's going to be holding your leash.'

'I didn't realise I was up there in your estimation.'

'John, you're a year away from retirement. I know you want one last go at Cafferty ...'

'And it seems I'm transparent, too.'

'Look, I'm just trying to—'

'I know, and I'm touched.'

'You really think Cafferty could be responsible?'

'If he's not, he'll want whoever was. Look, if it all gets a bit fraught with your parents ...' Now who was changing the subject? 'Send me a text and we'll meet for a drink.'

'All right, I will. You can turn the Elbow CD up now.'

'Well spotted. Talk to you later.'

Rebus cut the connection; did as he was told.

2

The barriers were going up. Down George IV Bridge and all along Princes Street, workmen were busy putting them in place. Road repairs and building projects had been put on hold, scaffolding removed so it couldn't be taken apart and used as missiles. Postboxes had been sealed shut and some shops boarded up. Financial institutions had been forewarned, staff advised not to wear formal clothing – it would make them easy targets. For a Friday evening, the town was quiet. Police vans cruised the central streets, metal grilles fixed to their windscreens. More vans were parked out of sight in unlit side roads. The cops on board wore riot gear and laughed among themselves, swapping stories from previous engagements. A few veterans had seen action during the last wave of miners' strikes. Others tried to match these memories with stories of soccer battles, poll tax demos, the Newbury bypass. They exchanged rumours about the expected size of the Italian anarchist contingent.

'Genoa toughened them up.'

'Just the way we like it, eh, lads?'

Bravado and nerves and camaraderie. The talk faltering whenever a radio crackled into life.

The uniformed police working the train station wore bright yellow jackets. Here, too, barriers were being erected. They were blocking exits, so there remained a single route in and out. Some officers carried cameras with which to record the faces of arrivals from the London trains. Special carriages had been laid on for the protesters, which made

28

it easy to identify them. Not that such skills were really needed: they sang songs, carried rucksacks, wore badges and T-shirts and wristbands. They carried flags and banners, were dressed in baggy trousers, camouflage jackets, hiking boots. Intelligence reports said busloads had already left from the south of England. First estimates had stated fifty thousand. The latest guess was north of a hundred thousand. Which, added to the summer tourists, would swell Edinburgh's population nicely.

Somewhere in the city there was a rally signalling the start of G8 Alternatives, a week-long series of marches and meetings. More police would be there. If needed, some of these would be on horseback. Plenty of dog-handlers, too, including four on Waverley Station's concourse. The plan was simple: visible strength. Let any potential troublemakers know what they'd be dealing with. Visors and truncheons and handcuffs; horses and dogs and patrol vans.

Force of numbers.

Tools of the trade.

Tactics.

Earlier in its history, Edinburgh was prone to invasion. Its inhabitants hid behind walls and gates, and when those were breached retreated to the warren-like tunnels below the Castle and the High Street, leaving the city empty and the victory hollow. It was a talent the denizens continued to bring to the annual August Festival. As the population swelled, the locals became less visible, blending into the background. It might also explain Edinburgh's reliance on 'invisible' industries such as banking and insurance. Until lately, it was said that St Andrews Square was the richest in Europe, boasting several corporate HQs. But with space at a premium, new building projects had prospered on Lothian Road and further west towards the airport. The Royal Bank's HQ at Gogarburn, recently completed, was seen as a target. So too buildings owned and staffed by Standard Life and Scottish Widows. Driving through the streets, killing some time, Siobhan reckoned the city would be tested as never before in the coming days.

A police convoy, sirens blaring, pulled out to pass her. No mistaking the schoolboy grin on the driver's face: loving every minute, Edinburgh providing his own personal racetrack. A purple Nissan was riding the slipstream, filled with local youths. Siobhan gave it ten seconds, then signalled to move back out into the flow of traffic. She was on her way to a temporary campsite in Niddrie. One of Edinburgh's less genteel areas. Instead of pitching their tents in people's gardens, this was where marchers were being told to go.

Niddrie.

The council had chosen the grasslands around the Jack Kane Centre. They were planning for ten thousand visitors, maybe even fifteen. Portaloos and showers had been provided, and a private security firm put in charge. Probably, Siobhan couldn't help thinking, to keep the neighbourhood gangs *out* rather than the marchers in. The local joke was that there'd be a lot of tents and camping gear for sale around the pubs in the next few weeks. Siobhan had offered to let her parents stay in her flat. Of course she had: they'd helped her buy it. They could have her bed; she'd crash on the sofa. But they'd been adamant: they would be travelling by bus, and camping 'with the others'. They'd been students in the 1960s, and had never quite shaken themselves free of the period. Though now nearing sixty – Rebus's generation – her dad still kept his hair tied back in a sort of ponytail. Her mum still wore dresses that were mostly kaftan. Siobhan thought of her words to Rebus earlier: *you're just the sort of cop they're afraid I'll grow into*. Thing was, part of her felt now that she'd joined the police mostly because she'd felt they wouldn't approve. After all the care and affection they'd doled out on her, she'd needed to rebel. Payback for the times their teaching jobs had led to yet another house-move, another

30

new school. Payback simply because it was in her power. The first time she'd told them out loud, their looks had almost made her recant. But that would have been weak. They'd been supportive, of course, while hinting that police work might not be the most fulfilling use of her skills. That was enough to make her dig her heels in.

So she'd become a cop. Not in London, where her parents lived, but in Scotland, which she hadn't really known at all until attending college there. One final heartfelt plea from her mum and dad:

'Anywhere but Glasgow.'

Glasgow: with its hard-man image and knife culture, its sectarian divide. Yet, as Siobhan had found, a great place to shop. A place she sometimes went with friends – hen parties which led to them staying the night at some boutique hotel or other, sampling the nightlife, steering clear of any bars with bouncers on the door – a point of drinking protocol on which she and John Rebus were agreed. While Edinburgh, meantime, had proved more deadly than her parents could ever have imagined.

Not that she would ever tell them that. During Sunday phone calls she tended to brush off her mum's enquiries, asking her own questions instead. She'd offered to meet them off the bus, but they'd said they would need time to get the tent ready. Stopped at traffic lights, the image made her smile. Nearly sixty, the pair of them, and messing about with a tent. They'd taken early retirement the previous year from their teaching jobs. Owned a fair-sized house in Forest Hill, the mortgage paid off. Always asking her if she needed money ...

'I'll pay for a hotel room,' she'd told them on the phone, but they'd remained resolute. Pulling away from the lights, she wondered if it might be some form of dementia.

She parked on The Wisp, ignoring the orange traffic cones, and stuck a Police Business notice on her windscreen. At the sound of her idling engine, a yellow-jacketed security guard had come for a look. He shook his head and pointed at the notice. Then he drew a hand across his throat and nodded towards the nearest housing scheme. Siobhan removed the sign, but left the car where it was.

'Local gangs,' the guard was saying. 'Sign like that's a red rag to a bull.' He slid his hands into his pockets, puffing up his already substantial chest. 'So what brings you here, Officer?'

His head was shaved, but he sported a full, dark beard and a tangle of eyebrows.

'Social call, actually,' Siobhan said, showing him her ID. 'A couple by the name of Clarke. Need a word with them.'

'In you come then.' He led her to a gate in the perimeter fence. In miniature, it was a bit like the Gleneagles security. There was even a sort of watch-tower. Every ten yards or so along the fence stood another guard. 'Here, put this on,' her new friend was saying, handing her a wrist-strap. 'Makes you less conspicuous. It's how we keep tabs on our band of happy campers.'

'Quite literally,' she said, taking it from him. 'How's everything going so far?'

'Local youth don't like it much. They've tried coming in, but that's about it.' He shrugged. They were walking along a metal walkway, stepping off it for a moment as a young girl rollerskated past, her mother watching cross-legged from the ground next to her tent.

'How many are here?' Siobhan found it hard to judge.

'Maybe a thousand. There'll be more tomorrow.'

'You're not keeping count?'

'Not taking names either – so I'm not sure where you're going to find your friends. Only thing we're allowed to take from them is the fee for their pitch.'

Siobhan looked around. The summer had been dry, and the earth underfoot was solid. Beyond the skyline of flats and houses she could make out other, more ancient shapes:

Holyrood Park and Arthur's Seat. She could hear some low chanting, and a few guitars and penny whistles. Children's laughter, and a baby ready for its next feed. Handclaps and chatter. Silenced suddenly by a megaphone, carried by a man with his hair crammed into an outsize woolly hat. Patchwork trousers lopped off at the knees and flip-flops on his feet.

'Big white tent, people – that's where it's happening. Vegetable curry at four quid, thanks to the local mosque. Only four quid ...'

'Maybe that's where you'll find them,' Siobhan's guide said. She thanked him and he headed back to his post.

The 'big white tent' was a marquee, and seemed to serve as a general meeting-place. Someone else was calling out that a group would be heading into town for a drink. Meet in five minutes by the red flag. Siobhan had passed a row of portable toilets and some standpipes and showers. All that was left for her to explore now were tents. The queue for curry was orderly. Someone tried to hand her a plastic spoon, and she shook her head, before remembering that it was a while since she'd eaten. Her polystyrene plate heaped high, she decided to take a slow walk through the camp. People were cooking their own food on camp-stoves. One pointed at her.

'Remember me from Glastonbury?' they called. Siobhan just shook her head. And then she saw her parents, and broke into a smile. They were doing the camping thing with style: a big red tent with windows and a covered porch. Foldaway table and chairs, and an open bottle of wine with real glasses next to it. They got up when they saw her, exchanged hugs and kisses, apologised that they'd only brought two chairs.

'I can sit on the grass,' Siobhan assured them. There was another young woman already doing just that. She hadn't moved at Siobhan's approach.

'We were just telling Santal about you,' Siobhan's mum

33

said. Eve Clarke looked young for her years, only the laughter lines giving the game away. The same could not be said for Siobhan's dad, Teddy. He'd grown paunchy, and the skin drooped from his face. His hairline had receded, the ponytail sparser and greyer than ever. He refilled the wine glasses with gusto, his gaze never leaving the bottle.

'I'm sure Santal's been riveted,' Siobhan said, accepting a glass.

The young woman gave the beginnings of a smile. Her hair was neck-length and dirty blonde, gelled or mistreated so that it emerged in clumps and braids from her scalp. No make-up, but multiple piercings to her ears and one to the side of her nose. Her dark-green sleeveless T-shirt displayed Celtic tattoos on either shoulder, and her bare midriff showed another piercing to her navel. Plenty of jewellery strung around her neck, and hanging lower still what looked like a digital video camera.

'You're Siobhan,' she said with a trace of a lisp.

'Afraid so.' Siobhan toasted the company with her glass. Another had been produced from a picnic basket, along with a second bottle of wine.

'Steady on, Teddy,' Eve Clarke said.

'Santal needs a top-up,' he explained, though Siobhan couldn't help noticing that Santal's glass was actually almost as full as her own.

'Did the three of you travel up together?' she asked.

'Santal hitched from Aylesbury,' Teddy Clarke said. 'After the bus ride we've just endured, I think next time I'd do the same.' He rolled his eyes and fidgeted in his seat, then unscrewed the wine bottle. 'Screw-top wine, Santal. Don't say the modern world doesn't have its pluses.'

In fact, she didn't reply at all. Siobhan couldn't say why she'd taken such an immediate dislike to this stranger, except that Santal was just that: a stranger. Siobhan had wanted some time with her mum and dad. Just the three of them.

'Santal's got the pitch next to us,' Eve was explaining. 'We needed a bit of help with the tent ...'

Her husband laughed suddenly and loudly, filling his own glass. 'Been a while since we camped,' he said.

'Tent looks new,' Siobhan commented.

'Borrowed from neighbours,' her mother said quietly.

Santal was rising to her feet. 'I should go ...'

'Not on our account,' Teddy Clarke protested.

'There's a bunch of us heading to a pub ...'

'I like your camera,' Siobhan said.

Santal looked down at it. 'Any of the plod take my picture, I want theirs in return. Fair's fair, isn't it?' Her unblinking look demanded agreement.

Siobhan turned towards her father. 'You've told her what I do,' she stated quietly.

'Not ashamed, are you?' Santal all but spat the words out.

'Just the opposite, to be honest.' Siobhan's eyes shifted from father to mother. Suddenly both her parents seemed intent on the wine in front of them. When she looked back at Santal, she saw that the young woman was pointing the camera at her.

'One for the family album,' Santal said. 'I'll send you a jpeg.'

'Thanks,' Siobhan replied coldly. 'Odd name, isn't it, Santal?'

'Means sandalwood,' Eve Clarke answered.

'At least people can spell it,' Santal herself added.

Teddy Clarke laughed. 'I was telling Santal about how we lumbered you with a name nobody down south could pronounce.'

'Shared any more family history?' Siobhan bristled. 'Any embarrassing stories I need to be aware of?'

'Touchy, isn't she?' Santal commented to Siobhan's mother.

'You know,' Eve Clarke admitted, 'we never really wanted her to become—'

'Mum, for Christ's sake!' Siobhan broke in. But her further complaint was cut short by sounds from the direction of the fence. She saw guards jogging towards the scene. There were kids on the outside, making Nazi salutes. They wore regulation dark hooded tops and wanted the guards to send out 'all the hippy scum'.

'The revolution starts here!' one of them yelled. 'Up against the wall, wankers!'

'Pathetic,' Siobhan's mother hissed.

But now there were objects sailing through the darkening sky.

'Get down,' Siobhan warned, all but pushing her mother into the tent, unsure what protection it would offer from the volley of rocks and bottles. Her father had taken a couple of steps towards the trouble, but she hauled him back, too. Santal was standing her ground, pointing her camera towards the mêlée.

'You're just a bunch of tourists!' one of the locals was yelling. 'Piss off home on the rickshaws that brought you here!'

Raucous laughter; jeers and gestures. If the campers wouldn't come outside, they wanted the guards. But the guards weren't that stupid. Instead, Siobhan's friend was on his radio for reinforcements. Situation like this, it could die down in moments or flare into all-out war. The guard found her standing by his shoulder.

'Don't worry,' he said. 'I'm sure you're insured ...'

It took her a second to get his meaning. 'My car!' she shouted, heading for the gate. Had to elbow her way past two more guards. Ran out on to the road. Her bonnet was dented and scored, back window fractured. *NYT* sprayed on one door panel.

Niddrie Young Team.

They stood there in a line, laughing at her. One of them held up his mobile phone to get a snap.

'Take all the photos you want,' she told him. 'Makes you even easier to trace.'

'Fuckin' polis!' another of them spat. He was in the centre, a lieutenant behind either shoulder.

The leader.

'Polis is right,' she said. 'Ten minutes in Craigmillar cop-shop and I'll know more about you than your own mother.' She was pointing for emphasis, but all he did was sneer. Only a third of his face visible, but she would file it away. A car was drawing up, three men inside. Siobhan recognised the one in the back: local councillor.

'Away you go!' he was yelling as he emerged, waving both arms as if putting sheep back in a pen. The gang's leader pretended to tremble, but could see that his fellow soldiers were wavering. Half a dozen of the security had come from behind the fence, the bearded guard at their head. Sirens in the distance, growing closer.

'Go on, bugger off with you!' the councillor persisted.

'Camp full of lezzas and poofs,' the gang's leader snarled in reply. 'And who's paying for it, eh?'

'I very much doubt you are, son,' the councillor said. The other two men from the car were flanking him now. They were big men, probably hadn't backed down from a fight in their lives. Just the sort of pollsters a Niddrie politician would need.

The gang leader spat on the ground, then turned and walked off.

'Thanks for that,' Siobhan said, holding out a hand for the councillor to shake.

'Not a problem,' he replied, seeming to dismiss the whole incident from his mind, Siobhan included. He was shaking the bearded guard's hand now, the two obviously known to one another.

'Quiet night otherwise?' the councillor asked. The guard chuckled a response.

'Was there something we can do for you, Mr Tench?'

Councillor Tench looked around him. 'Just thought I'd drop by, let all these lovely people know that my ward stands firmly behind them in the fight to end poverty and injustice in the world.' He had an audience now: fifty or so campers standing just the other side of the fence. 'We know something about both in this part of Edinburgh,' he bellowed, 'but that doesn't mean we've no time for those worse off than us. Big-hearted I like to think we are.' He saw that Siobhan was examining the damage to her car. 'Few wild ones in our midst, naturally, but then what community hasn't?' Smiling, Tench opened his arms again, this time like a brimstone preacher.

'Welcome to Niddrie!' he told his congregation. 'Welcome one and all.'

Rebus was alone in the CID suite. It had taken him half an hour to find the notes for the murder inquiry: four boxes and a series of folders; floppy disks and a single CD-ROM. He'd left these latter items on their shelf in the storeroom, and now had some of the paperwork spread out in front of him. He'd made use of the half-dozen desks available, pushing in-trays and computer keyboards aside. By walking through the room, he could shift between the different stages of the inquiry: crime scene to initial interviews; victim profile to further interviews; prison record; connection with Cafferty; autopsy and toxicology reports ... The phone in the DI's little booth had rung a few times, but Rebus had ignored it. He wasn't the senior DI here: Derek Starr was. And the smarmy little bastard was out on the town somewhere, it being a Friday night. Rebus knew Starr's routine because Starr himself shared it with all and sundry each Monday morning: couple of drinks at the Hallion Club, then maybe home for a shower and change of clothes before coming back into town; back to the Hallion if it was lively, but always heading to George Street afterwards – Opal Lounge; Candy Bar; Living Room. Nightcap at Indigo Yard if he hadn't 'struck lucky' before then. There was a new jazz place opening on Queen Street, owned by Jools Holland. Starr had already made enquiries about membership.

The phone rang again; Rebus ignored it. If it was urgent, they'd try Starr's mobile. If it was being transferred from the front desk ... well, they knew Rebus was up here. He'd wait till they tried his extension rather than Starr's. Could be they were winding him up, hoping he'd answer so they could apologise and say it was DI Starr they were after. Rebus knew his place in the food-chain: somewhere down amongst the plankton, the price for years of insubordination and reckless conduct. Never mind that there'd been results along the way, too: far as the High Hiedyins were concerned, these days it was all about *how* you got the result; about efficiency and accountability, public perceptions, strict rules and protocols.

Rebus's translation: covering your own arse.

He stopped by a folder of photographs. Some he had already removed and spread out across the surface of the desk. Now he sifted through the others. Cyril Colliar's public history: newspaper clippings, Polaroids offered by family and friends, the official photos from his arrest and trial. Someone had even snapped a grainy shot of him during his time in prison, reclining on his bed, arms behind his head as he watched TV. It had made the front page of the tabloids: *Could Life Be Any Cushier for Rape Beast?*

Not any longer.

Next desk: details of the rape victim's family. Name kept secret from the public. She was Victoria Jensen, eighteen at the time of the attack. Vicky to those closest to her. Followed from a nightclub ... followed as she walked with two pals to the bus stop. Night bus: Colliar had found himself a seat a couple of rows behind the three. Vicky got off the bus alone. Not much more than five hundred yards from home when he'd struck, hand over her mouth, hauling her into an alley ...

CCTV images showed him leaving the club straight after her. Showed him boarding the bus and taking his seat. DNA from the attack sealed his fate. Some of his associates had attended the trial, made threats towards the victim's family. No charges brought.

Vicky's father was a vet; his wife worked for Standard Life. Rebus himself had delivered the news of Cyril Colliar's demise to the family home in Leith.

'Thanks for telling us,' the father had said. 'I'll break it to Vicky.'

'You don't understand, sir,' Rebus had responded. 'There are questions I need to ask you ...'

Did you do it?

Hire someone to do it for you?

Know anyone who might've been compelled?

Vets had access to drugs. Maybe not heroin, but other drugs which could be exchanged for heroin. Dealers sold ketamine to clubbers – Starr himself had made the point. It was used by vets to treat horses. Vicky had been raped in an alley, Colliar killed in one. Thomas Jensen had appeared outraged by the insinuations.

'You mean you've really never thought of it, sir? Never planned any sort of revenge?'

Of course he had: images of Colliar rotting in a cell or burning in hell. 'But that doesn't happen, does it, Inspector? Not in *this* world ...'

Vicky's friends had been questioned too, none of them ready to own up.

Rebus moved to the next table. Morris Gerald Cafferty stared back at him from photographs and interview transcripts. Rebus had needed to argue his case before Macrae would let him anywhere near. Feeling was, their shared history ran too deep. Some knew them for enemies; others thought them too similar ... and way too familiar with one another. Starr for one had voiced his concerns in front of both Rebus and DCI Macrae. Rebus's snarled attempt to grab his fellow DI by the shirt-front had been, in Macrae's later words, 'Just another own goal, John.'

Cafferty was dextrous: fingers in every imaginable criminal pie. Saunas and protection; muscle and intimidation. Drugs, too, which would give him access to heroin. And if not him personally, Colliar's fellow bouncers for sure. It wasn't unknown for clubs to be shut down when it emerged that the so-called doormen were controlling the flow of dope into the premises. Any one of them could have decided to get rid of the 'Rape Beast'. Might even have been personal: a disrespectful remark; a slight against a girlfriend. The many and varied possible motives had been explored at length and in detail. On the surface, then, a by-the-book investigation. Nobody could say otherwise. Except ... Rebus could see the team's heart hadn't been in it. A few questions missed here and there; avenues left unexplored. Notes typed up sloppily. It was the sort of thing only someone close to the case would spot. Effort had been spared throughout, just enough to show what the officers really thought of their 'victim'.

The autopsy, however, had been scrupulous. Professor Gates had said it before: didn't bother him who it was lying on his slab. They were human beings, and somebody's daughter or son.

'Nobody's born bad, John,' he'd muttered, leaning over his scalpel.

'Well, nobody makes them do bad things either,' Rebus had retorted.

'Ah,' Gates had conceded. 'A conundrum pored over by wiser heads than ours down the centuries. What makes us keep doing these terrible things to each other?'

He hadn't offered an answer. But something else he'd pointed out resonated with Rebus as he moved to Siobhan's desk and picked up one of the post-mortem photographs of Colliar. *In death we all return to innocence, John ...* It was true that Colliar's face seemed at peace, as though nothing had ever troubled it.

The phone was ringing again in Starr's office. Rebus let it ring, picked up Siobhan's extension instead. There was a Post-it note affixed to the side of her hard drive: rows of names and phone numbers. He knew better than to try the lab; punched in the mobile instead.

Picked up almost immediately by Ray Duff.

'Ray? It's DI Rebus.'

'Inviting me to join him on a Friday night pub crawl?' Rebus's silence was answered with a sigh. 'Why am I not surprised?'

'I'm surprised at *you*, though, Ray, shirking your duties ...'

'I don't sleep in the lab, you know.'

'Except we both know that's a lie.'

'Okay, I work the odd night ...'

'And that's what I like about you, Ray. See, we're both driven by that passion for the job.'

'A passion I'm jeopardising by showing my face at my local pub's quiz-night?'

'Not my place to judge you, Ray. Just wondering how this new Colliar evidence is shaping up.'

Rebus heard a tired chuckle at the other end of the phone. 'You never let up, do you?'

'It's not for me, Ray. I'm just helping out Siobhan. This could mean a big step-up for her if she nails it. *She's* the one who found the patch.'

'The evidence only came in three hours ago.'

'Ever heard of striking while the iron is hot?'

'But the beer in front of me is cold, John.'

'It would mean a lot to Siobhan. She's looking forward to you claiming that prize.'

'What prize?'

'The chance to show off that car of yours. A day out in the country, just the two of you on those winding roads.

42

Who knows, maybe even a hotel room at the end of it if you play your cards right.' Rebus paused. 'What's that music?'

'One of the quiz questions.'

'Sounds like Steely Dan. "Reeling in the Years".'

'But how did the band get their name?'

'A dildo in a William Burroughs novel. Now tell me you're heading to the lab straight after ...'

Well satisfied with the outcome, Rebus treated himself to a mug of coffee and a stretch of the legs. The building was quiet. The desk sergeant had been replaced by one of his juniors. Rebus didn't know the face, but nodded anyway.

'Been trying to get CID to take a call,' the young officer said. He ran a finger along his shirt collar. His neck was pitted with acne or some species of rash.

'That'll be me then,' Rebus told him. 'What's the emergency?'

'Trouble at the Castle, sir.'

'Have the protests started early?'

The uniform shook his head. 'Reports of a scream and a body landing in the Gardens. Looks like someone fell from the ramparts.'

'Castle's not open this time of night,' Rebus stated, brow creasing.

'Dinner for some of the bigwigs ...'

'So who ended up going over the edge?'

The constable just shrugged. 'Shall I tell them there's no one available?'

'Don't be daft, son,' Rebus announced, heading off to fetch his jacket.

As well as being a major tourist attraction, Edinburgh Castle also acted as a working barracks, something Commander David Steelforth stressed to Rebus when he intercepted him just inside the portcullis.

'You get about a bit,' Rebus said by way of response.

43

The Special Branch man was dressed formally: bow tie and cummerbund, dinner jacket, patent shoes.

'Thing is, that means it is quite properly under the aegis of the armed forces ...'

'I'm not sure what "aegis" means, Commander.'

'It means,' Steelforth hissed, losing patience, 'Military Police will be looking into the whys and wherefores of what occurred here.'

'Good dinner, was it?' Rebus was still walking. The path wound uphill, fierce gusts whipping around both men.

'There are important people here, DI Rebus.'

As if on cue, a car appeared from some sort of tunnel ahead. It was making for the gates, forcing Rebus and Steelforth to stand aside. Rebus caught a glimpse of the face in the back: a glint from metal-rimmed glasses, long, pale, worried-looking face. But then the Foreign Secretary often seemed to look worried, as Rebus pointed out to Steelforth. The Special Branch man frowned, disappointed at the recognition.

'Hope I don't need to interview him,' Rebus added.

'Look, Inspector ...'

But Rebus was moving again. 'Here's the thing, Commander,' he said over his shoulder. 'Victim may have fallen – or jumped, or any other "why" or "wherefore" – and I'm not disputing he was on army turf when he did ... but he landed a few hundred feet further south in Princes Street Gardens.' Rebus proffered a smile. 'And that makes him mine.'

Rebus kept walking, trying to remember the last time he'd been inside the Castle walls. He'd brought his daughter here, of course, but twenty-odd years ago. The Castle dominated the Edinburgh skyline. You could see it from Bruntsfield and Inverleith. On the drive in from the airport, it took on the aspect of a louring Transylvanian lair, and made you wonder if you'd lost your colour vision. From Princes Street, Lothian Road and Johnston

Terrace its volcanic sides seemed sheer and impregnable – and so they had proved down the years. Yet approaching from the Lawnmarket, you climbed a gentle slope to its entrance, with little hint of its enormous presence.

The drive from Gayfield Square had almost stymied Rebus. Uniformed cops hadn't wanted to let him use Waverley Bridge. A great grinding and clanking of metal as the barriers were dragged into position for tomorrow's march. He'd sounded his horn, ignoring gestures that he should find another route. When one officer had approached, Rebus had wound down the window and opened his warrant card.

'This route's closed,' the man stated. English accent, maybe Lancashire.

'I'm CID,' Rebus told him. 'And behind me there's going to be maybe an ambulance, a pathologist, and a Scene of Crime van. Want to tell them the same story?'

'What's happened?'

'Someone's just landed in the Gardens.' Rebus nodded towards the Castle.

'Bloody protesters ... one got stuck on the rocks earlier. Fire brigade had to winch him down.'

'Well, much as I'd like nothing better than a chinwag ...'

The officer scowled, but moved the barrier aside.

Now another barrier had placed itself in front of Rebus: Commander David Steelforth.

'This is a dangerous game, Inspector. Better left to those of us specialising in intelligence.'

Rebus's eyes narrowed. 'You calling me thick?'

A short, barked laugh. 'Not at all.'

'Good.' Rebus moved past him again. He saw where he was supposed to go. Military guards peering over the edge of the battlements. A cluster of elderly and distinguished-looking men, dressed for dinner, lurked nearby, smoking cigars.

45

'This where he fell?' Rebus asked the guards. He had his ID open, but had decided not to identify himself as civvy police.

'Must be about the spot,' someone answered.

'Anyone see it?'

There were shakes of the head. 'There was an incident earlier,' the same soldier said. 'Some idiot got stuck. We were warned more of them might try.'

'And?'

'And Private Andrews thought he saw something round the other side.'

'I said I wasn't sure,' Andrews defended himself.

'So you all skedaddled to the other side of the Castle?' Rebus made a show of sucking in breath. 'That used to be called "deserting your post".'

'Detective Inspector Rebus has no jurisdiction here,' Steelforth was telling the group.

'And *that* would have counted as treason,' Rebus warned him.

'Do we know who's unaccounted for?' one of the older men was asking.

Rebus heard another car making for the portcullis. Headlamps threw wild shadows across the wall ahead. 'Hard to say, with everyone doing a runner,' he said quietly.

'No one's "doing a runner",' Steelforth snapped.

'Just a bunch of prior engagements?' Rebus guessed.

'These are hellish busy people, Inspector. Decisions are being taken that may change the world.'

'Won't change whatever happened to the poor sod down there.' Rebus nodded towards the wall, then turned to face Steelforth. 'So what was going on here tonight, Commander?'

'Discussions over dinner. Moves towards ratification.'

'Good news for all rats. What about the guests?'

'G8 representatives – foreign ministers; security personnel; senior civil servants.'

'Probably rules out pizza and a case or two of beer.'

'A lot gets done at these get-togethers.'

Rebus was peering over the edge. He'd never much liked heights, and didn't linger. 'Can't see a damned thing,' he said.

'We heard him,' one of the soldiers said.

'Heard what exactly?' Rebus asked.

'The scream as he fell.' He looked around his comrades for support. One of them nodded.

'Seemed to scream all the way down,' he added with a shiver.

'Wonder if that rules out suicide,' Rebus speculated. 'What do you think, Commander?'

'I think there's nothing for you to learn here, Inspector. I also think it odd that you seem to pop up like this whenever there's bad news to find.'

'Funny, I was just thinking the same thing,' Rebus said, eyes boring into Steelforth's, 'about you ...'

The search party had comprised yellow-jacketed officers from barricade duty. Kitted out with torches, it hadn't taken them long. Paramedics declared the man dead, though anyone could have done the job. Neck twisted at an unnatural angle; one leg folded in half from the impact; blood seeping from the skull. He had lost a shoe on the way down and his shirt had been ripped open, probably by an overhang. Police HQ had spared a single SOCO, who was photographing the body.

'Want to place a small wager on cause of death?' the SOCO asked Rebus.

'Not a chance, Tam.' Tam the SOCO had not lost a bet like that in fifty or sixty cases.

'Did he jump or was he pushed, that's what you're asking yourself.'

'You're a mind-reader, Tam. Do you do palms as well?'

'No, but I take photos of them.' And to prove his point,

he got close up on one of the victim's hands. 'Nicks and scratches can be very useful, John. Know why?'

'Impress me.'

'If he's been pushed, he'll have scrabbled for purchase, clawed at the sides of the rock.'

'Tell me something I don't know.'

The SOCO let off another flash. 'His name's Ben Webster.' He turned to gauge Rebus's reaction, seemed satisfied with the result. 'I recognise his face – what's left of it anyway.'

'You know him?'

'I know who he is. Member of Parliament from up Dundee way.'

'The Scottish Parliament?'

Tam shook his head. 'The one in London. He's something to do with International Development – leastways he was last time I looked.'

'Tam …' Rebus sounded exasperated. 'How the hell do you know all this?'

'Got to keep up with politics, John. It's what makes the wheels turn. And besides, our young friend here shares a name with my favourite tenor player.'

Rebus was already tottering back down the grassy slope. The body had come to rest against a shelf of rock fifteen feet above one of the narrow paths that snaked around the base of the ancient volcanic plug. Steelforth was on the path itself, taking a call on his mobile. He flipped the phone shut as Rebus neared.

'Remember,' Rebus reminded him, 'how we saw the Foreign Secretary leaving in his chauffeured car? Funny that he'd go without one of his men.'

'Ben Webster,' Steelforth stated. 'That was the Castle on the phone; seems he's the only one missing.'

'International Development.'

'You're well informed, Inspector.' Steelforth made a show of looking Rebus up and down. 'Maybe I've misjudged you. But International Development is a separate department from the FO. Webster was a PPS – Parliamentary Private Secretary.'

'Meaning what?'

'The minister's right-hand man.'

'Excuse my ignorance.'

'Don't worry about it. I'm still impressed.'

'Is this where you make an offer to keep me off your back?'

Steelforth smiled. 'That's usually not necessary.'

'Might be in my case.'

But Steelforth was shaking his head. 'I doubt you can be bought in that particular way. Nevertheless, we both know this will be wrenched from your hands in the next few hours, so why waste energy? Battlers like yourself usually know when it's time to rest and refuel.'

'Are you inviting me to the Great Hall for port and cigars?'

'I'm telling you the truth as I see it.'

Rebus was watching another van arrive on the roadway below them. It would be from the mortuary, here to collect the body. Another job for Professor Gates and his staff.

'You know what I think really bothers you, Inspector?' Steelforth had taken a step closer. His phone was ringing but he chose to ignore it. 'You see all this as an incursion. Edinburgh is *your* town, and you wish we'd all just sod off back home. Does that about sum it up?'

'Just about,' Rebus was prepared to admit.

'A few days and it'll all be over, like a bad dream you'll wake up from. But in the meantime ...' His lips were almost touching Rebus's ear. '*Get used to it,*' he whispered, moving away.

'Seems a nice sort,' Tam commented. Rebus turned towards him.

'How long've you been there?'

'Not long.'

'Any news for me?'

'Pathologist's the one with the answers.'

Rebus nodded slowly. 'All the same, though ...'

'Nothing points to him doing anything but jumping.'

'He screamed all the way down. Reckon a suicide would do that?'

'I know I would. But then I'm scared of heights.'

Rebus was rubbing the side of his jaw. He stared up at the Castle. 'So either he fell or he jumped.'

'Or was given a sudden push,' Tam added. 'No time to even think about clawing his way to safety.'

'Thanks for that.'

'Could be there was bagpipe music between courses. Might've broken his will to live.'

'You're a jazz snob, Tam.'

'Wouldn't have it any other way.'

'No note tucked away inside his jacket?'

Tam shook his head. 'But I did have half a mind to give you this.' He held up a small cardboard wallet. 'Seems he was staying at the Balmoral.'

'That's nice.' Rebus opened the wallet and saw the plastic key-card. Closing the wallet, he examined Ben Webster's signature and room number.

'Might be a goodbye-cruel-world waiting for you there,' Tam said.

'Only one way to find out.' Rebus slipped the key into his own pocket. 'Thanks, Tam.'

'Just remember: it was *you* that found it. I don't want any grief.'

'Understood.' The two men stood in silence for a moment. A pair of old pros who'd seen everything the job could throw at them. The mortuary attendants were approaching, one of them carrying a body-bag.

'Nice night for it,' he commented. 'All done and dusted, Tam?'

'Doctor's not arrived yet.'

The attendant checked his watch. 'Think he'll be long?'

Tam just shrugged. 'Depends who's drawn the short straw.'

The attendant puffed air out from his cheeks. 'Going to be a long night,' he said.

'Long night,' his partner echoed.

'Know they've had us move some of the bodies out of the mortuary?'

'Why's that?' Rebus asked.

'In case any of these rallies and marches turns nasty.'

'Courts and cells are empty and waiting too,' Tam added.

'A and E on stand-by,' the attendant countered.

'You make it sound like *Apocalypse Now*,' Rebus said. His mobile sounded and he moved away a little. Caller ID: Siobhan.

'What can I do for you?' he said into the phone.

'I need a drink,' her voice explained.

'Trouble with the folks?'

'My car's been vandalised.'

'Catch them in the act?'

'In a manner of speaking. So how about the Oxford Bar?'

'Tempting, but I'm on something. Tell you what though ...'

'What?'

'We could rendezvous at the Balmoral.'

'Spending your overtime?'

'I'll let you be the judge of that.'

'Twenty minutes?'

'Fine.' He snapped shut the phone.

'Tragedy runs in that family,' Tam was musing.

'Which one?'

The SOCO nodded in the direction of the corpse. 'Mum was attacked a few years back, died as a result.' He paused.

'Reckon something could prey on your mind all that time?'

'Just needs the right trigger,' one of the mortuary attendants added. Everyone, Rebus decided, was a bloody psychologist these days ...

He decided to leave the car and walk. Quicker than trying to negotiate the barriers again. He was at Waverley in a couple of minutes; had to clamber over a couple of obstacles. Some unlucky tourists had just arrived by train. No taxis to be had, so they stood behind the railings, bemused and abandoned. He gave them a body-swerve, turned the corner into Princes Street and was outside the Balmoral Hotel. Some locals still called it the North British, though it had changed its name years back. Its large illuminated clock-tower still ran a few minutes fast, so passengers would be sure to catch their train. A uniformed doorman ushered Rebus inside, where a keen-eyed concierge immediately spotted him as trouble of some kind.

'How can I be of assistance this evening, sir?'

Rebus held out his ID in one hand, key-card in the other. 'I need to take a look at this room.'

'And why's that, Inspector?'

'Seems the guest checked out early.'

'That's unfortunate.'

'I dare say someone else is picking up his tab. Actually, that's something you could look into for me.'

'I'll need to clear it with the duty manager.'

'Fine. Meantime, I'll be upstairs ...' He waved the key-card.

'I need to clear that too, I'm afraid.'

Rebus took a step back, the better to size up his opponent. 'How long will it take?'

'Just need to track down the duty manager ... couple of minutes is all.' Rebus followed him to the reception desk. 'Sara, is Angela about?'

'Think she went upstairs. I'll page her.'

'And I'll check the office,' the concierge told Rebus, moving off again. Rebus waited and watched as the receptionist punched numbers into her phone before putting down the receiver. She looked up at him and smiled. She knew something was up, and wanted to know more.

'Guest just dropped dead,' Rebus obliged.

Her eyes widened. 'That's terrible.'

'Mr Webster, Room 214. Was he here on his own?'

Her fingers busied themselves on her keyboard. 'Double room, but just the one key issued. I don't think I remember him ...'

'Is there a home address?'

'London,' she stated.

Rebus guessed this would be a weekday pied-à-terre. He was leaning across the reception desk, trying to seem casual, unsure how many questions he'd get away with. 'Was he paying by credit card, Sara?'

She studied her screen. 'All charges to—' She broke off, aware that the concierge was approaching.

'All charges to ...?' Rebus nudged.

'Inspector,' the concierge was calling, sensing something was going on.

Sara's phone was ringing. She lifted the receiver. 'Reception,' she trilled. 'Oh, hello, Angela. There's another policeman here ...'

Another?

'Will you come down, or shall I send him up?'

The concierge was behind Rebus now. 'I'll take the Inspector up,' he was telling Sara.

Another policeman ... up ... Rebus was getting a bad feeling. When the lift doors signalled that they were opening, he turned towards the sound. Watched David Steelforth step out. The Special Branch man gave the beginnings of a smile as he shook his head slowly. His meaning couldn't

53

have been clearer: Matey, you're not getting anywhere *near* Room 214. Rebus turned round and grabbed the computer monitor, swivelling it towards him. The concierge locked on to his arm. Sara gave a little shriek into the telephone, probably deafening the duty manager. Steelforth bounded forward to join the fray.

'That's definitely out of order,' the concierge hissed. His grip was vice-like. Rebus decided the man had seen some action in his time; decided not to make an issue of it. He lifted his hand from the monitor. Sara swung it back towards her.

'You can let go now,' Rebus said. The concierge released his grip. Sara was staring at him in shock, the phone still held in one hand. Rebus turned to Steelforth.

'You're going to tell me I can't see Room 214.'

'Not at all.' Steelforth's smile broadened. 'But the duty manager is: that's her prerogative, after all.'

As if on command, Sara put the phone to her ear. 'She's on her way,' she said.

'I'll bet she is.' Rebus's eyes were still on Steelforth, but there was another figure a little way behind him: Siobhan. 'Bar still open, is it?' Rebus asked the concierge. The man desperately wanted to say no, but the lie would have been blatant. He gave a little nod instead. 'I won't ask you to join me,' Rebus said to Steelforth. He brushed past both men and climbed the steps to the Palm Court. Stood at the bar and waited for Siobhan to catch up. He took a deep breath and reached into his jacket for a cigarette.

'Little problem with the management?' Siobhan asked.

'You saw our friend from SO12?'

'Nice perks they get in Special Branch.'

'I don't know if he's staying here, but a guy called Ben Webster was.'

'The Labour MP?'

'That's the one.'

'I feel there's a story behind this.' Her shoulders seemed

to slump a little, and Rebus remembered that she too had had adventures this evening.

'You go first,' he insisted. The barman had placed bowls of nibbles in front of them. 'Highland Park for me,' Rebus told him. 'Vodka tonic for the lady.' Siobhan nodded her agreement. As the barman turned away, Rebus reached for one of the paper napkins. Took a pen from his pocket and jotted something down. Siobhan angled her head to get a better look.

'Who or what is Pennen Industries?'

'Whoever they are, they've got deep pockets and a London postcode.' From the corner of his eye, Rebus could see Steelforth watching from the doorway. He made a show of waving the napkin at him before folding and pocketing it.

'So who was it took against your car – CND, Greenpeace, Stop the War?'

'Niddrie,' Siobhan stated. 'More specifically, the Niddrie Young Team.'

'Think we can persuade the G8 to list them as a terror cell?'

'Few thousand Marines would sort things nicely.'

'Sadly, however, Niddrie has yet to strike oil.' Rebus reached a hand out towards the tumbler of malt. Slightest of tremors, that was all. Toasted his drinking partner, the G8, and the Marines ... and would have toasted Steelforth too.

Had the doorway not been empty.

Saturday 2 July

3

Rebus awoke to daylight and realised he hadn't closed the curtains the previous night. The TV was showing early morning news. Seemed mostly to be about the concert in Hyde Park. They were talking to the organisers. No mention of Edinburgh. He switched it off and went into the bedroom. Changed out of the previous day's clothes and into a short-sleeved shirt and chinos. Splashed some water on his face, studied the results and knew he needed something more. Grabbed his keys and phone – he'd left it charging overnight; couldn't have been that drunk – and left his flat. Down two flights of stairs to the tenement's main door. His area of town, Marchmont, was a student enclave, the up side of which was that it was quiet during the summer. He'd watched them decant at the end of June, loading cars belonging to them or their parents, stuffing duvets into the chinks of spare space. There had been parties to celebrate the end of exams, meaning Rebus had twice had to remove parking cones from the roof of his car. He stood now on the pavement and sucked in what was left of the overnight chill, then headed for Marchmont Road, where the newsagent's was just opening. A couple of single-decker buses trundled past. Rebus thought they must be lost, until he remembered. And now he could hear it: workmen's hammers; a PA system being tested. He paid the shopkeeper and unscrewed the top from the Irn-Bru bottle. Downed it in one, which was fine: he'd added a back-up to his purchases. Unpeeled and ate the banana as he walked – not straight back to the flat, but down to the bottom of Marchmont Road, where it connected with The Meadows. The Meadows had been just that, several centuries back: meadowland on the outskirts of the city, Marchmont itself not much more than a farm with surrounding fields. Nowadays The Meadows was used for games of football and cricket, for jogging or picnics.

But not today.

Melville Drive had already been cordoned off, turning an important traffic artery into a bus park. There were dozens of them, stretching to the curve of the road and beyond, three abreast in some places. They were from Derby and Macclesfield and Hull, Swansea and Ripon, Carlisle and Epping. People dressed in white were descending from them. White: Rebus remembered that everyone had been asked to wear the same colour. It meant that when they marched around the city, they would create a vast and visible ribbon. He checked his own clothes: the chinos were fawn, the shirt pale blue.

Thank Christ for that.

A lot of the bus people looked elderly, some quite frail. But they all sported their wristbands and their sloganed shirts. Some carried home-made banners. They looked delighted to be there. Further along, marquees had been constructed. Vans were arriving, ready to sell chips and meat-free burgers to the hungry masses. Stages had been erected, and there was a display of huge wooden jigsaw pieces laid out next to a series of cranes. It took Rebus only a matter of seconds to spell out the words MAKE POVERTY HISTORY. There were uniformed cops in the vicinity, but nobody Rebus knew; probably not even local. He looked at his watch. It had just gone nine, another three hours till kick-off. Hardly a cloud in the sky. A police van had decided that its quickest route would entail mounting the kerb, forcing Rebus to backtrack on to the grass. He scowled at the driver, who returned the look. The side window opened.

'What's your problem, Grandad?'

Rebus stuck two fingers up, willing the driver to stop. The pair of them could have a nice little chat. But the van had other ideas; kept moving. Rebus had finished his banana, thought about dropping the skin but reckoned he'd be pounced on by the Recycling Police. Headed over to a bin instead.

'Here you go,' a young woman said, holding out a carrier bag. Rebus looked inside: a couple of stickers and a Help the Aged T-shirt.

'Hell do I want this for?' he growled. She took it back, trying hard to retain the traces of her original smile.

He moved away, opening the reserve bottle of Irn-Bru. His head felt less gummy, but there was sweat on his back. A memory had been trying to force its way through, and now he grasped it: Mickey and himself, church outings to Burntisland links. Buses took them there, trailing streamers from their windows. Lines of buses waiting to take them home after the picnic and the organised races across the grass – Mickey always able to beat him from a standing start, so that Rebus had stopped trying, eventually, his only weapon against his kid brother's sinewy determination. White cardboard boxes containing their lunch: jam sandwich; iced cake; maybe a hard-boiled egg.

They always left the egg.

Summer weekends, appearing endless and unchangeable. Nowadays, Rebus hated them. Hated that so little would happen to him. Monday mornings were his true release, a break from the sofa and the bar-stool, the supermarket and curry-house. His colleagues returned to work with stories of shopping exploits, football games, bike rides with the family. Siobhan would have been to Glasgow or Dundee, seeing friends, catching up. Cinema trips and walks by the Water of Leith. Nobody asked Rebus any more how he spent the furlough. They knew he'd just shrug.

Nobody'd blame you for coasting …

Except that coasting was the one thing he had no time for. Without the job, he almost ceased to exist. Which was why he punched a number into his phone and waited. Listened to the pick-up: messaging service.

'Good morning, Ray,' he said when prompted, 'this is your alarm call. Every hour on the hour till I start to get some answers. Speak to you soon.' He ended the call, immediately making another, leaving the same message on Ray Duff's home machine. Mobile and land-line taken care of, there wasn't much he could do but wait. The Live 8 concert started around two, but he didn't think either The Who or Pink Floyd would appear until evening. Plenty of time for him to go over the Colliar case-notes. Plenty of time for follow-up on Ben Webster. Pushing Saturday along until it turned into Sunday.

Rebus reckoned he would survive.

The only things directory enquiries could give him on Pennen Industries were a phone number and an address in central London. Rebus called, but got a message telling him the switchboard would open again on Monday morning. He reckoned he could do better than that, so placed a call to Operation Sorbus HQ in Glenrothes.

'It's CID here, B Division in Edinburgh.' He crossed the floor of his living room and peered out of the window. A family, kids with their faces painted, was making its way down the street towards The Meadows. 'We've been hearing rumours about the Clown Army. Seems they might have their sights trained on something called …' he paused for effect, as though consulting a document, 'Pennen Industries. We're in the dark, wondered if your boffins could shed some light.'

'Pennen?'

Rebus spelled it.

'And you are …?'

'DI Starr ... Derek Starr,' Rebus lied blithely. No way of knowing what would get back to Steelforth.

'Give me ten minutes.'

Rebus was about to offer thanks, but the line was dead. It had been a male voice, noises off: the sounds of a busy hub. He realised the officer hadn't needed to ask for his phone number ... must've come up on some sort of display, making it a matter of record.

And traceable.

'Oops,' he said quietly, heading for the kitchen and some coffee. He recalled that Siobhan had left the Balmoral after two drinks. Rebus had added a third, before crossing the road to the Café Royal for a nightcap. Vinegar on his fingers this morning, which meant he'd eaten chips on the way home. Yes: taxi driver dropping him at the end of The Meadows, Rebus saying he'd walk from there. He thought of calling Siobhan, make sure she got home all right. But it always annoyed her when he did that. She'd probably be out already: meeting her parents at the march. She was looking forward to seeing Eddie Izzard and Gael Garcia Bernal. Others were making speeches too: Bianca Jagger; Sharleen Spiteri ... She'd made it sound like a carnival. He hoped she was right.

Had to get her car to the garage too, see about fixing the damage. Rebus knew Councillor Tench; knew *of* him, at least. Some sort of lay preacher, used to have a spot at the foot of The Mound, calling out for the weekend shoppers to repent. Rebus used to see him when he was on his way to the Ox for a lunchtime session. Had a good rep in Niddrie, harvesting development grants from local government, charities, even the EU. Rebus had told Siobhan as much, then given her a number for a panel-beater off Buccleuch Street. Guy specialised in VWs but owed Rebus a favour ...

His phone was ringing. He took the coffee through to the living room and picked up.

'You're not at the station,' the same voice in Glenrothes said warily.

'I'm at home.' He could hear a helicopter somewhere overhead, outside his window. Maybe surveillance; maybe news. Or could it be Bono parachuting in with a sermon?

'Pennen doesn't have any offices in Scotland,' the voice was saying.

'Then we don't have a problem,' Rebus replied, trying to sound casual. 'Time like this, the rumour-mill's on overtime, same as the rest of us.' He laughed, and was about to add a fresh question, but the voice made it unnecessary.

'They're a defence contractor, so the rumours might still have force.'

'Defence?'

'Used to belong to the MoD; sold off a few years back.'

'I think I remember,' Rebus made a show of saying. 'London-based, right?'

'Right. Thing is, though ... their MD is up here just now.'

Rebus whistled. 'Potential target.'

'We had him risk-flagged anyway. He's secure.' The words didn't sound right in the young officer's mouth. Rebus reckoned he'd learned the phrases only recently.

Maybe from Steelforth.

'He's not based at the Balmoral, is he?' Rebus asked.

'How do you know that?'

'Rumours again. But he's got protection?'

'Yes.'

'His own or ours?'

The caller paused. 'Why do you want to know?'

'Just looking out for the taxpayer.' Rebus laughed again. 'Think we should talk to him?' Asking advice ... as if the caller was the boss.

'I can pass the message along.'

'Longer he's in town, tougher it is ...' Rebus broke off. 'I don't even know his name,' he admitted.

Suddenly another voice broke into the call. 'DI Starr? Is that Detective Inspector Starr speaking?'

Steelforth ...

Rebus sucked in air.

'Hello?' Steelforth was saying. 'Gone shy all of a sudden?'

Rebus cut the call. Cursed under his breath. Punched in more numbers and was connected to the switchboard at the local newspaper.

'Features, please,' he said.

'I'm not sure anyone's in,' the operator told him.

'What about the news desk?'

'Bit of a ghost ship, for obvious reasons.' She sounded as if she, too, would rather be elsewhere, but put him through anyway. It took a while for someone to pick up.

'My name's DI Rebus, Gayfield CID.'

'Always happy to talk to an officer of the law,' the reporter said brightly. 'Both on *and* off the record ...'

'I'm not touting for business, son. I just need to speak to Mairie Henderson.'

'She's gone freelance. And she's features, not news.'

'Didn't stop you putting her and Big Ger Cafferty on the front page, did it?'

'I thought about it years back, you know ...' The reporter sounded as if he was getting comfortable, ready for a natter. 'Not just Cafferty, though – interviews with all the gangsters, east coast and west. How they got started, codes they live by ...'

'Well, thanks for that, but have I tuned into *Parkinson* here or what?'

The reporter snorted. 'Just making conversation.'

'Don't tell me: it's a ghost ship there, am I right? They're all out with their laptops, trying to transform the march into elegant prose? Here's the thing, though ... a guy fell from the Castle ramparts last night, and I didn't see anything about it in your paper this morning.'

'We didn't get wind of it till too late.' The reporter paused. 'Straight suicide though, right?'

'What do you think?'

'I asked you first.'

'Actually, it was me that asked first – for Mairie Henderson's number.'

'Why?'

'Give me her number, and I'll tell you something I'm not going to tell her.'

The reporter thought for a moment, then asked Rebus to hang on. He was back half a minute later. Meantime, the receiver had been making a noise, letting him know someone else was trying to reach him. He ignored it, jotted down the number the reporter gave him.

'Thanks,' he said.

'Now do I get my little treat?'

'Ask yourself this: straight suicide, why is a Special Branch slimeball called Steelforth clamping down on it?'

'Steelforth? How do you spell—?'

But Rebus had cut the connection. His phone began ringing immediately. He didn't answer; had more than half an idea who it would be – Operation Sorbus had his number; would have taken about a minute for Steelforth to work out whose home address it belonged to. Another minute to call Derek Starr and ascertain he didn't know anything about anything.

Brreeep-brreeep-brreeeppp.

Rebus put the TV on again; pressed the mute button on the remote. No news, just kids' programmes and pop videos. The chopper was circling again. He made sure it wasn't his tenement.

'Just because you're paranoid, John ...' he muttered to himself. His phone had stopped ringing; he made the call to Mairie Henderson. They'd been close friends a few years back; traded gen for stories, stories for gen. Then she'd gone and written a book about Cafferty – written it with the gangster's full cooperation. Asked Rebus for an interview, but he'd refused. Asked again later.

'Way Big Ger talks about you,' she'd cajoled, 'I really think you need to give your side.'

Rebus hadn't felt that need at all.

Which hadn't stopped the book being a roaring success, not just in Scotland but further afield. USA, Canada, Australia. Translations into sixteen languages. For a time, he couldn't pick up the paper without reading about it. Couple of prizes; TV talk shows for journalist and subject. Wasn't enough that Cafferty had spent his life ruining people and their communities, terrorising them ... now he was a full-scale celebrity.

She'd sent Rebus a copy of the book; he'd sent it back by return. Then had gone out two weeks later and bought himself a copy – half-price on Princes Street. Flicked through it but hadn't had the stomach for the whole thing. Nothing brought the bile up quicker than a penitent ...

'Hello?'

'Mairie, it's John Rebus.'

'Sorry, the only John Rebus I know is dead.'

'Now that's hardly fair.'

'You sent my book back! After I'd signed it to you and everything!'

'Signed it?'

'You didn't even read the inscription?'

'What did it say?'

'It said, "Whatever it is you're wanting, get stuffed."'

'Sorry about that, Mairie. Let me make it up to you.'

'By asking a favour?'

'How did you guess?' He smiled into the receiver. 'You going to the march?'

'Thinking about it.'

'I could buy you a tofu burger.'

She gave a snort. 'Long time since I was *that* cheap a date.'

'I'll throw in a mug of decaf ...'

'What the hell do you want, John?' The words cold, but the voice thawing a little.

'I want some info on an outfit called Pennen Industries. Used to be Ministry of Defence. I think they're in town right now.'

'And why am I interested?'

'You're not, but I am ...' He paused to light a cigarette; exhaled smoke as he spoke. 'Did you hear about Cafferty's chum?'

'Which one?' Trying not to sound interested.

'Cyril Colliar. That missing scrap from his jacket has turned up.'

'With Cafferty's confession written on it? He told me you wouldn't give up.'

'Just thought I'd let you know – it's not exactly common knowledge.'

She was silent for a moment. 'And Pennen Industries?'

'Something else entirely. You heard about Ben Webster?'

'It was on the news.'

'Pennen were paying for his stay at the Balmoral.'

'So?'

'So I'd like to know a bit more about them.'

'Their MD's name is Richard Pennen.' She laughed, sensing his bemusement. 'Ever heard of Google?'

'And you just did that while we're talking?'

'Do you even have a computer at home?'

'I bought a laptop.'

'So you're on the internet?'

'In theory,' he confessed. 'But hey, I play a mean game of Minesweeper ...'

She laughed again, and he knew it was going to be all right between them. He heard something hissing in the background; the clinking of cups.

'Which café are you in?' he asked.

'Montpelier's. There are people outside, all dressed in white.'

Montpelier's was in Bruntsfield; five minutes by car. 'I could come buy you that coffee. You can show me how to use my laptop.'

'I'm just leaving. Want to meet later at The Meadows?'

'Not especially. How about a drink?'

'Maybe. I'll see what I can find about Pennen, call you when I'm finished.'

'You're a star, Mairie.'

'And a bestseller to boot.' She paused. 'Cafferty's share went to charity, you know.'

'He can afford to be generous. Talk to you later.' Rebus finished the call, decided to check for messages. There was only the one. Steelforth's voice had got just a dozen words out when Rebus cut it off. The unfinished threat echoed in his head as he crossed to the hi-fi and filled the room with the Groundhogs ...

Don't ever presume to be able to outsmart me, Rebus, or I'll—

' ... break most of the major bones,' Professor Gates was saying. He gave a shrug. 'Fall like that, what else can you expect?'

He was in work because Ben Webster was news. Rush job: everyone wanted the case closed as soon as possible.

'A nice suicide verdict,' was how Gates had put it earlier. He was joined in the autopsy suite by Dr Curt. In Scots law, two pathologists were needed: corroboration the result. Kept things tidy in court. Gates was the heavier of the two men, face red-veined, nose misshapen by early abuse on the rugby pitch (his version) or an ill-judged student fight. Curt, his junior by only four or five years, was slightly taller and a good deal thinner. Both men had tenure at the University of Edinburgh. With the term finished, they could have been sunning themselves elsewhere, but Rebus had never known them to take holidays – either would have regarded it as a sign of weakness in the other.

'Not on the march, John?' Curt asked. The three men were gathered around a steel slab in the mortuary on Cowgate. Just behind them, an assistant was moving pans and instruments with a series of metallic scrapes and clatterings.

'Too tame for me,' Rebus answered. 'Monday, that's when I'll be out.'

'With all the other anarchists,' Gates added, slicing into the body. There was an area for spectators, and Rebus would usually have stayed there, shielded by Perspex, distanced from this ritual. But, 'this being the weekend', Gates had said, they could 'rise to a certain informality'. Rebus had seen the insides of a human before, but averted his gaze nonetheless.

'What was he – thirty-four, thirty-five?' Gates asked.

'Thirty-four,' the assistant confirmed.

'In pretty good nick ... considering.'

'Sister says he kept fit: jogging, swimming, gym.'

'Is that who did the formal ID?' Rebus asked, happy to turn his head in the assistant's direction.

'Parents are dead.'

'It was in the papers, wasn't it?' Curt drawled, keeping a beady eye on his colleague's work. 'Scalpel sharp enough, Sandy?'

Gates ignored this. 'Mother was killed during a break-in. Tragic really; father couldn't go on without her.'

'Just wasted away, didn't he?' Curt added. 'Want me to take over, Sandy? Can't blame you for feeling tired, the week we've had ...'

'Stop fussing.'

Curt offered a sigh and a shrug, both for Rebus's benefit.

'Did the sister come down from Dundee?' Rebus asked the assistant.

'Works in London. She's a cop, nicer-looking than most.'

'No valentine for you next year,' Rebus retorted.

'Present company excepted, obviously.'

'Poor girl,' Curt commented. 'To lose your family ...'

'Were they close?' Rebus couldn't help asking. Gates thought it an odd question; glanced up from his work. Rebus ignored him.

'Don't think she'd seen much of him lately,' the assistant was saying.

Like me and Michael ...

'Pretty cut up about it all the same.'

'She didn't travel up on her own, did she?' Rebus asked.

'Wasn't anyone with her at the ID,' the assistant said matter-of-factly. 'I left her in the waiting area after, gave her a mug of tea.'

'She's not still there, is she?' Gates snapped.

The assistant looked around him, unsure what rule he'd broken. 'I had to get the cutters ready ...'

'Place is deserted apart from us,' Gates barked. 'Go see she's all right.'

'I'll do it,' Rebus stated.

Gates turned towards him, hands cradling a pile of glistening innards. 'What's the matter, John? Lost the stomach?'

There was no one in the waiting area. An empty mug, decorated with the badge of Glasgow Rangers FC, sat on the floor beside a chair. Rebus touched it: still warm. He walked towards the main door. Members of the public entered the building from an alley off the Cowgate. Rebus looked up and down the road, but saw no one. Walked around the corner into Cowgate itself and saw the figure seated on the low wall which fronted the mortuary. She was staring at the children's nursery across the street. Rebus stopped in front of her.

71

'Got a cigarette?' she asked.

'You want one?'

'Seems as good a time as any.'

'Meaning you don't smoke.'

'So?'

'So I'm not about to corrupt you.'

She looked at him for the first time. She had short fair hair, and a round face with prominent chin. Her skirt was knee-length, an inch of leg showing above brown boots with fur edging. On the wall next to her sat an oversized bag, probably everything she'd packed – hurriedly, haphazardly – before rushing north.

'I'm DI Rebus,' he told her. 'I'm sorry about your brother.'

She nodded slowly, eyes returning to the nursery school. 'Is that working?' she asked, gesturing in its direction.

'As far as I know. It's not open today, of course ...'

'But it *is* a nursery.' She turned to examine the building behind her. 'And right across the road from *this*. Short journey, isn't it, DI Rebus?'

'I suppose you're right. I'm sorry I wasn't there when you ID'd the body.'

'Why? Did you know Ben?'

'No ... I just thought ... How come nobody's with you?'

'Such as?'

'From his constituency ... the party.'

'Think Labour gives two hoots about him now?' She gave a short laugh. 'They'll all be lining up at the head of that bloody march, ready for the photo-op. Ben kept saying how close he was getting to what he called "the power". Little good it did him.'

'Careful there,' Rebus warned her. 'You sound like you'd fit right in with the marchers.' She gave a snort, but didn't say anything. 'Any idea why he would ...?' Rebus broke off. 'You know I need to ask?'

'I'm a cop, same as you.' She watched him bring out the packet. 'Just one,' she begged. How could he refuse? He lit both their cigarettes and leaned against the wall next to her.

'No cars,' she stated.

'Town's locked down,' he explained. 'You'll have trouble getting a taxi, but my car's parked ...'

'I can walk,' she told him. 'He didn't leave a note, if that's what you wanted to know. Seemed fine last night, very relaxed, et cetera. Colleagues can't explain ... no problems at work.' She paused, raising her eyes skywards. 'Except he *always* had problems at work.'

'Sounds like the two of you were close.'

'He was in London most weekdays. We hadn't seen one another for maybe a month – actually, probably more like two – but there were texts, emails ...' She took a drag on the cigarette.

'He had problems at work?' Rebus prompted.

'Ben worked on foreign aid, deciding which decrepit African dictatorships deserved our help.'

'Explains what he was doing here,' Rebus said, almost to himself.

She gave a slow, sad nod. 'Getting closer to the power – a slap-up dinner at Edinburgh Castle while you discuss the world's poor and hungry.'

'He'd be aware of the irony?' Rebus guessed.

'Oh yes.'

'And the futility?'

She fixed her eyes on his. 'Never,' she mouthed quietly. 'Wasn't in Ben's nature.' She blinked back tears, sniffed and sighed, and flipped most of the cigarette on to the roadway. 'I need to go.' She brought a wallet from her shoulder bag, handed Rebus a business card. Nothing on it but her name – Stacey Webster – and a mobile number.

'How long have you been in the police, Stacey?'

'Eight years. The last three at Scotland Yard.' Her eyes

73

fixed on his. 'You'll have questions for me: did Ben have any enemies? Money problems? Relationships gone bad? Maybe later, eh? A day or so, give me a call.'

'Okay.'

'Nothing in the ...' She had trouble getting the next word out; sucked in some air and tried again. 'Nothing to suggest he didn't just fall?'

'He'd had a glass or two of wine – might've made him woozy.'

'Nobody saw anything?'

Rebus offered a shrug. 'Sure I can't give you a lift?'

She shook her head. 'I need to walk.'

'Word of advice: steer clear of the parade route. Maybe I'll see you again ... and I really am sorry about Ben.'

Her eyes bored into his. 'You actually sound as if you mean that.'

He almost opened up to her – *I left my own brother in a box only yesterday* – but gave a twitch of the mouth instead. She might have started asking questions: *Were you close? Are you okay?* Questions he didn't really know the answers to. He watched her start her long and lonely walk along Cowgate, then went back inside for the autopsy's closing act.

4

By the time Siobhan arrived at The Meadows, the queue of waiting marchers stretched all the way down the side of the old infirmary and across the playing-fields to where the rows of buses sat. Someone with a megaphone was warning that it might be two hours before those at the back of the line actually started moving.

'It's the pigs,' someone explained. 'Only letting us go in batches of forty or fifty.'

Siobhan had been about to defend the tactic, but knew it would give her away. She moved down the patient queue, wondering how she was expected to meet her parents. There had to be a hundred thousand people here, maybe even double that. She'd never known a crowd like it; T in the Park only got sixty thousand. The local football derby might attract eighteen on a good day. Hogmanay in and around Princes Street, you could get close to a hundred.

This was bigger.

And everyone was smiling.

Hardly a uniform to be seen; not many stewards either. Families streaming down from Morningside and Tollcross and Newington. She'd bumped into half a dozen acquaintances and neighbours. The Lord Provost was leading the procession. Some said Gordon Brown was there too. Later he'd be addressing a rally, the Police Protection Squad in attendance, though Operation Sorbus had graded him 'low risk' due to his active pronouncements on aid and fair trade. She'd been shown a list of celebrities who were expected to hit the city: Geldof and Bono, of course; maybe

Ewan McGregor (who was due at an event in Dunblane anyway); Julie Christie; Claudia Schiffer; George Clooney; Susan Sarandon ...

Having worked her way down the line, she headed for the main stage. A band was playing, a few people dancing enthusiastically. Most just sat on the grass and watched. The small tented village nearby offered activities for children, first aid, petitions and exhibits. Crafts were being sold, flyers handed out. One of the tabloids seemed to have been distributing Make Poverty History placards. Recipients were now tearing across the top section of each placard, removing the tabloid's masthead. Helium-filled balloons rose into the sky. A makeshift brass band was circumnavigating the field, followed by an African steel band. More dancing; more smiles. She knew then, knew that it was going to be all right. There'd be no riots today, not on this march.

She looked at her mobile. No messages. She'd tried her parents twice, but they weren't answering. So she commenced another tour of the site. A smaller stage had been erected in front of a stationary open-topped bus. There were TV cameras here, and people were being interviewed. She recognised Pete Postlethwaite and Billy Boyd; caught a glimpse of Billy Bragg. The actor she really wanted to see was Gael Garcia Bernal, just in case he really did look as good in the flesh ...

The queues at the vegetarian food vans were longer than the ones for burgers. She'd been vegetarian herself at one time, but had lapsed several years back, blaming Rebus and the bacon rolls he'd kept wafting in her face. She thought of texting him, dragging him down here. What else would he be doing? Either slumped on the sofa, or resting on a stool at the Oxford Bar. But she sent a text to her parents instead, then headed towards the waiting lines again. Banners had been hoisted high; whistles were being blown, drums beaten. All that energy in the air ...

Rebus would say it was being wasted. He'd say the political deals had already been done. And he'd be right: the guys at Sorbus HQ had told her as much. Gleneagles was for private confabs and public photo-ops. The real business had been thrashed out in advance by lesser mortals, chief among them the Chancellor of the Exchequer. All of it done on the quiet and ratified by eight signatures on the final day of the G8.

'And how much is it all costing?' Siobhan had wondered.

'A hundred and fifty mil, give or take.'

The answer had produced a sharp intake of breath from DCI Macrae. Siobhan had pursed her lips, saying nothing.

'I know what you're thinking,' her informant had continued. 'Same sort of money buys a lot of vaccine ...'

Every path across The Meadows was now four deep with waiting marchers. A new line had formed stretching back to the tennis courts and Buccleuch Street. As Siobhan squeezed her way past, still no sign of her parents, she caught a blur of colour at the edge of her vision. Bright yellow jackets hurrying down Meadow Lane. She followed them, rounding the corner into Buccleuch Place.

And was stopped dead.

Sixty or so black-clad demonstrators had been encircled by double that number of police. The protesters had airhorns, which rasped a deafening complaint. They wore sunglasses, black scarves muffling their faces. Some wore hooded tops. Black combat trousers and boots, a few bandannas. They didn't carry placards and none of them were smiling. Riot shields were all that separated them from the police lines. Someone had spray-painted the anarchist symbol on at least one translucent shield. The mass of demonstrators pressed forward, demanding access to The Meadows. But police tactics said different: containment above all else. A demo contained was a demo controlled. Siobhan was impressed: her colleagues had to have known the protesters were on their way. They'd taken up position fast, and weren't about to let the situation develop any further than here and now. There were a few other bystanders, torn between this spectacle and a need to join the march. Some of them had their camera-phones out. Siobhan looked around, making sure no fresh intake of riot officers tried corralling *her*. The voices from within the cordon seemed foreign, maybe Spanish or Italian. She knew some of the names: Ya Basta; Black Bloc. No sign of anything as outlandish as the Wombles or Rebel Clown Army.

Her hand went into her pocket, clutching her warrant card. Wanted to be ready to show ID if things got heated. Helicopter hovering overhead, and a uniformed officer videotaping proceedings from the steps of one of the university buildings. He scanned the street with his camera, pausing on her for a moment before moving on to the other bystanders. But Siobhan was suddenly aware of another camera, focused on *him*. Santal was inside the cordon, recording everything with her own digital video. She was dressed like the others, backpack slung over one shoulder, concentrating on her task rather than joining in with the chants and slogans. The demonstrators wanted their own record: to watch later and enjoy; so they could learn police tactics and how to counter them; and just in case of – maybe even in the hope of – heavy-handedness. They were media-savvy, counted lawyers among their activist friends. Film from Genoa had been beamed around the world. No reason fresh film of violent policing wouldn't be just as efficacious.

Siobhan realised Santal had seen her. The camera was pointed her way, and the mouth below the viewfinder broke into a scowl. Siobhan didn't think it the right time to wander over and ask for her parents' whereabouts ... Her phone started to vibrate, telling her she had an incoming call. She checked the number, but didn't recognise it.

'Siobhan Clarke,' she said, holding the slim little box to her ear.

'Shiv? It's Ray Duff. Reckon I'm bloody well earning that day out.'

'What day out?'

'The one you're due me ...' He paused. 'Except that's not the deal you made with Rebus, is it?'

Siobhan smiled. 'All depends. Are you at the lab?'

'Working my arse off on your behalf.'

'The stuff from Clootie Well?'

'Might have something for you, though I'm not sure you're going to like it. How soon can you get here?'

'Half an hour.' She turned away from the sudden blare of the air-horn.

'No prizes for guessing where you are,' Duff's voice said. 'I've got it on the news channel here.'

'The march or the demo?'

'Demo, naturally. Happy, law-abiding marchers hardly make for a story, even when they number quarter of a million.'

'Quarter of a million?'

'That's what they're saying. See you in half an hour.'

'Bye, Ray.' She ended the call. A figure like that ... more than half the population of Edinburgh. It was like three million on the streets of London. And sixty black-clad figures hogging the news cycle for the next hour or two.

Because after that, all eyes would turn to the Live 8 concert in London.

No, no, no, she thought, too cynical, Siobhan; you're thinking like John bloody Rebus. Nobody could ignore a human chain encircling the city, a ribbon of white, all that passion and hope ...

Minus one.

Had she ever planned to stick around, add her own small self to the statistics? No chance of that now. She could apologise later to her parents. For now, she was on

79

the move, walking away from The Meadows. Her best bet: St Leonard's, the nearest police station. Hitch a lift in a patrol car; hijack one if need be. Her own car was sitting in the garage Rebus had recommended. Mechanic had said to call him on Monday. She remembered how one owner of a 4x4 had apparently moved her car out of town for the duration, lest rioters should target it. Just one more scare story, or so she'd thought at the time.

Santal didn't appear to notice her leave.

'... can't even mail a letter,' Ray Duff was saying. 'They've locked up all the postboxes in case someone decides to put a bomb in one.'

'Some of the shop-fronts on Princes Street are boarded up,' Siobhan added. 'What do you reckon it is Ann Summers is afraid of?'

'Basque separatists?' Rebus guessed. 'Any chance of us getting to the point?'

Duff snorted. 'He's afraid he'll miss the big reunion.'

'Reunion?' Siobhan looked at Rebus.

'Pink Floyd,' Rebus answered. 'But if it's anything like McCartney and U2, I'm well shot of it.'

The three were standing in one of the labs belonging to the Lothian and Borders Forensic Science Unit on Howdenhall Road. Duff, mid-thirties with short brown hair and a pronounced widow's peak, was polishing his glasses on a corner of his white lab-coat. The rise of television's *CSI* franchise had had, to Rebus's mind, a detrimental effect on all the Howdenhall boffins. Despite their lack of resources, glamour and pounding soundtrack, they all seemed to think they were actors. Moreover, some of the CID had started to agree, and would ask them to replicate the TV shows' most far-fetched forensic techniques. Duff had apparently decided that his own role would be that of eccentric genius. As a result, he had dispensed with his contact lenses and reverted to NHS-style specs with Eric

Morecambe frames, the better to complement the row of multicoloured pens in his top pocket. Additionally, a line of bulldog clips was attached to one lapel. As Rebus had pointed out on arrival, he looked like he'd walked out of a Devo video.

And now he was stringing them along.

'In your own time,' Rebus encouraged him. They were standing in front of a workbench on which various pieces of cloth had been laid out. Duff had placed numbered squares beside each one, and smaller squares – apparently colour-coded – next to any stains or blemishes on each article. 'Sooner we're done, sooner you can get back to polishing the chrome on your MG.'

'That reminds me,' Siobhan said. 'Thanks for offering me to Ray.'

'You should have seen first prize,' Rebus muttered. 'What are we looking at, Prof?'

'Mud and bird shit mostly.' Duff rested his hands on his hips. 'Brown for the former, grey for the latter.' He nodded at the coloured squares.

'Leaving blue and pink ...'

'Blue is for stuff that needs further analysis.'

'Tell me pink is for lipstick,' Siobhan said quietly.

'Blood, actually.' Duff spoke with a flourish.

'Oh good,' Rebus responded, eyes fixing on Siobhan. 'How many?'

'Two so far ... Numbered one and two. One is a pair of brown cord trousers. Blood can be a bugger to make out against a brown background – resembles rust. Two belongs to a sports shirt, pale yellow as you can see.'

'Not really,' Rebus said, leaning over for a closer look. The shirt was caked with dirt. 'What's that on the left breast? Badge of some kind?'

'What it actually says is Keogh's Garage. The blood spatter is on the back.'

'Spatter?'

81

Duff nodded. 'Consistent with a blow to the head. Something like a hammer, you make contact, break the skin, and when you draw the hammer away, the blood flies off in all directions.'

'Keogh's Garage?' Siobhan's question was directed at Rebus, who merely shrugged. Duff, however, cleared his throat.

'Nothing in the Perthshire phone book. Or Edinburgh, come to that.'

'Fast work, Ray,' Siobhan said approvingly.

'Another brownie point there, Ray,' Rebus added with a wink. 'How about contestant number one?'

Duff nodded. 'Not spatter this time – dollops on the right-hand leg, around the level of the knee. Whack someone on the head, you'll get some drips like that.'

'You're saying we've got three victims, one attacker?'

Duff shrugged. 'No way to prove it, of course. But ask yourself: what are the chances of *three* victims having three different attackers, all ending up in the same obscure location?'

'You've got a point, Ray,' Rebus conceded.

'And *we've* got a serial killer,' Siobhan said into the silence. 'Different blood types, I take it?' She watched Duff nod. 'Any idea which order they might have died in?'

'CC Rider is the freshest. I'd guess the sports shirt is the oldest.'

'And no other clues from the cords?'

Duff shook his head slowly, then dug into his lab-coat pocket and produced a clear polythene envelope. 'Unless you count this, of course.'

'What is that?' Siobhan asked.

'Cash-machine card,' Duff told her, relishing the moment. 'Name of Trevor Guest. So never let me hear you say I don't earn my little rewards ...'

*

Back in the fresh air, Rebus lit a cigarette. Siobhan paced the length of a parking bay, arms folded.

'One killer,' she stated.

'Yep.'

'Two named victims, the other a mechanic ...'

'Or a car salesman,' Rebus mused. 'Or just someone who had access to a shirt advertising a garage.'

'Thanks for refusing to narrow the search.'

He shrugged. 'If we'd found a Hibs scarf, would we be homing in on the first team?'

'All right, point taken.' She stopped in her tracks. 'Do you need to get back to the autopsy?'

He shook his head. 'One of us is going to have to break the news to Macrae.'

She nodded. 'I'll do it.'

'Not a hell of a lot more to be done today.'

'Back to Live 8 then?'

He gave another shrug. 'And The Meadows for yourself?' he guessed.

She nodded, her mind elsewhere. 'Can you think of a worse week for this to happen?'

'Why they pay us the big bucks,' Rebus told her, drawing the nicotine deep.

A fat parcel was waiting for Rebus at the door of his flat. Siobhan was heading back down to The Meadows. Rebus had told her to drop by later for a drink. He realised his living room was stuffy, so forced open the window. He could hear sounds from the march: echoey, amplified voices; drums and whistles. Live 8 was on TV, but not a band he recognised. He kept the sound down, opened the parcel. There was a note inside from Mairie – *YOU DON'T DESERVE IT* – followed by pages and pages of printout. News stories about Pennen Industries, dating right back to its separation from the MoD. Snippets from the business pages, detailing rising profits. Praiseworthy profiles of Richard Pennen, accompanied by photos of him. Every inch the successful businessman: well groomed, pinstriped, coiffeured. Salt-and-pepper hair, even though he was still in his mid-forties. Steel-rimmed glasses, and a square-set jaw below perfect-looking teeth.

Richard Pennen had been an MoD employee, something of a whiz with microchips and software programs. He stressed that his company didn't sell arms as such, just the components to make them as efficient as possible. 'Which has to be better than the alternative, for all concerned,' he was quoted as saying. Rebus flicked quickly through interviews and background features. Nothing to link Pennen to Ben Webster, except that both dealt with aspects of 'trade'. No reason why the company *wouldn't* treat MPs to five-star hotel rooms. Rebus turned to the next set of stapled sheets and gave a silent thank-you to Mairie. She'd added a screed of stuff about Ben Webster himself. Not that there was much about his career as an MP. But five years back the media had shown sudden interest in the family, following the shocking attack on Webster's mother. She and her husband had been holidaying in the Borders, renting a cottage in the countryside outside Kelso. He'd gone into town one afternoon for supplies, and had returned to find the cottage ransacked, his wife dead, strangled with a cord from the window blinds. She had been beaten but not sexually assaulted. Money was missing from her bag, as was her mobile phone. Nothing else had been taken.

Just some loose cash and a phone.

And a woman's life.

The inquiry had dragged on for weeks. Rebus looked at photos of the isolated cottage, the victim, her grieving husband, the two children – Ben and Stacey. He lifted from his pocket the card Stacey had given him, rubbed its edges with his fingers as he continued to read. Ben the MP for Dundee North; Stacey the cop from the Met, whom colleagues described as 'diligent and well liked'. The cottage was placed on the edge of woodland, amidst rolling hills, no other habitation visible. Husband and wife had liked to take long walks, and were regularly to be seen in Kelso's bars and eateries. The region had been their destination of choice for many holidays. Councillors for the area were quick to point out that the Borders 'remains largely crime-free and a haven of peace'. Didn't want the tourists scared off ...

The killer was never caught. The story drifted to the inside pages, then deeper into the paper, reappearing sporadically as a paragraph or two when Ben Webster was being profiled. There was one in-depth interview with him, dating back to when he'd been made PPS. He hadn't wanted to talk about the tragedy.

Tragedies plural, actually. The father hadn't lasted long after his wife's murder. His death came from natural causes. 'The will to live just left him' was how one neighbour in Broughty Ferry had put it. 'And now he's at peace with the love of his life.'

Rebus looked again at the photograph of Stacey, taken on the day of her mother's funeral. She'd gone on TV, apparently, appealing for information. Stronger than her brother, who'd decided not to join her at the press conference. Rebus really hoped she would stay strong.

Suicide seemed the obvious conclusion, grief finally catching up with the orphaned son. Except that Ben Webster had screamed as he fell. And the guards had been alerted to an intruder. Besides, why *that* particular night? *That* location? The world's media hitting town ...

A very public gesture.

And Steelforth ... well, Steelforth wanted it all swept away. Nothing must deflect attention from the G8. Nothing must be allowed to perturb the various delegations. Rebus had to admit, the reason he was holding on to the case was simply to piss off the Special Branch man. He got up from the table and went into the kitchen, made himself another mug of coffee and brought it back through to the living room. He changed channels on the TV, but couldn't find any feeds from the march. The Hyde Park crowd looked to be enjoying themselves, though there was some sort of enclosure directly in front of the stage, sparsely filled. Security maybe; either that or media. Geldof wasn't asking for money this time round; what Live 8 wanted was to focus hearts and minds. Rebus wondered how many concert-goers would afterwards heed the call and trek the four hundred miles north to Scotland. He lit a cigarette to go with his coffee, sat down in an armchair and stared at the screen. He thought again of the Clootie Well, of the ritual played out there. If Ray Duff was right, they had at least three victims, and a killer who had made a shrine of sorts. Did that mean someone local? How well known was the Clootie Well outside Auchterarder? Did it appear in travel books, tourist brochures? Had it been chosen for its proximity to the G8 summit, the killer guessing that all those extra police patrols were bound to mean his grim little offering was found? In which case, was his spree now finished?

Three victims ... no way they were going to keep that away from the media. CC Rider ... Keogh's Garage ... a cash card ... The killer was making it easy for them; he *wanted* them to know he was out there. World's press gathered in Scotland as never before, giving him an international stage. And Macrae would relish the opportunity. He'd be out there in front of them, chest puffed up as he answered their questions, Derek Starr right beside him.

Siobhan had said she would call Macrae from the march, let him know the lab's findings. Ray Duff meantime would be doing more tests, trying for DNA fingerprints from the blood, seeing if any hairs or fibres could be isolated and identified. Rebus thought about Cyril Collar again. Hardly a typical victim. Serial killers tended to prey on the weak and the marginalised. A case of wrong place, wrong time? Killed in Edinburgh, but the scrap from his jacket ends up in woods in Auchterarder, just as Operation Sorbus is getting started. Sorbus: a kind of tree ... the CC Rider's patch left in a wooded glade ... If there was any hint of a connection with the G8, Rebus knew the spooks would wrench the case out of Siobhan's hands and out of his. Steelforth wouldn't have it any other way. The killer taunting them ...

Leaving calling cards.

There was a knock at his door. Had to be Siobhan. He stubbed out the cigarette, stood up and took a look around the room. It wasn't too bad: no empty beer cans or pizza boxes. Whisky bottle by the chair: he picked it up, put it on the mantelpiece. Switched the TV to a news channel and headed for the door. Swung it open and recognised the face, felt his stomach clench.

'That's your conscience salved then, is it?' he asked, feigning indifference.

'Pure as the driven fuckin' snow, Rebus. But can you say the same?'

Not Siobhan. Morris Gerald Cafferty. Dressed in a white T-shirt bearing the slogan *Make Poverty History*. Hands in trouser pockets. Slid them out slowly and held them up, to show Rebus they were empty. A head the size of a bowling ball, shiny and all but hairless. Small, deep-set eyes. Glistening lips. No neck. Rebus made to shut the door on him, but Cafferty pressed a hand to it.

'That any way to treat an old pal?'

'Go to hell.'

'You look like you've beaten me to it – did that shirt come off a scarecrow?'

'And who dresses you – Trinny and Susannah?'

Cafferty snorted. 'I did meet them on breakfast TV, actually ... See, isn't this better? We're having a nice wee chinwag.'

Rebus had stopped trying to close the door. 'Hell are you doing here, Cafferty?'

Cafferty was examining his palms, brushing imaginary grime from them. 'How long have you been living here, Rebus? Got to be thirty years.'

'So?'

'Ever hear of the housing ladder?'

'Christ, now it's *Location, Location, Location* ...'

'You've never tried to improve your situation, that's what I can't understand.'

'Maybe I should write a book about it.'

Cafferty grinned. 'I'm thinking of a follow-up, charting a few more of our little "disagreements".'

'Is that why you're here? Memory needs refreshing, does it?'

Cafferty's face darkened. 'I'm here about my boy Cyril.'

'What about him?'

'I hear there's been some progress. I want to know how much.'

'Who told you?'

'It's true then?'

'Think I'd tell you even if it was?'

Cafferty gave a snarl, hands shooting forward, propelling Rebus backwards into the hall, where he collided with the wall. Cafferty grabbed at him again, teeth bared, but Rebus was ready, managed to get a handful of the T-shirt. The two men wrestled, twisting and turning, moving further down the hall until they were in the doorway to the living room. Neither had said a word, eyes and limbs doing their talking. But Cafferty glanced into the room and seemed to freeze. Rebus was able to free himself from his grasp.

'Jesus Christ ...' Cafferty was staring at the two boxes on the sofa – part of the Colliar case-notes, brought home from Gayfield the previous night. Lying on the top was one of the autopsy photos, and, just visible beneath, an older photograph of Cafferty himself. 'What's all this stuff doing here?' Cafferty asked, breathing heavily.

'None of your damned business.'

'You're still trying to pin this on me ...'

'Not as much as I was,' Rebus admitted. He walked over to the mantelpiece and grabbed the whisky. Lifted his glass from the floor and poured. 'It'll be public knowledge soon enough,' he said, pausing to drink. 'We think Colliar's not the only victim.'

Cafferty's eyes narrowed as he tried to take this in. 'Who else?'

Rebus shook his head slowly. 'Now get the hell out.'

'I can help,' Cafferty said. 'I know people ...'

'Oh aye? Trevor Guest ring a bell?'

Cafferty thought for a moment before conceding defeat.

'What about a garage called Keogh's?'

Cafferty stiffened his shoulders. 'I can find things out, Rebus. I've got contacts in places that would frighten you.'

'Everything about you frightens me, Cafferty: fear of contamination, I suppose. How come you're so het up about Colliar?'

Cafferty's eyes strayed to the whisky bottle. 'Got a spare glass?' he asked.

Rebus fetched one from the kitchen. When he returned, Cafferty was reading Mairie's covering note.

'I see Ms Henderson's been lending a hand.' Cafferty gave a cold smile. 'I recognise her handwriting.'

Rebus said nothing; poured a small measure into the glass.

'I prefer malt,' Cafferty complained, wafting the contents under his nose. 'What's your interest in Pennen Industries?'

Rebus ignored this. 'You were going to tell me about Cyril Colliar.' Cafferty made to sit down. 'Stay on your feet,' Rebus commanded. 'You're not going to be here that long.'

Cafferty sank the drink and placed the glass on the table. 'It's not Cyril I'm interested in as such,' he admitted. 'But when something like that happens ... well, rumours get started. Rumours that someone's out there with a grudge. Never very good for business. As you well know, Rebus, I've had enemies in the past ...'

'Funny how I never see them any more.'

'Plenty of jackals out there who'd like a share of the spoils ... *my* spoils.' He stabbed a finger into his own chest.

'You're getting old, Cafferty.'

'Same as you. But there's no retirement package in my line of business.'

'And meantime the jackals get younger and hungrier?' Rebus guessed. 'And you need to keep proving yourself.'

'I've never backed down, Rebus. Never will.'

'It'll come out soon enough, Cafferty. If there's no connection between you and the other victims, then there's no reason for anyone to see it as a vendetta.'

'But meantime ...'

'Meantime what?'

Cafferty gave a wink. 'Keogh's Garage and Trevor Guest.'

'Leave them to us, Cafferty.'

'Who knows, Rebus, maybe I'll see what I can turn up about Pennen Industries too.' Cafferty started to walk out of the room. 'Thanks for the drink and the wee spot of exercise. Think I'll go join the tail-end of the march. Poverty's always been a great concern of mine.' He paused in the hall, taking in his surroundings. 'Never seen it as bad as this, though,' he added, heading for the stairwell.

5

The Right Honourable Gordon Brown MP, Chancellor of the Exchequer, had already started to speak when Siobhan entered the room. An audience of nine hundred had gathered in the Assembly Hall at the top of The Mound. The last time Siobhan had been there, the place was acting as temporary home to the Scottish Parliament, but the Parliament now had lavish premises of its own opposite the Queen's residence at Holyrood, leaving the Assembly Hall once again the exclusive property of the Church of Scotland, who, along with Christian Aid, had organised the evening's event.

Siobhan was there for a meeting with Edinburgh's Chief Constable, James Corbyn. Corbyn had been in charge just over a year, having replaced Sir David Strathern. There had been mutters of dissent over the appointment. Corbyn was English, a 'bean-counter', and 'too bloody young'. But he had proved himself a hands-on copper who made regular visits to the front line. He was seated a few rows back, in full dress uniform, cap resting on his lap. Siobhan knew she was expected, so found a space by the doors, content to listen to the Chancellor's vows and pledges. When he announced that Africa's poorest thirty-eight countries would see a debt write-off, there was spontaneous applause. But when the clapping died down, Siobhan was aware of a voice of dissent. A lone protester had stood up. He was wearing a kilt, and lifted it to reveal a cut-out picture of Tony Blair's face on the front of his underpants. Stewards moved in quickly, and those around the man helped with the process. As he was dragged to the doors, the fresh applause was for the stewards. The Chancellor, who had busied himself tidying his notes, continued where he'd left off.

The commotion, however, provided useful cover for James Corbyn to make his move. Siobhan followed him out of the hall and introduced herself. There was no sign of the protester or his captors, just a few civil servants pacing the floor, waiting for their master to finish. They carried document files and mobile phones, and seemed exhausted by the day's events.

'DCI Macrae says we have a problem,' Corbyn stated. No niceties; straight to the heart of the matter. He was in his early forties, with black hair parted to the right. Solidly built, just over six feet in height. There was a large mole on his right cheek, which Siobhan had been forewarned not to stare at.

'Bloody hard to keep eye contact,' Macrae had told her, 'with that thing in your sight-line ...'

'We may have three victims,' she said now.

'And a locus on the G8's doorstep?' Corbyn snapped.

'Not exactly, sir. I don't think we'll find bodies there, just trace evidence.'

'They'll be out of Gleneagles by Friday. We can stall the investigation till then.'

'On the other hand,' Siobhan offered, 'the leaders don't start arriving till Wednesday. Three full days away ...'

'What are you proposing?'

'We keep things low-key, but do as much as we can. Forensics can have made a full sweep by then. The one definite victim we have is an Edinburgh remit, no need to go disturbing the bigwigs.'

Corbyn studied her. 'You're a DS, am I right?'

Siobhan nodded.

'Bit junior to be heading something like this.' It didn't sound like criticism; he was simply stating a fact.

'A DI from my station was with me, sir. We both worked the original inquiry.'

'How much help will you need?'

'I'm not sure much can be spared.'

Corbyn smiled. 'It's a sensitive time, DS Clarke.'

'I appreciate that.'

'I'm sure you do. And this DI of yours ... he's reliable?'

Siobhan nodded, maintaining eye contact, not blinking. Thinking: *Maybe he's too new to have heard of John Rebus.*

'Happy to work a Sunday?' he asked.

'Absolutely. Not so sure about the SOCOs ...'

'A word from me should help.' He grew thoughtful. 'The march passed off without incident ... perhaps we'll have it easier than we feared.'

'Yes, sir.'

His eyes regained their focus. 'Your accent's English,' he remarked.

'Yes, sir.'

'Ever given you problems?'

'A few jibes along the way ...'

He nodded slowly. 'All right.' Straightening his back. 'See what you can get done before Wednesday. Any problems, let me know. But do try not to step on any toes.' He glanced in the direction of the civil servants.

'There's an SO12 officer called Steelforth, sir. He may raise a few objections.'

Corbyn looked at his watch. 'Direct him to my office.' He fixed his braided cap to his head. 'Time I was elsewhere. You do realise the enormous responsibility ...?'

'Yes, sir.'

'Make sure your colleague gets the message.'

'He'll understand, sir.'

He held out his hand. 'Very well. Let's shake on it, DS Clarke.'

They shook.

*

On the radio news there was a report from the march and, in a postscript, mention that the death of International Development minister Ben Webster was 'being treated as a tragic accident'. The chief story, however, was the Hyde Park concert. Siobhan had heard plenty of complaints from the hordes gathered at The Meadows. They felt the pop stars would upstage them.

'Limelight and album sales, that's what they're after,' one man had said. 'Ego-tripping bastards ...'

The latest estimate of numbers on the march was two hundred and twenty-five thousand. Siobhan didn't know how many were at the London concert, but she doubted it was even half that. The nighttime streets were busy with cars and pedestrians. Plenty of coaches, too, heading south out of the city. Some of the shops and restaurants she passed had put signs in their windows: *We Support Make Poverty History ... We Only Use Fairtrade Produce ... Small Local Retailer ... Marchers Welcome ...* There was graffiti, too: anarchy symbols and messages exhorting the passers-by to 'Activ8, Agit8, Demonstr8'. Another statement stated simply that 'Rome Wasn't Sacked in One Day'. She hoped the Chief Constable would be proved right, but there was a long way to go ...

Buses were parked outside the Niddrie campsite. The tented village had grown. The same guard as the previous night was in charge. She asked him his name.

'Bobby Greig.'

'Bobby, I'm Siobhan. Looks busy tonight.'

He shrugged. 'Maybe a couple of thousand. I reckon that's as busy as it'll get.'

'You sound disappointed.'

'Council's spent a million on this place – could have given them all a hotel room for that, never mind a pitch in the wilderness.' He nodded towards the car she'd just locked. 'I see you've got a replacement.'

'Borrowed from the car park at St Leonard's. Had any

more trouble from the natives?'

'Nice and quiet,' he told her. 'Dark now, mind ... that's when they come out to play. Know what it feels like in here?' He scanned the compound. 'One of those zombie films ...'

Siobhan offered a smile. 'That makes you mankind's last great hope, Bobby. You should be flattered.'

'My shift ends at midnight!' he called after her as she made her way to her parents' tent. There was no one home. She unzipped the opening and looked in. The table and stools had been folded away, sleeping-bags rolled tight. She tore a sheet of paper from her notebook and left a message. No sign of life in the surrounding tents either. Siobhan began to wonder if her mum and dad had maybe gone out drinking with Santal.

Santal: last seen at the demo in Buccleuch Place. Which meant she might be trouble ... might *get* into trouble.

Listen to yourself, girl! Afraid your trendy leftie parents will be led astray!

She tutted to herself and decided to kill some time walking around the camp. It was little changed from the previous night: a strummed guitar, a cross-legged circle of singers, kids playing barefoot on the grass, cheap food doled out at the marquee. New arrivals, weary after the march, were being handed their wristbands and shown where to pitch camp. There was still some light left in the sky, making a startling silhouette of Arthur's Seat. She thought maybe she would climb it tomorrow, take an hour to herself. The view from the top was always a thrill ... supposing she could afford an hour to herself. She knew she should call Rebus, let him know the score. He was probably still at home in front of the box. Time enough yet to give him the news.

'Saturday night, eh?' Bobby Greig said. He was standing just behind her, holding a torch and his two-way. 'You should be out enjoying yourself.'

'Seems to be what my friends are up to.' She nodded in the direction of her parents' tent.

'I'll be having a drink myself when I finish,' he hinted.

'I've got work tomorrow.'

'Hope you're on overtime.'

'Thanks for the offer, though ... maybe another night.'

He gave a huge shrug. 'I'm trying not to feel rejected here.' His radio burst into life with a jolt of static. He raised it to his mouth. 'Say again, tower.'

'Here they come again,' came the distorted voice.

Siobhan looked towards the fence; couldn't make anything out. She followed Bobby Greig towards the gate. Yes: a dozen of them, hooded tops drawn tight around their heads, eyes shaded by baseball caps. No sign of weapons, other than a litre bottle of cheap booze being passed between them. Half a dozen guards had gathered inside the gate, waiting for Greig to give the word. The gang outside was gesturing: come and have a go. Greig stared back, seeming bored with the performance.

'Should we call it in?' one of the other security men asked.

'No sign of missiles,' Greig replied. 'Nothing we can't handle.'

The gang had steadily been approaching the fence. Siobhan recognised the one in the middle as the leader from Friday night. The mechanic at Rebus's recommended workshop had said it might end up costing six hundred to fix her car.

'Insurance might do some of it,' had been his only crumb of comfort. In reply she'd asked him if he'd ever heard of Keogh's Garage, but he'd shaken his head.

'Can you ask around?'

He'd said he would do that, then had asked for a deposit. A hundred gone from her bank account, just like that. Five hundred still to go, and here were the culprits, not twenty feet from her. She wished she had Santal's camera ... fire off a few shots and see if anyone at Craigmillar CID could put names to faces. Had to be CCTV cameras around here somewhere. Maybe she could ...

Sure she could. But she knew she wouldn't.

'Off you go now,' Bobby Greig was calling out in a firm voice.

'Niddrie's *ours*,' the leader spat. 'It's *youse* should fuck off!'

'Point taken, but we can't do that.'

'Makes you feel big, eh? Playing babysitter to a bunch of gyppo scum.'

'Happy-clappy hippy shite,' one of his followers concurred.

'Thanks for sharing,' was all Bobby Greig said.

The leader barked out a laugh; one of the gang spat at the fence. Another joined him.

'We can take them, Bobby,' one of the security-men said softly.

'No need to.'

'Fat bastard,' the gang's leader goaded.

'Fat bum-bandit bastard,' one of his lieutenants added.

'Paedo.'

'Alky.'

'Pop-eyed baldie arse-licking ...'

Greig's eyes were on Siobhan. He seemed to be making up his mind. She shook her head slowly. *Don't let them win.*

'Jakey.'

'Beardie.'

'Bloated ba'-bag.'

Bobby Greig turned his head towards the guard next to him, gave a brief nod. 'Count of three,' he said in an undertone.

'Save your breath, Bobby.' The guard leapt for the gate, his comrades right behind him. The gang scattered, but regrouped at the other side of the road.

'Come on then!'

'Any time you like!'

'You want us? Here we are ...'

Siobhan knew what they wanted. They wanted the security men to chase them into the labyrinth of streets. Jungle warfare, where local knowledge could defeat firepower. Weapons – ready-made or improvised – could be waiting there. A larger army could be hidden behind hedges and down shadowy closes. And meantime, the camp was left unguarded ...

She didn't hesitate; called it in on her mobile. 'Officer requiring assistance.' Brief details of where she was. Two, three minutes, they'd start arriving. Craigmillar cop-shop wasn't further away than that. The gang's leader was bending over, making a show of offering his backside to Bobby Greig. One of Greig's men accepted the insult on his behalf, ran at the leader, who did what Siobhan had feared: appeared to retreat further down the walkway.

Into the heart of the housing scheme.

'Careful!' she warned, but no one was listening. Turning, she saw that some of the campers were watching the action. 'Police will be here in a minute,' she assured them.

'Pigs,' one of the campers said in evident disgust.

Siobhan jogged out into the road. The gang really had scattered now; at least that was what it looked like. She traced Bobby Greig's route, down the path and into a cul-de-sac. Low-rise blocks all around, some of the last and worst of the old streets. The skeleton of a bike lay on the pavement. A supermarket-trolley's carcass sat kerbside. Shadows and scuffles and yells. The sound of breaking glass. If there was fighting, she couldn't see it. Back gardens were the battleground. Stairwells, too. Faces at some of the windows, but they withdrew quickly, leaving only the cold blue glare of TV sets. Siobhan kept walking, checking to left and right. She was wondering how Greig would have acted had she not been there to witness the taunts. Bloody men and their bloody machismo ...

End of the street: still nothing. She took a left, then a right. In one front garden a car sat on bricks. A lamp-post had had its inspection-cover removed, its wiring ripped out. The place was a bloody maze, and how come she couldn't hear sirens? She couldn't hear any yells now either, apart from an argument in one of the houses. A kid on a skateboard came towards her, maybe ten or eleven at most, staring hard at her until he was past. She reckoned she could take a left and be back at the main road. But she entered another cul-de-sac, and cursed under her breath – not even a footpath to be seen. Knew the quickest route might be to skirt around the end-terrace and climb the fence. Next block over and she'd be back where she started.

Maybe.

'In for a pound,' she said, heading down the cracked paving-slabs. There wasn't much of anything behind the row of houses: weeds and ankle-high grass and the twisted remains of a rotary clothes-line. The fence was broken-backed, easy to cross into the next set of back gardens.

'That's my flower bed,' a voice called in mock complaint. Siobhan looked around. Stared into the milky blue eyes of the gang's leader.

'Tasty,' he said, eyeing her from top to toe.

'Don't you think you're in enough trouble?' she asked.

'What trouble's that then?'

'It was my car you got at last night.'

'Don't know what you're talking about.' He'd taken a step closer. Two shapes behind him to left and right.

'Your best bet right now's to start walking,' she warned them. The response: low laughter.

'I'm CID,' she said, hoping her voice would hold up. 'Anything happens here, we're talking a lifetime's pay-back.'

'So how come you're quaking in your boots?'

Siobhan hadn't moved, hadn't retreated an inch. He was nose-to-nose with her now. Knee-in-the-groin close. She felt some of her confidence return.

'Walk away,' she said quietly.

'Maybe I don't want to.'

'Then again,' came a deep, booming voice, 'maybe you do.'

Siobhan looked behind her. It was Councillor Tench. He had his hands clasped in front of him, legs slightly apart. He seemed to fill Siobhan's vision.

'Nothing to do with you,' the gang leader complained, stabbing a finger in Tench's direction.

'Everything around here's got *something* to do with me. Those that know me know that. Now scarper back to your rabbit-holes and we'll say no more.'

'Thinks he's the big man,' one of the gang sneered.

'Only one "big man" in my universe, son, and he's up there.' Tench gestured skywards.

'Dream on, preacher,' the leader said. But he turned and walked into the encroaching darkness, his men following.

Tench unclasped his hands and let his shoulders relax. 'Could have turned nasty,' he said.

'Could have,' Siobhan agreed. She introduced herself, and he nodded.

'Thought to myself last night – that lassie looks like a copper.'

'Seems you're on regular peace-keeping duties,' she told him.

He made a face, as if to play down his role. 'Quiet around here most nights. You just picked a bad week for a visit.' His ears picked out a single siren, growing closer. 'Your idea of the cavalry?' Tench offered, leading the way back to the camp.

*

The car – her loaner from St Leonard's – had been sprayed with the letters NYT.

'Beyond a damned joke,' Siobhan told herself through gritted teeth. She asked Tench if he had names for her.

'No names,' he stated.

'But you know who they are.'

'What difference does that make?'

She turned instead to the uniforms from Craigmillar, gave them her description of the leader's build, clothes, eyes. They shook their heads slowly.

'Camp's in one piece,' one of them said. 'That's what matters.' His tone said it all – *she* was the one who'd summoned them here, and there was nothing for them to see or do. Some name-calling and a few (alleged) thrown punches. None of the security men had any injuries to report. They looked exhilarated, brothers in arms. No real threat against the camp, and no damage to report – other than Siobhan's car.

In other words: a wild-goose chase.

Tench was moving among the tents, introducing himself all over again and shaking hands, rubbing the kids' heads and accepting a beaker of herbal tea. Bobby Greig was nursing bruised knuckles, though all he'd connected with, according to one of his team, was a gable-end.

'Livens things up, eh?' he said to Siobhan.

She didn't reply. Walked to the marquee and someone poured her out a cup of camomile. She was outside again, blowing on it, when she saw that Tench had been joined by someone with a hand-held tape machine. She recognised the journalist, used to be pals with Rebus ... Mairie Henderson, that was the name. Siobhan moved closer and heard Tench talking about the area.

'G8's all fine and well, but the Executive should be looking a damn sight closer to home. Kids here, they can't see any sort of a future. Investment, infrastructure, industry – what we need here is the rebuilding of a shattered community. Blight's done for this place, but blight is reversible. An injection of aid and these kids will have something to be proud of, something to keep them busy and productive. Like the slogan says, it's fine and dandy to think global ... but we shouldn't forget to act *local*. Thank you very much.'

And he was moving again, shaking another hand, rubbing another child's head. The reporter had spotted Siobhan and came bounding over to her, holding out the tape machine.

'Care to add a police perspective, DS Clarke?'

'No.'

'I hear that's two nights running you've been here ... What's the attraction?'

'I'm not in the mood, Mairie.' Siobhan paused. 'You're really going to write a story about this?'

'Eyes of the world are on us.' She shut off the machine. 'Tell John I hope he got the package.'

'What package?'

'The stuff about Pennen Industries and Ben Webster. Still not sure what he thinks he can make of it.'

'He'll come up with something.'

Mairie nodded. 'Just hope he remembers me when he does.' She was studying Siobhan's cup. 'Is that tea? I'm gasping.'

'From the marquee,' Siobhan said, nodding in that direction. 'It's a bit weak, though. Tell them you want it strong.'

'Thanks,' the reporter said, moving away.

'Don't mention it,' Siobhan said quietly, pouring the contents of her cup on to the ground.

The Live 8 concert was on the late-night news. Not just London, but Philadelphia and the Eden Project and elsewhere. Viewing figures in the hundreds of millions, and worries that with the concert over-running the crowds would be forced to sleep rough for a night.

'Tut-tut,' Rebus said, draining the dregs from a last can of beer. The Make Poverty History march was on the screen now, a noisy celeb stating that he just felt the need to be 'here on this day, making history by helping make poverty a thing of the past'. Rebus flipped to Channel 5 – *Law and Order: Special Victims Unit*. He didn't understand the title: wasn't every victim special? But then he thought of Cyril Colliar and realised the answer was 'no'.

Cyril Colliar, muscle for Big Ger Cafferty. Looking like a targeted hit at first, but now almost certainly not. Wrong place, wrong time.

Trevor Guest ... so far only a piece of plastic, but all those coded numbers would yield an identity. Rebus had been through the phone book for Guests, found almost twenty. Called half of those, with only four answering – and none of them knew a Trevor.

Keogh's Garage ... There were a dozen Keoghs in the Edinburgh phone book, but by then Rebus had given up on the notion that all three victims would be from the city. Draw a wide enough circumference around Auchterarder and you would take in Dundee and Stirling as easily as Edinburgh – Glasgow and Aberdeen too, at a push. The victims could have come from anywhere. Nothing to be done about it till Monday.

Nothing except sit and brood, sinking beers and making a sortie to the corner shop for an oven-ready dinner of Lincolnshire Sausage with Onion Gravy and Parmesan Mash. Plus four more beers. The people queueing at the till had smiled at him. They were still dressed in their white T-shirts. They were talking about the 'whole amazing afternoon'.

Rebus had nodded his agreement.

One autopsy on a Member of Parliament. Three victims of some anonymous killer.

Somehow, 'amazing' didn't quite do it justice.

SIDE TWO

Dance with the Devil

Sunday 3 July

6

'So how were The Who?' Siobhan asked. It was late morning on Sunday, and she'd invited Rebus over for brunch. His contribution: a packet of sausages and four floury rolls. She'd put them to one side and made scrambled eggs instead, topping each helping with slices of smoked salmon and a few capers.

'The Who were good,' Rebus said, using his fork to manoeuvre the capers to the side of his plate.

'You should try one,' she admonished him. He wrinkled his nose and ignored the advice.

'Floyd were good too,' he told her. 'No major fallings-out.' They were facing one another across the small fold-away table in her living room. She lived in a tenement just off Broughton Street, five minutes' walk from Gayfield Square. 'What about you?' he asked, looking around the room. 'No signs of Saturday night debauchery.'

'Chance would be a fine thing.' Her smile grew thoughtful, and she told him about Niddrie.

'Lucky to get out in one piece,' Rebus commented.

'Your friend Mairie was there, writing a piece on Councillor Tench. She said something about some notes she'd sent you.'

'Richard Pennen and Ben Webster,' he confirmed.

'So are you getting anywhere?'

'Onward and upward, Shiv. I also tried phoning a few Guests and Keoghs – with nothing to show for it. Been as well chasing a few hoodies around the houses.' He'd cleared his plate – capers aside – and was leaning back in his chair. Wanted a cigarette, but knew he should wait till she'd finished eating. 'Oh, and I had an interesting encounter myself, as it happens.'

So he told her about Cafferty, and by the time he was done her plate was empty.

'He's the last thing we need,' she said, rising to her feet. Rebus made the beginnings of an offer to clear the table, but she nodded towards the window instead. Smiling, he made his way over and eased it open. Cool air wafted in and he crouched down, lighting up. Made sure to direct the smoke through the gap; held the cigarette out of the window between puffs.

Siobhan's rules.

'More coffee?' she called.

'Keep it coming,' he answered.

She came in from the kitchen carrying a fresh cafetiere. 'There's another march later on,' she said. 'Stop the War Coalition.'

'Bit late for all that, I'd have thought.'

'And the G8 Alternatives ... George Galloway's going to be speaking.'

Rebus gave a snort, stubbed out his cigarette on the windowsill. Siobhan had wiped clean the table, lifted one of the boxes on to it. The boxes she'd asked Rebus to bring.

The Cyril Colliar case.

The offer of double pay – sanctioned by James Corbyn – had persuaded Scene of Crimes to put a team together. They were on their way to the Clootie Well. Siobhan had warned them to keep a low profile: 'Don't want local CID getting sniffy.' Advised that SOCOs from Stirling had covered the same area two days before, one of the Edinburgh team had given a chuckle.

'Time we let the grown-ups in about it then,' was all he'd said.

Siobhan wasn't hopeful. All the same, on Friday all they'd been doing was bagging evidence of one crime.

Now the signs pointed to two more. It was worth a bit of sifting and lifting.

She started unloading files and folders from the boxes. 'You've been through this lot already?' she asked.

Rebus slid the window closed. 'And all I learned was that Colliar was a big bad bastard. Chances are, he had more enemies than friends.'

'And the odds of him falling prey to a random killing …?'

'Slim – we both know that.'

'And yet that appears to be what happened.'

Rebus held up a finger. 'We're reading a lot into a couple of items of clothing, owners unknown.'

'I tried Trevor Guest with Missing Persons.'

'And?'

She shook her head. 'Not on any local register.' She tossed an emptied box on to the sofa. 'It's a Sunday morning in July, John … not a hell of a lot we can do before tomorrow.'

He nodded. 'Guest's bank card?'

'It's HSBC. They've only one branch in Edinburgh – precious few in Scotland as a whole.'

'Is that good or bad?'

She gave a sigh. 'I got through to one of their call centres. They told me to try the branch on Monday morning.'

'Isn't there some sort of branch code on the card?'

Siobhan nodded. 'Not the sort of information they give out over the phone.'

Rebus sat down at the table. 'Keogh's Garage?'

'Directory enquiries did what they could. No listing on the web.'

'The name's Irish.'

'There are a dozen Keoghs in the phone book.'

He looked at her and smiled. 'So you checked too?'

'Soon as I'd sent the SOCOs off.'

'You've been busy.' Rebus opened one of the folders; nothing in it he hadn't seen before.

'Ray Duff's promised me he'll go to the lab today.'

'He has his eyes on the prize ...'

She gave him a hard look before emptying the final box. The amount of paperwork caused her shoulders to slump.

'Day of rest, eh?' Rebus said. A phone started ringing.

'Yours,' Siobhan said. He went over to the sofa, lifted the mobile from his jacket's inside-pocket.

'Rebus,' he announced. Listened for a moment, face darkening. 'That's because I'm not there ...' Listening again. 'No, I'll meet you. Where is it you need to be?' Glancing at his watch. 'Forty minutes?' Eyes on Siobhan. 'I'll be there.'

He snapped the phone shut.

'Cafferty?' she guessed.

'How did you know?'

'He does something to you ... your voice, your face. What does he want?'

'He went to my flat. Says there's something I need to see. No way I was letting him come here.'

'Much appreciated.'

'He's got some land deal going on, needs to get to the site.'

'I'm coming with you.'

Rebus knew there was no way to refuse.

Queen Street ... Charlotte Square ... Lothian Road. Rebus's Saab, Siobhan the wary passenger, gripping the door-sill with her left hand. They'd been stopped at barriers, made to show ID to various uniforms. Reinforcements were on their way into the city: Sunday was when the big exodus of officers north was due to happen. Siobhan had learned as much during her two days with Macrae, passed the info along to Rebus.

'You've just found yourself a new specialist subject,' he told her, 'for *Masterbore*.'

112

As they waited at lights on Lothian Road, they saw people waiting outside the Usher Hall.

'The Alternative Summit,' Siobhan said. 'That's where Bianca Jagger's due to speak.'

Rebus just rolled his eyes. In return, she smacked a fist into the side of his thigh.

'Did you *see* the march on TV? Two hundred thousand!'

'Nice day out for all concerned,' Rebus commented. 'Doesn't change the world *I'm* living in.' He looked at her. 'What about Niddrie last night? Have the ripples from all those positive vibes managed to stretch that far?'

'There were only a dozen of them, John, against two thousand in the camp.'

'I know which side my money'd be on ...'

After which they sat in silence until reaching Fountainbridge.

Once an area of breweries and factories, where Sean Connery had spent his early years, Fountainbridge was changing. The old industries had all but vanished. The city's financial district was encroaching. Style bars were opening. One of Rebus's favourite old watering-holes had already been demolished, and he reckoned the bingo hall next door – the Palais de Danse as was – would soon follow. The canal, not much more than an open sewer at one time, had been cleaned up. Families would go there for bike rides or to feed the swans. Not far from the CineWorld complex stood the locked gates of one mothballed brewery. Rebus stopped the car and sounded his horn. A young man in a suit appeared from behind the wall and released the padlock, swinging one half of the gate open – enough to squeeze the Saab through.

'You're Mr Rebus?' he asked through the driver's-side window.

'That's right.'

The young man waited to see if Rebus was about to

113

introduce Siobhan. Then he gave a nervous smile and handed over a brochure. Rebus glanced at it before passing it on.

'You're an estate agent?'

'I work for Bishops Solicitors, Mr Rebus. Commercial property. Let me give you my card ...' He was reaching into his jacket.

'Where's Cafferty?'

The tone of voice made the young man more nervous still. 'Parked around the side ...'

Rebus didn't wait to hear more.

'He obviously thinks you're one of Cafferty's team,' Siobhan said. 'And from the line of sweat on his top lip, I'd say he knows who Cafferty is.'

'Whatever he thinks, it's good news he's here.'

'Why?'

Rebus turned to her. 'Makes it less likely we're walking into a trap.'

Cafferty's car was a dark blue Bentley GT. He was standing over it, pressing a plan of the site against the bonnet so it couldn't blow away.

'Here, take a corner, will you?' he said. Siobhan obliged. Cafferty gave her a smile. 'DS Clarke. A pleasure as ever. Promotion can't be too far off, eh? Especially when the Chief Constable's trusting you with something this big.'

Siobhan glanced towards Rebus, who shook his head, letting her know he wasn't Cafferty's source.

'CID leaks like a sieve,' was Cafferty's explanation. 'Always has, always will.'

'What do you want with this place?' Siobhan couldn't help asking.

Cafferty slapped a hand against the unruly sheet of paper. 'Land, DS Clarke. We don't always realise how precious it is in Edinburgh. You've got the Firth of Forth to the north, North Sea to the east, and the Pentland Hills to the south. Developers are scrabbling about for projects

... putting pressure on the council to free up the Green Belt. And here's a twenty-acre plot only five minutes' walk from the financial district.'

'So what would you do with it?'

'Apart,' Rebus interrupted, 'from burying a few bodies in the foundations.'

Cafferty decided to laugh at this. 'That book made me a bit of money. Need to invest it somehow.'

'Mairie Henderson thinks your share went to charity,' Rebus said.

Cafferty ignored him. 'Did you read it, DS Clarke?'

She hesitated, giving Cafferty his answer. 'Like it?' he asked.

'Don't really remember.'

'They're thinking of turning it into a film. The early chapters, at any rate.' He lifted the plan and folded it, tossed it on to the Bentley's seat. 'I'm not sure about this place ...'. He turned his attention to Rebus. 'You mentioned bodies, and that's what I get a sense of. All the people who used to work here ... all of them gone, and Scottish industry along with them. A lot of my family were miners – I'll bet you didn't know that.' He paused. 'You're from Fife, Rebus. I'm betting you grew up surrounded by coal.' He paused. 'I was sorry to hear about your brother.'

'Sympathy from the devil,' Rebus said. 'That's all I need.'

'A killer with a social conscience,' Siobhan added in an undertone.

'I wouldn't be the first ...' Cafferty's voice drifted off. He rubbed a finger along the underside of his nose. 'In fact, maybe that's what's landed on your plate.' He reached into the car again, opening the glove-box this time. Drew out some rolled-up sheets of paper and made to hand them to Siobhan.

'Tell me what they are,' she asked, hands on hips.

'They're your case, DS Clarke. Proof that we're dealing

with a bad bastard. A bad bastard who likes other bad bastards.'

She took the papers but didn't look at them. '"We're dealing with"?' Quoting his own words back at him.

Cafferty's attention turned to Rebus. 'Doesn't she know that's the deal?'

'There was never a deal,' Rebus stated.

'Like it or not, I'm on your side in this one.' Cafferty's eyes were on Siobhan again. 'These papers cost me some substantial favours. If they help you catch him, I'll accept that. But I'll be hunting him too ... with you or without you.'

'Then why help us?'

Cafferty's mouth twitched. 'Makes the race that bit more exciting.' He pushed the passenger seat forward. 'Bags of space in the rear ... make yourselves at home.'

Rebus joined Siobhan on the back seat, while Cafferty sat in the front. Both detectives were aware of Cafferty's gaze. He wanted them to be impressed.

Rebus, for one, was finding it hard not to give anything away. He wasn't just impressed: he was amazed.

Keogh's Garage was in Carlisle. One of the mechanics, Edward Isley, had been found murdered three months back, his body dumped on waste ground just outside the city. A blow to the head and a toxic injection of heroin. The body had been naked from the waist up. No witnesses, no clues, no suspects.

Siobhan met Rebus's eyes.

'Does he have a brother?' Rebus asked.

'Some obscure musical reference?' she guessed.

'Read on, Macduff,' Cafferty said.

The notes were just that – culled from police records. Those same police records went on to report that Isley had been in employment only a little over a month, having been released from a six-year prison stretch for rape and sexual assault. Both Isley's victims had been prostitutes:

116

one picked up in Penrith and the other further south in Lancaster. They worked the M6 motorway, catering to lorry drivers. It was believed there might be other victims out there, scared either of testifying or of being identified.

'How did you get these?' The question burst from Rebus. It caused Cafferty to chuckle.

'Networks are wonderful things, Rebus – you should know that.'

'Plenty of palms greased along the way, no doubt.'

'Christ, John,' Siobhan was hissing, 'look at this.'

Rebus started reading again. Trevor Guest. The notes started with bank details and home address – in Newcastle. Guest had been unemployed ever since being released from a three-year term for aggravated burglary and an assault on a man outside a pub. During one break-in, he'd attempted to sexually assault a teenage babysitter.

'Another piece of work,' Rebus muttered.

'Who went the same way as the others.' Siobhan traced the relevant words with her index finger. Body found dumped by the shore at Tynemouth, just east of Newcastle. Head smashed in ... lethal dose of heroin. The killing had happened two months back.

'He'd only been out of the nick a fortnight ...'

Edward Isley: three months past.

Trevor Guest: two.

Cyril Colliar: six weeks.

'Looks like maybe Guest put up a fight,' Siobhan commented.

Yes: four broken fingers; lacerations to the face and chest. Body pummelled.

'So we've got a killer who's only after scumbags,' Rebus summed up.

'And you're thinking "More power to him"?' Cafferty guessed.

'A vigilante,' Siobhan said. 'Tidying up all the rapists ...'

'Our burglar friend didn't rape anyone,' Rebus felt it necessary to point out.

'But he tried to,' Cafferty said. 'Tell me, does all of this make your job easier or harder?'

Siobhan just shrugged. 'He's working at pretty regular intervals,' she said to Rebus.

'Twelve weeks, eight and six,' he agreed. 'Means we should have had another one by now.'

'Maybe we just haven't looked.'

'Why Auchterarder?' Cafferty asked. It was a good question.

'Sometimes they take trophies.'

'And hang them on public display?' Cafferty's brow furrowed.

'The Clootie Well doesn't get that many visitors ...' Siobhan grew thoughtful, turned back to the top of the first sheet and started reading again. Rebus got out of the car. The leather smell was beginning to get to him. He tried to light a cigarette, but the breeze kept extinguishing the flame. Heard the door of the Bentley open and close.

'Here,' Cafferty said, handing him the car's chrome-plated lighter. Rebus took it, got the cigarette going, gave it back with the briefest of nods.

'It was always business with me, Rebus, back in the old days ...'

'That's a myth all you butchers use. You forget, Cafferty, I've *seen* what you did to people.'

Cafferty gave a slow shrug. 'A different world ...'

Rebus exhaled smoke. 'Anyway, looks like you can rest easy. Your man was picked out all right, but not because of any connection to you.'

'Whoever did it, he carries a grudge.'

'A big one,' Rebus conceded.

'And he knows about convicts ... knows release dates and what happens to them after.'

Rebus nodded, scraping the heel of one shoe over the rutted tarmac.

'And you'll go on trying to catch him?' Cafferty guessed.

'It's what I'm paid for.'

'But it's never been about the money to you, Rebus ... never just been a *job*.'

'You don't know that.'

'Actually I do.' Cafferty was nodding now. 'Otherwise I'd have tempted you on to my payroll, like dozens of your colleagues down the years.'

Rebus flicked the remains of his cigarette on to the ground. Flecks of ash blew back, dotting Cafferty's coat. 'You really going to buy this shit-hole?' Rebus asked.

'Probably not. But I could if I wanted to.'

'And that gives you a buzz?'

'Most things are within reach, Rebus. We're just scared what we'll find when we get there.'

Siobhan was out of the car, finger stabbing the bottom of the final sheet. 'What's this?' she was asking as she walked around the Bentley towards them. Cafferty narrowed his eyes in concentration.

'I'm guessing a website,' he said.

'Of course it's a website,' she snapped. 'That's where half this stuff comes from.' She shook the sheets in his face.

'You mean it's a clue?' he asked archly.

She'd turned her back, making for Rebus's Saab, signalling to him with her arm that it was time to go.

'She's really shaping up, isn't she?' Cafferty told Rebus in an undertone. It didn't just sound like praise either: to Rebus's mind, it was as if the gangster was taking at least a portion of the credit.

On the way back into town, Rebus found a local news station. An alternative children's summit was being held in Dunblane.

'I can't hear the name of that place without shivering,' Siobhan admitted.

'I'll let you into a secret: Professor Gates was one of the pathologists.'

'He's never said.'

'Won't talk about it,' Rebus told her. He turned up the radio volume a little. Bianca Jagger was speaking to the audience at the Usher Hall.

They have been brilliant at hijacking our campaign to make poverty history ...'

'She means Bono and Co.' Siobhan said. Rebus nodded agreement.

'Bob Geldof has not just danced with the devil, but slept with the enemy ...'

As applause broke out, Rebus turned the volume down again. The reporter was saying that there was little evidence the Hyde Park audience was making its way north. Indeed, many of Saturday's marchers had already returned home from Edinburgh.

'Dance with the devil,' Rebus mused. 'Cozy Powell song, I seem to remember.' He broke off, slamming his feet on brake and clutch. A convoy of white vans was racing towards the Saab on the wrong side of the road. Headlights flashing, but no sirens. The windshield of each van was covered with a mesh grille. They'd streamed into the Saab's lane to get past a couple of other vehicles. Cops in riot gear could be seen through the side windows. The first van careered back into its own lane, missing the Saab's front wing by an inch. The others followed.

'Bloody hell,' Siobhan gasped.

'Welcome to the police state,' Rebus added. The engine had stalled, so he started the ignition again. 'Not a bad emergency stop, though.'

'Were they some of our lot?' Siobhan had turned in her seat to examine the disappearing convoy.

'No markings that I could see.'

'Think there's been trouble somewhere?' She was thinking of Niddrie.

Rebus shook his head. 'If you ask me, they're scooting back to Pollock Halls for tea and biscuits. And they pulled that little stunt just because they could.'

'You say "they" as if we're not on the same side.'

'Remains to be seen, Siobhan. Fancy a coffee? I need something to get the old heart pumping ...'

There was a Starbucks on the corner of Lothian Road and Bread Street. Hard to find a parking space. Rebus speculated that they were too close to the Usher Hall. He opted for a double-yellow line, stuck a POLICE notice on the dashboard. Inside the café, Siobhan asked the teenager behind the till if he wasn't scared of protesters. He just shrugged.

'We've got our orders.'

Siobhan dropped a pound coin into the tips box. She'd brought her shoulder-bag with her. At the table, she slid her laptop out and switched it on.

'This me getting my tutorial?' Rebus asked, blowing across the surface of his coffee. He'd gone for filter, complaining that he could buy a whole jar for the price of one of the costlier options. Siobhan scooped whipped cream from her hot chocolate with a finger.

'Can you see the screen all right?' she asked. Rebus nodded. 'Then watch this.' Within seconds she was on line and typing names into a search engine:

Edward Isley.

Trevor Guest.

Cyril Colliar.

'Plenty of hits,' she commented, scrolling down a page. 'But only one with all three.' Her cursor ran back up to the first entry. She tapped the touch-pad twice and waited.

'We'd have checked this, of course,' she said.

'Of course.'

'Well ... *some* of us would. But first we'd have needed

121

Isley's name.' Her eyes met Rebus's. 'Cafferty has saved us a long day's slog.'

'Doesn't mean I'm about to join his fan club.'

The welcome screen from a website had appeared. Siobhan studied it. Rebus moved a little closer for a better view. The site seemed to be called BeastWatch. There were grainy head-and-shoulders shots of half a dozen men, with chunks of text to the right.

'Listen to this,' Siobhan said, tracing the words on the screen with her finger. '*As the parents of a rape victim, we feel it is our right to know the whereabouts of her attacker after his release from prison. The aim of this site is to allow families and friends – and victims themselves – to post details of release dates, along with photos and descriptions, the better to prepare society for the beasts in our midst ...*' Her voice died away, lips moving silently as she read the rest to herself. There were links to a photo gallery called Beast In View and a noticeboard and discussion group, as well as an online petition. Siobhan moved the cursor to Edward Isley's photo and tapped the pad. A page of details came up, showing Isley's expected release date from prison, nickname – 'Fast Eddie' – and areas he would most likely frequent.

'It says "expected release date",' Siobhan pointed out.

Rebus nodded. 'And nothing more up-to-date ... no sign they knew where he was working.'

'But it does say he was trained as a car mechanic ... mentions Carlisle, too. Posted by ...' Siobhan sought out the relevant details. 'It just says "Concerned".'

She tried Trevor Guest next.

'Same set-up,' Rebus commented.

'And posted anonymously.'

She returned to the home page and clicked on Cyril Colliar. 'That same photo's in our files,' she said.

'It's from one of the tabloids,' Rebus explained, watching more photos of Colliar pop up. Siobhan swore under her breath. 'What is it?'

'Listen: *This is the animal who put our beloved daughter through hell, and who has blighted our lives ever since. He's up for release soon, having shown no remorse, or even admitting his guilt despite all the evidence. We were so shocked that he will soon be back in our midst that we had to do something, and this site is the result. We want to thank all of you for your support. We believe this may be the first site of its kind in Britain, though others like it exist elsewhere, and our friends in the USA in particular have given us such help in getting started.'*

'Vicky Jensen's parents did all this?' Rebus said.

'Looks like.'

'How come we didn't know?'

Siobhan shrugged, concentrated on finishing the page.

'He's picking them off,' Rebus went on. 'That's what he's doing, right?'

'He or she,' Siobhan corrected him.

'So we need to know who's been accessing this site.'

'Eric Bain at Fettes might help.'

Rebus looked at her. 'You mean Brains? Is he still talking to you?'

'I haven't seen him in a while.'

'Not since you gave him the brush-off?'

She glowered at Rebus, who held up his hands in surrender. 'Got to be worth a punt, all the same,' he admitted. 'I can do the asking if you like.'

She sat back in her chair, folded her arms. 'Bugs you, doesn't it?'

'What?'

'I'm the DS, you're the DI, yet Corbyn's put *me* in charge.'

'No skin off my nose.' He tried to sound slighted by the accusation.

'Sure about that? Because if we're going to work together on this ...'

'I only asked if you wanted me to speak to Brains.' His irritation showing now.

123

Siobhan unfolded her arms, bowed her head. 'Sorry, John.'

'Just as well you didn't have espresso,' was all he said in reply.

'A day off would have been nice,' Siobhan stated with a smile.

'Well, you could always go home and put your feet up.'

'Or?'

'Or we could go talk to Mr and Mrs Jensen.' He wafted a hand towards the laptop. 'See what they can tell us about their little contribution to the World Wide Web.'

Siobhan nodded slowly, dipped her finger back into the whipped cream. 'Then that's what we should probably do,' she said.

The Jensens lived in a rambling four-storey house overlooking Leith Links. The basement flat was daughter Vicky's domain. It had its own separate entrance, reached by a short flight of stone steps. The gate at the top of the steps boasted a lock, and there were bars on the windows either side of the door, plus a sticker warning potential intruders of an alarm system.

None of this had been deemed necessary before Cyril Colliar's attack. Back then, Vicky had been a bright eighteen-year-old studying at Napier College. Now, ten years later, she still lived at home, as far as Rebus was aware. He stood on the doorstep, hesitated a moment.

'Diplomacy's never been my strong point,' he advised Siobhan.

'Then let me do the talking.' She reached past him and pushed the bell.

Thomas Jensen was removing his reading-glasses as he opened the door. He recognised Rebus and his eyes widened.

'What's happened?'

'Nothing to worry about, Mr Jensen,' Siobhan assured him, showing her warrant card. 'Just need to ask a few questions.'

'You're still trying to find his killer?' Jensen guessed. He was medium height and in his early fifties, hair greying at the temples. The red V-necked jumper looked new and expensive. Cashmere, maybe. 'Why the hell do you think I'd want to help you?'

'We're interested in your website.'

Jensen frowned. 'Pretty standard practice these days if you're a vet ...'

'Not your surgery, sir,' Rebus explained.

'BeastWatch,' Siobhan added.

'Oh, that.' Jensen looked down at the floor, gave a sigh. 'Dolly's pet project.'

'Dolly being your wife?'

'Dorothy, yes.'

'Is she at home, Mr Jensen?'

He shook his head. Looked past them as if scanning the outside world for a sign of her. 'She was going to the Usher Hall.'

Rebus nodded as if this explained everything. 'Thing is, sir, we've got a bit of a problem ...'

'Oh?'

'It's to do with the website.' Rebus gestured in the direction of the hallway. 'If we could come in and tell you about it ...?'

Jensen seemed reluctant, but good manners prevailed. He led them into the living room. There was a dining room off, its table spread with newspapers. 'Seem to spend all of Sunday reading them,' Jensen explained, tucking his spectacles into his pocket. He motioned for them to sit down. Siobhan settled herself on the sofa, while Jensen himself took an armchair. Rebus, however, stayed standing by the glass doors to the dining room, peering through them towards the array of newsprint. Nothing out of the ordinary ... no particular stories or paragraphs marked.

'The problem is this, Mr Jensen,' Siobhan was saying in measured tones. 'Cyril Colliar is dead, and so are two other men.'

'I don't understand.'

'And we think we're looking at a single culprit.'

'But ...'

'A culprit who may have plucked the names of all three victims from your website.'

'All three?'

'Edward Isley and Trevor Guest,' Rebus recited. 'Plenty more names in your hall of shame ... I wonder who'll be next.'

'There must be some mistake.' The blood had drained from Jensen's face.

'Do you know Auchterarder at all, sir?' Rebus asked.

'No ... not really.'

'Gleneagles?'

'We did go there once ... a veterinarians' conference.'

'Was there maybe a bus run to the Clootie Well?'

Jensen shook his head. 'Just some seminars and a dinner-dance.' He sounded befuddled. 'Look, I don't think I can help you ...'

'The website was your wife's idea?' Siobhan asked quietly.

'It was a way of dealing with ... She'd gone online looking for help.'

'Help?'

'Victims' families. She wanted to know how to help Vicky. Along the way, the idea came to her.'

'She had help to construct the site?'

'We paid a firm of designers.'

'And the other sites in America ...?'

'Oh yes, they helped with layout. Once it was up and running ...' Jensen shrugged. 'I think it almost manages itself.'

'Do people subscribe?'

Jensen nodded. 'If they want the newsletter. It's supposed to be every quarter, but again, I'm not sure Dolly's kept it up.'

'So you have a list of subscribers?' Rebus asked.

Siobhan looked at him. 'Not that you need to be a subscriber to look at the site.'

'There'll be a list somewhere,' Jensen was saying.

'How long has the site been active?' Siobhan asked.

'Eight or nine months. It was when his release date started to come closer ... Dolly was getting more and more anxious.' He paused, glanced at his watch. 'For Vicky, I mean.'

As if on cue, the front door opened and closed. An excited, breathless voice came from the hallway.

'I did it, Dad! The Shore and back!' The woman who filled the door-frame was red-faced and overweight. She shrieked when she saw that her father was not alone.

'It's all right, Vicky ...'

But she'd turned on her heels and fled. Another door opened and slammed shut. They heard her footsteps as she padded down to her basement refuge. Thomas Jensen's shoulders slumped.

'That's as far as she's managed on her own,' he explained.

Rebus nodded. The Shore was barely half a mile away. He knew now why Jensen had been so anxious at their arrival, and why he had scanned the world outside.

'We pay someone to stay with her weekdays,' Jensen went on, hands in his lap. 'Means we can both keep working.'

'You told her Colliar's dead?' Rebus asked.

'Yes,' Jensen confirmed.

'She was interviewed about it?'

Now Jensen shook his head. 'The officer who came to ask us questions ... he was very understanding when we explained about Vicky.' Rebus and Siobhan shared a look: *going through the motions … not trying too hard* … 'We didn't kill him, you know. Even if he'd been standing there in front of me …' Jensen's eyes grew unfocused. 'I'm not sure I could bring myself to do it.'

'They all died of injections, Mr Jensen,' Siobhan stated.

The vet blinked a couple of times, raised a hand slowly and squeezed the skin either side of his nose, just below the eyes. 'If you're going to accuse me of anything, I'd like my lawyer to hear it.'

'We just need your help, sir.'

He stared at her. 'And that's the one thing I'm determined not to give you.'

'We'll need to talk to your wife and daughter,' Siobhan said, but Jensen was on his feet.

'I want you to leave now. I have to look after Vicky.'

'Of course, sir,' Rebus said.

'But we'll be back,' Siobhan added. 'Lawyer or no lawyer. And remember, Mr Jensen, tampering with evidence can get you locked up.' She strode towards the door, Rebus following in her wake. Outside, he lit a cigarette, staring towards a makeshift game of football on the links.

'See when I said diplomacy wasn't my strong point …?'

'What?'

'Five more minutes in there, you'd've been roughing him up.'

'Don't be stupid.' But the blood had risen to her face. She puffed out her cheeks and made an exasperated sound.

'What did you mean about evidence?' Rebus asked.

'Websites can be wound down,' she explained. 'Subscriber lists can be "lost".'

'Which means the sooner we speak to Brains, the better.'

Eric Bain was watching the Live 8 concert on his computer

– at least, that was what it looked like to Rebus, but Bain soon corrected him.

'Editing it, actually.'

'A download?' Siobhan guessed, but Bain shook his head.

'Burnt it on to DVD-ROM; now I'm taking out anything I don't need.'

'That would take some time in my case,' Rebus said.

'It's easy enough once you get the hang of the tools.'

'I think,' Siobhan broke in, 'DI Rebus means he'd be deleting a lot of stuff.'

Bain smiled at this. He hadn't got up since they'd arrived, hadn't so much as glanced up from the screen. It was his girlfriend, Molly, who'd opened the door for them; Molly who'd asked if they'd like a cup of tea. She was in the kitchen now, boiling the kettle, while Bain stuck to his task in the living room.

It was a top-floor flat in a warehouse conversion off Slateford Road. The brochure had probably referred to it as the 'penthouse'. There were expansive views from the small windows, mostly of chimneys and clapped-out factories. The top of Corstorphine Hill was just visible in the distance. The room was neater than Rebus had expected. No lengths of wiring, cardboard boxes, soldering irons or games consoles. Hardly the typical residence of a self-confessed gadget geek.

'How long you been here, Eric?' Rebus asked.

'Couple of months.'

'Pair of you decided to move in together?'

'That's about the size of it. I'll be finished here in a minute ...'

Rebus nodded, went over to the sofa and made himself comfortable. Molly shuffled in with the tea-tray, fizzing with energy. She was wearing mules on her feet. Tight blue jeans which only reached as far as her calves. A red T-shirt with Che Guevara on it. Great figure, and long blonde hair – dyed that colour, but still suiting her. Rebus had to admit he was impressed. He'd risked several glances towards Siobhan, who on each occasion had been studying Molly the way a scientist would a lab rat. Clearly she too thought Bain had done well for himself.

And Molly had made her mark on Brains: the boy had been house-trained. What was that Elton John line? *You nearly had me roped and tied* ... Bernie Taupin actually. The original Brown Dirt Cowboy to Reg's Captain Fantastic.

'Place looks great,' Rebus said to Molly as she handed him a mug. His reward: her pink lips and perfect white teeth breaking into a smile. 'Didn't catch your surname ...?'

'Clark,' she said.

'Same as Siobhan here,' Rebus informed her. Molly looked to Siobhan for confirmation.

'I've an "e" at the end,' Siobhan offered.

'Not me,' Molly replied. She'd settled on the sofa next to Rebus, but kept moving her bottom, as if unable to get comfortable.

'Still, it gives you something else in common,' Rebus added teasingly, receiving a scowl from Siobhan for his effort. 'How long have you two been an item then?'

'Fifteen weeks,' she said breathlessly. 'Doesn't seem long, does it? But sometimes you just *know*.'

Rebus nodded agreement. 'I'm always saying, Siobhan here should settle down. It can be the making of you, can't it, Molly?'

Molly didn't seem convinced, but still looked at Siobhan with something like sympathy. 'It really can,' she stressed. Siobhan gave Rebus a hard stare and accepted her own mug.

'Actually,' Rebus went on, 'for a wee while back there, Siobhan and Eric looked like becoming an item.'

'We were just friends,' Siobhan said, forcing out a laugh. Bain seemed frozen in front of the computer screen, hand unmoving on the mouse.

'Is that right, Eric?' Rebus called to him.

'John's just teasing,' Siobhan was assuring Molly. 'Take no notice of him.'

Rebus offered Molly a wink. 'Lovely spot of tea,' he said. She was still fidgeting.

'And we're really sorry to disturb your Sunday,' Siobhan added. 'If it wasn't an emergency ...'

Bain's chair creaked as he rose from it. Rebus noticed he had lost a good bit of weight, maybe as much as a stone. His pale face was still fleshy, but the gut had shrunk.

'Still based at the Forensic Computer Branch?' Siobhan asked him.

'That's right.' He accepted some tea and sat down next to Molly. She slid an arm protectively around him, stretching the material of her T-shirt, further accentuating her breasts. Rebus concentrated all the harder on Bain. 'Been busy with G8,' he was saying, 'sifting intelligence reports.'

'What sort of stuff?' Rebus asked, getting up as if to stretch his legs. With Bain on the sofa, it was getting crowded there. He began sauntering towards the computer.

'The secret sort,' Bain replied.

'Come across anyone called Steelforth?'

'Should I have?'

'He's SO12 ... seems to be running the show.'

But Bain just shook his head slowly and asked them what they wanted. Siobhan handed him the sheet of paper.

'It's a website,' she explained. 'Might suddenly disappear. We need everything you can get: subscription lists; anyone who's been looking at it, maybe downloading stuff ...'

'That's a big ask.'

'I know it is, Eric.' The way she said his name seemed to hit a nerve. He got up and walked to the window, perhaps to hide from Molly the flush of colour which had risen up his neck.

Rebus had picked up a piece of paper from beside the computer. It was a letter, headed Axios Systems, signed by someone called Tasos Symeonides. 'Sounds Greek,' he said. Eric Bain seemed relieved to be changing the subject.

'Based right here,' he said. 'An IT outfit.'

Rebus wafted the letter in front of him. 'Sorry to be nosy, Eric ...'

'It's a job offer,' Molly explained. 'Eric gets them all the time.' She had risen to her feet and crossed to the window, sliding an arm around Bain. 'I have to keep persuading him that his police work is crucial.'

Rebus put the letter back and returned to the sofa. 'Any chance of a refill?' he asked. Molly was happy to pour. Bain seized the moment, fixed Siobhan with a stare, dozens of unspoken words transmitted in a few seconds.

'Lovely,' Rebus said, accepting a spot of milk. Molly was seated next to him again.

'How soon could it be shut down?' Bain asked.

'I don't know,' Siobhan admitted.

'Tonight?'

'More likely tomorrow.'

Bain studied the piece of paper. 'All right,' he said.

'Isn't this nice?' Rebus seemed to be asking the question of the whole room, but Molly wasn't listening. She'd slapped both of her hands to her face, mouth falling open.

'I forgot the biscuits!' She jumped back to her feet. 'How could I have done that? And nobody said ...' She turned to Bain. 'You could have *said*!' Colour was flushing her cheeks as she flew from the room.

And for the first time Rebus realised that the place wasn't just tidy.

It was neurotically so.

Siobhan had watched the procession, with its anti-war chants and banners. The route was lined with police, waiting for trouble. Siobhan caught the sweet smell of cannabis in her nostrils, but doubted anyone would be arrested for it: the Sorbus briefings had said as much.

If they're shooting up as they pass you, take them in; otherwise, let it go ...

Whoever was targeting the BeastWatch website had access to high-grade heroin. She thought again of the mild-seeming Thomas Jensen. Vets might not have access to H, but they could always trade for something.

Access to heroin, and a grudge. Vicky's two pals, the ones who'd been with her at the club and on the bus ... maybe they needed to be questioned.

The blow to the head ... always from behind. Someone less physically strong than those being attacked. Wanting them prone before the injection. Lashing out at Trevor Guest because he'd not been KO'd? Or did it show the killer becoming more unhinged, more brazen, starting to enjoy the process?

But Guest had been the second victim. The third, Cyril Colliar, hadn't been dealt with so harshly. Meaning someone had stumbled on the scene perhaps, the killer fleeing before he'd had a chance to get his jollies?

Had he killed again? If so ... Siobhan gave a little cluck. 'He *or* she,' she reminded herself.

'Bush, Blair, CIA, how many kids did you kill today?'

The chant was taken up by the crowd. They were

streaming up Calton Hill, Siobhan following. A few thousand of them, heading for their rally. The wind was biting, the hilltop exposed to the elements. Views towards Fife and across the city to the west. Views south to Holyrood and the Parliament, cordoned day and night by police. Calton Hill, Siobhan seemed to recall, was another of Edinburgh's extinct volcanoes. The Castle sat on one; Arthur's Seat was another. There was an observatory at the top, and a series of public monuments. Best of all was the 'folly': a single side of what had been meant as a full-scale replica of the Parthenon in Athens. The mad donor had died, leaving the thing unfinished. Some marchers were clambering on to it. Others were gathering around to hear the speeches. One young woman, in a world of her own, danced around the periphery, singing to herself.

'Didn't expect to see you here, dear.'

'No, but I thought I might see you.' Siobhan gave her parents a hug. 'Couldn't find you at The Meadows yesterday.'

'Wasn't it fantastic?'

Siobhan's father gave a laugh. 'Your mum was in tears throughout.'

'*So* emotional,' his wife agreed.

'I came looking for you last night.'

'We went out for a drink.'

'With Santal?' Siobhan tried to make the question sound casual. She ran a hand over her head, as if trying to erase the voice within: *I'm your bloody daughter, not her!*

'She was there for a little while ... didn't seem to appeal to her.' The crowd were clapping and cheering the first speaker.

'Billy Bragg's on later,' Teddy Clarke said.

'I thought we could get something to eat,' Siobhan was saying. 'There's a restaurant on Waterloo Place ...'

'Are you hungry, dear?' Eve Clarke asked her husband.

'Not really.'

'Me neither.'

Siobhan shrugged her shoulders. 'Maybe later, eh?'

Her father put a finger to his lips. 'They're starting,' he whispered.

'Starting what?' Siobhan asked.

'The Naming of the Dead.'

And so they were: reading out the names of a thousand victims of the warfare in Iraq, people from all sides of the conflict. A thousand names, the speakers taking it in turn, their audience silent. Even the young woman stopped dancing. She stood staring into space instead. Siobhan retreated a little at one point, realising her mobile was still on. Didn't want Eric Bain calling with news. She took it from her pocket and switched it to vibrate. Drifted a little further away, still in earshot of the roll-call. She could see the Hibernian stadium below, empty now that the season was over. The North Sea was calm. Berwick Law to the east, looking like yet another extinct volcano. And still the names continued, forcing a secret, rueful smile from her.

Because this was what she did, her whole working life. She named the dead. She recorded their last details, and tried to find out who they'd been, why they'd died. She gave a voice to the forgotten and the missing. A world filled with victims, waiting for her and other detectives like her. Detectives like Rebus, too, who gnawed away at every case, or let it gnaw at them. Never letting go, because that would have been the final insult to those names. Her phone was buzzing. She lifted it to her ear.

'They were quick,' Eric Bain told her.

'The site's gone?'

'Yep.'

She cursed under her breath. 'Did you get anything?'

'Bits and pieces. I couldn't burrow far enough in, not with the gear at home.'

'No subscriber list?'

'Afraid not.'

Another speaker had taken over at the microphone ... the names kept coming.

'Anything else you can try?' she asked.

'From the office, yes, maybe one or two little tricks.'

'Tomorrow then?'

'If our G8 masters can spare me.' He paused. 'It was good to see you, Siobhan. Sorry you had to meet—'

'Eric,' she warned, 'don't.'

'Don't what?'

'All of it ... none of it. Let's just not, okay?'

There was a long silence on the line. 'Still friends?' he asked eventually.

'Absolutely. Call me again tomorrow.' She ended the call. Had to, otherwise she'd have been telling him, Stick to your nervy, pouting, bosomy girlfriend ... you might end up having a future.

Stranger things had happened.

She studied her parents from behind. They were holding hands, her mother leaning her head against her father's shoulder. Tears threatened to well up in Siobhan's eyes, but she forced them back down. She remembered Vicky Jensen, running from the room; and Molly, doing the self-same thing. Both of them scared of life itself. In her teens, Siobhan had run from plenty of rooms, rooms her parents had been in. Tantrums, bust-ups, battles of wits, power-plays. And all she wanted now was to be standing right there between them. Wanted it, but couldn't do it. Instead she stood fifty feet behind them, willing them to turn their heads.

Instead of which, they listened to the names ... the names of people they'd never known.

'I appreciate this,' Steelforth said, rising to shake Rebus's hand. He'd been waiting in the lobby of the Balmoral Hotel, sitting with one leg crossed over the other. Rebus had kept him waiting quarter of an hour, using that time to walk past the doors of the Balmoral several times, glancing inside to see what traps might await. The Stop the War march had been and gone, but he'd spotted its rump, moving slowly up Waterloo Place. Siobhan had told him she was headed there, thought she might catch up with her parents.

'You've not had much time for them,' Rebus had sympathised.

'And vice versa,' she'd muttered.

There was security on the door of the hotel: not just the liveried doorman and concierge – a different one from Saturday night – but what Rebus assumed were plainclothes officers, probably under Steelforth's control. The Special Branch man was looking more dapper than ever in a double-breasted pinstripe. Having shaken hands, he was gesturing towards the Palm Court.

'A small whisky perhaps?'

'Depends who's paying.'

'Allow me.'

'In which case,' Rebus advised, 'I might manage a large one.'

Steelforth's laugh was loud enough, but empty at its core. They found a corner table. A cocktail waitress appeared as if conjured into being by their very arrival.

'Carla,' Steelforth informed her, 'we'd like a couple of whiskies. Doubles.' He turned his attention to Rebus.

'Laphroaig,' Rebus obliged. 'The older the better.'

Carla bowed her head and moved off. Steelforth was adjusting the line of his jacket, waiting for her to leave before he spoke. Rebus decided not to give him the chance.

'Managing to hush up our dead MP?' he enquired loudly.

'What's to hush up?'

'You tell me.'

'As far as I can establish, DI Rebus, your own investigation so far has consisted of one unofficial interview with the deceased's sister.' Having finished toying with his jacket, Steelforth clasped his hands in front of him. 'An interview conducted, moreover, lamentably soon after she had made formal identification.' He paused theatrically. 'No offence intended, Inspector.'

'None taken, Commander.'

'Of course, it may be that you've been busy in other ways. I've had no fewer than two local journalists raking over the coals.'

Rebus tried to look surprised. Mairie Henderson, plus whoever it was he'd spoken to on the *Scotsman* news desk. Favours now owed to both ...

'Well,' Rebus said, 'since there's nothing to hush up, I don't suppose the press will get very far.' He paused. 'You said at the time that the investigation would be taken out of my hands ... that doesn't seem to have happened.'

Steelforth shrugged. 'Because there's nothing to investigate. Verdict: accidental death.' He unclasped his hands as the drinks arrived, and with them a small jug of water and a bowl brimming with ice cubes.

'Do you want to leave the bill open?' Carla asked. Steelforth looked at Rebus, then shook his head.

'We'll just be having the one.' He signed for the drinks with his room number.

'Is it the taxpayer picking up the tab,' Rebus enquired, 'or do we have Mr Pennen to thank?'

'Richard Pennen is a credit to this country,' Steelforth stated, adding too much water to his drink. 'The Scottish economy in particular would be the poorer without him.'

'I didn't realise the Balmoral was so expensive.'

Steelforth's eyes narrowed. 'I mean defence jobs, as you well know.'

'And if I interview him about Ben Webster's demise, he'll suddenly send the work elsewhere?'

Steelforth leaned forward. 'We need to keep him sweet, surely you can see that?'

Rebus savoured the aroma of the malt, then lifted it to his mouth.

'Cheers,' Steelforth said grudgingly.

'*Slainte*,' Rebus replied.

'I've heard you enjoy a drop of the hard stuff,' Steelforth added. 'Maybe even more than a drop.'

'You've been talking to the right people.'

'I don't mind a man who drinks ... just so long as it doesn't interfere with his work. But then I also hear it's been known to affect your judgement.'

'Not my judgement of character,' Rebus said, putting the glass down. 'Sober or pissed, I'd know you for a prick of the first order.'

Steelforth made a mock toast with his glass. 'I was going to offer you something,' he said, 'to make up for your disappointment.'

'Do I look disappointed?'

'You're not going to get anywhere with Ben Webster, suicide or not.'

'Suddenly you're ruling in suicide again? Does that mean there's a note?'

Steelforth lost patience. 'There's no bloody note!' he spat. 'There's nothing at all.'

'Makes it an odd suicide, wouldn't you say?'

'Accidental death.'

'The official line.' Rebus lifted his glass again. 'What were you going to offer me?'

Steelforth studied him for a moment before answering. 'My own men,' he said. 'This murder case you've got ... I hear tell the count is now three victims. I'd imagine you're stretched. Right now it's just you and DS Clarke, isn't it?'

'More or less.'

'I've plenty of men up here, Rebus – very good men. All sorts of skills and specialisms between them.'

'And you'd let us borrow them?'

'That was the intention.'

'So we'd be able to focus on the murders and give up on the MP?' Rebus made a show of thinking the proposal over; went so far as to press his hands together and rest his chin on his fingertips. 'Sentries at the Castle said there was an intruder,' he said quietly, as if thinking aloud.

'No evidence of that,' Steelforth was quick to reply.

'Why was Webster on the ramparts ... that's never really been answered.'

'A breath of air.'

'He excused himself from the dinner?'

'It was winding down ... port and cigars.'

'He said he was going outside?' Rebus's eyes were on Steelforth now.

'Not as such. People were getting up to stretch their legs ...'

'You've interviewed all of them?' Rebus guessed.

'Most of them,' the Special Branch man qualified.

'The Foreign Secretary?' Rebus waited for a response which didn't come. 'No, I didn't think so. The foreign delegations then?'

'Some of them, yes. I've done pretty much everything *you'd* have done, Inspector.'

'You don't know *what* I'd have done.'

Steelforth accepted this with a slight bow of the head. He had yet to touch his drink.

'You've no qualms?' Rebus added. 'No questions?'

'None.'

'And yet you don't know why it happened.' Rebus shook his head slowly. 'You're not much of a cop, are you, Steelforth? You might be a whizz at the handshakes and the briefings, but when it comes to policing, I'd say you haven't a fucking clue. You're window-dressing, that's all.' Rebus rose to his feet.

'And what are you exactly, DI Rebus?'

'Me?' Rebus considered for a moment. 'I'm the janitor, I suppose ... the one who sweeps up after you.' He paused, found his punchline. 'After you *and* around you, if it comes to that.'

Exit stage right.

Before leaving the Balmoral, he'd wandered downstairs to the restaurant, breezing through the anteroom despite the best efforts of the staff. The place was busy, but there was no sign of Richard Pennen. Rebus climbed the steps to Princes Street and decided he might as well drop into the Café Royal. The pub was surprisingly quiet.

'Trade's been lousy,' the manager confided. 'Lot of locals keeping their heads down the next few days.'

After two drinks, Rebus headed along George Street. The workmen had stopped digging the roads – council orders. A new one-way system was being introduced, and with it confusion for motorists. Even the traffic cops thought it ham-fisted, and weren't going out of their way to enforce the new No Entry signs. Again, the street was quiet. No hint of Geldof's army. The bouncers outside the Dome told him the place was three-quarters empty. On Young Street, the narrow lane's one-way routeing had been switched from one direction to the other. Rebus pushed open the door to the Oxford Bar, smiling at something he'd been told about the new system.

They're doing it in easy stages: you can go in either direction for a while ...

'Pint of IPA, Harry,' Rebus said, reaching for his cigarettes.

'Eight months and counting,' Harry muttered, pulling the pump.

'Don't remind me.'

Harry was counting the days till Scotland's smoking ban took effect ...

'Anything happening out there?' one of the regulars

asked. Rebus shook his head, knowing that in the drinker's sealed-off world, news of a serial killer wouldn't quite qualify for the category of 'anything happening'.

'Isn't there some march on?' Harry added.

'Calton Hill,' one of the other drinkers confirmed. 'Money this is costing, we could've sent every kid in Africa a Jenner's hamper.'

'Putting Scotland on the world stage,' Harry reminded him, nodding in the direction of Charlotte Square, home to the First Minister. 'A price Jack says is worth every penny.'

'It's not his money, though,' the drinker grumbled. 'My wife works at that new shoe shop on Frederick Street, says they'd be as well shutting for the week.'

'Royal Bank's going to be closed all tomorrow,' Harry stated.

'Aye, tomorrow's going to be the bad one,' the drinker muttered.

'And to think,' Rebus complained, 'I came in here to cheer myself up.'

Harry stared at him in mock disbelief. 'Should know better than that by now, John. Ready for another?'

Rebus wasn't sure, but he nodded anyway.

A couple of pints later, and having demolished the last filled roll on display, he decided he might as well head home. He'd read the *Evening News*, watched the Tour de France highlights on TV, and listened to further opposition to the new road layout.

'If they don't change it back, my wife says they might as well pull down the shutters where she works. Did I tell you? She's in that new shoe shop on Frederick Street ...'

Harry was rolling his eyes as Rebus made for the door. He considered walking home, or calling Gayfield to see if anyone was out in a patrol car, could maybe pick him up. A lot of the taxis were steering clear of the centre, but he knew he could take a chance outside the Roxburghe

Hotel, try to look like a wealthy tourist ...

He heard the doors opening, but was slow to turn around. Hands grabbed at his arms, pulling them behind his back.

'Had a bit too much to drink?' a voice barked. 'Night in the cells will do you, matey.'

'Get off me!' Rebus twisted his body, to no effect. He felt the plastic restraints going around his wrists, pulled tight enough to cut off circulation. No way to loosen them once they were on: you had to slice them off.

'Hell's going on?' Rebus was hissing. 'I'm bloody CID.'

'Don't look like CID,' the voice was telling him. 'Stink of beer and fags, clothes like rags ...' It was an English accent; London maybe. Rebus saw a uniform, then two more. The faces shadowy – maybe tanned – but chiselled and stern. The van was small and unmarked. Its back doors were open, and they pushed him in.

'I've got ID in my pocket,' he said. There was a bench for him to sit on. The windows were blacked out and covered on the outside by a metal grille. There was a faint smell of sick. Another grille separated the back of the van from the front, with a sheet of chipboard blocking any access.

'This is a big mistake!' Rebus yelled.

'Tell it to the Marines,' a voice called back.

The van started moving. Rebus saw headlights through the back window. Stood to reason: three of them couldn't fit in the front; had to be another vehicle. Didn't matter where they took him – Gayfield Square, West End or St Leonard's – he'd be a known face. Nothing to worry about, except the swelling of his fingers as the blood failed to circulate. His shoulders were agony too, drawn back by the tightness of the cuffs. He had to slide his legs apart to stop himself careering around the enclosure. They were doing maybe fifty, not stopping for lights. He heard two pedestrians squeal at a near-miss. No siren, but the roof-light was flashing. Car behind seemed to have neither siren nor flasher. Not a patrol car then ... and this wasn't exactly a regulation vehicle either. Rebus thought they were heading east, meaning Gayfield, but then they took a sharp left towards the New Town, barrelling downhill so that Rebus's head thumped the roof as they went.

'Where the hell ...?' If he'd been drunk before, he was sober now. Only destination he could think of was Fettes, but that was HQ. You didn't take drunks there to sleep off their binge. It was where the brass hung out, James Corbyn and his cronies. Sure enough, they took a left into Ferry Road, but didn't make the turn to Fettes ...

Which left only Drylaw police station; a lonely outpost in the north of the city – Precinct Thirteen, some called it. A gloomy shed of a place, and they were pulling to a halt at its door. Rebus was hauled out and taken inside, his eyes adjusting to the sudden glare of the strip-lighting. There was no one on the desk; place seemed deserted. They marched him into the back where two holding-cells waited, both with their doors wide open. He felt the pressure on one hand ease, the blood tingling its way back down the fingers. A push in the back sent him stumbling into one of the cells. The door slammed shut.

'Hey!' Rebus called out. 'Is this some sick kind of joke?'

'Do we look like clowns, matey? Think you've wandered into an episode of *Dirty Sanchez*?' There was laughter from behind the door.

'Get a good night's kip,' another voice added, 'and don't go giving us any trouble, else we might have to come in there and administer one of our special sedatives, mightn't we, Jacko?'

Rebus thought he could hear a hiss. Everything went quiet, and he knew why. They'd made a mistake, given him a name.

Jacko.

He tried to remember their faces, the better to exact his eventual revenge. All that came to him was that they'd been either tanned or weatherbeaten. But there was no way he was going to forget those voices. Nothing unusual about the uniforms they'd been wearing ... except the badges on the epaulettes had been removed. No badges meant no easy means to ID them.

Rebus kicked the door a few times, then reached into his pocket for his phone.

And realised it wasn't there. They'd taken it from him, or he'd dropped it. Still had his wallet and warrant card, cigarettes and lighter. He sat on the cold concrete shelf which served as a bed and looked at his wrists. The plastic cuff was still encircling his left hand. They'd sliced open the one around his right. He tried to run his free hand up and down the arm, massaging the wrist, the palm and fingers, trying to get some blood going. Maybe the lighter could burn its way through, but not without searing his flesh in the process. He lit a cigarette instead, and tried to slow his heartbeat. Walked over to the door again and banged on it with his fist, turned his back to it and hammered his heel into it.

All the times he'd visited the cells in Gayfield and St Leonard's ... hearing these self-same tattoos. Thum-thum-thum-thum-thum. Making jokes with the lock-key about it.

Thum-thum-thum-thum-thum.

The sound of hope over experience. Rebus sat down again. There was neither toilet nor basin, just a metal pail in one corner. Ancient faeces smeared on the wall next to it. Messages gouged into the plasterwork: *Big Malky Rules*; *Wardie Young Team*; *Hearts Ya Bass*. Hard to believe, but someone with a bit of Latin had even been holed up here: *Nemo Me Impune Lacessit*. In the Scots: 'Whau Daur Meddle Wi' Me?' Modern equivalent: 'Screw Me and I'll Screw You Right Back'.

Rebus got to his feet again, knew now what was going on, should have realised from the word go.

Steelforth.

Easy for him to get his hands on some spare uniforms ... dispatching three of his men on a mission ... same men he'd offered to Rebus earlier. They'd probably been watching as he'd left the hotel. Followed him from pub to pub until they picked their spot. The lane outside the Oxford Bar was perfect.

'Steelforth!' Rebus yelled at the door. 'Come in here and talk to me! Are you a coward as well as a bully?' He pressed his ear to the door but heard nothing. The spyhole was closed. The hatch which would be opened at meal-times was locked shut. He paced the cell, opened his cigarette packet but decided he needed to conserve supplies. Changed his mind and lit one anyway. The lighter spluttered – not much petrol left ... a toss-up which would run out first. Ten o'clock his watch said. A long time till morning ...

Monday 4 July

8

The turning of the lock awoke him. The door creaked open. First off, he saw a young uniform, mouth agape in amazement. And to his left, Detective Chief Inspector James Macrae, looking irate and with his hair uncombed. Rebus checked his watch: just shy of four, which meant Monday was dawning.

'Got a blade?' he asked, mouth dry. He showed them his wrist. It was swollen, the palm and knuckles discoloured. The constable produced a penknife from his pocket.

'How did you get in here?' he asked, voice shaking.

'Ten o'clock last night, who was holding the fort?'

'We had a call-out,' the constable said, 'locked the place before we left.'

Rebus had no reason to disbelieve the story. 'How did the call-out go?'

'False alarm. I'm really sorry ... Why didn't you shout or something?'

'I assume there's nothing in the log?' The cuffs fell to the floor. Rebus started rubbing life back into his fingers.

'Nothing. And we don't check the cells when they're empty.'

'You knew they were empty?'

'Kept that way so we can stick any rioters in them.'

Macrae was studying Rebus's left hand. 'Need to get that seen to?'

'I'll be fine.' Rebus grimaced. 'How did you find me?'

'Text message. I'd left the phone to charge in my study. The beeping woke my wife.'

'Can I see it?'

Macrae handed over the phone. At the top of the screen was the caller's number, and below it a capitalised message – REBUS IN DRYLAW CELLS. Rebus punched the Return Call option, but when connected all he got was a machine telling him the number was not in use. He handed the phone back to Macrae.

'Screen says the call was sent at midnight.'

Macrae failed to meet Rebus's gaze. 'It was a while before we heard it,' he said quietly. But then he remembered who he was, and stiffened his spine. 'Care to tell me what happened here?'

'Some of the lads having a laugh,' Rebus improvised. He kept flexing his left wrist, trying not to show how much it was flaring with pain.

'Names?'

'No names, no pack-drill, sir.'

'So if I were to return their little text message ...?'

'Number's already been cancelled, sir.'

Macrae studied Rebus. 'Few drinks last night, eh?'

'A few.' He turned his attention back to the uniform. 'Nobody's left a mobile at the front desk, by any chance?'

The young officer shook his head. Rebus leaned in towards him. 'Something like this gets out ... well, there'll be a few laughs at my expense, but *you'll* be the ones the joke's really on. Cells unchecked, station left unmanned, front door unlocked ...'

'The door was locked,' the constable argued.

'Still doesn't look good for you, does it?'

Macrae patted the officer's shoulder. 'So let's keep this to ourselves, eh? Now come on, DI Rebus, I'll drop you home before the barricades go up again.'

Outside, Macrae paused before unlocking his Rover. 'I can see why you'd want this kept quiet, but rest assured – if *I* find the culprits, there'll be hell to pay.'

'Yes, sir,' Rebus agreed. 'Sorry to have been the cause.'

'Not your fault, John. Now hop in.'

They drove southwards in silence through the city, dawn breaking to the east. A few delivery vans and bleary pedestrians, but little clue as to what the day might bring. Monday meant the 'Carnival of Full Enjoyment'. The police knew it was a euphemism for trouble. This was when the Clown Army, the Wombles and the Black Bloc were expected to make their move. They would try to shut the city down. Macrae had switched the radio to a local station, just in time to catch a news flash – an attempt to padlock the pumps at a petrol station on Queensferry Road.

'The weekend was just for starters,' Macrae commented as he drew to a halt on Arden Street. 'So I hope you enjoyed it.'

'Nice and relaxing, sir,' Rebus said, opening his door. 'Thanks for the lift.' He patted the roof of the car and watched it drive off, then climbed the two flights, searching his pockets for his keys.

No keys.

Of course not: they were hanging from the lock on his door. He swore and opened up, withdrew the keys and held them in a bunch in his right fist. Walked into the hall on tiptoe. No noises or lights. Padded past the kitchen and bedroom doorways. Into the living room. The Colliar case-notes weren't there, of course: he'd taken them to Siobhan's. But the stuff Mairie Henderson had found for him – about Pennen Industries and Ben Webster MP – was strewn about the place. He picked his mobile phone up from the table. Nice of them to bring it back. He wondered how thoroughly they had scoured it for calls in and out, messages and texts. Didn't really bother him: he deleted stuff at the end of each day. Didn't mean it wasn't still hidden on the chip somewhere ... And they'd have the authority to ask his phone company for records. When you were SO12, you could do most things.

He went into the bathroom and ran the tap. It always

151

took a while for the water to run hot. He was going to spend a good fifteen or twenty minutes under the shower. He checked the kitchen and both bedrooms: nothing seemed out of place, which in itself also meant nothing. Filled the kettle and switched it on. Might the place be bugged? He'd no way of telling; didn't think it was as easy these days as unscrewing the base from the telephone to find out. The paperwork on Pennen had been tossed about, but not taken. Why? Because they knew it would be easy for him to get the same information again. It was all in the public domain after all, only a mouse-click or two away.

They'd left it because it was meaningless.

Because Rebus wasn't anywhere near getting to whatever it was Steelforth was trying to protect.

And they'd left his keys in the lock, his phone in plain view, to add insult to injury. He flexed his left hand again, wondering how you could tell if you had a blood clot or thrombosis. He took the tea through to the bathroom, turned off the tap at the sink, shed his clothes, and climbed into the shower. He tried to empty his mind of the previous seventy-two hours. Started listing his 'Desert Island Discs' instead. Couldn't decide which track off *Argus* to choose. He was still busy debating with himself as he got out and towelled himself dry; found himself humming 'Throw Down the Sword'.

'Not on your life,' he declared to the mirror.

He was determined to get some sleep. Five restless hours curled up on a slab hardly counted. But first he had to charge his phone. Plugged it in and decided to see what messages there were. One text – same anonymous caller as before.

LETS CALL A TRUCE

Sent barely half an hour before. Which meant two things. They knew he was home. And the 'out of service' number was somehow back in play. Rebus could think of a dozen replies, but decided to switch the phone off again instead. Another mug of tea and he made for the bedroom.

Panic on the streets of Edinburgh.

Siobhan had never known the place so tense. Not during the local Hibs/Hearts derby; not even during Republican and Orange marches. The air was somehow heightened, as if an electrical current ran through it. Not just Edinburgh either: a peace camp had been established in Stirling. There had been short, sharp outbursts of violence. Still two days to go before the G8 opened, but the protesters knew that a number of delegations had already arrived. A lot of the Americans were based at Dunblane Hydro, a short drive from Gleneagles. Some foreign journalists had found themselves much further away in hotels in Glasgow. Japanese officials had taken over many of the rooms in the Edinburgh Sheraton, just across the road from the financial district. Siobhan's instinct had been to use the hotel's car park, but there was a chain across its entrance. A uniformed officer approached as she wound down her window. She showed him her ID.

'Sorry, ma'am,' he apologised in a polite English voice. 'No can do. Orders from on high. Your best bet is to do a U-turn.' He pointed further down the Western Approach Road. 'There's some idiots on the carriageway ... we're trying to herd most of them into Canning Street. Bunch of clowns, by all accounts.'

She did as instructed, finally finding a space on a yellow line outside the Lyceum Theatre. Crossed at the lights, but instead of going into the Standard Life HQ, decided to walk past it, down the concrete lanes which ran mazily through the whole area. Turned a corner into Canning Street and found herself stopped by a cordon of police, on the other side of which black-clad demonstrators mixed with figures from the Big Top. A bunch of clowns: quite literally. This was Siobhan's first real sighting of the Rebel Clown Army. They wore red and purple wigs, faces painted white. Some brandished feather dusters, others waved carnations. A smiley face had been drawn on one of the riot shields. The cops were in black too, protected by knee and elbow pads, stab-proof vests, visored helmets. One of the demonstrators had somehow scrambled up a high wall and was shaking his bared buttocks at the police below. There were windows all around, office workers peering out. Plenty of noise, but no real fury as yet. As more officers jogged into view, Siobhan retreated as far as the pedestrian bridge which crossed over the Western Approach Road. Again, the protesters were heavily outnumbered. One of them was in a wheelchair, a lion rampant attached to the back, fluttering in the breeze. Traffic heading into town was at a standstill. Whistles were being blown, but the police horses looked unfazed. As a line of officers marched beneath the footbridge, they held their shields above their heads to protect them.

The situation seemed under control, and unlikely to change, so Siobhan headed for her final destination.

The revolving door which led to the Standard Life reception area was locked. A guard stared out at her before buzzing her in.

'Can I see your pass, miss?'

'I don't work here.' Siobhan showed her ID instead.

He took it from her to study it. Handed it back and nodded towards the reception desk.

'Any problems?' she asked.

'Couple of goons tried to get in. One's scaled the west side of the building. Seems to be stuck three floors up.'

'Fun for all concerned.'

'It pays the bills, miss.' He gestured once more towards the desk. 'Gina there will sort you out.'

Gina did indeed sort Siobhan out. First a visitor's pass – 'to be kept in view at all times, please' – and then a call upstairs. The waiting area was plush, with sofas and magazines, coffee and a flat-screen TV showing some mid-morning design show. A woman came striding towards Siobhan.

'Detective Sergeant Clarke? I'll take you upstairs.'

'Mrs Jensen?'

But the woman shook her head. 'Sorry to've kept you waiting. As you can imagine, things are a bit fraught ...'

'That's okay. I've been learning which floor lamp to buy.'

The woman smiled, without really comprehending, and led Siobhan to the lifts. As they waited, she studied her own clothes. 'We're all in mufti today,' she said, explaining the slacks and blouse.

'Good idea.'

'It's funny seeing some of the men in jeans and T-shirts. Hardly recognisable, some of them.' She paused. 'Is it the riots you're here about?'

'No.'

'Only Mrs Jensen seemed in the dark ...'

'Up to me to shed some light then, isn't it?' Siobhan replied with a smile, as the lift doors opened.

The name-plate on Dolly Jensen's office stated that she was Dorothy Jensen, but gave no indication of her job title. Had to be quite high-powered, Siobhan reckoned. Jensen's assistant had knocked on the door, then retreated to her own desk. The main floor was open-plan, plenty of faces peering up from their computers to study the new arrival. A few stood by the available windows, coffee mugs in hand, watching the outside world.

'Come in,' a voice called. Siobhan opened the door and closed it behind her, shook Dorothy Jensen's hand and was invited to take a seat.

'You know why I'm here?' Siobhan asked.

Jensen leaned back in her chair. 'Tom told me all about it.'

'You've been busy since, haven't you?'

Jensen scanned her desk. She was the same age as her husband. Broad-shouldered and with a masculine face. Thick black hair – the grey dyed out of it, Siobhan guessed – fell in immaculate waves to her shoulders. Around her neck hung a simple pearl necklace.

'I don't mean here, Mrs Jensen,' Siobhan explained, allowing the irritation to show. 'I mean at home, wiping all trace of your website.'

'Is that a crime?'

'It's called "impeding an investigation". I've seen people go to court for it. Sometimes we can up the ante to criminal conspiracy, if we're of a mind ...'

Jensen took hold of a pen from her desk, twisted its barrel, opening and closing it. Siobhan was satisfied that she had breached the woman's defences.

'I need everything you've got, Mrs Jensen – any paperwork, email addresses, names. We need to clear all those people – you and your husband included – if we're going to catch this killer.' She paused. 'I know what you're thinking – your husband told us pretty much the same – and I can appreciate you'd feel that way. But you've got to understand . . . whoever did this, they're not going to stop. They could have downloaded everyone listed on your site, and that turns those men into victims – not so very different from Vicky.'

At mention of her daughter's name, Jensen's eyes burned into Siobhan's. But they soon grew liquid. She dropped the pen and opened a drawer, bringing out a handkerchief and blowing her nose.

'I tried, you know ... tried to forgive. It's supposed to make us divine after all, isn't it?' She forced a nervous laugh. 'These men, they go to jail to be punished, but we hope they'll change, too. The ones who don't ... what use are they? They come back to us and do the same things over and over again.'

Siobhan knew the argument well, and had found herself many times on both sides of it. But she stayed silent.

'He showed no remorse, no sense of guilt, no sympathy ... What kind of creature is that? Is it even human? At the trial, the defence kept on about the broken home he came from, the drugs he took. They called it a "chaotic lifestyle". But it was *his* choice to destroy Vicky, *his* little power-trip. Nothing chaotic about that, let me tell you.' Jensen's voice had grown tremulous. She took a deep breath, adjusting her posture, calming by degrees. 'I work in insurance. We deal with choice and risk. I do know a *little* of what I'm talking about.'

'Is there any paperwork, Mrs Jensen?' Siobhan asked quietly.

'Some,' Jensen admitted. 'Not very much.'

'What about emails? You must have corresponded with the site's users?'

Jensen nodded slowly. 'The families of victims, yes. Are they all suspects too?'

'How soon can you get everything to me?'

'Do I need to talk to my lawyer?'

'Might be an idea. Meantime, I'd like to send someone to your home. He knows about computers. If he comes to you, it saves us having to take your hard drive elsewhere.'

'All right.'

'His name's Bain.' *Eric Bain of the pneumatic girlfriend ...* Siobhan shifted in her chair and cleared her throat. 'He's a detective sergeant, like me. What time this evening would suit?'

'You look rough,' Mairie Henderson said, as Rebus tried to squeeze himself into the passenger seat of her sports car.

'Restless night,' he told her. What he didn't add was that her ten a.m. call had woken him. 'Does this thing go back any further?'

She bent down and tugged at a lever, sending Rebus's seat flying backwards. Rebus turned to examine what space was left behind him.

'I've heard all the Douglas Bader jokes,' she warned him. 'And the ones about "getting legless".'

'Then I'm stymied,' Rebus said, fastening his seat-belt. 'Thanks for the invite, by the way.'

'In that case, you can pay for the drinks.'

'What drinks are those?'

'Our excuse for being there in the first place ...' She was heading for the top of Arden Street. Left, right and left would put her on Grange Road and only five minutes away from Prestonfield House.

Prestonfield House Hotel was one of the city's better-kept secrets. Surrounded by 1930s bungalows and with views across to the schemes of Craigmillar and Niddrie, it seemed an unpromising location for a grand house in the baronial style. Its substantial grounds – including an adjacent golf course – gave plenty of privacy. The only time the place had been in the news, to Rebus's knowledge, was when a Member of the Scottish Parliament had tried setting fire to the curtains after a party.

'I meant to ask on the phone ...' Rebus said to Mairie.

'What?'

'How do you know about this?'

'Contacts, John. No journalist should ever leave home without them.'

'Tell you something you've left at home, though ... the brakes on this bloody death-trap.'

'It's a road-racer,' she told him. 'Doesn't sound right when you dawdle.' But she eased her foot back a little.

'Thanks,' he said. 'So what's the occasion?'

'Morning coffee, then he gives his pitch, and then lunch.'

'Where exactly?'

She shrugged. 'A meeting room, I suppose. Maybe the

restaurant for the actual lunch.' She signalled left into the hotel driveway.

'And we are ...?'

'Looking for some peace and quiet amid the madness. Plus a pot of tea for two.'

Staff were awaiting them at the front door. Mairie explained the situation. There was a room off to the left where their needs could be met, or another to the right, just past a closed door.

'Something on in there?' Mairie asked, pointing.

'Business meeting,' the employee revealed.

'Well, just so long as they're not kicking up a fuss, we'll be fine in here.' She entered the adjoining room. Rebus heard peacocks squawking outside on the lawn.

'Is it tea you're wanting?' the young man asked.

'Coffee for me,' Rebus told him.

'Tea – peppermint if you've got it; otherwise camomile.' The employee disappeared, and Mairie pressed her ear to the wall.

'I thought eavesdropping had gone electronic,' Rebus commented.

'If you can afford it,' Mairie whispered. She lifted her ear away. 'All I can hear is muttering.'

'Hold the front page.'

She ignored him, pulled a chair over towards the doorway, making sure she'd have a view of anyone entering or leaving the meeting.

'Lunch sharpish at twelve, that's my guess. Get them feeling good about their host.' She checked her watch.

'I brought a woman here for dinner once,' Rebus mused. 'Had coffee in the library after. It's upstairs. Walls a sort of curdled red. I think someone told me they were leather.'

'Leather wallpaper? Kinky,' Mairie said with a smile.

'By the way, I never did thank you for going straight to Cafferty with news of Cyril Colliar ...' His eyes drilled into hers, and she had the good grace to allow some red to creep up her neck.

'You're welcome,' she said.

'Nice to know that when I come to you with confidential information, you'll feed it to the city's biggest villain.'

'Just that once, John.'

'Once too often.'

'The Colliar killing has been gnawing away at him.'

'Just the way I like it.'

She gave a tired smile. 'Just the once,' she repeated. 'And please bear in mind the huge favour I'm currently doing you.'

Rebus decided not to answer, walked back out into the hall instead. The reception desk was at the far end, past the restaurant. It had changed a bit in the years since Rebus had spent half his pay-packet on that meal. The drapes were heavy, the furniture exotic, tassels everywhere. A dark-skinned man in a blue silk suit made to pass Rebus, giving a little bow.

'Morning,' Rebus said.

'Good morning,' he said crisply, coming to a stop. 'Is the meeting already closing?'

'I wouldn't know.'

The man bowed his head again. 'My apologies. I thought perhaps . . .' But he left the sentence unfinished and walked the rest of the way to the door, tapping once before disappearing inside. Mairie had come out for a look.

'Not much of a secret knock,' Rebus informed her.

'It's not the Masons.'

Rebus wasn't so sure about that. What was the G8, after all, if not a very private club?

The door was opening again, two more men stepping out. They made for the driveway, stopping to light their cigarettes.

'Breaking up for lunch?' Rebus guessed. He followed Mairie back to the doorway of their own little room and watched the men filter out. Maybe twenty of them. Some looked African, others Asian and Middle Eastern. A few wore what Rebus took to be their national dress.

'Maybe Kenya, Sierra Leone, Niger ...' Mairie was whispering.

'Meaning that really you've got no idea whatsoever?' Rebus whispered back.

'Geography was never my strong point ...' She broke off and clutched his arm. A tall, imposing figure was now mingling with the others, shaking hands and exchanging some words. Rebus recognised him from Mairie's press pack. His elongated face was tanned and lined, and some brown had been added to his hair. Pinstripe suit with an inch of crisp white shirt-cuff. He had a smile for everyone, seemed to know them personally. Mairie had retreated a few steps further into the room, but Rebus stayed in the doorway. Richard Pennen took a good photograph. In the flesh, the face was slightly scrawnier, the eyes heavy-lidded. But he did look disgustingly healthy, as though he had spent the previous weekend on a tropical beach. Assistants stood either side of him, whispering information into his ear, making sure this part of the day, like those before and after, went without a hitch of any kind.

Suddenly, a member of staff was blocking Rebus's view. He bore a tray with the tea and coffee. As Rebus moved to let him pass, he saw that he'd come to Pennen's notice.

'Your shout, I believe,' Mairie was saying. Rebus turned into the room and paid for the drinks.

'Would it be Detective Inspector Rebus?' The deep voice came from Richard Pennen. He was standing just a few feet away, still flanked by his assistants.

Mairie took a couple of steps towards him and held out her hand.

'Mairie Henderson, Mr Pennen. Terrible tragedy at the Castle the other night ...'

'Terrible,' Pennen agreed.

'I believe you were there.'

'I was.'

'She's a journalist, sir,' one of the assistants said.

'I'd never have guessed,' Pennen answered with a smile.

'Just wondering,' Mairie ploughed on, 'why you were paying for Mr Webster's hotel room.'

'I wasn't – my company was.'

'What's your interest in debt relief, sir?'

But Pennen's focus was on Rebus. 'I was told I might be seeing you.'

'Nice to have Commander Steelforth on your team ...'

Pennen looked Rebus up and down. 'His description didn't do you justice, Inspector.'

'Still, it's nice that he took the trouble.' Rebus could have added: *because it means I've got him rattled*.

'You're aware, of course, of how much flak you might get if I were to report this intrusion?'

'We're just enjoying a cuppa, sir,' Rebus said. 'Far as I'm aware, *you're* the one doing the intruding.'

Pennen smiled again. 'Nicely put.' He turned to Mairie. 'Ben Webster was a fine MP and PPS, Miss Henderson, and scrupulous with it. As you know, any gifts in kind received from my company would be listed in members' interests.'

'Doesn't answer my question.'

Pennen's jawline twitched. He took a deep breath. 'Pennen Industries does most of its business overseas – get your economics editor to fill you in. You'll see what a major exporter we've become.'

'Of arms,' Mairie stated.

'Of *technology*,' Pennen countered. 'What's more, we put money back into some of the poorest nations. That's why Ben Webster was involved.' He turned his gaze back on to Rebus. 'No cover-up, Inspector. Just David Steelforth doing his job. A lot of contracts could get signed during these next few days ... huge projects green-lit. Contacts

162

made, and jobs saved as a result. Not the sort of feelgood story our media seem to be interested in. Now, if you'll excuse me ...' He turned away, and Rebus was gratified to see that there was a blob of something on the heel of one black leather brogue. No expert, Rebus would still have bet heavily on it being peacock shit.

Mairie slumped on to a sofa which creaked beneath her, as if unused to such mistreatment.

'Bloody hell,' she said, pouring out some tea. Rebus could smell the peppermint. He poured himself coffee from the small cafetiere.

'Remind me,' he said, 'how much is this whole thing costing?'

'The G8?' She waited till he'd nodded, puffed out her cheeks as she tried to remember. 'A hundred and fifty?'

'As in millions?'

'As in millions.'

'And all so businessmen like Mr Pennen can keep plying their trade.'

'There might be a *bit* more to it than that ...' Mairie was smiling. 'But you're right in a sense: the decisions have already been taken.'

'So what's Gleneagles all about but a few nice dinners and some handshakes for the cameras.'

'Putting Scotland on the map?' she offered.

'Aye, right.' Rebus finished his coffee. 'Maybe we should stay for lunch, see if we can rile Pennen more than we already have.'

'Sure you can afford it?'

Rebus looked around him. 'Which reminds me, that flunkey's not come back with my change.'

'Change?' Mairie gave a laugh. Rebus caught her meaning, and decided he was going to drain the cafetiere to its last drop.

*

According to the TV news, central Edinburgh was a war zone.

Half past two on a Monday afternoon. Normally, there would have been shoppers in Princes Street, laden with purchases; people in the adjacent Gardens, enjoying a promenade or resting on one of the commemorative benches.

But not today.

The newsroom cut to protests at the Faslane naval base, home to Britain's four Trident-class submarines. The place was under siege from about two thousand demonstrators. Police in Fife had been handed control of the Forth Road Bridge for the first time in its history. Cars heading north were being stopped and searched. Roads out of the capital had been blocked by sit-down protests. There had been scuffles near the Peace Camp in Stirling.

And a riot was kicking off in Princes Street. Baton-wielding police making their presence felt. They carried circular shields of a kind Siobhan hadn't seen before. The area around Canning Street was still causing trouble. Marchers still bringing traffic to a halt on the Western Approach. The studio cut back to Princes Street. The pro-testers seemed to be outnumbered not only by police but by cameras, too. A lot of pushing on both sides.

'They're trying to start a fight,' Eric Bain said. He'd come to Gayfield to show her what little he'd been able to find so far.

'It could have waited till after you'd seen Mrs Jensen,' she'd told him, to which all he'd done was shrug.

They were alone in the CID office. 'See what they're doing?' Bain asked, pointing at the screen. 'A rioter wades in, then backs off. The nearest cop raises his truncheon, and the papers get a photo of him striking out at some poor sod who's first in line. Meantime, the real trouble-maker is tucked away somewhere behind, ready to do the same thing again.'

Siobhan nodded. 'Makes it look like we're being heavy-handed.'

'Which is what the rioters want.' He folded his arms. 'They've learned a few tricks since Genoa ...'

'But so have we,' Siobhan said. 'Containment, for one thing. That's four hours now the group in Canning Street have been corralled.'

Back in the studio, one of the presenters had a live feed to Midge Ure. He was telling the troublemakers to go home.

'Shame none of them are watching,' Bain commented.

'Are you going to speak with Mrs Jensen?' Siobhan hinted.

'Yes, boss. How hard should I push her?'

'I've already warned we could do her for obstruction. Remind her of that.' Siobhan wrote the Jensens' address on a sheet of her notebook, ripped it out and handed it over. Bain's attention was back on the TV screen. More live pictures from Princes Street. Some protesters had climbed on to the Scott Monument. Others scrambled over the railings into the Gardens. Kicks were aimed at shields. Divots of earth were being thrown. Benches and rubbish bins were next.

'This is getting bad,' Bain muttered. The screen flickered. A new location: Torphichen Street, site of the city's West End police station. Sticks and bottles were being hurled. 'Glad we're not stuck there,' was all Bain said.

'No, we're stuck here instead.'

He looked at her. 'You'd rather be in the thick of things?'

She shrugged, stared at the screen. Someone was calling into the studio by mobile phone, a shopper, trapped like so many others in the branch of British Home Stores on Princes Street.

'We're just bystanders,' the woman was shrieking. 'All we want to do is get out, but the police are treating us all the same ... mothers with babies ... old folk ...'

'You're saying the police are overreacting?' the journalist in the studio asked. Siobhan used the remote to change channels: *Columbo* on one side, *Diagnosis: Murder* on another ... And a film on Channel Four.

'That's *Kidnapped*,' Bain said. 'Brilliant.'

'Sorry to disappoint you,' she said, finding another of the news channels. Same riots; different angles. The same protester she'd seen in Canning Street was still on top of his wall. He sat swinging his feet, only his eyes showing through the gap in his balaclava. He was holding a mobile phone to his ear.

'That reminds me,' Bain said, 'I had Rebus on the blower, asking how an out-of-service number could still be active.'

Siobhan looked at him. 'Did he say why?' Bain shook his head. 'So what did you tell him?'

'You can clone the SIM card, or specify outgoing calls only.' He gave a shrug. 'All kinds of ways to do it.'

Siobhan nodded, eyes back on the TV screen. Bain ran a hand across the back of his neck.

'So what did you think of Molly?' he asked.

'You're a lucky man, Eric.'

He gave a huge grin. 'Pretty much my thinking.'

'But tell me,' Siobhan asked, hating herself for being led down this route, 'does she always twitch so much?'

Bain's grin melted away.

'Sorry, Eric, that was out of order.'

'She said she likes you,' he confided. 'She's not got a bad bone in her body.'

'She's great,' Siobhan agreed. Even to her ears, the sentiment sounded hollow. 'So how did you two meet?'

Bain froze for a moment. 'A club,' he said, recovering.

'Never took you for a dancer, Eric.' Siobhan glanced in his direction.

'Molly's a great dancer.'

'She's got the body for it ...' Relief washed over her as her own mobile sounded. She hoped to hell it would offer the excuse to be anywhere but here ... It was her parents' number.

'Hello?'

At first she mistook the noise on the line for static, then she realised: yells and catcalls and whistles. Same noises she'd just been hearing on the report from Princes Street.

'Mum?' she said. 'Dad?'

And now a voice: her father's. 'Siobhan? Can you hear me?'

'Dad? What the hell are you doing down there?'

'Your mum ...'

'What? Dad, put her on, will you?'

'Your mum's ...'

'Has something—'

'She was bleeding ... ambulance ...'

'Dad, you're breaking up! Where are you exactly?'

'Kiosk ... Gardens.'

The line went dead. She looked at its small rectangular screen. Connection lost.

'Connection lost,' she echoed.

'What's going on?' Bain asked.

'My mum and dad . . . that's where they are.' She nodded towards the TV. 'Can you give me a lift?'

'Where?'

'There.' She stabbed a finger at the screen.

'*There?*'

'There.'

9

They didn't get any further than George Street. Siobhan got out of the car and told Bain not to forget the Jensens. He was telling her to be careful as she slammed shut the door.

There were protesters here too, spilling down Frederick Street. Staff watched in fascinated horror from behind the doors and windows of their shops. Bystanders pressed themselves to walls in the hope of blending in. There was debris underfoot. The protesters were being pushed back down into Princes Street. Nobody tried to stop Siobhan crossing the police line in that direction. Easy enough to get in; getting out was the problem.

There was only one kiosk she knew of – just along from the Scott Monument. The gates to the Gardens had been closed, so she made for the fence. The skirmishes had moved from the street into the Gardens themselves. Rubbish flew through the air, along with stones and other missiles. A hand grabbed at her jacket.

'No you don't.'

She turned to face a policeman. Just above his visor were the letters XS. For a brief moment she read it as *Excess* – just perfect. She had her warrant card ready.

'I'm CID,' she yelled.

'Then you must be crazy.' He released his grip.

'It has been said,' she told him, clambering over the spikes. Looking around, she saw that the rioters had been reinforced by what looked like local hooligans: any excuse for a rammy. Wasn't every day they could lash out at the cops and have a good chance of getting away with it. They were disguising their identities with football scarves around their mouths, jackets zipped all the way to the chin. At least these days they all wore trainers rather than Doc Marten boots.

The kiosk: it sold ice cream and cold drinks. Shards of glass lay strewn around it, and it was closed. She circled it in a crouch: no sign of her father. Spots of blood on the ground, and she followed them with her eyes. They stopped short of the gates. Circled the kiosk again. Banged on the serving-hatch. Tried again. Heard a muffled voice from inside.

'Siobhan?'

'Dad? You in there?'

The door to the side was yanked open. Her father was standing inside, and next to him the kiosk's terrified owner.

'Where's Mum?' Siobhan asked, voice shaking.

'They took her in the ambulance. I couldn't ... they wouldn't let me past the cordon.'

Siobhan couldn't remember ever seeing her father in tears, but he was crying now. Crying, and obviously in shock.

'We need to get you out.'

'Not me,' his companion said with a shake of her head. 'I'm guarding the fort. But I saw what happened ... bloody police. She was only standing there ...'

'It was one of their sticks,' Siobhan's father added. 'Right across her head.'

'Blood was gushing out ...'

Siobhan silenced the woman with a look. 'What's your name?' she asked.

'Frances ... Frances Neagley.'

'Well, Frances Neagley, my advice is to get out.' Then, to her shivering father: 'Come on, let's get going.'

'What?'

169

'We need to go see Mum.'

'But what about ...?'

'It'll be all right. Now *come on*.' She tugged at his arm, felt she would have hauled him out of there bodily if need be. Frances Neagley closed the door on them and locked it.

Another divot flew past. Siobhan knew that tomorrow, this being Edinburgh, the major complaint would be of destruction of the famed flowerbeds. The gates had been forced open by the demonstrators from Frederick Street. A man dressed as a Pictish warrior was being dragged by his arms behind the police lines. Directly in front of the cordon, a young mother was calmly changing the nappy on her pink-clad baby. A placard was being waved: NO GODS, NO MASTERS. The letters X and S ... the baby in pink ... the message on the placard ... they all seemed incredibly vivid to her, snapshots bright with a significance she couldn't quite determine.

There's a pattern here, a meaning of sorts ...

Something to ask Dad later ...

Fifteen years ago, he'd tried explaining semiotics to her, supposedly helping with a school essay, but just getting her more confused. Then, in class, she'd called it 'semenotics', her teacher laughing out loud ...

Siobhan sought out faces she might know. She saw none. But one officer's vest bore the words 'Police Medic'. She pulled her father towards him, warrant card held open in front of her.

'CID,' she explained. 'This man's wife's been taken to hospital. I need to get him there.'

The officer nodded, and guided them through the police line.

'Which hospital?' the medic asked.

'What's your guess?'

He looked at her. 'Dunno,' he admitted. 'I'm down here from Aberdeen.'

'Western General's closest,' Siobhan said. 'Any transport available?'

He pointed up Frederick Street. 'The road that crosses at the top.'

'George Street?'

He shook his head. 'Next one.'

'Queen Street?' She watched him nod. 'Thanks,' she said. 'You better get back there.'

'Suppose so,' he said, with no real enthusiasm. 'Some of them are going in a bit strong ... Not our lot – the ones from the Met.'

Siobhan turned to face her father. 'Any chance you can ID him?'

'Who?'

'The one who hit Mum.'

He rubbed a hand across his eyes. 'I don't think so.'

She made a small, angry sound and led him up the hill towards Queen Street.

There was a line of parked patrol cars. Unbelievably, there was also traffic: all the cars and lorries diverted from the main drag, crawling past as if it was just another day, another commute. Siobhan explained to one police driver what she wanted. He seemed relieved at the thought of being elsewhere. She got into the back with her dad.

'Blues and twos,' she ordered the driver. Cue flashing lights and siren. They pulled past the queue of traffic and got going.

'Is this the right way?' the driver shouted.

'Where are you from?'

'Peterborough.'

'Straight ahead, I'll tell you when to turn.' She squeezed her father's hand. 'You're not hurt?'

He shook his head, fixed her with his eyes. 'How about you?'

'What about me?'

'You're amazing.' Teddy Clarke gave a tired smile. 'Way you acted back there, taking control ...'

'Not just a pretty face, eh?'

'I never realised ...' There were tears in his eyes again. He bit his bottom lip, blinked them back. She gave his hand a tighter squeeze.

'I never really appreciated,' he said, 'how good you might be at this.'

'Just be thankful I'm not in uniform, or it might've been me wielding one of those batons.'

'You wouldn't have hit an innocent woman,' her father stated.

'Straight across at the lights,' she told the driver, before turning her attention back to her father. 'Hard to say, isn't it? We don't know what we'll do till we're there.'

'You wouldn't,' he said determinedly.

'Probably not,' she conceded. 'What the hell were you doing there anyway? Did Santal take you?'

He shook his head. 'I suppose we were ... we thought we'd be spectators. The police didn't see it that way.'

'If I find whoever ...'

'I didn't really see his face.'

'Plenty of cameras there – hard to hide under that sort of coverage.'

'Photographs?'

She nodded. 'Plus CCTV, the media, and us, of course.' She looked at him. 'The police will have filmed everything.'

'But surely ...'

'What?'

'You can't sift through the whole lot?'

'Want to bet on it?'

He studied her for a moment. 'No, I'm not sure I do.'

Almost a hundred arrests. The courts would be busy on Tuesday. By evening, the stand-off had moved from

Princes Street Gardens to Rose Street. Cobbles were torn from the road surface, becoming missiles instead. There were skirmishes on Waverley Bridge, Cockburn Street and Infirmary Street. By nine thirty, things were calming. The final bit of trouble had been outside McDonald's on South St Andrew Street. The uniforms were back at Gayfield Square now, and had brought burgers with them, the aroma making its way into the CID suite. Rebus had the TV playing – a documentary about an abattoir. Eric Bain had just forwarded a list of email addresses – regular users of BeastWatch. His email had ended with the words 'Shiv, let me know how you got on!!' Rebus had tried calling her mobile, but no one was answering. Bain's email had stipulated that the Jensens had given him no grief but had been only 'grudgingly cooperative'.

Rebus had the *Evening News* open beside him. On its cover, a picture of Saturday's march and the headline 'Voting With Their Feet'. They'd be able to use the headline again tomorrow, with a photo of a rioter kicking at a police shield. The TV page gave him the title of the abattoir film – *Slaughterhouse: the Task of Blood*. Rebus stood up and walked to one of the free desks. The Colliar notes stared up at him. Siobhan had been busy. They'd been joined by police and prison reports on Fast Eddie Isley and Trevor Guest.

Guest: burglar, thug, sexual predator.

Isley: rapist.

Colliar: rapist.

Rebus turned to the BeastWatch notes. Details of twenty-eight further rapists and child molesters had been posted. There was a long and angry article from someone calling herself 'Tornupinside' – felt to Rebus as if the author was female. She railed against the court system and its iron-clad ruling on 'rape' versus 'sexual assault'. Hard enough to get a conviction for rape anyway – but 'sexual assault' could be every bit as ugly, violent and degrading, yet with lesser penalties attached. She seemed to know her law: hard to tell if she was from north or south of the border. He skimmed through the text again, looking for examples of 'burglar' or 'burglary' – the term in Scotland was 'housebreaking'. But all she'd used were 'assault' and 'assailant'. Still, Rebus decided a reply was merited. He logged on to Siobhan's terminal and accessed her Hotmail account – she used the same password for everything: Hibsgirl. Ran a finger down Eric Bain's list until he found an address for Tornupinside. Started typing:

I've just finished reading your piece at BeastWatch. It really interested me, and I would like to talk to you about it. I have some information that you may find interesting. Please call me on ...

He thought for a moment. No way of knowing how long Siobhan's mobile would be out of commission. So he typed in his own number instead, but signing off as 'Siobhan Clarke'. More chance, he felt, of the writer replying to another woman. He read the message through, decided it looked as if it had been written by a cop. Gave it another go:

I saw what you said on BeastWatch. Did you know they've shut the site down? I'd like to talk to you, maybe by phone.

Added his number and Siobhan's name – just her first name this time; less formal. Clicked on 'send'. When his phone started trilling only a few minutes later, he knew it was too good to be true – and so it proved.

'Strawman,' the voice drawled: Cafferty.

'Think you'll ever get fed up of that nickname?'

Cafferty chuckled. 'How long has it been?'

Maybe sixteen years ... Rebus giving evidence, Cafferty in the dock ... one of the lawyers confusing Rebus for a previous witness called Stroman ...

'Anything to report?' Cafferty was asking.

'Why should I tell you?'

Another chuckle, even colder than the first. 'Say you

catch him and it goes to court ... how would it look if I suddenly piped up that I'd helped you out? Lot of explaining to do ... could even lead to a mistrial.'

'I thought you wanted him caught?' Cafferty stayed silent. Rebus weighed up what to say. 'We're making progress.'

'How much progress?'

'It's slow.'

'Only natural, with the city in chaos.' That chuckle again; Rebus wondered if Cafferty had been drinking. 'I could have pulled off any size of heist today, and you lot would have been too stretched to notice.'

'So why didn't you?'

'Changed man, Rebus. On *your* side now, remember? So, if there's anything I can do to help ...'

'Not right now.'

'But if you needed me, you'd ask?'

'You said it yourself, Cafferty – more you're involved, harder it might be to get a conviction.'

'I know how the game's played, Rebus.'

'Then you'll know when it's best to miss a turn.' Rebus turned away from the TV. A machine was flaying the skin from a carcass.

'Keep in touch, Rebus.'

'Actually ...'

'Yes?'

'There are some cops I could do with talking to. They're English, but here for the G8.'

'So talk to them.'

'Not so easy. They don't wear any insignia, run around town in an unmarked car and van.'

'Why do you want them?'

'I'll tell you later.'

'Descriptions?'

'I think they might be the Met. Work in a team of three. Tanned faces—'

175

'Meaning they'll stand out from the crowd up here,' Cafferty interrupted.

'Leader's called Jacko. Could be working for a Special Branch guy called David Steelforth.'

'I know Steelforth.'

Rebus leaned back against one of the desks. 'How?'

'He's put away a number of my acquaintances down the years.' Rebus remembered: Cafferty had links to the old-school London mob. 'Is he here too?'

'Staying at the Balmoral.' Rebus paused. 'I wouldn't mind knowing who's picking up his room tab.'

'Just when you think you've seen it all,' Cafferty said, 'John Rebus comes asking you to go sniffing around Special Branch ... I get the feeling this has got nothing to do with Cyril Colliar.'

'Like I said, I'll tell you later.'

'So what are you up to just now?'

'Working.'

'Want to meet for a drink?'

'I'm not that desperate.'

'Me neither, just thought I'd offer.'

Rebus considered for a moment, almost tempted. But the line had gone dead. He sat down and drew a pad of paper towards him. The sum total of his evening's efforts was listed there:

Grudge against?

Poss victim?

Access to H ...

Auchterarder – local connection?

Who's next?

He narrowed his eyes at this last line. Interesting wording – it was the title of a Who album, another of Michael's favourites. Home to 'Won't Get Fooled Again', which they were using these days as the theme on one of those *CSI* shows ... He felt the sudden urge to talk to someone, maybe his daughter or his ex-wife. The tug of family.

He thought of Siobhan and her parents. Tried not to feel slighted that she hadn't wanted him to meet them. She never spoke about them; he didn't really know how much family she had.

'Because you never ask,' he chided himself. His phone beeped, telling him he had a message. Sender: Shiv. He opened it.

Cn u meet me @ WGH?

WGH meant the Western General Hospital. He hadn't heard reports of any police injuries ... no reason she'd have been in Princes Street or anywhere near.

Let me know how you got on!!

He tried her number again on his way out to the car park. Nothing but the busy signal. Jumped into his car, tossing the phone on to the passenger seat. It rang before he'd gone fifty yards. He grabbed at it, flipped it open.

'Siobhan?' he asked.

'What?' A female voice.

'Hello?' Gritting his teeth as he tried to steer with one hand.

'Is this ... I was looking for ... No, never mind.' The phone died in his hand and he threw it towards the seat next to him. It bounced once and hit the floor. He wrapped both fists around the steering wheel and hit the accelerator hard.

10

There were tailbacks at the Forth Road Bridge. Neither of them really minded. There was plenty to talk about; plenty of thinking to be done, too. Siobhan had told Rebus all about it. Teddy Clarke would not be budged from his wife's bedside. Staff had said they could make up a temporary bed for him. They were planning to give her a scan first thing in the morning, checking for brain damage. The baton had caught her across the top half of her face: both eyes swollen and bruised, one of them closed altogether. Her nose covered with gauze: not broken. Rebus had asked, was there any danger she could lose her sight? Maybe in one eye, Siobhan had admitted.

'After the scan, they'll take her to the Eye Pavilion. Know what the hardest thing was, though, John?'

'Realising your mum's only human?' he'd guessed.

Siobhan had shaken her head slowly. 'They came and questioned her.'

'Who?'

'Police.'

'Well, that's something.'

At which she'd laughed harshly. 'They weren't looking to find out who'd hit her. They were asking what *she'd* done ...'

Yes, of course, because hadn't she been one of the rioters? Hadn't she been in the vanguard?

'Christ,' Rebus had muttered. 'Were you there?'

'If I had been, there'd've been hell to pay.' And a little later, just above a whisper: 'I saw it down there, John.'

'Looked hairy, judging by the TV.'

'Police overreacted.' Staring hard at him, willing him to contradict her.

'You're angry,' was all he'd said, winding down his window for the security check.

By the time they reached Glenrothes, he'd told her about his own evening, warning her that she might get an email from Tornupinside. She hardly seemed to be listening. At the Fife Police HQ, they had to show ID three times before they could gain entry to Operation Sorbus. Rebus had decided not to mention his night in the cells – not her problem. His left hand was back to something like normal at last. It had only taken a box of ibuprofen ...

It was a control room much like any other: CCTV pictures; civilian staff at computers, headsets on; maps of central Scotland. There was a live feed from the perimeter fence at Gleneagles, cameras posted at each watch-tower. Other feeds from Edinburgh, Stirling, the Forth Bridge. And traffic video from the M9, the motorway passing alongside Auchterarder.

Night-shift had kicked in, which meant voices were lowered, the atmosphere muted. Quiet concentration and a lack of hurry. No brass that Rebus could see, and no Steelforth. Siobhan knew one or two faces from her visit of the week before. She went to ask her favour, leaving Rebus to cross the room at his own pace. Then he too, spotted someone. Bobby Hogan had been promoted DCI after a result in a South Queensferry shooting. But with the promotion had come a move to Tayside. Rebus hadn't seen him for a year or so, but recognised the wiry silver hair, the way the head sank into the shoulders.

'Bobby,' he said, holding out a hand.

Hogan's eyes widened. 'Christ, John, tell me we're not that desperate.' He returned Rebus's grip.

'Don't worry, Bobby, I'm only acting as chauffeur. How's life treating you?'

'Can't complain. Is that Siobhan over there?' Rebus nodded. 'Why is she chatting up one of my officers?'

'She's after some surveillance footage.'

'That's one thing we've no shortage of. What does she want it for?'

'A case we're working, Bobby ... suspect might have been at that riot today.'

'Needle in a haystack,' Hogan commented, creasing his forehead. He was a couple of years younger than Rebus, but had more lines on his face.

'Enjoying being DCI?' Rebus asked, trying to deflect his friend's attention.

'You should try it some time.'

Rebus shook his head. 'Too late for me, Bobby. How's Dundee treating you?'

'I've got quite the bachelor pad.'

'I thought you and Cora were getting back together?'

Hogan's face creased further. He shook his head vigorously, letting Rebus know it was a subject best avoided.

'This is quite an ops room,' he said instead.

'Command post,' Hogan said, puffing out his chest. 'We're in contact with Edinburgh, Stirling, Gleneagles.'

'And if the shit really does hit the fan?'

'The G8 moves to our old stomping ground – Tulliallan.'

Meaning the Scottish Police College. Rebus nodded to show he was impressed.

'Direct line to Special Branch, Bobby?'

Hogan just shrugged. 'End of the day, John, it's *us* in charge, not them.'

Rebus nodded again, this time feigning agreement. 'Bumped into some of them, all the same ...'

'Steelforth?'

'He's strutting around Edinburgh like he owns the place.'

'He's a piece of work,' Hogan admitted.

'I could put it another way,' Rebus confided, 'but I better not … you two might be bestest pals.'

Hogan hooted. 'Fat chance.'

'See, it's not just him.' Rebus lowered his voice still further. 'I had a run-in with some of his men. They're in uniform, but no badges. Unmarked car, plus a van with lights but no siren.'

'What happened?'

'I was trying to be nice, Bobby …'

'And?'

'Let's just say I hit a wall.'

Hogan looked at him. 'Literally?'

'As good as.'

Hogan nodded his understanding. 'You'd like a few names to go with their faces?'

'I can't offer much of a description,' Rebus said apologetically. 'They'd been in the sun, and one of them's called Jacko. I think they're from the south-east.'

Hogan thought for a moment. 'Let me see what I can do.'

'Only if it means *you* staying under the radar, Bobby.'

'Relax, John. I told you, this is *my* show.' He placed a hand on Rebus's arm, as if by way of reassurance.

Rebus nodded his thanks; decided it wasn't his job to pierce his friend's bubble …

Siobhan had narrowed her search. She was only interested in footage from the Gardens, after all, and only within a thirty-minute period. Even so, there would be over a thousand photographs to look at, and film from a dozen different viewpoints. Which still left any CCTV evidence, plus video and stills shot by protesters and onlookers.

'Then there's the media,' she'd been told. BBC News, ITV, Channels 4 and 5, plus Sky and CNN. Not to mention photographers working for the main Scottish newspapers.

'Let's start with what we've got,' she'd said.

'There's a booth you can use …'

She'd thanked Rebus for the lift and told him he'd best get home. She'd cadge a ride back to Edinburgh somehow.

'You're staying here all night?'

'Maybe it won't come to that.' Both knowing it might. 'Canteen's open twenty-four/seven.'

'And your parents?'

'I'll head there first thing.' She'd paused. 'If you can spare me …'

'We'll just have to see, won't we?'

'Thanks.' And she'd hugged him, not exactly sure why. Maybe just to feel human, the night stretching in front of her.

'Siobhan . . . always supposing you find him, what then? He'll say he was doing his job.'

'I'll have proof that he wasn't.'

'If you push it too hard …'

She'd nodded, given him a wink and a smile. Gestures she'd learned from him, used whenever he was planning on crossing the line.

A wink and a smile, and then she was gone.

Someone had painted a large anarchy symbol on the doors of the C Division police HQ in Torphichen Place. It was an old, crumbling building, with twice the atmosphere of Gayfield Square. Street-sweepers were gathering debris and overtime outside. Broken glass, bricks and stones, fast-food cartons.

The desk sergeant buzzed Rebus in. Some of the Canning Street protesters had been brought here for processing. They'd spend the night in cells cleared for the purpose. Rebus didn't like to think how many junkies and muggers were roaming the Edinburgh streets, having been ejected from their rightful lock-ups. The CID room was long and narrow and always had about it the faint musk of human odour, something Rebus put down to the regular presence of DC Ray 'Rat-Arse' Reynolds. He was slouched there now with his feet crossed on the desk in front of him, tie undone and a can of lager in his fist. At another desk sat his boss, DI Shug Davidson. Davidson's tie was all the way off, but he appeared to be still working, pounding with two fingers at his computer keyboard. The can of lager next to him had yet to be opened.

Reynolds didn't bother to stifle a belch as Rebus walked into the room. 'It's the spectre at the feast!' he called out in recognition. 'I hear you're about as welcome near the G8 as the Rebel Clown Army.' But he raised his can in a toast anyway.

'That cuts to the quick, Ray. Been hectic, has it?'

'We should be on bonuses.' Reynolds held up a fresh beer, but Rebus shook his head.

'Come to see where the action is?' Davidson added.

'Just need a word with Ellen,' Rebus explained, nodding in the direction of the room's only other occupant. DS Ellen Wylie looked up from the report she was hiding behind. Her blonde hair was cut short, with a centre parting. She'd put on some weight since the days when Rebus had worked a couple of cases with her. Her cheeks had filled out, and were now flushed, something Reynolds could not resist referring to by rubbing his hands together and then holding them out in her direction, as though warming them at an open fire.

She was rising to her feet, but without making eye contact with the intruder. Davidson asked if it was anything he should know about. Rebus just shrugged. Wylie had lifted her jacket from the back of her chair, picked up her shoulder-bag.

'I was calling it a night anyway,' she announced to the room. Reynolds gave a whistle and nudged the air with his elbow.

'What do you reckon, Shug? Nice when love blossoms

between colleagues.' Laughter followed her out of the room. In the corridor, she leaned against the wall and let her head drop.

'Long day?' Rebus guessed.

'You ever tried questioning a German anarcho-syndicalist?'

'Not recently.'

'All had to be processed tonight so the courts could have them tomorrow.'

'Today,' Rebus corrected her, tapping his watch. She checked her own.

'Is that really the time?' She sounded exhausted. 'I'll be back here in six hours.'

'I'd offer to buy you a drink if the pubs were still open.'

'I don't need a drink.'

'A lift home?'

'My car's outside.' She thought for a moment. 'No, it's not – didn't bring it in today.'

'Good move, considering.'

'We were warned not to.'

'Foresight is a wonderful thing. And it means I can give you that lift home after all.' Rebus waited until her eyes met his. He was smiling. 'You still haven't asked what I want.'

'I *know* what you want.' She bristled slightly, and he raised his hands in surrender.

'Easy now,' he told her. 'Don't want you getting all …'

'All what?'

Walking straight into his punch-line. 'Torn up inside,' he obliged.

Ellen Wylie shared a house with her divorced sister.

It was a mid-terrace in Cramond. The back garden ended in a sheer drop to the River Almond. The night being mild, and Rebus needing to smoke, they sat at a table outside.

Wylie kept her voice low – didn't want the neighbours complaining, and besides, her sister's bedroom window was open. She brought out mugs of milky tea.

'Nice spot,' Rebus told her. 'I like that you can hear the water.'

'There's a weir just over there.' She pointed into the darkness. 'Masks the noise of the planes.'

Rebus nodded his understanding: they were directly under the flight-path into Turnhouse Airport. This time of night, it had only taken them fifteen minutes from Torphichen Place. On the way, she'd told him her story.

'So I wrote something for the website . . . not against the law, is it? I was just so pissed off at the system. We bust a gut to get these animals to court, and then the lawyers do their damnedest to get their sentences whittled away to nothing.'

'Is that all it was?'

She'd shifted in the passenger seat. 'What else?'

'Tornupinside – sounds like it was more personal.'

She'd stared through the windscreen. 'No, John, just angry. Too many hours spent on rape cases, sexual assault, domestic abuse – maybe it takes a woman to understand.'

'Which is why you phoned Siobhan back? I recognised your voice straight off.'

'Yes, that was particularly devious of you.'

'My middle name . . .'

Now, seated in her garden with a cold breeze blowing, Rebus buttoned his jacket and asked about the website. How did she find it? Did she know the Jensens? Had she ever met with them?

'I remember the case,' was all she said.

'Vicky Jensen?' She nodded slowly. 'Did you work on it?'

A shake of the head. 'But I'm glad he's dead. Show me where he's buried and I'll dance a little jig.'

'Edward Isley and Trevor Guest are dead too.'

185

'Look, John, all I did was write a bit of a blog ... I was letting off steam.'

'And now three of the men listed on the site are dead. A dunt to the head and a smack overdose. You've worked murders, Ellen ... what does that MO tell you?'

'Someone with access to hard drugs.'

'Anything else?'

She thought for a moment. 'You tell me.'

'Killer didn't want a face-to-face with the victims. Maybe because they were bigger and stronger. Didn't really want them to suffer either – a straight KO and then the injection. Doesn't that sound like a woman to you?'

'How's your tea, John?'

'Ellen ...'

She slapped a palm against the tabletop. 'If they were listed on BeastWatch, they were Grade A scumbags ... don't expect me to feel sorry for them.'

'What about catching the killer?'

'What about it?'

'You want them to get away with it?'

She was staring into the darkness again. The wind was rustling the trees nearby. 'Know what we had today, John? We had a war, cut and dried – good guys and bad ...'

Rebus's thought: *Tell that to Siobhan.*

'But it isn't always like that, is it?' she went on. 'Sometimes the line blurs.' She'd turned her gaze on him. '*You* should know that better than most, number of corners I've seen you cut.'

'I make a lousy role-model, Ellen.'

'Maybe so, but you're planning to find him, aren't you?'

'Him or her. That's why I need to get a statement from you.' She opened her mouth to complain, but he held up a hand. 'You're the only person I know who used the site. The Jensens have closed it down, so I can't be sure what might have been on there.'

186

'You want me to help?'

'By answering a few questions.'

She gave a harsh, quiet laugh. 'You know I've got court later today?'

Rebus was lighting another cigarette. 'Why Cramond?' he asked. She seemed surprised by the change of subject.

'It's a village,' she explained. 'A village inside a city – best of both worlds.' She paused. 'Has the interview already started? Is this you getting me to drop my guard?'

Rebus shook his head. 'Just wondered whose idea it was.'

'It's my house, John. Denise came to live with me after she ...' She cleared her throat. 'Think I swallowed a bug,' she apologised. 'I was going to say, after her divorce.'

Rebus nodded at the explanation. 'Well, it's a peaceful spot, I'll give you that. Easy out here to forget all about the job.'

The light from the kitchen caught her smile. 'I get the feeling it wouldn't work for you. I'm not sure anything short of a sledgehammer would.'

'Or a few of those,' Rebus countered, nodding towards the row of empty wine bottles lined up beneath the kitchen window.

He took it slow, driving back into town. Loved the city at night, the taxi-cabs and lolling pedestrians, warm sodium glare from the streetlamps, darkened shops, curtained tenements. There were places he could go – a bakery; a night-porter's desk; a casino – places where he was known and where tea would be brewed, gossip exchanged. Years back, he could have stopped for a chat with the working girls on Coburg Street, but most of them had either moved on or died. And after he, too, was gone, Edinburgh would remain. These same scenes would be enacted, a play whose run was never-ending. Killers would be caught and punished; others would remain at large. The world and the underworld, co-existing down the generations. By week's end, the G8 circus would have trundled elsewhere. Geldof and Bono would have found new causes. Richard Pennen would be in his board room, David Steelforth back at Scotland Yard. Sometimes it felt to Rebus that he was close to seeing the mechanism which connected everything.

Close ... but never quite close enough.

The Meadows seemed deserted as he turned up Marchmont Road. Parked at the top of Arden Street and walked back downhill to his tenement. Two or three times a week he got flyers through his letter box, firms keen to sell his flat for him. The one upstairs had gone for two hundred K. Add that sort of money to his CID pension and he was, as Siobhan herself had said, 'on Easy Street'. Problem was, it wasn't a destination that appealed. He stooped to pick up the mail from inside the door. There was a menu from a new Indian takeaway. He'd pin it up in the kitchen, next to the others. Meantime, he made himself a ham sandwich, ate it standing in the kitchen, staring at the array of empty cans on the work surface. How many bottles had there been in Ellen Wylie's garden? Fifteen, maybe twenty. A lot of wine. He'd seen an empty Tesco's carrier in the kitchen. She probably did a regular recycling run, same time she did the shopping. Say every fortnight ... Twenty bottles a fortnight; ten a week – *Denise came to stay with me after she ... after her divorce*. Rebus hadn't seen any nighttime insects illuminated against the kitchen window. Ellen had looked washed out. Easy to blame it on the day's events, but Rebus knew it went deeper. The lines under her bloodshot eyes had taken weeks to accumulate. Her figure had been thickening for some time. He knew that Siobhan had once seen Ellen as a rival – two DSs who'd have to fight tooth and nail for promotion. But lately Siobhan had stopped saying as much. Maybe because Ellen didn't look quite so dangerous to her these days ...

He poured a glass of water and took it into the living

room, gulped it down until only half an inch was left, then added a slug of malt to the remainder. Tipped it back and felt the heat work its way down his throat. Topped it up and settled into his chair. Too late now to put any music on. He rested the glass against his forehead, closed his eyes.

Slept.

Tuesday 5 July

11

The best Glenrothes could offer was a lift to the railway station at Markinch.

Siobhan sat on the train – too early yet for the commuter rush – and looked out at the passing countryside. Not that she saw any of it: her mind was replaying footage of the riot, the same hours of footage she had just walked away from. Sound and fury, swearing and swinging, the clatter of hurled objects and the grunts of exertion. Her thumb was numb from pressure on the remote control. Pause ... slow back ... slow forward ... play. Fast forward ... rewind ... pause ... play. In some of the still photographs, faces had been circled – people the force would want to question. The eyes burned with hatred. Of course, some of them weren't demonstrators at all – just local troublemakers ready to rumble, smothered in Burberry scarves and baseball caps. Down south, they'd probably be called chavs, but up here they were neds. One of the team, bringing her coffee and a chocolate bar, had said as much as he stood behind her shoulder.

'Neddy the Ned from Nedtown.'

The woman across from Siobhan on the train had the morning paper open. The riot had made the front page. But so too had Tony Blair. He was in Singapore, pitching for London to win the Olympic bid. 2012 seemed a long way off; so did Singapore. Siobhan couldn't believe he was going to make it back to Gleneagles in time to shake all those hands – Bush and Putin, Schroeder and Chirac. The paper also said there was little sign of Saturday's Hyde

Park crowd heading north.

'Sorry, is this seat taken?'

Siobhan shook her head and the man squeezed in beside her.

'Wasn't yesterday terrible?' he said. Siobhan grunted a reply, but the woman across the table said she'd been shopping in Rose Street and had only just escaped being caught up in it. The two then started trading war stories, while Siobhan stared out of the window again. The skirmishes had been just that. Police tactics had been unchanged: go in hard; let them know the city's ours, not theirs. From the footage, there'd been obvious provocation. But they'd been forewarned – no point in joining a demo if it didn't make the news. Anarchists couldn't afford ad campaigns. Baton charges were their equivalent of free publicity. The photos in the paper proved it: cops with gritted teeth swinging their truncheons; rioters defenceless on the ground, being dragged away by faceless uniforms. All very George Orwell. None of it got Siobhan any closer to finding out who had attacked her mother, or why.

But she wasn't about to give up.

Her eyes stung when she blinked, and every few blinks the world seemed to swim out of focus. She needed sleep, but was wired on caffeine and sugar.

'Sorry, but are you all right?'

It was her neighbour again. His hand was brushing her arm. When she blinked her eyes open, she could feel the single tear running down her cheek. She wiped it away.

'I'm fine,' she said. 'Just a bit tired.'

'Thought maybe we'd upset you,' the woman across the table was saying, 'going on about yesterday ...'

Siobhan shook her head, saw that the woman had finished with her paper. 'Mind if I ...?'

'No, pet, you go ahead.'

Siobhan managed a smile and opened the tabloid, studying the pictures, looking for the photographer's name ...

At Haymarket she queued for a cab. Pitched up at the Western General and went straight to the ward. Her father was slurping tea in the reception area. He'd slept in his clothes and hadn't managed a shave, the bristles grey on his cheeks and chin. He looked old to her, old and suddenly mortal.

'How is she?' Siobhan asked.

'Not too bad. Due to get the scan just before lunch. How about you?'

'Still haven't found the bastard.'

'I meant, how are you feeling?'

'I'm all right.'

'You were up half the night, weren't you?'

'Maybe a bit more than half,' she conceded with a smile. Her phone beeped: not a message, just warning her its battery was low. She switched it off. 'Can I see her?'

'They're getting her ready. Said they'd tell me when they'd finished. How's the outside world?'

'Ready to face another day.'

'Can I buy you a coffee?'

She shook her head. 'I'm swimming in the stuff.'

'I think you should get some rest, love. Come see her this afternoon, after the tests.'

'I'll just say hello first.' She nodded towards the ward doors.

'Then you'll go home?'

'Promise.'

The morning news: yesterday's arrests were being sent to the sheriff court on Chambers Street. The court itself would be closed to the public. A protest was taking place outside the Dungavel Immigration Centre. Forewarned, the Immigration Service had already moved the waiting deportees elsewhere. The demo would go ahead anyway, organisers said.

Trouble at the Peace Camp in Stirling. People were

starting to head for Gleneagles, the police determined to stop them, using Section 60 powers to stop and search without suspicion. In Edinburgh, the clean-up was well advanced. A vehicle loaded with ninety gallons of cooking oil had been detained – the oil would have formed a road-slick, causing traffic chaos. Wednesday's 'Final Push' concert at Murrayfield was coming together. The stage had been built, lighting-rig installed. Midge Ure was hoping for some 'decent Scottish summer weather'. Performers and celebrities had started arriving in the city. Richard Branson had flown one of his jets to Edinburgh. Prestwick Airport was gearing up for the next day's arrivals. An advance guard of diplomats had already arrived. President Bush would be bringing his own sniffer dog, plus a mountain bike so he could maintain his daily exercise regime. Back in the newsroom, the TV presenter read out an email from a viewer, suggesting the summit could have been held on one of the North Sea's many decommissioned oil platforms, 'saving a small fortune in security, and making protest marches an interesting proposition'.

Rebus finished his coffee and turned down the sound. Vans were arriving in the police station car park, ready to transport prisoners to the court. Ellen Wylie was due in around ninety minutes to make her statement. He'd tried Siobhan's mobile a couple of times, but it went straight to messaging, meaning she'd switched it off. He'd called Sorbus HQ, only to be told she'd left for Edinburgh. Tried the Western General, but learned only that 'Mrs Clarke has had a comfortable night'. Number of times he'd heard that in his life ... A comfortable night: meaning 'she's still alive, if that's what's worrying you'. He looked up and saw that a man had entered the CID room.

'Help you?' Rebus asked. Then he recognised the uniform. 'Sorry, sir.'

'We've not met,' the Chief Constable said, holding out his hand. 'I'm James Corbyn.'

Rebus returned the handshake, noting that Corbyn wasn't a Freemason. 'DI Rebus,' he said.

'Are you working with DS Clarke on the Auchterarder case?'

'That's right, sir.'

'I've been trying to reach her. She owes me an update.'

'Some interesting developments, sir. There's a website set up by a local couple. Might be how the killer chose his victims.'

'You've got names for all three?'

'Yes, sir. Same MO each time.'

'Could there be others?'

'No way of knowing.'

'Will he stop at three?'

'Again, sir, hard to tell.'

The Chief Constable was patrolling the room, inspecting wallcharts, desks, computer monitors. 'I told Clarke she had until tomorrow. After that, we shut the case down till the G8 is done and dusted.'

'I'm not sure that's a good idea.'

'Media haven't got hold of it yet. No reason we can't sit on it for a few days.'

'Trails have a way of going cold, sir. If we give suspects that bit of extra time to get their stories straight ...'

'You've got suspects?' Corbyn had turned towards Rebus.

'Not as such, sir, but there are people we're talking to.'

'G8 has to take priority, Rebus.'

'Mind if I ask why, sir?'

Corbyn glared at him. 'Because the world's eight most powerful men are going to be in Scotland, staying at the country's best hotel. That's the story everyone wants. The fact that a serial killer is stalking the central belt might just get in the way, don't you think?'

'Actually, sir, only one of the victims is from Scotland.'

The Chief Constable walked to within a few inches of

Rebus. 'Don't try to be smart, DI Rebus. And don't think I haven't dealt with your kind before.'

'What kind is that, sir?'

'The kind that thinks because he's been around a while, he knows better than anyone else. You know what they say about cars – more miles on the clock, closer they are to being scrapped.'

'Thing is, sir, I prefer vintage cars to the stuff they're churning out today. Shall I pass your message along to DS Clarke? I expect you've got better things to be doing with your time. Off to Gleneagles yourself at any point?'

'None of your bloody business.'

'Message received.' Rebus gave the Chief Constable something that could have been construed as a salute.

'You'll shut this thing down.' Corbyn slapped a hand against some of the paperwork on Rebus's desk. 'And remember – DS Clarke is in charge, not you, Inspector.' His eyes narrowed a little. Then, seeing that Rebus wasn't about to reply, he stalked out of the room. Rebus waited the best part of a minute before exhaling, then made a phone call.

'Mairie? Any news for me?' He listened to her apology. 'Well, never mind. I've got a wee bonus-ball here for you, if you can manage the price of a cuppa ...'

Multrees Walk took him less than ten minutes on foot. It was a new development adjacent to the Harvey Nichols department store, and some of the shops were still to let. But the Vin Caffe was open for snacks and Italian coffee, and Rebus ordered a double espresso.

'And she's paying,' he added as Mairie Henderson arrived.

'Guess who's covering the sheriff court this afternoon?' She slid into her seat.

'And that's your excuse for treading water on Richard Pennen?'

She glared at him. 'John, what does it matter if Pennen

paid for an MP's hotel room? There's nothing to prove it was cash-for-contracts. If Webster's remit was arms procurement, I might have the beginnings of a story.' She made an exasperated sound and gave a theatrical shrug of the shoulders. 'Anyway, I'm not giving up yet. Let me talk to a few more people about Richard Pennen.'

Rebus ran a hand across his face. 'It's just the way they're going about protecting him. Not just Pennen, actually – everyone who was there that night. No way we're going to get near them.'

'You really think Webster was given a shove over that wall?'

'It's a possibility. One of the guards thought there was an intruder.'

'Well, if it was an intruder, reason dictates it wasn't anyone at the actual dinner.' She angled her face, seeking his agreement. When he failed to concede, she straightened again. 'Know what I think? I think all of this is because there's a bit of the anarchist in you. You're on *their* side, and it annoys you that you've somehow ended up working for "The Man".'

Rebus snorted a laugh. 'Where did you get that from?'

She laughed with him. 'I'm right though, aren't I? You've always seen yourself as being on the outside ...' She broke off as their coffees arrived, dug her spoon into her cappuccino and scooped foam into her mouth.

'I do my best work on the margins,' Rebus said thoughtfully.

She nodded. 'That's why we used to get along so well.'

'Until you chose Cafferty instead.'

She gave another shrug. 'He's more like you than you care to admit.'

'And I was just about to do you this huge favour ...'

'Okay.' She narrowed her eyes. 'The pair of you are chalk and cheese.'

'That's better.' He handed her an envelope. 'Typed by

my own fair hands, so the spelling might not be up to your own high journalistic standard.'

'What is it?' She was unfolding the single sheet of paper.

'Something we were keeping the lid on: two more victims, same killer as Cyril Colliar. I can't give you everything we've got, but this'll get you started.'

'Christ, John ...' She looked up at him.

'What?'

'Why are you giving me this?'

'My latent anarchic streak?' he pretended to guess.

'It might not even make the front page, not this week.'

'So?'

'Any week of the year except this ...'

'Are you checking my gift horse's mouth?'

'This stuff about the website ...' She was scanning the sheet for a second time.

'It's all kosher, Mairie. If you don't have a use for it ...' He held out his hand to take it back.

'What's a "serial kilter"? Is that someone who can't stop making kilts?'

'Give me it back.'

'Who is it that's pissed you off?' she asked with a smile. 'You wouldn't be doing this otherwise.'

'Just hand it over and we'll say no more.'

But she slid the page back into the envelope and folded it into her pocket. 'If things stay calm for the rest of the day, maybe my editor can be persuaded.'

'Stress the link with the website,' Rebus advised. 'Might help the others on the list be a bit more cautious.'

'They've not been told?'

'Haven't got around to it. And if the Chief Constable gets his way, they won't find out till next week.'

'By which time the killer could strike again?'

Rebus nodded.

'So really you're doing this to save these scuzzballs' lives?'

'To protect and serve,' Rebus said, trying another salute.

'And not because you've had a falling-out with the Chief Constable?'

Rebus shook his head slowly, as if disappointed in her. 'And I thought I was the one with the cynical streak ... You'll really keep looking at Richard Pennen?'

'For a little while longer.' She waved the envelope at him. 'Got to retype all of this first, though. Didn't realise English wasn't your first language.'

Siobhan had headed home and run a bath, closing her eyes after getting in, then waking with a jolt, chin touching the surface of the tepid water. She'd got out and changed her clothes, ordered a taxi and headed for the garage where her car was ready. She'd driven to Niddrie, trusting that lightning wouldn't strike twice ... actually, three times, though she'd managed to get the St Leonard's loaner back to its berth without being spotted. If anyone came asking, she could always say the damage must have been done in the car park.

There was a single-decker bus idling next to the pavement, its driver busy with his newspaper. A few campers passed Siobhan on their way out to it, rucksacks bulging. They gave sleepy smiles. Bobby Greig was watching them leave. Siobhan looked around and saw that others were busy dismantling their tents.

'Saturday was our busiest night,' Greig explained. 'Each day since has been a bit quieter.'

'You didn't have to turn people away, then?'

His mouth twitched. 'Facilities for fifteen thousand, and only two could be bothered to show.' He paused. 'Your "friends" didn't come home last night.' The way he said it let her know he'd worked something out.

'My parents,' she confirmed.

'And why didn't you want me to know that?'

'I'm not sure, Bobby. Maybe I didn't think a cop's mum and dad would be safe here.'

'So they're staying with you?'

She shook her head. 'One of the riot police cracked my mum across her face. She spent the night in a hospital bed.'

'Sorry to hear that. Anything I can do?'

She shook her head again. 'Any more trouble with the locals?'

'Another stand-off last night.'

'Persistent little sods, aren't they?'

'Councillor happened by again and made the truce.'

'Tench?'

Greig nodded. 'He was showing a bigwig around. Some urban regeneration thing.'

'Area could use it. What sort of bigwig?'

Greig shrugged. 'Government.' He ran his fingers over his shaved head. 'This place'll be dead soon. Good riddance to it.'

Siobhan didn't ask if he meant the camp or Niddrie itself. She turned and made for her parents' tent. Unzipped the flap and looked inside. Everything was intact, but with a few additions. It looked as if those who were moving out had decided to leave gifts of leftover food, candles, and water.

'Where are they?'

Siobhan recognised Santal's voice. She backed out of the tent and straightened up. Santal too was toting a rucksack and holding a bottle of water.

'Heading out?' Siobhan asked.

'Bus to Stirling. I wanted to say goodbye.'

'You're off to the Peace Camp?' Siobhan watched Santal's braids flex as she nodded. 'Were you at Princes Street yesterday?'

'Last time I saw your parents. What's happened to them?'

'Someone belted my mum. She's in hospital.'

'Christ, that's hellish. Was it ...' She paused. 'One of your lot?'

'One of my lot,' Siobhan echoed. 'And I want him caught. Lucky you're still here.'

'Why?'

'Did you get any film? I thought maybe I could look at it.'

But Santal was shaking her head.

'Don't worry,' Siobhan assured her, 'I'm not looking to ... It's the uniforms I'm interested in, not the demo itself.' But Santal kept shaking her head.

'I didn't have my camera.' A bald lie.

'Come on, Santal. Surely you want to help.'

'Plenty of others taking photos.' She gestured around the camp with an outstretched arm. 'Ask them.'

'I'm asking you.'

'The bus is leaving ...' She pushed her way past Siobhan.

'Any message for my mum?' Siobhan called after her. 'Shall I bring them to see you at the Peace Camp?' But the figure kept moving. Siobhan cursed under her breath. Should have known better: to Santal she was still a 'pig', 'the filth', 'the plod', a 'rozzer'. Still the enemy. She found herself standing beside Bobby Greig as the bus filled, its door closing with a hiss of air. The sound of communal singing came from inside. A few of the passengers waved out at Greig. He waved back.

'Not a bad bunch,' he observed to Siobhan, offering her a piece of gum, 'for hippies, I mean.' Then he slid his hands into his pockets. 'Got a ticket for tomorrow night?'

'Failed in the attempt,' she admitted.

'Only, my firm's doing security ...'

She stared at him. 'You've got a spare?'

'Not exactly, but I'll be there, meaning you could be "plus one".'

'You're joking, right?'

'Not a date or anything ... offer's there if you want it.'

'It's very generous, Bobby.'

'Up to you.' He was looking everywhere but at her.

'Can I take your number, let you know tomorrow?'

'Thinking something better might come up?'

She shook her head. '*Work* might come up,' she corrected him.

'Everyone's allowed a night off, DS Clarke.'

'Call me Siobhan,' she insisted.

'Where are you?' Rebus asked into the mobile.

'On my way to the *Scotsman*.'

'What's at the *Scotsman*?'

'More photos.'

'Your phone's been switched off.'

'I needed to charge it.'

'Well, I've just been taking a statement from Tornupinside.'

'Who?'

'I told you yesterday ...' But then he remembered that she'd had other things on her mind. So he explained again about the blog and how he'd sent a message, and Ellen Wylie had called back ...

'Whoah, back up,' Siobhan said. '*Our* Ellen Wylie?'

'Wrote a long and angry piece for BeastWatch.'

'But why?'

'Because the system's letting the sisterhood down,' Rebus answered.

'Are those her exact words?'

'I've got them on tape. Of course, the one thing I don't have is corroboration, since there was no one around to assist with the interview.'

'Sorry about that. So is Ellen a suspect?'

'Listen to the tape, then you can tell me.' Rebus looked around the CID room. The windows needed a clean, but what was the point when all they looked down on was the rear car park? A lick of paint would cheer up the walls, but soon be covered by scene-of-crime photos and victim details.

'Maybe it's because of her sister,' Siobhan was saying.

'What?'

'Ellen's sister Denise.'

'What about her?'

'She moved in with Ellen a year or so back ... maybe a bit less, actually. Left her partner.'

'So?'

'Her *abusive* partner. That was the story I heard. They lived in Glasgow. Police were called in a few times but never got a charge to stick. Had to get a restraint order on him, I think.'

Came to live with me after she ... after the divorce. Suddenly, the 'bug' Ellen had swallowed made sense.

'I didn't know,' Rebus said quietly.

'No, well ...'

'Well what?'

'It's the sort of thing women talk to other women about.'

'But not to men, is that what you're saying? And *we're* the ones who're supposed to be sexist.' Rebus rubbed his free hand over the back of his neck. The skin felt tight. 'So Denise goes to live with Ellen, and next thing Ellen's on the net, looking for sites like BeastWatch ...'

And staying in at night with her sister, overeating, drinking too much ...

'Maybe I could talk to them,' Siobhan suggested.

'Haven't you enough on your plate? How is your mum anyway?'

'She's having a scan. I was planning to go see her next.'

'Then do it. I'm assuming you didn't get anything from Glenrothes?'

'Nothing but a sore back.'

'There's another call coming in. I better go. Can we meet up later?'

'Sure thing.'

'Because the Chief Constable stopped by.'

'Sounds ominous.'

'But it can wait.' Rebus pushed the button to pick up the next caller. 'DI Rebus,' he stated.

'I'm at the courts,' Mairie Henderson said. 'Come see what I've got for you.' There were hoots and cheers in the background. 'Got to go,' she said.

Rebus headed downstairs and hitched a lift in a patrol car. Neither uniform had been involved in yesterday's running battles.

'Back-up,' they explained gloomily. 'Sat on a bus for four hours listening to it on the radio. You giving evidence, Inspector?'

Rebus said nothing until the car turned in to Chambers Street. 'Drop me here,' he ordered.

'You're welcome,' the driver informed him in a growl, but only after Rebus had climbed out.

The patrol car did a screeching U-turn, drawing the attention of the media positioned outside the sheriff court. Rebus stood across the street, lighting a cigarette next to the steps of the Royal Scottish Museum. Another protester was leaving the court building to cheers and whoops from his comrades. His fist punched the air as they slapped him on the back, press photographers capturing the moment.

'How many?' Rebus asked, aware that Mairie Henderson was standing next to him, notebook and tape-recorder in hand.

'About twenty so far. Some of them have been farmed out to other courts.'

'Any quotes I should be looking out for tomorrow?'

'How about "Smash the system"?' She glanced at her

notes. 'Or "Show me a capitalist and I'll show you a blood-sucker"?'

'Seems like a fair swap.'

'It's Malcolm X, apparently.' She flipped her notebook shut. 'They're all being issued with exclusion orders. Can't go anywhere near Gleneagles, Auchterarder, Stirling, central Edinburgh ...' She paused. 'Nice touch, though: one guy said he had a ticket for T in the Park this weekend, so the judge said he could go to Kinross.'

'Siobhan's going to that,' Rebus said. 'Be nice to have the Colliar inquiry wrapped up in time.'

'In which case this may not be good news.'

'What is it, Mairie?'

'The Clootie Well. I got a mate at the paper to do some background.'

'And?'

'And there are others.'

'How many?'

'At least one in Scotland. It's on the Black Isle.'

'North of Inverness?'

She nodded. 'Follow me,' she said, turning and heading for the museum's main door. Inside she took a right, into the Museum of Scotland. The place was busy with families – school holidays, kids with too much energy. The smaller ones were squealing and bouncing on their toes.

'What are we doing here?' Rebus asked. But Mairie was already at the lifts. They got off and climbed some stairs. Through the windows, Rebus had a great view down on to the sheriff court. But Mairie was leading him into the furthest corner of the building. 'I've been here before,' Rebus told her.

'The section on death and belief,' she explained.

'There are some wee coffins with dolls inside ...'

This was the very display she stopped at, and Rebus realised there was an old black and white photograph behind the glass.

A photo of the Black Isle's Clootie Well ...

'Locals have been hanging bits of cloth there for centuries. I've got my mate widening the search to England and Wales, on the off-chance. Reckon it's worth a recce?'

'Black Isle's got to be a two-hour drive,' Rebus mused, eyes still on the photo. The scraps of material looked almost bat-like, clinging to thin, bare branches. Next to the photo sat witches' casting-sticks, bits of bone protruding from hollowed pebbles. Death and belief ...

'More like three, this time of year,' Mairie was telling him. 'All those caravans to get past.'

Rebus nodded. The A9 north of Perth was notoriously slow. 'Might just get the locals to take a look. Thanks, Mairie.'

'I got these from the net.' She handed over a few sheets detailing the history of the Clootie Well near Fortrose. There were grainy photographs – including a copy of the one on display – which showed it to be almost identical to its namesake in Auchterarder.

'Thanks again.' He rolled the sheets up and put them in his jacket pocket. 'Did your editor take the bait?' They started retracing their steps to the lift.

'Depends. A riot tonight might see us relegated to page five.'

'A gamble worth taking.'

'Is there anything else you can tell me, John?'

'I've given you a scoop – what else do you want?'

'I want to know you're not just using me.' She pushed the lift button.

'Would I do a thing like that?'

'Of course you bloody well would.' They were quiet all the way back out to the steps. Mairie watched the action across the street. Another protester, another clenched-fist salute. 'You've kept the lid on this since Friday. Aren't you scared the killer will go deep cover once he sees it in the paper?'

'Can't get any deeper than he is right now.' He looked at her. 'Besides, all we had on Friday was Cyril Colliar. It was Cafferty gave us the rest.'

Her face hardened. 'Cafferty?'

'You told him the patch from Colliar's jacket had turned up. He paid me a visit. Went away with the other two names and came back with the news they were dead.'

'You've been using Cafferty?' She sounded incredulous.

'Without him telling *you*, Mairie – that's what I'm getting at. Try trading with him, you'll find it's all one-way traffic. Everything I've given you on the killings, he had it first. But he wasn't going to tell you.'

'You seem to be under some sort of misapprehension that the two of us are close.'

'Close enough for you to go straight to him with the news about Colliar.'

'That was a promise of long standing – any new developments, he wanted to know. Don't think I'm about to apologise.' Her eyes narrowed and she pointed across the street. 'What's Gareth Tench doing here?'

'The councillor, you mean?' Rebus followed the path of her finger. 'Preaching to the heathen, maybe,' he offered, watching as Tench shuffled along crab-like behind the line of photographers. 'Maybe he wants you to do another interview.'

'How did you know about ...? I suppose Siobhan told you.'

'No secrets between Siobhan and me.' Rebus gave a wink.

'So where is she now?'

'She's down at the *Scotsman*.'

'My eyes must be deceiving me then.' Mairie was pointing again. Sure enough, it was Siobhan ... and Tench had stopped right in front of her, the two of them exchanging a handshake. 'No secrets between you two, eh?'

But Rebus was already on his way. This end of the street

had been closed to traffic, easy enough to cross.

'Hiya,' he said. 'Sudden change of mind?'

Siobhan gave a little smile, and introduced him to Tench.

'Inspector,' the councillor said with a bow of his head.

'You're a fan of street theatre, Councillor Tench?'

'I don't mind it at festival time,' Tench said with a chuckle.

'Used to do a bit yourself, didn't you?'

Tench turned to Siobhan. 'The Inspector means my little Sunday morning sermons at the foot of The Mound. Doubtless he paused a moment on his way to communion.'

'Don't seem to see you there any more,' Rebus added. 'Did you lose your faith?'

'Far from it, Inspector. But there are ways of getting a point across besides preaching.' His face composed itself into a more serious professionalism. 'I'm here because a couple of my constituents got caught up in all that trouble yesterday.'

'Innocent bystanders, I don't doubt,' Rebus commented.

Tench's eyes flitted to him, then back to Siobhan. 'The Inspector must be a joy to work with.'

'Nonstop laughs,' Siobhan agreed.

'Ah! And the Fourth Estate too!' Tench exclaimed, holding out a hand towards Mairie, who'd finally decided to join them. 'When is our article running? I'll assume you know these two guardians of truth.' He gestured towards Rebus and Siobhan. 'You did promise me a wee keek at the contents before publishing,' he reminded Mairie.

'Did I?' She was trying to look surprised. Tench wasn't falling for it. He turned to the two detectives.

'I think I need to have a word in private ...'

'Don't mind us,' Rebus told him. 'Siobhan and I need a minute too.'

'We do?' But Rebus had already turned away, leaving

Siobhan little option but to follow.

'Sandy Bell's will be open,' he told her, once they were out of earshot. But she was checking the crowd.

'Someone I need to see,' she explained. 'Photographer I know ... apparently he's here somewhere.' She stood on tiptoe. 'Ahh ...' Pushed her way into the scrum of journalists. The photographers were checking the backs of each other's cameras, examining the digital screens to see what they'd got. Rebus waited impatiently while Siobhan talked to a wiry figure with cropped salt-and-pepper hair. At least he had an explanation now: she'd gone to the *Scotsman* only to be told that the person she needed to see was right here. The photographer took a bit of persuading, but eventually followed her back to where Rebus was standing with arms folded.

'This is Mungo,' Siobhan said.

'Would Mungo like a drink?' Rebus asked.

'I'd like that very much,' the photographer decided, wiping a sheen of sweat from his forehead. The grey in his hair was premature – he probably wasn't much older than Siobhan herself. He had a chiselled, weatherbeaten face and an accent to match.

'Western Isles?' Rebus guessed.

'Lewis,' Mungo confirmed, as Rebus led the way to Sandy Bell's. There was another cheer from behind them, and they turned to see a young man exiting the gates of the sheriff court.

'I think I know him,' Siobhan said quietly. 'He's the one who's been tormenting the campsite.'

'Bit of respite last night then,' Rebus stated. 'He'll have been in the cells.' As he spoke, he realised he was rubbing his left hand with his right. When the young man gave a salute to the spectators, it was returned by several of the crowd.

Including, watched by a bemused Mairie Henderson, Councillor Gareth Tench.

12

Sandy Bell's had only been open ten minutes, but a couple of regulars had already settled themselves at the bar.

'Just a half of best,' Mungo said, when asked what he was drinking. Siobhan wanted orange juice. Rebus decided he could tackle a pint. They sat around a table. The bar's narrow, shadowy interior smelled of brass polish and bleach. Siobhan explained to Mungo what she wanted, and he opened his camera bag, lifting out a small white box.

'iPod?' Siobhan guessed.

'Useful for storing pictures,' Mungo explained. He showed her how to work it, and then apologised that he hadn't captured the whole day.

'So how many photos are on there?' Rebus asked, as Siobhan demonstrated the small colour screen to him, using the flywheel to flip to and fro between stills.

'A couple of hundred,' Mungo said. 'I've weeded out the no-hopers.'

'Is it all right if I look at them now?' Siobhan asked. Mungo just shrugged. Rebus offered him the pack of cigarettes.

'Actually, I'm allergic,' the photographer warned. So Rebus took his addiction to the other end of the bar, next to the window. As he stood there, staring out on to Forrest Road, he saw Councillor Tench walking towards The Meadows, busy talking with the young man from the court. Tench was giving his constituent's back a pat of reassurance: no sign of Mairie. Rebus finished his cigarette and returned to the table. Siobhan turned the iPod around so he could see its screen.

'My mum,' she said. Rebus took the device from her and peered at it.

'Second row back?' he said. Siobhan nodded excitedly. 'Looks like she's trying to get out.'

'Exactly.'

'Before she was hit?' Rebus was studying the faces behind the riot shields, cops with their visors down, teeth bared.

'It seems I failed to capture that particular moment,' Mungo admitted.

'She's definitely trying to push her way back through the crowd,' Siobhan stressed. 'She wanted to get away.'

'So why give her a whack across the face?' Rebus asked.

'The way it worked,' Mungo offered, enunciating each syllable, 'the leaders would lash out at the police line, then retreat. Chances are, anyone left at the front would suffer the consequences. Picture desks then have to choose what to publish.'

'And it's usually the riot cops retaliating?' Rebus guessed. He held the screen a little further from his face. 'Can't really identify any of the police.'

'No ID on their epaulettes either,' Siobhan pointed out. 'All nice and anonymous. Can't even tell which force they're from. Some of them have letters stencilled above their visors – XS, for example. Could that be a code?'

Rebus shrugged. He was remembering Jacko and his pals ... no insignia on show there either.

Siobhan seemed to remember something and gave her watch a quick check. 'I need to call the hospital ...' She rose from her seat and headed outdoors.

'Another?' Rebus asked, pointing at Mungo's glass. The photographer shook his head. 'Tell me, what else are you covering this week?'

Mungo puffed out his cheeks. 'Bits and pieces.'

'The VIPs?'

'Given the chance.'

'Don't suppose you were working Friday night?'

'As a matter of fact, I was.'

'That big dinner at the Castle?'

Mungo nodded. 'Editor fancied a pic of the Foreign Secretary. The ones I got were pretty feeble – that's what happens when you aim a flash gun at a windscreen.'

'What about Ben Webster?'

Mungo shook his head. 'Didn't even know who he was, more's the pity – it would have been the last ever photo of him.'

'We took a few at the mortuary, if that makes you feel any better,' Rebus said. Then, as Mungo smiled a soulful smile: 'I wouldn't mind a look at the ones you did get ...'

'I'll see what I can do.'

'They're not on your little machine then?'

The photographer shook his head. 'That lot are on my laptop. It's mostly just cars whizzing up Castle Hill – we weren't allowed as far as the Esplanade.' He had a thought. 'You know, they'll have taken an official portrait at the dinner itself. You could always ask to see that, if you're really interested.'

'I doubt they'd just hand it over.'

Mungo gave a wink. 'Leave it with me,' he said. Then, as he watched Rebus drain his glass: 'Funny to think it'll be back to old clothes and porridge next week.'

Rebus smiled and wiped his thumb across his mouth. 'My dad used to say that when we came back from holiday.'

'Don't suppose Edinburgh will ever see anything like this again.'

'Not in my lifetime,' Rebus conceded.

'Think any of it will make a difference?' Rebus just shook his head. 'My girlfriend gave me this book, all about 1968 – the Prague Spring and the Paris riots.'

Think we dropped the baton, Rebus thought to himself. 'I lived through 1968, son. Didn't mean anything at the time.' He paused. 'Or since, come to that.'

'You didn't tune in and drop out?'

'I was in the Army – short hair and an attitude.' Siobhan was returning to the table. 'Any news?' he asked her.

'They've not found anything. She's off to the Eye Pavilion for some tests, and that's that.'

'Western's discharged her?' Rebus watched Siobhan nod. She picked up the iPod again. 'Something else I wanted to show you.' Rebus heard the wheel click. She turned the screen towards him. 'See the woman at the far right? The one with the braids?'

Rebus saw. Mungo's camera was focused on the line of riot shields, but at the top of the picture he'd caught some onlookers, most holding camera phones in front of their faces. The woman with the hair braids, however, was toting some sort of video.

'That's Santal,' Siobhan stated.

'And who's Santal when she's at home?'

'Didn't I tell you? She was camping next door to my mum and dad.'

'Funny sort of name ... reckon she was born with it?'

'Means sandalwood,' Siobhan told him.

'Lovely-smelling soap,' Mungo added. Siobhan ignored him.

'See what she's doing?' she asked Rebus, holding the iPod close to him.

'Same as everyone else.'

'Not exactly.' Siobhan turned the machine towards Mungo.

'They're all pointing their phones towards the police,' he answered, nodding.

'All except Santal.' Siobhan angled the screen towards Rebus again, and rubbed the flywheel with her thumb, accessing the next photo. 'See?'

Rebus saw, but wasn't sure what to make of it.

'Mostly,' Mungo obliged, 'they want photos of the police – useful propaganda.'

'But Santal's photographing the protesters.'

'Meaning she might have caught your mum,' Rebus offered.

'I asked her at the campsite, she wouldn't show me. What's more, I saw her at that demo on Saturday – she was taking pictures then too.'

'I'm not sure I get it,' Rebus admitted.

'Me neither, but it could mean a trip to Stirling.' She looked at Rebus.

'Why?' he asked.

'Because that's where she was headed this morning.' She paused. 'Think my absence will be noted?'

'Chief Constable wants the Clootie Well put on ice anyway.' He reached into his pocket. 'I meant to say ...' Handing her the scrolled sheets. 'We've another Clootie Well on the Black Isle.'

'It's not really an island, you know,' Mungo piped up. 'The Black Isle, I mean.'

'You'll be telling us next it's not black either,' Rebus scolded him.

'The soil's supposed to be black,' Mungo conceded, 'but not so you'd notice. I know the spot you're talking about, though – we had a holiday up there last summer. Bits of rags hanging from the trees.' He screwed his face up in distaste. Siobhan had finished reading.

'You want to take a look?' she asked. Rebus shook his head.

'But someone should.'

'Even when the case is supposed to be "on ice"?'

'Not until tomorrow,' Rebus said. 'That's what the Chief Constable specified. But you're the one he put in charge ... up to you how we play it.' He leaned back in his seat, the wood creaking in protest.

'Eye Pavilion's five minutes' walk,' Siobhan mused. 'I was thinking I might head over there.'

'And a wee drive to Stirling thereafter?'

'Think I'll pass for a hippy chick?'

'Might be problematic,' Mungo chipped in.

'I've got a pair of combats in the wardrobe,' Siobhan argued. Her eyes fixed on Rebus. 'Means I'm leaving *you* in charge, John. Any ructions you cause, I'll be the one with the bruises.'

'Understood, boss,' Rebus said. 'Now, whose round is it?'

But Mungo had to get to his next job, and Siobhan was heading for the hospital ... leaving Rebus alone in the pub.

'One for the road,' he muttered to himself. Standing at the bar, waiting for his drink to be poured, staring at the optics, he thought again of that photo ... the woman with the braids. Siobhan called her Santal, but she reminded Rebus of someone. Screen had been too small for him really to get a good look. Should have asked Mungo for a print ...

'Day off?' the barman asked as he placed the pint in front of Rebus.

'Man of leisure, that's me,' Rebus confirmed, lifting the glass to his mouth.

'Thanks for coming back in,' Rebus said. 'How was court?'

'I wasn't needed.' Ellen Wylie placed her shoulder-bag and attaché case on the floor of the CID room.

'Can I fix you a coffee?'

'Got an espresso machine?'

'In here, we call it by its proper Italian name.'

'And what's that?'

'A kettle.'

'That joke's as weak as I suspect the coffee will be. How

can I help you, John?' She eased her jacket off. Rebus was already in shirtsleeves. Summer, and the station's heating was on. No apparent means of adjusting the radiators. Come October, they'd be lukewarm. Wylie was looking at the case-notes spread across three desks.

'Am I in there?' she asked.

'Not yet.'

'But I will be ...' She picked up one of the Cyril Colliar mug-shots, held it by its corner, as if fearing contamination of some kind.

'You didn't tell me about Denise,' Rebus commented.

'I don't remember you asking.'

'She had an abusive partner?'

Wylie's face twisted. 'He was a piece of work.'

'Was?'

She stared at him. 'All I mean is, he's out of our lives. You're not going to find bits of him at the Clootie Well.' A photo of the site was pinned to the wall; she studied it, angling her head. Then she turned and cast her gaze around the room. 'Got your work cut out, John,' she stated.

'Some help wouldn't go amiss.'

'Where's Siobhan?'

'Other business.' He was looking at her meaningfully.

'Why the hell should I help you?'

Rebus shrugged. 'Only one reason I can think of – you're curious.'

'Just like you, you mean?'

He nodded. 'Two killings in England, one in Scotland ... I'm finding it hard to work out how he's choosing them. They weren't listed together on the site ... didn't know each other ... crimes they committed are similar but not identical. They chose all sorts of victims ...'

'All three served time, right?'

'Different jails, though.'

'All the same, word travels. Ex-cons might talk to other

ex-cons, pass along the name of a particular sleazeball. Sex offenders aren't liked by other inmates.'

'It's a point.' Rebus pretended to consider it. Really, he didn't see it, but he wanted her thinking.

'You've spoken to the other police forces?' she asked.

'Not yet. I think Siobhan sent written requests.'

'Don't you need the personal touch? See what they can tell you about Isley and Guest?'

'I'm a bit swamped.'

Their eyes met. He could see she was hooked – for the moment.

'You really want me helping?' she asked.

'You're not a suspect, Ellen,' he said, trying for sincerity. 'And you know more about all of this than Siobhan and me.'

'How's she going to feel about me coming on board?'

'She'll be fine.'

'I'm not so sure about that.' She thought for a moment, then gave a sigh. 'I posted one message on the site, John. I never met the Jensens ...'

Rebus merely shrugged. She took a minute to make the decision. 'They arrested him, you know – Denise's ...' Swallowed back the next word, couldn't bring herself to say 'partner' or 'man'. 'Nothing ever came of it.'

'What you mean is, he was never jailed.'

'She's still terrified of him,' she said quietly, 'and he's still out there.' She unbuttoned the sleeves of her blouse and started rolling them up. 'Okay, tell me who I should be calling.'

He gave her numbers for Tyneside and Cumbria, then got on the phone himself. Inverness sounded disbelieving at first. 'You want us to what?' Rebus could hear a hand unsuccessfully smothering the mouthpiece at the other end. 'Edinburgh want us taking snaps o' the Clootie Well. We used to go there for picnics when I was a lad ...' The receiver changed hands.

'This is DS Johnson. Who am I speaking to?'

'DI Rebus, B Division in Edinburgh.'

'Thought you lot had your hands full with all the Trots and Chairman Maos.' There was laughter in the background.

'That may be so, but we also have three murders. Evidence from all three was found in Auchterarder, at a local spot known as the Clootie Well.'

'There's only one Clootie Well, Inspector.'

'Apparently not. Might be that the one you've got up there also has bits of evidence draped over its branches.'

Bait the detective sergeant could not refuse. Few enough moments of excitement in the Northern Constabulary.

'Let's start with photos of the scene,' Rebus went on. 'Plenty of close-ups, and check for anything intact – jeans, jackets ... we found a cash card in a pocket. Best if you can send me the photos as an email. If I can't open it, somebody here will be able to.' He looked across to Ellen Wylie. She sat on the corner of a desk, skirt straining at the thigh. She was playing with a pen as she talked into her receiver.

'Your name again?' DS Johnson was asking.

'DI Rebus. I'm based at Gayfield Square.' Rebus gave a contact number and his email. He could hear Johnson writing the information down.

'And if we *do* have anything up here ...?'

'Means our guy has been busy.'

'All right with you if I call this in? Just want to be sure you're not winding me up.'

'Be my guest. My Chief Constable's called James Corbyn – he knows all about it. But don't waste more time than you have to.'

'There's a constable here, his dad does portraits and graduations.'

'Doesn't mean to say the constable knows one end of a camera from the other.'

'I wasn't thinking of him – I was thinking of his dad.'

'Whatever works,' Rebus said, putting down the phone just as Ellen Wylie was doing the same.

'Any joy?' she asked.

'They're going to send a photographer, if he's not too busy at a wedding or a kid's birthday. How about you?'

'The officer in charge of the Guest investigation, I couldn't speak to him personally but one of his colleagues filled me in. There's some additional paperwork on its way to us. Reading between the lines, they weren't busting a gut on the case.'

'It's what they always tell you in training – the perfect murder is where nobody's looking for the victim.'

Wylie nodded. 'Or in this case, where no one's grieving. They thought maybe it was a drug deal gone wrong.'

'Now that's original. Any evidence that Mr Guest was a user?'

'Apparently so. Could have been dealing too, owed money for goods and couldn't—' She saw the look on Rebus's face.

'Lazy thinking, Ellen. Same thing might explain why no one thought to connect the three killings.'

'Because nobody was trying very hard?' she guessed.

Rebus nodded slowly.

'Well,' she said, 'you can ask him yourself.'

'Ask who?'

'Reason I couldn't talk to the boss is that he's right here.'

'Here?'

'Seconded to Lothian and Borders CID.' She glanced down at her notes. 'He's a detective sergeant, name of Stan Hackman.'

'So where can I find him?'

'His pal suggested the student residences.'

'Pollock Halls?'

She shrugged, picked up the notepad and turned it towards him. 'I've got his mobile, if that helps.' As Rebus stalked towards her, she tore off the sheet and held it out to him. He snatched at it.

'Get on to whoever led the Isley inquiry,' he said. 'See what you can get from them. I'll go have a word with Hackman.'

'You forgot to say thank you.' Then, watching him shrug his arms back into the sleeves of his jacket: 'Remember Brian Holmes?'

'I used to work with him.'

She nodded. 'He told me once you had a nickname for him. Used to call him "Shoeleather" because he did all the donkey work.'

'Donkeys don't wear shoes, do they?'

'You know what I mean, John. You're swanning off and leaving me here – it's not even my office! What does that make me?' She had picked up the telephone receiver and was waving it as she spoke.

'Switchboard maybe?' he pretended to guess, heading for the exit.

13

Siobhan wouldn't take no for an answer.

'I think,' Teddy Clarke said to his wife, 'maybe we should listen to her this time.'

Siobhan's mother wore a gauze patch over one eye. Her other eye was bruised, and there was a cut to the side of her nose. The painkillers seemed to have dulled her resolve; she just nodded when her husband spoke.

'What about clothes?' Mr Clarke said as they got into the taxi.

'You can go to the camp later,' Siobhan told him, 'bring back what you need.'

'We'd booked places on the bus for tomorrow,' he mused as Siobhan gave the driver directions to her flat. She knew he meant one of the protest buses: a convoy heading to the G8. His wife said something which he didn't quite catch. He leaned closer, squeezing her hand, and she repeated it for him.

'We're still going.' Her husband looked hesitant. 'Doctor doesn't see a problem,' Eve Clarke went on, clearly enough for Siobhan to hear.

'You can decide in the morning,' Siobhan said. 'Let's concentrate on today first, eh?'

Teddy Clarke smiled at his wife. 'Told you she'd changed,' he reminded her.

When they reached the flat, Siobhan paid for the taxi, waving aside her father's offer of money, then headed upstairs ahead of her parents, checking the living room and bedroom. No knickers on the floor or empty Smirnoff bottles lying around.

'In you come,' she told them. 'I'll get the kettle on. Make yourselves at home.'

'Must be ten years since we've been here,' her father commented, making a little tour of the living room.

'I couldn't have bought the place without your help,' Siobhan called from the kitchen. She knew what her mother would be looking for: signs of male occupation. Whole point of giving her money towards the deposit had been to help her 'get settled', that great euphemism. Steady boyfriend, then marriage, then kids. Not a route Siobhan had ever managed to start on. She took through the teapot and mugs, her father rising to help.

'You can pour,' she told him. 'I just need to sort some things in the bedroom ...'

She opened the wardrobe and hauled out her overnight bag. Tugged open drawers as she considered what she would need. With a bit of luck, she might not need any of it, but it was best to be safe. Change of clothes, tooth-brush, shampoo ... She delved to the bottom of a couple of drawers, finding the scruffiest, least-ironed items. Dungarees she'd painted the hall in, one shoulder-strap held on with a safety pin; a cheesecloth shirt which had been left behind by a three-night stand.

'We're driving you out,' her father said. He was in the doorway, holding a mug of tea towards her.

'There's a trip I have to make, nothing to do with the two of you being here. I might not be back till tomorrow.'

'We could be gone to Gleneagles by then.'

'Might see you there,' she answered with a wink. 'The pair of you will be all right tonight? Plenty of shops and places to eat. I'll leave you a key ...'

'We'll be fine.' He paused. 'This trip, is it to do with what happened to your mother?'

'Might be.'

'Because I've been thinking ...'

'What?' She looked up from her packing.

'You're a cop too, Siobhan. If you keep on with this, chances are you'll just make enemies.'

'It's not a popularity contest, Dad.'

'All the same ...'

She zipped the bag shut, left it on the bed and took the mug from him. 'I just want to hear him say he was wrong.' She took a sip of the lukewarm tea.

'Is that likely to happen?'

She shrugged. 'Maybe.'

Her father had settled himself on a corner of the bed. 'She's determined to go to Gleneagles, you know.'

Siobhan nodded. 'I'll drive you to the camp, bring your things back here before I leave.' She crouched down in front of him, pressing her free hand to his knee. 'You're sure you'll be all right?'

'We'll be fine. What about you?'

'Nothing's going to happen to me, Dad. I've got a force-field around me, or hadn't you noticed?'

'I think I might have caught a glimpse of it in Princes Street.' He placed his own hand over hers. 'All the same, take care, eh?'

She smiled and stood up, saw that her mother was watching from the hallway, and shared the smile with her too.

Rebus had been to the refectory before. In term-time it was crowded with students, many of them just starting at university, looking wary and even downright scared. A few years back, a second-year undergraduate had been dealing drugs, Rebus arresting him over breakfast.

The students who used the cafeteria brought laptops and iPods with them, so that even when busy the place was never noisy, except for the trilling of mobile phones.

But today the cafeteria rang with the sounds of harsh

raised voices. Rebus could sense the crackle of testosterone in the air. Two tables had been put together to form a temporary bar, from which small bottles of French lager were being sold. The No Smoking signs were being disregarded as uniformed officers slapped each other on the back and shared awkward approximations of the American 'high five'. Stab vests had been removed, lined up against one wall, and the busy female staff were dishing out plates of fried food, red-faced from either exertion or the exaggerated compliments of the visitors.

Rebus was on the hunt for visual clues, for some sort of Newcastle insignia. At the gatehouse, he'd been directed to an old baronial-style building behind it, where a civilian assistant had found a room number for Hackman. But Rebus had knocked on the door without answer, so had come here – the assistant's next suggestion.

'Of course, he could still be "in the field",' she'd cautioned, relishing the chance to use the phrase.

'Message received and understood,' Rebus had replied, helping to make her day even more satisfying.

There wasn't a single Scottish accent in the cafeteria. Rebus saw uniforms from the Met and the London Transport Police, South Wales and Yorkshire ... He decided to buy a mug of tea, only to be told there was no charge, having heard which he added a sausage roll and Mars Bar to his purchases. Asked a table if he could sit with them. They shifted to make some room.

'CID?' one of them guessed. Sweat had matted the man's hair, and his face was flushed.

Rebus nodded, realising he was the only bloke in the place not wearing a white shirt open at the neck. There was a smattering of female uniforms, too, but they were seated together, ignoring the various remarks launched in their direction.

'Looking for one of my number,' Rebus remarked casually. 'A DS called Hackman.'

'You from round here then?' one of the other uniforms asked, placing Rebus's accent. 'Bloody beautiful city you've got. Shame we had to mess it up a bit.' His laughter was shared by his colleagues. 'Don't know any Hackman, though.'

'He's a Geordie,' Rebus added.

'That lot over there are Geordies.' The officer was pointing to a table further towards the window.

'They're Scousers,' his neighbour corrected him.

'All look the bloody same to me.' There was more laughter at this.

'Where are you from then?' Rebus asked.

'Nottingham,' the first officer replied. 'Guess that makes us the sheriffs. Food's shit, though, isn't it?' He was nodding towards Rebus's half-eaten sausage roll.

'I've had worse – at least it's free.'

'That's a proper Jock talking and no mistake.' The man laughed again. 'Sorry we can't help you find your mate.'

Rebus just shrugged. 'Were you in Princes Street yesterday?' he asked, as if making conversation.

'Half the bloody day.'

'Nice bit of overtime,' his neighbour added.

'We had the same thing a few years back,' Rebus added. 'Commonwealth Heads of Government Meeting. Choggum, we called it. Few of the lads chipped a lump off their mortgages that week.'

'Mine's going towards a holiday,' the uniform said. 'Wife fancies Barcelona.'

'And while she's there,' his neighbour said, 'where will you be taking the girlfriend?' More laughter, elbows digging into ribs.

'You earned it yesterday, though,' Rebus stated, getting them back on track.

'Some did,' came the reply. 'Most of us sat on the bus waiting for things to really kick off.'

His neighbour nodded. 'Compared to what we'd been warned might happen, it was a walk in the park.'

'Photos in the paper this morning, at least some of you drew a bit of blood.'

'The Met boys probably. They train against Millwall fans, so yesterday was nothing special.'

'Can I try another name on you?' Rebus asked. 'Guy called Jacko, might be with the Met.'

They shook their heads. Rebus decided he wasn't going to get much more, so tucked his Mars Bar into his pocket and rose to his feet. Told them to take care and went for a wander. There were plenty of other uniforms milling about outside. If rain hadn't been threatening, he suspected they'd be lying on the lawns. He overheard nothing approximating a Newcastle accent, and nothing about giving innocent protesters a good hiding. He tried Hackman's mobile, but it was still switched off. On the verge of giving up, he decided to try Hackman's room one last time.

And the door was opened from within.

'DS Hackman?'

'Who the hell wants to know?'

'DI Rebus.' Rebus showed his ID. 'Can I have a word?'

'Not in here, there's barely room to swing a cat. Place could do with a bit of fumigating, too. Hang on a sec ...' As Hackman retreated into his room, Rebus made a quick examination: clothes strewn everywhere; empty cigarette packets; razzle mags; a personal hi-fi; can of cider sitting on the floor by the bed. Sound of horse-racing from the TV. Hackman had picked up a phone and lighter. Patted his pockets till he found his key. Back out into the hall again. 'Outside, yeah?' he suggested, leading the way whether Rebus liked it or not.

He was stocky: huge neck and close-cropped fair hair. Maybe early thirties, the face pitted and pock marked, nose squashed to one side. His white T-shirt had suffered too many washes. It rode up at the back, revealing the top of its owner's underpants. He wore jeans and trainers.

'Been working?' Rebus asked.

'Just back.'

'Undercover?'

Hackman nodded. 'Ordinary man in the street.'

'Any trouble getting in character?'

Hackman's mouth twitched. 'Local plod?'

'That's right.'

'I could do with a few tips.' Hackman glanced around at Rebus. 'Lap bars are on Lothian Road, right?'

'There and thereabouts.'

'Which one should I grace with my hard-earned cash?'

'I'm not an expert.'

Hackman looked him up and down. 'Sure about that?' he asked. They were outside now. Hackman offered Rebus a cigarette – readily received – and flicked his lighter open.

'Leith's got its share of knocking-shops too, right?'

'Right.'

'And it's legalised here?'

'We tend to turn a blind eye, so long as it's kept indoors.' Rebus paused to inhale. 'I'm glad to see it's not all work and no play ...'

Hackman gave a rasping laugh. 'We've got better-looking women in the Toon, and that's the truth of it.'

'Your accent's not Geordie, though.'

'Grew up near Brighton. Been in the north-east eight years.'

'See any action yesterday?' Rebus was making show of studying the view before them – Arthur's Seat rising skywards.

'Is this my debriefing?'

'Just wondering.'

Hackman narrowed his eyes. 'What can I do for you, DI Rebus?'

'You worked the Trevor Guest murder.'

'That was two months back; plenty more in my in-tray since.'

'It's Guest I'm interested in. His trousers have turned up near Gleneagles, cash card in the pocket.'

Hackman stared at him. 'He wasn't wearing any when we found him.'

'Now you know why: killer's been taking trophies.'

Hackman wasn't slow. 'How many?'

'Three victims so far. Two weeks after Guest, he struck again. Identical MO, and a little souvenir left at the same location.'

'Bloody hell ...' Hackman drew hard on his cigarette. 'We had it down as ... well, lowlife like Guest makes plenty enemies. He was a druggie too, hence the heroin – sending a message.'

'It went to the bottom of your in-tray?' Rebus watched the big man shrug. 'Any leads at all?'

'Interviewed those who owned up to knowing him. Traced his last night on earth, but didn't come up with any startling conclusions. I can have all the paperwork sent ...'

'Already in hand.'

'Guest was two months back. You say he struck again a couple of weeks later?' Hackman watched Rebus nod agreement. 'And the other vic?'

'Three months ago.'

Hackman thought it through. 'Twelve weeks, eight, then six. What you expect of killers once they get a taste for it – they speed up. Each new fix satisfies them that bit less than the one before. So what's happened between then and now? Six weeks without another killing?'

'Sounds unlikely,' Rebus agreed.

'Unless we've caught him for something else; or he's moved his business elsewhere.'

'I like the way you think,' Rebus admitted.

Hackman looked at him. 'You've already sussed every-thing I've just said, haven't you?'

'That's why I like your thinking.'

Hackman gave a scratch of his crotch. 'All I've been thinking about the past few days is minge – now you go and do this to me.'

'Sorry about that.' Rebus stubbed the remains of his cigarette. 'I wanted to ask if there was anything you could tell me about Trevor Guest – anything that sticks in your mind.'

'For the price of a cold beer, my head is your oyster.'

Problem with oysters, Rebus considered as they walked to the cafeteria, was that you were more likely to get a load of old grit than a pearl.

The place had quietened a little, and they found a table to themselves – though not before Hackman had made an effort to introduce himself to the female officers, formally taking each one by the hand.

'Lovely,' he announced as he returned to Rebus's table. He clapped his palms together and was rubbing them as he sat down.

'Bottoms up,' he said, raising his bottle. Then he gave a little chuckle. 'Should be the name of a lap-dancing club.'

Rebus refrained from revealing that it already was. Instead, he repeated Trevor Guest's name.

Hackman sank half his lager straight off. 'Like I said, lowlife. In and out of jail – burglaries, flogging the stuff he'd nicked, some other petty stuff and a bit of grievous bodily. He was up here for a time, few years back. Kept his nose clean, far as we could tell.'

'By "here" you mean Edinburgh?'

Hackman stifled a belch. 'Jockland generally ... no offence.'

'None taken,' Rebus lied. 'I wonder if there's any way he could have met the third victim – club bouncer called Cyril Colliar, got out of jail three months back.'

'Name doesn't register. Want another of these?'

'I'll get them.' Rebus was halfway out of his chair, but Hackman waved him back. Rebus watched as he first approached the women's table, asking if they were all right for drinks. He made one of them laugh, which probably counted as a result in his book. He carried four bottles back to the table.

'Pissy little things,' he explained, sliding two across towards Rebus. 'Besides, got to spend the loot somehow, eh?'

'I notice no one's paying for bed and board.'

'No one except the local taxpayer.' Hackman's eyes widened. 'I suppose that's *you*. So ta very much.' He toasted Rebus with a fresh bottle. 'Don't suppose you're free tonight to act the tour guide?'

'Sorry.' Rebus shook his head.

'I'd be buying ... hard offer for a Jock to turn down.'

'I'm turning it down anyway.'

'Suit yourself,' Hackman said with a shrug. 'This killer you're looking for ... got any leads?'

'He targets scum; maybe gets them from a victim-support website.'

'Vigilante, eh? Meaning someone with a grudge ...'

'That's the theory.'

'Clever money would say the connection's to the first victim. Should have been the beginning and end, but he caught the bug.'

Rebus nodded slowly, having considered the same conclusion. Fast Eddie Isley, attacker of prostitutes. Isley's killer maybe a pimp or boyfriend ... tracked him using BeastWatch, then asked himself a question – why stop with just one?

'How badly do you really want to find this guy?' Hackman asked. 'That's what I'd be wrestling with ... sounds like he's on *our* side.'

'You don't believe people can change? All three victims

had served their sentences, no sign of reoffending.'

'You're talking about redemption.' Hackman mimed the act of spitting. 'Could never be doing with that goody-good bullshit.' He paused. 'What are you smiling at?'

'It's a line from a Pink Floyd song.'

'Is it? I could never be doing with them either. A bit of Tamla or Stax, songs to seduce the crumpet by. Our Trev was a bit of a ladies' man.'

'Trevor Guest?'

'Liked them a bit on the young side, judging by the girlfriends we dug up.' Hackman snorted. 'Believe me, if they'd been any younger, we'd've been using a crèche and not an interview room.' He enjoyed this joke so much, he found it hard to take his next slug of lager. 'I like my meat that bit more mature,' he said finally, smacking his lips, seeming lost in thought. 'A lot of the escorts in the back of your local paper, they call themselves "mature" too. How old do you reckon that makes them? I mean, I'm not one for geriatrics ...'

'Guest attacked a babysitter, didn't he?' Rebus asked.

'Broke into a house, happened to find her there on the couch. Far as I remember, all he wanted was a blow-job. She hollered and he scarpered.' He offered a shrug.

Rebus's chair scraped against the floor as he stood up. 'I need to be going,' he said.

'Finish your drink.'

'I'm driving.'

'Something tells me you might get away with a misdemeanour or two this week. Still, waste not, want not.' Hackman slid the untouched bottle towards himself. 'What about a pint later on? I need a Sherpa to show me the way ...'

Rebus ignored him, kept walking. Back in the fresh air, he risked a glance through the window, saw Hackman doing a little improvised shuffle as he headed towards the women.

14

The so-called Camp Horizon on the edge of Stirling, sand-wiched between a football ground and a trading estate, reminded Siobhan of some of the temporary encampments she'd seen around the Greenham Common air base in the 1980s, when she'd hitched there as a teenager to protest about nuclear missiles. There weren't just tents here, but elaborate wigwams and structures made of osiers, resembling willow igloos. Canvases had been strung between the trees, daubed with rainbows and peace signs. Smoke was rising from camp-fires, and there was the pungent scent of cannabis in the air. Solar panels and a small wind turbine seemed to be generating electricity for strings of multicoloured light-bulbs. A static caravan was supplying legal advice and free condoms, while discarded leaflets provided additional information on everything from HIV to Third World debt.

She had been stopped at five separate checkpoints on the route from Edinburgh. Despite showing ID, one security man had even insisted she open the boot of her car.

'These people have all kinds of sympathisers,' he'd explained.

'They're well on their way to getting another,' Siobhan had muttered in response.

The inhabitants of the camp seemed to have split into distinct tribes, with the anti-poverty contingent remaining separate from the hard-core anarchists. Red flags appeared to be acting as a border between the two. Old-time hippies formed another sub-group, one of the wigwams their epicentre. Beans were cooking on a stove, while a makeshift sign announced Reiki and Holistic Healing between the hours of five and eight with 'special rates for unwaged/ students'.

Siobhan had asked one of the guards at the entrance about Santal. He'd shaken his head.

'No names, no pack-drill.' He'd looked her up and down. 'Mind a word of warning?'

'What?'

'You look like a cop working undercover.'

She'd followed his eyes. 'Is it the dungarees?'

He'd shaken his head again. 'The clean hair.'

So she'd ruffled it a bit, without seeming to convince him. 'Anyone else in there undercover?'

'Bound to be,' he'd said with a smile. 'But I'm not going to spot the good ones, am I?'

Her car was parked in the city centre. If the worst came to the worst, she'd sleep in the car rather than under the stars. The site was a lot bigger than the one in Edinburgh, the tents more densely grouped. As dusk encroached, she had to watch out for tent-pegs and guy-ropes. Twice she passed a young man with a straggly beard who was trying to interest people in 'herbal relaxation'. Third time, their eyes met.

'Lost somebody?' he asked.

'Friend of mine called Santal.'

He shook his head. 'Not a great one for names.' So she gave a brief description. He shook his head again. 'If you just sit and chill, maybe she'll come to you.' He held out a ready-rolled joint. 'On the house.'

'Only available to new customers?' she guessed.

'Even the forces of law and order need to relax at day's end.'

She stared at him for a moment. 'I'm impressed. Is it the hair?'

'The bag doesn't help,' he commented. 'What you really

want is a muddy rucksack. That thing …' indicating the guilty item, 'makes you look like you're off to the gym.'

'Thanks for the advice. You weren't scared I might want to bust you?'

He shrugged. 'You want a riot, go right ahead.'

She gave a brief smile. 'Maybe another time.'

'This "friend" of yours, any chance she might have been part of the advance guard?'

'Depends what you mean.'

He had paused to light the joint, inhaling deeply, then exhaling and speaking at the same time. 'Stands to reason there'll be blockades from first light, your lot trying to stop us getting near the hotel.' He offered her a hit, but she shook her head.

'You'll never know till you try,' he teased.

'Believe it or not, I was a teenager once … So the advance guard headed out of here earlier?'

'Ordnance Survey maps in hand. Only the Ochil Hills between us and victory.'

'Cross-country in the dark? Isn't that a bit risky?'

He offered a shrug, then drew on the joint again. A young woman was hovering nearby. 'Get you anything?' he asked her. The transaction took half a minute: a tiny shrink-wrapped package for three ten-pound notes.

'Cheers,' the woman said. Then, to Siobhan: 'Evening, Officer.' She was giggling as she left them. The dealer was looking at Siobhan's dungarees.

'I know when I'm beaten,' she admitted.

'So take my advice: sit and chill for a while. You might find something you didn't know you were looking for.' He stroked his beard as he spoke.

'That's … deep,' Siobhan told him, her tone letting him know she was thinking the exact opposite.

'You'll see,' he retorted, moving past her into the gloom. She walked back to the perimeter and decided to phone Rebus. He didn't pick up, so she left a message.

'Hi, it's me. I'm in Stirling, no sign of Santal. I'll see you tomorrow, but if you need me in the meantime, feel free to call.'

An exhausted but excited-looking group was entering the compound. Siobhan snapped shut her phone and moved to within earshot of them as they were met by some of their comrades.

'Heat-seeking radar ... dogs ...'

'Armed to the teeth, man ...'

'American accents ... Marines if you ask me ... no ID ...'

'Choppers ... searchlights ...'

'Had us for dead ...'

'Tracked us halfway back to base-camp ...'

Then the questions started. How close did they get? Any weak points in the security? Did they reach the perimeter? Was anyone still out there?

'We split up ...'

'Sub-machine guns, I reckon ... '

'Weren't messing ... '

'Split into ten groups of three ... easier to lay low ...'

'State of the art ...'

More questions flew at them. Siobhan started counting heads, stopped at fifteen. Meaning a further fifteen were still out on the Ochils somewhere. In the hubbub, she launched her own question.

'Where's Santal?'

A shake of the head. 'Didn't see her after we split up.'

One of them had unfolded a map, to show how far they'd got. He had a flashlight strapped to his forehead and was tracing the route with a muddied finger. Siobhan squeezed closer.

'It's a total exclusion zone ...'

'Has to be a weak spot ...'

'Force of numbers, that's all we've got ...'

'We'll be ten thousand strong by morning.'

'Herbal cigarettes for all our brave soldiers!' As the dealer started handing them out, there were bursts of laughter from the crowd – a release of tension. Siobhan retreated to the back of the throng. A hand grasped her arm. It was the young woman who'd bought from the dealer earlier.

'Pigs better get wings,' she hissed.

Siobhan glared at her. 'Or what?'

The young woman offered a malevolent smile. 'Or I might have to squeal.'

Siobhan said nothing; just hoisted her bag and backed away. The young woman waved her off. The same guard was on duty at the gate.

'Did the disguise hold?' he asked with something just shy of a smirk.

All the way back to her car, Siobhan tried to think of a comeback.

Rebus had acted the gentleman: returned to Gayfield Square bearing Pot Noodles and chicken tikka wraps.

'You're spoiling me,' Ellen Wylie said as he switched on the kettle.

'You also get first choice – chicken and mushroom or beef curry?'

'Chicken.' She watched him peel open the plastic containers. 'So how did it go?'

'I found Hackman.'

'And?'

'He wanted a tour of the fleshpots.'

'Yuck.'

'I told him I couldn't oblige, and in return he told me very little we don't already know.'

'Or couldn't have guessed?' She'd come over to join Rebus at the kettle. Picked up one of the wraps and examined its sell-by: 5 July. 'Half-price,' she commented.

'I knew you'd be impressed. But there's even more.'

He produced the Mars Bar from his pocket and handed it over. 'So what news of Edward Isley?'

'Again, there's more paperwork coming north,' she said, 'but the DI I spoke to was one of the brighter lights on the tree. Recited most of it from memory.'

'Let me guess: no shortage of enemies ... someone with a grudge ... keeping an open mind ... no progress to report?'

'Just about sums it up,' Wylie admitted. 'I got the impression a few stops had been left unpulled.'

'Nothing to connect Fast Eddie to Mr Guest?'

She shook her head. 'Different prisons, no sign of shared associates. Isley didn't know Newcastle, and Guest hadn't been hanging around Carlisle or the M6.'

'And Cyril Colliar probably knew neither of them.'

'Bringing us back to their shared appearance on BeastWatch.' Wylie watched Rebus pour water on to the noodles. He offered her a spoon and they stirred their individual pots.

'Have you spoken to anyone at Torphichen?' he asked. 'Told them you were short-handed.'

'Rat-Arse probably hinted we were involved in a bunk-up.'

'How well you know DC Reynolds,' she said with a smile. 'By the way, some jpegs arrived from Inverness.'

'That was quick.' He watched as she logged on at the computer. The photos appeared as thumbnails, but Wylie enlarged each one.

'It looks just like Auchterarder,' Rebus commented.

'Photographer got some close-ups,' Wylie said, bringing them up on screen. Tattered remnants of cloth, but none of it looking recent. 'What do you think?' she asked.

'I don't see anything for us, do you?'

'No,' she agreed. One of the phones started ringing. She picked up and listened.

'Send him up,' she said, replacing the receiver. 'Guy

called Mungo,' she explained. 'Says he has an appointment.'

'More of an open invitation,' Rebus said, sniffing the contents of the wrap he'd just opened. 'Wonder if he likes chicken tikka ...'

Mungo did indeed, and demolished the gift in two huge bites while Rebus and Wylie examined the photographs.

'You work fast,' Rebus said by way of thanks.

'What are we looking at?' Ellen Wylie asked.

'Friday night,' Rebus explained. 'A dinner at the Castle.'

'Ben Webster's suicide?'

Rebus nodded. 'That's him there,' he said, tapping one of the faces. Mungo had been as good as his word: not just his own snatched shots of the motorcade and its passengers, but copies of the official portraits. Lots of well-dressed smiling men shaking hands with other well-dressed smiling men. Rebus recognised only a few: the Foreign Secretary, Defence Secretary, Ben Webster ...

'How did you get these?' Rebus asked.

'Openly available to the media – just the sort of PR opportunity the politicos like.'

'Got any names to put to the faces?'

'That's a job for a sub,' the photographer said, swallowing the last of the wrap. 'But I dug out what I could.' He reached into his bag and pulled out sheets of paper.

'Thanks,' Rebus said. 'I've probably already seen them ...'

'But I haven't,' Wylie said, taking them from Mungo. Rebus was more interested in the photos from the dinner.

'I didn't realise Corbyn was there,' he mused.

'Who's he when he's at home?' Mungo asked.

'Our esteemed Chief Constable.'

Mungo looked to where Rebus was pointing. 'Didn't stay long,' he said, sifting through his own prints. 'Here he is leaving again. I was just packing up ...'

'So how long was that after it all kicked off?'

'Not even half an hour. I'd been biding my time in case of latecomers.'

Richard Pennen hadn't made it into any of the official portraits, but Mungo had snapped his car as it entered the compound, Pennen caught unawares, mouth agape.

'It says here,' Ellen Wylie piped up, 'that Ben Webster helped try to negotiate a truce in Sierra Leone. Also visited Iraq, Afghanistan and East Timor.'

'Racked up a few Air Miles,' Mungo commented.

'And liked a bit of adventure,' she added, turning a page. 'I didn't realise his sister was a cop.'

Rebus nodded. 'Met her a few days back.' He paused for a moment. 'Funeral's tomorrow, I think. I was supposed to be calling her ...' Then he went back to studying the official photographs. They'd all been posed, leaving little for him to glean: no tête-à-têtes caught in the background; nothing these powerful men didn't want the world to see. Just like Mungo said: a PR exercise. Rebus picked up the phone and called Mairie on her mobile.

'Any chance you could drop into Gayfield?' he asked her. He could hear the clacking of her keyboard.

'Need to polish this off first.'

'Half an hour?'

'I'll see what I can do.'

'There's a Mars Bar riding on it.' Wylie's face showed her displeasure. Rebus ended the call and watched Wylie unwrap the chocolate and bite into it.

'Bang goes my bribe,' Rebus told her.

'I'll leave these with you,' Mungo was saying, brushing flour from his fingers. 'They're yours to keep anyway – but not for publication.'

'Our eyes only,' Rebus agreed. He spread out the photos of the various back-seat passengers. Most were blurred, the result of vehicles refusing to slow for the photographer. A few of the foreign dignitaries were smiling, however, perhaps pleased to be noticed.

'And can you give these to Siobhan?' Mungo added, handing over a large envelope. Rebus nodded and asked what they were. 'The Princes Street demo. She was interested in the woman on the edge of the crowd. I've managed to zoom in a little.'

Rebus opened the envelope. The young woman with braided hair held her own camera to her face. Santal, was that what she was called? Meaning sandalwood. Rebus wondered if Siobhan had run the name past Operation Sorbus. The face seemed focused on its job, the mouth a thin line of concentration. Dedicated; maybe a professional. In other snaps she was holding the camera away from her, looking to left and right. As if on the lookout for something. Totally uninterested in the array of riot shields. Not scared of the flying debris. Not excited or in awe.

Just doing her job.

'I'll see she gets them,' Rebus told Mungo as the photographer strapped his bag shut. 'And thanks for these. I owe you.'

Mungo nodded slowly. 'Maybe a tip-off next time you're first at a scene?'

'Seldom happens, son,' Rebus warned him. 'But I'll keep it in mind.'

Mungo shook both officers' hands. Wylie watched him leave. 'You'll keep him in mind?' she echoed.

'Bugger is, Ellen, at my time of life the memory's not what it was.' Rebus reached for the noodles, only to find they'd gone cold.

Good as her word, Mairie Henderson turned up within the half-hour, her look turning sour as she saw the Mars Bar wrapper on the desk.

'Don't blame me,' Rebus apologised, holding up his hands.

'Thought you might like to see this,' she said, unfolding a printout of the next morning's front page. 'We got lucky: no big stories.'

POLICE PROBE G8 MURDER MYSTERY. Plus photos of the Clootie Well and Gleneagles Hotel. Rebus didn't bother reading the text.

'What was it you were just saying to Mungo?' Wylie teased.

Rebus ignored her, focusing instead on the dignitaries. 'Care to enlighten me?' he asked Mairie. She took a deep breath and started reeling off names. Government ministers from countries as diverse as South Africa, China and Mexico. Most had trade or economic portfolios, and when Mairie wasn't sure, she placed a call to one of the paper's pundits, who put her right.

'So we can assume they were talking about trade or aid?' Rebus asked. 'In which case what was Richard Pennen doing there? Or our own Defence Minister, come to that?'

'You can trade in weapons, too,' Mairie reminded him.

'And the Chief Constable?'

She shrugged. 'Probably invited as a courtesy. This man here ...' She tapped one of the portraits. 'He's Mr Genetic Modification. I've seen him on TV, arguing with the environmentalists.'

'We're selling genetics to Mexico?' Rebus wondered. Mairie shrugged again.

'You really think they're covering something up?'

'Why would they do that?' Rebus asked, as though surprised by her question.

'Because they can?' Ellen Wylie suggested.

'These men are cleverer than that. Pennen's not the only businessman on show.' Mairie pointed to two other faces. 'Banking and airlines.'

'They got the VIPs out of there in a hurry,' Rebus said, 'once Webster's body was discovered.'

'Standard procedure, I'd think,' Mairie answered.

Rebus slumped into the nearest chair. 'Pennen doesn't want us sticking our oars in, and Steelforth's been trying to give me a good skelp. What does that tell you?'

'That any publicity is bad publicity ... when you're trying to trade with *some* governments.'

'I like this guy,' Wylie said, coming to the end of the Webster notes. 'I'm sorry he's dead.' She looked at Rebus. 'You going to the funeral?'

'Thinking about it.'

'Another chance to rub Pennen and Special Branch up the wrong way?' Mairie guessed.

'Paying my respects,' Rebus countered, 'and telling his sister that we're getting nowhere.' He'd picked up one of Mungo's close-ups from Princes Street Gardens. Mairie was looking at them, too.

'Way I hear it,' she said, 'you guys went over the top.'

'We went in hard,' Wylie said, sounding prickly.

'Few dozen hot-heads versus a few hundred riot police.'

'And who is it gives them the oxygen of publicity?' Wylie sounded ready for the fight.

'You and your truncheons,' Mairie countered. 'If there was nothing to report, we wouldn't report it.'

'But it's the way the truth can be twisted ...' Wylie realised that they had lost Rebus. He was staring at one photograph in particular, eyes narrowed. 'John?' she said. When the name had no effect, she nudged him. 'Care to back me up here?'

'I'm sure you can fight your own battles, Ellen.'

'What's wrong?' Mairie asked, peering over his shoulder at the tableau. 'You look like you've seen a ghost.'

'In a manner of speaking,' Rebus said. He picked up the phone, but thought better of it, let it clatter back into its cradle again. 'After all,' he said, 'tomorrow is another day.'

'Not just "another" day, John,' Mairie reminded him. 'It's when everything finally kicks off.'

'And here's hoping London doesn't get the Olympics,' Wylie added. 'We'll be hearing about it from now till doomsday.'

Rebus had risen to his feet, still seemingly distracted. 'Beer time,' he stated. 'And I'm on the shout.'

'I thought you'd never ask,' Mairie sighed. Wylie went to fetch her jacket and bag. Rebus was leading the way.

'Not leaving that?' Mairie hinted, nodding at the photo he still held in his hand. He glanced down at it, then folded it into his pocket. Patted his other pockets before resting his palm on Mairie's shoulder.

'I'm a bit short, as it happens. Any chance of a sub ...?'

Later that evening, Mairie Henderson returned to her Murrayfield home. She owned the top two floors of a detached Victorian pile, and shared the mortgage with her boyfriend, Allan. Problem was, Allan was a TV cameraman, and she saw precious little of him at the best of times. This week was turning out to be pure murder. One of the spare bedrooms was now her office, and she made straight for it, throwing her jacket over the back of a chair. The coffee table didn't have room for even a single mug of the stuff, covered as it was with piles of newsprint. Her own cuttings files took up a whole wall, and her few precious journalism awards were framed above the computer. She sat down at her desk and wondered why she felt so comfortable in this cramped and stuffy room. The kitchen was airy, but she spent very little time there. The living room had been swamped by Allan's home cinema and hi-fi. This room – her office – was hers and hers alone. She looked at the racks of cassette tapes – interviews she'd done – each one encapsulating a life. Cafferty's story had demanded over forty hours of conversation, the transcripts stretching to a thousand pages. The resulting book had been compiled meticulously, and she knew she deserved a bloody medal for it. Not that one had been forthcoming. That the book sold by the truckload had done nothing to alter the flat fee she'd signed up to. And it was Cafferty who appeared on the chatshows, Cafferty who did the bookshop signings, the festivals, the circuit of celebrity parties in London. When the book had gone into its third printing, they'd even changed the jacket, magnifying his name and shrinking hers.

Bloody nerve.

And when she saw Cafferty these days, all he did was tease her with the notion of a further instalment, hinting that he might get 'another hack' this time round – because he knew damned well she wouldn't allow herself to be conned in the same way. What was the old saying? Fool me once, shame on you; fool me twice, shame on me.

Bastard.

She checked for emails, thinking back to the drink she'd just had with Rebus. She was still annoyed with him. Annoyed that he hadn't given her an interview for the Cafferty book. Without him, it had been Cafferty's word alone on so many events and incidents. So, yes, she was still annoyed with Rebus.

Annoyed because she knew he'd been right to refuse.

Her fellow journalists thought she'd made a packet on the Cafferty book. Some had stopped talking to her or answering her calls. Jealousy doubtless played a part, but they also felt they had nothing to offer her. Work had dried up. She found herself scratching around, penning pieces about councillors and charity workers – human interest stories with very little interest. Editors sounded surprised that she needed the work ...

Thought you'd cleaned up on Cafferty ...

Naturally, she couldn't tell them the truth, so made up lies instead about needing to keep her hand in.

Cleaned up ...

Her few remaining copies of the Cafferty book were stacked beneath the coffee table. She'd stopped handing them out to family and friends. Stopped after watching Cafferty share a joke with a daytime TV host, the audience lapping it up, Mairie feeling grubbier than ever. But when she thought about Cafferty, she couldn't help picturing Richard Pennen too – glad-handing at Prestonfield House, cosseted by yes-men, buffed to a spotless sheen. Rebus had a point about the Edinburgh Castle dinner. It wasn't so much that an arms dealer of sorts had found himself at the top table, but that no one had taken any notice. Pennen had said that anything he'd given to Ben Webster would have been declared in the register of members' interests. Mairie had checked, and it looked as though the MP had been scrupulous. It struck her now that Pennen had known she would look. He'd wanted her investigating Webster's affairs. But why? Because he'd known there was nothing for her to find? Or to tarnish a dead man's name?

I like this guy, Ellen Wylie had said. Yes, and after a few minutes' chat with Westminster insiders, Mairie had started to like him too. Which only made her trust Richard Pennen all the less. She fetched a glass of tap-water from the kitchen and settled again at her computer.

Decided to start from scratch.

Typed Richard Pennen's name into the first of her many search engines.

15

Rebus was three steps away from the tenement door when the voice called his name. Inside the pockets of his coat, his fingers curled into fists. He turned to face Cafferty.

'Hell do you want?'

Cafferty wafted a hand in front of his nose. 'I can smell the booze from here.'

'I drink to forget people like you.'

'Wasted your money tonight then.' Cafferty gave a flick of his head. 'Something I want to show you.'

Rebus stood his ground a moment, till curiosity got the better of him. Cafferty was unlocking the Bentley, gesturing for Rebus to get in. Rebus opened the passenger door and leaned inside.

'Where are we going?'

'Nowhere deserted, if that's what's worrying you. Point of fact, place we're going will be packed.'

The engine roared into life. With two beers and two whiskies under his belt, Rebus knew his wits weren't going to be the sharpest.

Nevertheless, he got in.

Cafferty offered chewing-gum and Rebus unwrapped a stick. 'How's my case going?' Cafferty asked.

'Doing just fine without your help.'

'As long as you don't forget who put you on the right track.' Cafferty gave a little smile. They were heading east through Marchmont. 'How's Siobhan shaping up?'

'She's fine.'

'Hasn't left you in the lurch, then?'

Rebus stared at Cafferty's profile. 'How do you mean?'

'I heard she was spreading herself a bit thin.'

'Are you keeping a watch on us?'

Cafferty just smiled again. Rebus noticed that his own fists were still clenched as they rested on his lap. One tug of the steering wheel, and he could put the Bentley into a wall. Or slide his hands around Cafferty's fat neck and squeeze ...

'Thinking evil thoughts, Rebus?' Cafferty guessed. 'I'm a taxpayer, remember – top-bracket at that – which makes me *your* employer.'

'Must give you a warm glow.'

'It does. That MP who jumped from the ramparts ... making headway?'

'What's it to you?'

'Nothing.' Cafferty paused a couple of beats. 'It's just that I know Richard Pennen.' He turned towards Rebus, pleased by the visible effect of this statement. 'Met him a couple of times,' he continued.

'Please tell me he was trying to flog you some dodgy weapons.'

Cafferty laughed. 'He has a stake in the firm that published my book. Meant he was at the launch party. Sorry you couldn't make it, by the way.'

'Invite came in handy when the bog-roll ran out.'

'Met him again over lunch when the book hit fifty thousand. Private room at the Ivy ...' He glanced at Rebus again. 'That's in London. I thought of moving there, you know. Used to have a lot of friends down south. Business acquaintances.'

'Same ones Steelforth put away?' Rebus thought for a moment. 'Why didn't you tell me you knew Pennen too?'

'There have to be *some* secrets between us,' Cafferty said, smiling. 'I ran a check on your pal Jacko by the way ... didn't get anywhere. You sure he's a cop?'

Rebus answered with another question of his own. 'What about Steelforth's bill at the Balmoral?'

'Picked up by Lothian and Borders Police.'

'That's generous of us.'

'You never let up, do you, Rebus?'

'Why should I?'

'Because sometimes you just have to let things go. What's past is another country – Mairie told me that when we were doing the book.'

'I just had a drink with her.'

'And not Ribena, by the smell of it.'

'She's a good kid. Shame she's got your claws in her back.'

The car was heading down Dalkeith Road, Cafferty signalling left towards Craigmillar and Niddrie. Either that or they were heading for the A1 south out of the city ...

'Where are we going?' Rebus asked again.

'Not far now. And Mairie's quite capable of looking after herself.'

'Does she pass everything along?'

'Probably not, but that doesn't stop me asking her. See, what Mairie really needs is another bestseller. This time she'd push for a percentage rather than a set fee. I keep tempting her with stories that didn't make it into the book ... The girl needs to keep me sweet.'

'More fool her.'

'It's funny,' Cafferty went on, 'but talking about Richard Pennen reminds me of a few tales about *him*, too. Not that you'd want to hear them.' He started chuckling again, his face lit from below by the dashboard. He seemed all shadows and smudges, a preparatory sketch for some grinning gargoyle.

I'm in hell, Rebus thought. This is what happens when you die and go downstairs. You get your own personal devil ...

'Salvation awaits!' Cafferty cried suddenly, turning the

steering wheel hard so that the Bentley slalomed through a set of gates, sending gravel flying skywards. It was a hall, lights glowing within. A hall attached to a church.

'Time to renounce the demon drink,' Cafferty teased, shutting off the engine and pushing open his door. But a sign next to the open doorway told Rebus this was a public meeting, part of G8 Alternatives – 'Communities in Action: the Future Crisis Averted'. Entry was free to students and the unwaged.

'Unwashed, more like,' Cafferty muttered, seeing the bearded figure holding a plastic bucket. The man had long, curly black hair and wore prescription glasses with thick black frames. He shook the bucket as the new arrivals approached. There were coins inside, but not many. Cafferty made a ritual of opening his wallet and extracting a fifty-pound note. 'Better be going to a good cause,' he warned the collector. Rebus followed him indoors, pointing out to the bucket-holder that his share could come out of Cafferty's contribution.

There were three or four rows of empty chairs at the back, but Cafferty had made the decision to stand, arms folded and legs apart. The room was busy, but the audience looked bored, or maybe just lost in contemplation. Up on the stage, four men and two women were squeezed behind a trestle table, sharing a single distortion-prone microphone. There were banners behind them stating that CRAIGMILLAR WELCOMES G8 PROTESTERS and OUR COMMUNITY IS STRONG WHEN WE SPEAK WITH ONE VOICE. The one voice speaking at that particular moment belonged to Councillor Gareth Tench.

'It's all very well,' he boomed out, 'saying give us the tools and we will do the job. But there need to be jobs there in the first place! We need concrete proposals for the betterment of our communities, and that's what I'm striving for in my own small way.'

There was nothing small about the councillor's delivery.

A hall this size, someone like Tench barely needed a microphone in the first place.

'He's in love with his own voice,' Cafferty commented. Rebus knew it was true. It had been the same when he'd stopped to watch Tench deliver his sermons on The Mound. He hadn't shouted to be heard; he'd shouted because the noise confirmed for him his own importance in the world.

'But friends ... comrades ...' Tench continued without seeming to draw breath, 'we're all prone to see ourselves as cogs in the vast political machine. How can we be heard? How can *we* make a difference? Well, think about it for a moment. The cars and buses you used when you travelled here tonight ... remove just one small cog from the engine and the machinery breaks down. Because every single moving part has equal worth – equal importance ... and that's as true in human life as it is with the infernal congestion engine.' He paused long enough to smile at his own pun.

'Preening little prick,' Cafferty muttered to Rebus. 'He couldn't love himself any better if he was double-jointed and giving himself a gam.'

Rebus was powerless to prevent the sudden choking laugh which escaped him. He tried camouflaging it as a cough, but to little avail. Some in the audience had turned in their seats to seek out the commotion's cause. Even Tench had been pulled up short. What he saw from the stage was Morris Gerald Cafferty patting the back of Detective Inspector John Rebus. Rebus knew he'd been recognised, despite the hand he was holding over his mouth and nose. Tench, put off his stride, worked hard to regain the momentum of his speech, but some of his previous forcefulness had evaporated into the night. He handed the microphone to the woman next to him, who emerged from her trance-like state and started reciting in a monotone from the copious notes in front of her.

Cafferty passed in front of Rebus and stepped outside. After a moment, Rebus followed. Cafferty was pacing the car park. Rebus lit a cigarette and bided his time till his nemesis was standing before him.

'I still don't get it,' Rebus admitted, flicking ash from the cigarette.

Cafferty shrugged. 'And you're supposed to be the detective.'

'A clue or two would help.'

Cafferty stretched out his arms. 'This is his territory, Rebus, his little fiefdom. But he's getting itchy, planning to *expand*.'

'You mean Tench?' Rebus narrowed his eyes. 'You're saying he's the one muscling in on your turf?'

'Mr Fire and Brimstone himself.' Cafferty lowered his arms so that his hands slapped his thighs, as if placing a full stop on proceedings.

'I still don't get it.'

Cafferty glared at Rebus. 'The thing is, he sees nothing wrong with shouldering me aside, because he's got right-eousness on *his* side. By controlling the illicit, he makes it a force for good.' Cafferty gave a sigh. 'Sometimes I think that's how half the globe operates. It's not the underworld you should be watching – it's the *over*world. Men like Tench and his ilk.'

'He's a councillor,' Rebus argued. 'I mean, they may take the occasional back-hander ...'

Cafferty was shaking his head. 'He wants *power*, Rebus. He wants *control*. See how much he loves being able to make his speeches? The stronger he is, the more talking he can do – and be listened to.'

'So set some of your thugs on him, make sure he gets the message.'

Cafferty's eyes bored into him. 'That's your best shot, is it?'

Rebus shrugged. 'This is between you and him.'

'I'm owed a favour ...'

'You're owed the square root of bugger all. Good luck to him if he takes you out of the game.' Rebus flicked the remains of the cigarette to the ground and crushed it beneath his heel.

'You sure about that?' Cafferty asked quietly. 'You sure you'd rather have him running the show? Man of the people ... man with political clout? Think he'll be an easier target than me? But then, you're just shy of retirement, so maybe it's Siobhan we should be thinking of. What is it they say?' Cafferty angled his head upwards, as if the words were somewhere up there. '"Better the devil you know ...",' he declared.

Rebus folded his arms. 'You didn't bring me here to show me Gareth Tench,' he said. 'You did it to show *me* to *him* – the two of us side by side, you patting me on the back ... a nice little portrait we must have made. You want him to think I'm in your pocket, and the rest of CID with me.'

Cafferty tried to look hurt by the accusation. 'You overestimate me, Rebus.'

'I doubt that. You could have told me all this back in Arden Street.'

'But then you'd have missed the show.'

'Aye, and so would Councillor Tench. Tell me, how's he going to finance this takeover? And where are the soldiers to back him up?'

Cafferty stretched his arms out again, this time spinning three hundred and sixty degrees. 'He *owns* this whole district – the bad as well as the good.'

'And the money?'

'He'll *talk* his way into the money, Rebus. It's what he does best.'

'I do talk a good game, it's true.' Both men turned to see Gareth Tench standing in the doorway, illuminated from behind. 'And I'm not easily scared, Cafferty – not by you, not by your friends.' Rebus was about to protest, but Tench hadn't finished. 'I'm cleaning up this area, no reason I can't do the same job elsewhere in the city. If your pals in the force won't put you out of business, the community might have to.'

Rebus noted the two thick-set men standing further back in the doorway, either side of Tench. 'Let's go,' he suggested to Cafferty. Last thing he wanted was to step in between Cafferty and a beating.

All the same, he knew he'd have to step in.

His hand was on Cafferty's arm. The gangster shrugged him off. 'I've never fought a battle and lost,' Cafferty warned Tench. 'Think about that before you start.'

'I don't need to do anything,' Tench shot back. 'Your little empire's turning to dust. Time you woke up to the fact. Having trouble recruiting bouncers for your pubs? Can't find tenants for your death-trap flats? Taxi firm short a few drivers?' A smile was spreading across Tench's face. 'You're in the twilight zone, Cafferty. Wake up and smell the coffin ...'

Cafferty made to spring forward. Rebus grabbed him, just as Tench's men pushed past their boss. Rebus turned Cafferty so his own back was facing the door. He gave the gangster a shove towards the Bentley.

'Get in and get going,' he ordered.

'Never lost a battle!' Cafferty was raging, face puce. But he yanked open the door and dumped himself into the driving seat. As Rebus walked around to the passenger side, he looked towards the doorway. Tench was waving a gloating goodbye. Rebus wanted to say something, if only to let Tench know he wasn't Cafferty's man, but the councillor was already turning away, leaving his minions to monitor proceedings.

'I'm going to rip his fucking eyeballs out and make him suck them like gobstoppers,' Cafferty was snarling, flecks of saliva pocking the inside of the windscreen. 'And if he wants concrete fucking proposals, I'll mix the cement myself before I whack him with the shovel – now *that's* "betterment of the community"!'

Cafferty stopped talking as he manoeuvred out of the car park. But his breathing remained fast and noisy. Eventually he turned towards his passenger. 'I swear to God, when I get my hands on that prick ...' His knuckles were white as they wrapped themselves around the steering wheel.

'But if you do say anything,' Rebus intoned, 'which may be used against you as evidence in a court of law ...'

'They'd never convict,' Cafferty roared with a wild laugh. 'Forensics will have to scoop up what's left of him with a teaspoon.'

'But if you do say anything ...' Rebus repeated.

'It started three years back,' Cafferty said, making an effort to control his breathing. 'Gaming licences knocked back, bar applications knocked back ... I was even going to open a cab office on his patch, take a few of the locals off the dole. He made sure the council bounced me out every time.'

'So it's not just that you've finally met someone with the guts to stand up to you?'

Cafferty glanced at Rebus. 'I thought that was *your* job?'

'Maybe it is.'

Eventually Cafferty broke the resulting silence. 'I need a drink,' he said, licking his lips. The corners of his mouth were coated with white flecks.

'Good idea,' Rebus told him. 'Like me, maybe you'll drink to forget ...'

He kept watching Cafferty during the rest of the silent ride back into town. The man had killed and got away with it – probably more times than Rebus knew. He'd fed victims to the hungry pigs on a Borders farm. He'd ruined countless lives, served four jail terms. He'd been a savage since his teenage years, served an apprenticeship as enforcer to the London mob ...

So why the hell was Rebus feeling sorry for him?

'I've got some thirty-year-old malt at the house,' Cafferty was saying. 'Butterscotch and heather and melted butter ...'

'Drop me in Marchmont,' Rebus insisted.

'What about that drink?'

But Rebus shook his head. 'I'm supposed to be renouncing it, remember?'

Cafferty snorted, but said nothing. All the same, Rebus could tell the man wanted him to change his mind. Wanted them to have that drink together, sitting opposite one another as the night circled them on tiptoe.

Cafferty wouldn't insist, though. Insisting would sound like begging.

He wouldn't beg.

Not just yet.

It struck Rebus that what Cafferty feared was a loss of power. Tyrants and politicians alike feared the self-same thing, whether they belonged to the underworld or the overworld. The day would come when no one listened to them any more, their orders ignored, reputation diminished. New challenges, new rivals and predators. Cafferty probably had millions stashed away, but a whole fleet of luxury cars was no substitute for status and respect.

Edinburgh was a small city; easy for one man to exert control over the greater part of it. Tench or Cafferty? Cafferty or Tench?

Rebus couldn't help wondering if he would have to choose.

The overworld.

Everyone from G8 leaders to Pennen and Steelforth. All of them driven by the will to power. A chain of command affecting every person on the planet. Rebus was still thinking about it as he watched the Bentley drive away. But then he became aware of a shadowy figure standing next to his tenement door. He clenched his fists and looked around, in case Jacko had brought his mates. But it wasn't Jacko who stepped forward. It was Hackman.

'Evening, all,' he said.

'I nearly took a swipe at you then,' Rebus replied, relaxing his shoulders. 'How the hell did you find me?'

'Couple of phone calls is all it took. Very helpful, the local plod. Must say though, I wouldn't have thought a street like this was your style.'

'So where am I supposed to live?'

'Dockside conversion,' Hackman stated.

'Is that right?'

'Nice young blonde thing to cook you breakfast at weekends.'

'I only see her at weekends, do I?' Rebus couldn't help smiling.

'That's all the time you can give her. Clean out the old pipes and then it's back to the daily grind.'

'You've got it all worked out. Doesn't explain what you're doing here this time of night.'

'Couple of bits and pieces I've remembered about Trevor Guest.'

'And they're mine for the price of a drink?' Rebus guessed.

Hackman nodded. 'But there's got to be a floor-show, mind.'

'A floor-show?'

'*Birds!*'

'You've got to be joking ...' But Rebus could tell from Hackman's face that he was quite, quite serious.

They hailed a cab on Marchmont Road and headed for Bread Street. The driver gave a little smile into his rearview: two middle-aged men with a few drinks under their belts heading for the fleshpots.

'So tell me,' Rebus said.

'What?' Hackman asked.

'The info on Trevor Guest.'

But Hackman wagged a finger. 'If I tell you now, what's to stop you jumping ship?'

'My word as a gentleman?' Rebus offered. He'd had enough for tonight; no way he was embarking on a lap-dance crawl of Lothian Road. He'd get the gen, then leave Hackman kerbside, point him in the right direction.

'All the hippies are shipping out tomorrow, you know,' the Englishman said. 'Busloads heading for Gleneagles.'

'What about you?'

Hackman shrugged. 'I do what I'm told.'

'Well, I'm telling you to cough up what you know about Guest.'

'Okay, okay ... so long as you promise not to hoof it as soon as the taxi stops.'

'Scout's honour.'

Hackman leaned back in the seat. 'Trevor Guest had a short fuse, made a lot of enemies. Headed south to London once, but it didn't work out. Ripped off by some tart or other ... seemed to take against the fairer sex after that. You said he ended up on some website?'

'BeastWatch.'

'Any idea who posted his details?'

'They did it anonymously.'

'But Trev was predominantly a burglar ... a burglar with a temper – that's why he went into the nick.'

'So?'

'So who put him on the website – and why?'

'You tell me.'

Hackman gave another shrug, gripping on to the hand-rail as the taxi made a sharp turn. 'One more story,' he said, checking he had Rebus's attention. 'When Trev went to London, rumour was that a consignment of tasty drugs went with him – could even have been smack.'

'He was an addict?'

'Occasional user. I don't think he injected ... until the night he died, that is.'

'Did he rip someone off?'

'Could be. See ... I'm wondering if there's a connection you're not getting.'

'And what connection might that be?'

'Small-time villains, maybe getting too big for their boots or ripping off those they shouldn't.'

Rebus was thoughtful. 'The Edinburgh victim worked for our local mobster.'

Hackman clapped his hands together. 'There you are then.'

'I suppose Eddie Isley might have had ...' But he broke off, unconvinced. The taxi was pulling to a stop, the driver telling them it would be a fiver. Rebus realised that they were directly outside the Nook, one of the city's more respectable lap-dance bars. Hackman had jumped out and was paying the cabbie through the passenger-side window – a sure sign he was a visitor: locals paid up from the back seat. Rebus considered his options: stay in the cab, or get out and tell Hackman he was calling it a night.

The door was still open, the Englishman gesturing impatiently.

Rebus got out – just as the door of the Nook burst open, a man staggering from its darkened interior. The two doormen were right behind him.

'I'm telling you, I didn't touch her!' the man was protesting. He was tall, well-dressed and dark-skinned. Rebus seemed to know the blue suit from somewhere ...

'Bloody liar!' one of the doormen yelled, stabbing a finger at the customer.

'She robbed me,' the suit was protesting. 'Her hand was

trying to extract my wallet from my jacket. It was only when I stopped her that she started to complain.'

'Another bloody lie!' the same doorman spat.

Hackman had given Rebus a dig in the ribs. 'You don't half know some classy joints, John.' But he seemed happy enough. The other doorman was talking into his wrist-microphone.

'She was attempting to take my wallet,' the suit kept arguing.

'So she didn't rob you then?'

'Given the chance, she most certainly—'

'Did she rob you? You swore blind a minute ago that she did. And I've got witnesses to prove it.' The doorman's head twitched towards Rebus and Hackman. The customer turned towards them and recognised Rebus straight off.

'My friend, do you see the situation I am in?'

'Sort of,' Rebus was forced to admit. The suit was shaking his hand.

'We met at the hotel, yes? At that delicious lunch hosted by my good friend Richard Pennen.'

'I wasn't at lunch,' Rebus reminded him. 'We chatted in the hallway.'

'You do get around, John,' Hackman chuckled, giving Rebus's ribs another dunt.

'This is a most unfortunate and serious situation,' the suit was saying. 'I felt myself to be thirsty, and entered what I assumed would be a tavern of some description—'

Both doormen gave a snort. 'Yeah,' the angrier of the two said, 'after we'd told you the admission charge ...'

Even Hackman had to laugh at that. But he was cut off by the door swinging open again. This time, it was a woman who emerged. One of the dancers obviously, dressed in bra, G-string and high heels. Her hair was piled atop her head and she was wearing too much make-up.

'Says I mugged him, does he?' she roared. Hackman looked as though he'd found the best ever ringside seat.

'We're handling it,' the angry doorman said, staring daggers at his partner, who'd obviously passed the accusation along.

'He owes me fifty for the dances!' the woman shouted. She had a hand stretched out, ready to collect payment. 'Then he starts pawing me! Right out of order ...'

A marked patrol car cruised past, faces inside staring out. Rebus saw its brake-lights come on, and knew it would be doing a U-turn.

'I am a diplomat,' the suit was declaring. 'I have a right to protection from false allegations.'

'Swallowed a dictionary and all,' Hackman commented, laughing to himself.

'Legal immunity,' the suit went on, 'as a member of the Kenyan delegation ...'

The patrol car had stopped, two officers climbing out, fixing their caps to their heads.

'Seems to be the trouble here?' the driver asked.

'Just escorting this gentleman from the premises,' the no-longer-angry doorman said.

'I was forcibly removed!' the Kenyan protested. 'And almost robbed of my wallet also!'

'Calm down, sir. Let's get this sorted out.' The uniform had turned towards Rebus, aware of movement from the corner of his eye.

Rebus's warrant-card, shoved into his face.

'I want these two taken to the nearest cop-shop,' Rebus stated.

'No need for that,' the doorman began to argue.

'You want to go with them, pal?' Rebus demanded, shutting him up.

'Which cop-shop's that then?' the uniform asked. Rebus stared at him.

'Where you from?'

'Hull.'

Rebus made an exasperated sound. 'West End,' he said.

262

'It's on Torphichen Place.'

The uniform nodded. 'Near Haymarket, yeah?'

'That's the one,' Rebus confirmed.

'Diplomatic immunity,' the Kenyan was stressing. Rebus turned to him.

'There's a necessary procedure,' he explained, trying to find words long enough to satisfy the man.

'You don't want me,' the woman was saying, pointing to her ample breasts. Rebus daren't look at Hackman, fearing he'd be salivating.

'Afraid I do,' Rebus told her, gesturing to the uniforms. Client and dancer were ushered towards the patrol car.

'One in the front, one in the back,' the driver told his partner. The dancer looked at Rebus as she clacked past him on her heels.

'Hang on,' he said, removing his jacket and slipping it over her shoulders. Then he turned to Hackman. 'I need to see to this,' he explained.

'Fancy your chances, eh?' the Englishman leered.

'Don't want a diplomatic incident,' Rebus corrected him. 'Will you be okay?'

'Never better,' Hackman confirmed, slapping Rebus on the back. 'I'm sure my friends here' – making sure the doormen could hear him – 'will waive their entry-fee for an officer of the law.'

'Just one thing, Stan,' Rebus cautioned.

'What's that then?'

'Don't let your hands wander ...'

The CID suite was deserted, no sign of Rat-Arse Reynolds or Shug Davidson. Easy enough to secure two interview rooms. Easy to get a couple of uniforms on overtime to act as babysitters.

'Glad of the business,' one of them said.

First, the dancer. Rebus took her a plastic beaker of tea. 'I even remember how you like it,' he told her. Molly

263

Clark sat with arms folded, still wearing his jacket and not much else. She was shuffling her feet, face twitching.

'Might have let me get changed,' she complained, giving a loud sniff.

'Afraid you'll catch a cold? Don't worry, a car will run you back in five minutes.'

She looked at him, eyes rimmed with kohl, cheeks rouged. 'You're not charging me?'

'What with? Our friend's not going to want to pursue it, trust me.'

'It's *me* should be pursuing *him*!'

'Whatever you say, Molly.' Rebus offered her a cigarette.

'There's a No Smoking sign,' she reminded him.

'So there is,' he agreed, lighting up.

She hesitated another moment. 'Go on then …' Took the cigarette from him, leaned across the table so he could light it for her. He knew her perfume would be clinging to his jacket for weeks. She inhaled and held the smoke deep within her.

'When we came to see you on Sunday,' Rebus began, 'Eric didn't mention how you met. I think I can guess now.'

'Bully for you.' She was examining the cigarette's glowing tip. Her body rocked a little, and Rebus realised she was pumping one knee up and down.

'So he knows what you do for a living?' Rebus asked.

'Is it any business of yours?'

'Not really.'

'Well, then …' Another drag on the cigarette, as if drawing nourishment from it. The smoke billowed into Rebus's face. 'No secrets between Eric and me.'

'Fair enough.'

She finally made eye contact. 'He *was* touching me up. And as for that line about me grabbing his wallet …' She snorted. 'Different culture, same shite.' She calmed a little. 'That's why Eric *means* something.'

Rebus nodded his understanding. 'It's our Kenyan friend who's in trouble, not you,' he assured her.

'Really?' She gave him that wide smile again, same as on Sunday. The whole dreary room seemed to brighten for an instant.

'Eric's a lucky man.'

'You're a lucky man,' Rebus told the Kenyan. Interview Room 2, ten minutes later. The Nook were sending a car for Molly – a car and some clothes. She'd promised to leave Rebus's jacket at the station's front desk.

'My name is Joseph Kamweze and I have diplomatic immunity.'

'Then you won't mind showing me your passport, Joseph.' Rebus held out his hand. 'If you're a diplomat, it'll say so.'

'I do not have it with me.'

'Where are you staying?'

'The Balmoral.'

'Now there's a surprise. Room paid for by Pennen Industries?'

'Mr Richard Pennen is a good friend to my country.'

Rebus leaned back in his chair. 'How's that then?'

'In matters of trade and humanitarian assistance.'

'He sticks microchips into weapons.'

'I do not see the connection.'

'What are you doing in Edinburgh, Joseph?'

'I am part of my nation's trade mission.'

'And what part of your remit took you into the Nook tonight?'

'I was thirsty, Inspector.'

'And maybe a wee bit randy?'

'I am not sure what it is that you are trying to insinuate. I have already told you that I have immunity ...'

'And I couldn't be happier for you. Tell me, do you know a British politician called Ben Webster?'

Kamweze nodded. 'I met him one time in Nairobi, at the High Commission.'

'You've not seen him this trip?'

'I did not have a chance to talk with him the night his life ended.'

Rebus stared at him. 'You were at the Castle?'

'Indeed, yes.'

'You saw Mr Webster there?'

The Kenyan nodded. 'I thought it unnecessary to speak with him on that occasion, as he would be joining us for lunch at Prestonfield House.' Kamweze's face fell. 'But then this great tragedy unfolded before our eyes.'

Rebus tensed. 'How do you mean?'

'Please do not misunderstand. I only say that his fall was a great loss to the international community.'

'You didn't see what happened?'

'No one did. But perhaps the cameras were of some assistance.'

'CCTV?' Rebus felt like slapping himself across the head. The Castle was an army HQ – of course there'd be CCTV.

'We were given a tour of the control room. It was impressively technical, but then terrorism is an everyday threat, is it not, Inspector?'

Rebus didn't answer for a moment.

'What's everyone saying about it?' he eventually asked.

'I'm not sure I understand ...' Kamweze's brow had furrowed.

'The other missions – that little League of Nations I saw you with at Prestonfield – any rumours about Mr Webster?'

The Kenyan shook his head.

'Tell me, does everyone feel as warmly towards Richard Pennen as you seem to?'

'Again, Inspector, I do not think I—' Kamweze broke off and rose hurriedly to his feet, the chair toppling behind him. 'I would like to leave now.'

'Something to hide, Joseph?'

'I feel you have brought me here under false pretences.'

'We could go back to the real ones – start discussing your little one-man delegation and its fact-finding tour of Edinburgh's lap-dancing bars.' Rebus leaned forwards, resting his arms on the table. 'These places have CCTV too, Joseph. They'll have you on tape.'

'Immunity ...'

'I'm not talking about charging you with anything, Joseph. I'm talking about the folks back home. I'm assuming you've got family in Nairobi ... mum and dad, maybe a wife and kids?'

'I want to leave now!' Kamweze slammed a fist down on the table.

'Easy there,' Rebus said, holding up his hands. 'Thought we were having a nice wee chat ...'

'Do you wish a diplomatic incident, Inspector?'

'I'm not sure.' Rebus seemed to ponder the notion. 'Do you?'

'I am outraged!' Another thump on the table and the Kenyan headed for the door. Rebus did nothing to stop him. Instead, he lit a cigarette and lifted his legs on to the table, crossing them at the ankles. Stretched back and stared at the ceiling. Naturally, Steelforth hadn't said anything about CCTV, and Rebus knew he'd have a hell of a time persuading anyone to hand the footage over. It was owned by the garrison and sited within the garrison – strictly out of Rebus's jurisdiction.

Which wouldn't stop him raising the issue ...

A minute passed before there was a knock at the door and a constable appeared from behind it.

'Our African friend says he wants a car back to the Balmoral.'

'Tell him the walk will do him good,' Rebus ordered. 'And warn him about getting thirsty again.'

'Sir?' The constable thinking he must have misheard.

'Just tell him.'

'Yes, sir. Oh, and one more thing ...'

'What?'

'No smoking in here.'

Rebus turned his head and stared the young officer out. When the door had closed, he reached into his trouser pocket for his mobile. Pushed the buttons and waited to be connected.

'Mairie?' he said. 'Got some information you might be able to find a use for ...'

SIDE THREE

No Gods, No Masters

Wednesday 6 July

16

Most of the G8 leaders touched down at Prestwick Airport, south-west of Glasgow. In all, nearly one hundred and fifty aircraft would land in the course of the day. The leaders, their spouses and their closest personnel would then be transferred to Gleneagles by helicopter, while fleets of chauffeured cars conveyed other members of the various delegations to their eventual destinations. George Bush's sniffer dog had its own car. Today was Bush's fifty-ninth birthday. Jack McConnell, First Minister of the Scottish Parliament, was on the tarmac to greet the world leaders. There were no visible protests or disruptions.

Not at Prestwick.

But in Stirling, morning TV news showed masked protesters hitting out at cars and vans, smashing the windows of a Burger King, blocking the A9, attacking petrol stations. In Edinburgh, demonstrators halted all traffic on Queensferry Road. Lothian Road was lined with police vans, a chain of uniformed officers protecting the Sheraton Hotel and its several hundred delegates. Police horses paraded down streets usually busy with the morning rush-hour, but today devoid of traffic. Buses queued the length of Waterloo Place, ready to convey marchers north to Auchterarder. But there were mixed signals, no one very sure that the official route had been sanctioned. The march was off, then on, then off again. Police ordered the bus drivers not to move their vehicles until the situation could be verified one way or the other.

And it was raining; looked like the 'Final Push' concert that evening might be a washout. The musicians and celebrities were at Murrayfield stadium, busy with sound-checks and rehearsals. Bob Geldof was at the Balmoral Hotel, but preparing to visit Gleneagles with his friend Bono. Always supposing the various demos would let them through. The Queen was on her way north too, and would host a dinner for the delegates.

The news journalists sounded breathless, wired on doses of caffeine. Siobhan, having spent a night in her car, was getting by on watery coffee from a local baker's. The other customers had been more interested in the events unfolding on the wall-mounted TV set behind the counter.

'That's Bannockburn,' one of them had said. 'And there's Springkerse. They're everywhere!'

'Circle the wagons,' her friend had advised, to a few smiles. The protesters had left Camp Horizon as early as two in the morning, literally catching the police napping.

'Can't understand how those bloody politicians can tell us this is good for Scotland,' a man in painter's overalls had muttered, waiting for his bacon roll to arrive. 'I've got jobs in Dunblane and Crieff today. Christ knows how I'm supposed to get there ...'

Back in her car, the heater soon warmed Siobhan up, though her spine remained creaky, her neck tight. She'd stayed in Stirling because going home would have meant coming back this morning, with the same security rigmarole – maybe even worse. She washed down two aspirin and headed for the A9. She hadn't made much progress along the dual carriageway when the flashers on a car ahead told her both lanes were at a dead stop. Drivers had emerged from their vehicles to shout at the men and women in clown costumes who were lying in the road, some chained to the central reservation's crash-barriers. Police were chasing other garish figures through the adjoining fields. Siobhan parked on the hard shoulder and walked to the head of the queue, where she showed her ID to the officer in charge.

'I'm supposed to be in Auchterarder,' she told him. He waved his short black baton in the direction of a police motorcycle.

'If Archie's got a spare helmet, he can have you there in two shakes.'

Archie produced the necessary helmet. 'You're going to be bloody cold on the back, mind,' he warned.

'I'll just have to snuggle up then, won't I?'

But as he accelerated away, the word 'snuggle' suddenly didn't fit. Siobhan was clinging to him for dear life. There was an earpiece inside her helmet, allowing her to listen in on messages from Operation Sorbus. Around five thousand demonstrators were descending on Auchterarder, preparing to march past the gates of the hotel. Futile, Siobhan knew: they'd still be hundreds of yards from the main building, their slogans evaporating on the wind. Inside Gleneagles, the dignitaries would have no scent of any march, any large-scale dissent. Protesters were heading across country from all directions, but the officers on the other side of the security cordon were prepared. Leaving Stirling, Siobhan had noticed fresh graffiti on a fast-food outlet: *10,000 Pharaohs, Six Billion Slaves*. She was still trying to work out who was meant to be who ...

Archie braked suddenly, tipping her forward so she could see over his shoulder the scene unfolding ahead.

Riot shields, dog handlers, mounted police.

A twin-engined Chinook helicopter scything the air overhead.

Flames licking from an American flag.

A sit-down protest stretching the full width of the carriageway. As officers started breaking it up, Archie gunned the bike towards the gap and squeezed through. If Siobhan's knuckles hadn't been rigid and numb with cold, she might have eased her grip on him long enough to offer a pat on the back. The earpiece was telling her that Stirling railway station might reopen shortly, but anarchists could be using the line as a shortcut to Gleneagles. She remembered that the hotel boasted its own railway station, doubted anyone would be using it today. There was better news from Edinburgh, where torrential rain had dampened the demonstrators' spirits.

Archie turned his head towards her. 'Scottish weather!' he yelled. 'What would we do without it?'

The Forth Road Bridge was operating with 'minimal disruption' and early road blocks on Quality Street and Corstorphine Road had been cleared. Archie slowed to negotiate another blockade, Siobhan taking the opportunity to wipe drizzle from her visor with the sleeve of her jacket. As they signalled to turn off the dual carriageway, another, smaller helicopter seemed to be following their progress. Archie brought his bike to a stop.

'End of the line,' he said. They hadn't quite reached the town's boundary, but she could see he was right. Ahead of them, past a police cordon, flew a sea of flags and banners. Chants, whistles and jeers.

Bush, Blair, CIA, how many kids did you kill today? Same chant she'd heard at the Naming of the Dead.

George Bush, we know you, your daddy was a killer, too. Okay, so that was a new one ...

Siobhan eased herself from the pillion, handed over the helmet and thanked Archie. He grinned at her.

'Won't get too many days as exciting as this,' he said, turning the bike around. Speeding off, he gave her a wave. Siobhan waved back, some of the feeling returning to her fingers. A red-faced cop bounded up to her. She already had her ID open.

'Which only makes you more of a bloody idiot,' he barked. 'You look like one of them.' He stabbed a finger in the direction of the stalled demo. 'They see you behind our lines, they'll think that's where *they* belong, too. So either make yourself scarce or get kitted up.'

'You're forgetting,' she told him, 'there *is* a third way.' And with a smile she walked up to the police line, squeezed between two of the black-clad figures and ducked under their riot shields. She was now in the front line of demonstrators. The red-faced officer looked aghast.

'Show your badges!' a protester was calling out to the police rank. Siobhan stared at the cop immediately in front of her. The thing he was wearing looked almost like a boilersuit. The letters ZH were painted in white on his helmet above the visor. She tried to remember if any of the squad from Princes Street Gardens boasted the same insignia. All she could remember was XS.

Police excess.

Sweat was running down both sides of the officer's face, but he seemed composed. Orders and encouragement were being called down the police line:

'Keep it tight!'

'Easy, lads.'

'Move it back!'

There was an element of agreed orchestration to the pushing on both sides. One of the demonstrators seemed to be in control, calling out that the march was official and the police were now in breach of all agreements. He could not, he said, be responsible for the consequences. Throughout, he held a mobile phone to his ear, while news photographers stood on tiptoe, cameras held aloft, to capture some of the drama.

Siobhan started back-pedalling, then shuffled sideways until she was on the edge of proceedings. From this vantage point she started scanning the crowd for any sign of Santal. There was a teenager next to her with bad teeth and a shaved head. When he started yelling abuse, the accent sounded local. His jacket flapped open at one point, and Siobhan caught a glimpse of something tucked into his waistband.

Something not unlike a knife.

He had his mobile phone out, using it to capture snippets of video, sending them to his mates. Siobhan looked around. No way she could alert the police officers. If they waded in to arrest him, all hell would break loose. Instead, she squeezed in behind him, waiting for the right moment. When a chant broke out, hands rose into the air and she seized her chance. Grabbed his arm and wrenched it around his back, pressing forward so he was sent down on to his knees. Her free hand went to his waist, removed the knife, then pushed him hard so he fell on all fours. She moved backwards briskly through the crowd, tossing the knife over a low wall into shrubbery. Melted into the crowd and raised her own arms into the air, clapping along. His face was purple with anger as he elbowed his way through the throng in front of her, seeking out his attacker.

He wasn't going to find her.

Siobhan almost allowed herself a smile, but knew her own search might well prove every bit as fruitless as his. And meantime she was in the middle of a demo, a demo which could at any moment turn into a riot.

I'd kill for a Starbucks latte, she thought.

Wrong place, and very definitely the wrong time ...

Mairie was in the foyer of the Balmoral Hotel. The lift door opened and she saw the man in the blue silk suit appear. She got up from her chair, and he walked towards her, holding out his hand.

'Mr Kamweze?' she asked.

He gave a bow of confirmation, and she returned his handshake.

'Good of you to see me at short notice,' Mairie said, trying not to sound too gushing. Her phone call had been just that: the cub reporter, overawed to be talking to such a senior figure in African politics ... and could he *possibly* spare five minutes to help with a profile she was doing?

The pose was no longer necessary: he was right there in front of her. All the same, she didn't want him bolting just yet.

'Tea?' he suggested, leading the way to the Palm Court.

'I love your suit,' she said as he drew out her chair for her. She smoothed her skirt beneath her as she sat. Joseph Kamweze seemed to enjoy the view.

'Thank you,' he said, sliding on to the banquette opposite her.

'Is it designer?'

'Purchased in Singapore, on my way back from a delegation to Canberra. Really rather inexpensive ...' He leaned towards her conspiratorially. 'But let's keep that to ourselves.' He gave a huge grin, showing one gold tooth at the back of his mouth.

'Well, I want to thank you again for seeing me.' Mairie was reaching into her bag for notebook and pen. She also had a little digital recorder, and asked him if he would mind.

'That will be dependent on your questions,' he said with another grin. The waitress arrived and he ordered Lapsang Souchong for both of them. Mairie hated the stuff but kept her mouth shut.

'You must let me pay,' she told him. He waved the offer aside.

'It is of no consequence.'

Mairie raised an eyebrow. She was still busying herself with the tools of her trade when she asked her next question.

'Your trip's being funded by Pennen Industries?'

The grin disappeared; the eyes hardened. 'I beg your pardon?'

She tried for a look of unsullied naivety. 'Just wondered who was paying for your stay here.'

'What is it you want?' The voice was chilled. His hands

brushed the edge of the table, the fingertips running along it.

Mairie made a show of consulting her notes. 'You are part of the Kenyan trade delegation, Mr Kamweze. What exactly is it that you're looking for from the G8?' She checked that the recorder was running and placed it on the table between them. Joseph Kamweze seemed thrown by the sheer ordinariness of the question.

'Debt relief is crucial to Africa's rebirth,' he recited. 'Chancellor Brown has indicated that some of Kenya's neighbours ...' He broke off, unable to keep going. 'Why are you here? Is Henderson even your real name? I'm a fool for not asking to see your identification.'

'I've got it right here.' Mairie made to rummage through her bag.

'Why did you mention Richard Pennen?' Kamwaze interrupted.

She blinked at him. 'I didn't.'

'Liar.'

'I *did* mention Pennen Industries, but that's a company, not an individual.'

'You were with the policeman at Prestonfield House.' It sounded like a statement, though he could have been guessing. Either way, she didn't deny it.

'I think you should go now,' he stated.

'Are you sure about that?' Her own voice had hardened, and she returned his stare. 'Because if you walk away from here, I'm going to splash a photo of you across the whole front page of my newspaper.'

'You are being ridiculous.'

'It's a bit grainy, and we'll need to blow it up, meaning it might be on the fuzzy side, too. But it will show a lap-dancer cavorting in front of you, Mr Kamweze. You'll have your hands on your knees and a big smile on your face as you stare at her naked chest. Her name's Molly and she works at the Nook on Bread Street. I took possession of the CCTV tape this morning.' Lies, all lies, but she loved the effect they were having on him. His fingernails were digging into the tabletop. His close-cropped hair glistened with sweat.

'You were then questioned at a police station, Mr Kamweze. I dare say there's footage of *that* little expedition, too.'

'What is it you want from me?' he hissed. But he had to compose himself as the tea-tray arrived, and with it some shortbread biscuits. Mairie bit into one: no breakfast this morning. The tea smelled like oven-baked seaweed, and she pushed her cup aside after the waitress had poured. The Kenyan did the same with his.

'Not thirsty?' she asked, and couldn't help smiling.

'The detective told you,' Kamweze realised. 'He, too, threatened me like this.'

'Thing is, *he* can't prosecute. Me, on the other hand ... Well, unless you give me a good reason to spike a front-page exclusive ...' She could see he hadn't yet taken the bait. 'A front page which will be seen around the world. How long till the press in your own country picks up the story and runs with it? How long till your government masters get to hear of it? Your neighbours, friends ...'

'Enough,' he growled. His eyes were focused on the table. It was highly polished, throwing his own reflection back at him. 'Enough,' he repeated, and his tone told her he was beaten. She bit into another of the biscuits. 'What do you want?'

'Not much really,' she assured him. 'Just everything you can tell me about Mr Richard Pennen.'

'Am I to be your Deep Throat, Miss Henderson?'

'If the thought excites you,' she offered.

Thinking to herself: but really, you're just another dupe who got caught ... another flawed civil servant ...

Another grass ...

*

His second funeral in a week.

He'd crawled out of the city – knock-on effect from earlier. At the Forth Bridge, Fife Constabulary were pulling over lorries and vans, checking their potential as barricades. Once over the bridge, however, traffic was fine. He was early as a result. Drove into the centre of Dundee, parked by the waterfront and smoked a cigarette with the radio tuned to rolling news. Funny, the English stations were on about London's Olympic bid; hardly a mention of Edinburgh. Tony Blair was jetting back from Singapore. Rebus pondered whether he collected Air Miles …

The Scottish news had picked up on Mairie's story: everyone was calling him the 'G8 Killer'. Chief Constable James Corbyn was making no public statements on the subject; SO12 were stressing that there was no danger to the leaders gathering at Gleneagles.

Two funerals inside a week. Rebus wondered if one reason why he was working so hard was so he wouldn't have time to think too much about Mickey. He'd brought a CD of *Quadrophenia* with him, played some of it on the drive north, Daltrey rasping the insistent question: *Can you see the real me?* He had the photos on the passenger seat: Edinburgh Castle, dinner jackets and bow ties. Ben Webster with about two hours to live, looking no different from anyone else. But then suicides didn't wear signs around their necks. Neither did serial killers, gangsters, bent politicians. Beneath all the official portraits was Mungo's close-up of Santal and her camera. Rebus studied it for a moment before placing it on top. Then he started the car and headed for the crem.

Place was packed. Family and friends, plus representatives from all the political parties. Labour MSPs too. The media kept their distance, huddled at the crematorium gates. Probably the office juniors, sour-faced with the knowledge that their elders and betters were busy at the G8, capturing Thursday's headlines and front pages. Rebus hung back as the real guests were ushered indoors. Some of them looked at him quizzically, thinking it unlikely he'd had any connection to the MP, taking him for some kind of vulture, preying on the grief of strangers.

Maybe they were right at that.

A hotel in Broughty Ferry was providing refreshments afterwards. 'The family,' the reverend was telling the assembly, 'have asked me to say that you'll all be most welcome.' But his eyes told another story: close family and bosom friends only, please. Quite right too: Rebus doubted any hotel in 'the Ferry' could cope with a crowd this size.

He was seated in the back row. The reverend had asked one of Ben Webster's colleagues to step up and say a few words. Sounded much like the eulogy at Mickey's funeral: a good man ... much missed by those who knew him, and many did ... devoted to his family ... well liked in the community. Rebus reckoned he'd given it long enough. There was no sign of Stacey. He hadn't really thought much about her since that meeting outside the mortuary. He guessed she'd gone back to London, or else was clearing out her brother's home, dealing with the banks and insurers and such like.

But to miss the funeral ...

There had been over a week between Mickey's death and his cremation. And Ben Webster? Not even five full days. Could the haste be classed as indecent? Stacey Webster's decision, or someone else's? Outside in the car park, he lit another cigarette and gave it five more minutes. Then he unlocked the driver's side and got in.

Can you see the real me ...

'Oh yes,' he said quietly, turning the ignition.

Mayhem in Auchterarder.

The rumour had gone around that Bush's helicopter was on its way. Siobhan had checked her watch, knowing he wasn't due to arrive at Prestwick till mid-afternoon.

283

Every chopper that came over, the crowd booed and bayed. They'd streamed down lanes and through fields, clambered over walls into people's gardens. One aim in mind: get to the cordon. Get *past* the cordon. That would be the real victory; no matter if they were still half a mile from the actual hotel. They would be on the Gleneagles estate. They would have beaten the police. She saw a few members of the Clown Army, and two protesters dressed in plus fours and carrying golf bags: the People's Golfing Association, whose mission was to play a hole on the hallowed championship course. She had heard American accents, Spanish voices, Germans. She had watched a huddle of black-clad, face-muffled anarchists planning their next move. An airship droning overhead, gathering surveillance ...

But no Santal.

Back on Auchterarder's main street, news had arrived that the Edinburgh contingent were being prevented from leaving the city.

'So they're marching there instead,' someone explained gleefully. 'Bully-boys are going to be stretched to breaking.'

Siobhan doubted it. All the same, she tried her parents' mobile. Her father answered, said they'd been sitting on the bus for hours, and were still there.

'Promise me you won't join any march,' Siobhan implored.

'Promise,' her father said. Then he put his wife on so Siobhan could hear the same pledge from her. As she ended the call, Siobhan suddenly felt an utter idiot. What was she doing here when she could be with her parents? Another march meant more riot cops; could be her mother would recognise her attacker, or something might nudge a nugget of remembrance to the surface.

She cursed herself quietly, then turned and was face to face with her quarry.

'Santal,' she said. The young woman lowered her camera.

'What are you doing here?' Santal asked.

'Surprised?'

'Just a little, yes. Are your parents …?'

'They're stranded in Edinburgh. I see your lisp's improved.'

'What?'

'Monday in the Gardens,' Siobhan went on, 'you were busy with your little camera. Only thing is, you weren't zeroing in on the cops. Why is that?'

'I'm not sure I know what you're getting at.' But Santal glanced to left and right, as if afraid they would be overheard.

'Reason you didn't want to show me any of your photos is that they would tell me something.'

'Like what?' She sounded neither scared nor wary, but genuinely curious.

'They'd tell me you were interested in your fellow rabble-rousers rather than the forces of law and order.'

'So?'

'So I got wondering why that might be. Should have come to me earlier. Everyone said so, after all – at the Niddrie camp and then again in Stirling.' Siobhan had taken a step closer, the two women nose to nose. She leaned in towards Santal's ear. 'You're undercover,' she whispered. Then she stood back, as if admiring the young woman's get-up. 'The earrings and piercings … mostly fake?' she guessed. 'Temporary tattoos, and …' staring at the coils of hair, 'a nicely-made wig. Why you bothered with the lisp, I've no idea – maybe to help you retain a sense of your own identity.' She paused. 'How am I doing?'

Santal just rolled her eyes. A phone was ringing, and she searched her pockets, bringing out two. The screen on one was lit up. She studied it, then stared over Siobhan's right shoulder. 'Gang's all here,' she said. Siobhan wasn't sure what she meant. Oldest trick in the book, but she turned and looked anyway.

John Rebus, standing there with a phone in one hand and what looked like a business card in the other.

'I'm not sure of the etiquette,' he commented, coming closer. 'If I light up something that's a hundred per cent tobacco, does that make me a slave to the evil empire?' He shrugged and brought out the packet of cigarettes anyway.

'Santal here is a plant,' Siobhan explained to him.

'This just might not be the safest place to announce that fact,' Santal hissed.

'Tell me something I don't know,' Siobhan snorted.

'I think I can oblige,' Rebus said. But his eyes were on Santal. 'Beyond the call of duty,' he told her, 'giving a body-swerve to your own brother's funeral.'

She glared at him. 'You were there?'

He nodded. 'I have to admit, though, I stared and stared at the photo of "Santal", and it still took an age to dawn on me.'

'I'll take that as a compliment.'

'You should.'

'I wanted to be there, you know.'

'What sort of excuse did you give?'

Only at this point did Siobhan butt in. 'You're Ben Webster's sister?'

'The penny drops,' Rebus commented. 'DS Clarke, meet Stacey Webster.' Rebus's eyes were still on Stacey. 'But I'm guessing we should keep calling you Santal?'

'Bit late for that now,' Stacey replied. As if on cue, a young man with a red bandanna around his forehead started towards them.

'Everything cool here?'

'Just catching up with an old friend,' Rebus warned him.

'You look like pigs to me.' His eyes shifting between Rebus and Siobhan.

'Hey, I can handle it.' Santal was back in character: the strong woman, able to fight her own battles. She stared the young man down.

'If you're sure ...' He was already retreating. As she turned back towards Rebus and Siobhan, she became Stacey again.

'You can't stay here,' she stated. 'I'm due to be relieved in an hour – we can talk then.'

'Where?'

She considered for a moment. 'Inside the perimeter. There's a field behind the hotel, that's where the drivers hang out. Wait for me there.'

Siobhan looked at the crowds surrounding them. 'And how exactly do we *get* there?'

Stacey offered a sour smile. 'Show some initiative.'

'I think,' Rebus explained, 'she's telling us to get ourselves arrested.'

17

It took Rebus a good ten minutes to push his way to the front of the throng, Siobhan tucking herself in behind him. With his body pressed to a scratched and scrawled riot shield, Rebus palmed his ID against the see-through reinforced plastic, level with the cop's eye-line.

'Get us out of here,' he mouthed. The cop wasn't falling for it. Called out instead for his boss to decide. The red-faced officer appeared over the cop's shoulder, recognised Siobhan straight off. She was trying to look suitably chastened.

The officer gave a sniff, then an order. The cordon of shields opened a fraction, and hands hauled at Rebus and Siobhan. The noise level rose perceptibly on the other side of the line.

'Show them your warrant cards,' the officer ordered. Rebus and Siobhan were happy to oblige. The officer held a loud-hailer in front of him and let the crowd know no arrests had been made. When he identified Rebus and Siobhan as police detectives, a huge jeer went up. All the same, the situation seemed to be easing.

'I should put you on report for that little escapade,' he told Siobhan.

'We're Murder Squad,' Rebus lied fluently. 'There was someone we needed to talk to – what else could we do?'

The officer stared at him, but suddenly found himself with more pressing concerns. One of his men had fallen over, and the protesters were aiming to exploit this breach in the barricade. He barked out orders on his loud-hailer, and Rebus gestured to Siobhan that maybe they should make themselves scarce.

Van doors were opening, more cops spilling out to provide back-up on the front line. A medic asked Siobhan if she was okay.

'I'm not injured,' she told him. A small helicopter was sitting on the roadway, rotor-blades turning. Rebus got into a crouch and went to talk to the pilot, then waved Siobhan across.

'He can take us to the field.'

The pilot was nodding from behind mirrored sunglasses. 'Not a problem,' he called out in an American accent. Thirty seconds later they were installed, and the machine was rising into the air, whipping up dust and litter below it. Rebus whistled a bit of Wagner – a nod to *Apocalypse Now* – but Siobhan ignored him. Hard to hear anything, which didn't stop her asking Rebus what he'd told the pilot. She read his lips as he replied:

Murder Squad.

The hotel was a mile to the south. From the sky, it was easy to make out the security fence and the watch-towers. Thousands of acres of deserted hillside, and pockets of demonstrators being corralled by black uniforms.

'I'm not allowed to go near the hotel itself,' the pilot was yelling. 'A missile would have us down if I did.'

He sounded serious, and took a wide arc around the hotel's perimeter. There were lots of temporary structures, probably to shelter the world's media. Satellite dishes on the tops of anonymous-looking vans. Television, or maybe the secret service. Rebus could make out a track which led from a large white canopy towards the perimeter. The field had been reduced to stubble, and someone had spray-painted a giant letter H to let the chopper know where to land. Their flight had taken only a couple of minutes. Rebus shook the pilot's hand and jumped out, Siobhan following.

'My day for travelling in style,' she mused. 'A motorbike brought me up the A9.'

'Siege mentality,' Rebus explained. 'This week, it's us and them as far as this lot are concerned.'

There was a soldier approaching, dressed in combat fatigues and toting a sub-machine gun. He looked far from pleased at their arrival. Both showed their ID, but this was not enough for the soldier. Rebus noted that there was no insignia on his uniform, nothing to identify his nationality, or which branch of the armed services he belonged to. He insisted on taking their warrant cards from them.

'Wait right there,' he ordered, pointing to where they were standing. As he turned away, Rebus did a little soft-shoe shuffle and gave Siobhan a wink. The soldier had disappeared into a huge caravan. Another armed soldier guarded its door.

'I get the feeling we're not in Kansas any more,' Rebus offered.

'Does that make me Toto?'

'Let's see what's over there,' Rebus suggested, heading for the canopy. Its roof was a fixed structure of plastic sections, held up by a series of poles. Beneath it sat rows of limousines. Liveried drivers shared cigarettes and stories. Strangest of all, a chef, dressed in white jacket and check trousers, and with a toque perched on his head, was cooking what appeared to be omelettes. He stood behind a sort of gantry, a large red bottle of Calor gas by his side. The food was being dished out on proper plates, with silver cutlery. Tables had been set up for the drivers' use.

'I heard about this when I was up here with the DCI,' Siobhan said. 'Hotel staff are using a back route into the compound, leaving their vehicles in the next field over.'

'I'm assuming they've all been vetted,' Rebus said, 'which is what's happening to us right now.' He glanced towards the caravan, then nodded a greeting to one group of drivers. 'Omelettes all right, lads?' he asked, receiving replies in the affirmative. The chef was awaiting fresh orders.

'One with everything,' Rebus told him, turning towards Siobhan.

'Same,' she said.

The chef got busy with his little plastic containers of cubed ham, sliced mushrooms, chopped peppers. Rebus picked up a knife and fork while he was waiting.

'Bit of a change for you,' he said to the chef. The man just smiled. 'All mod cons, though,' Rebus went on, sounding impressed. 'Chemical toilets, hot food, a bit of shelter for when it rains ...'

'Half the cars have got tellies,' one of the drivers informed him. 'Signal's not up to much, mind.'

'It's a hard life,' Rebus commiserated. 'Ever allowed inside the caravans?'

The drivers shook their heads. 'They're choc-a-bloc with gizmos,' one man offered. 'I caught a glimpse. Computers and stuff.'

'That aerial on the roof probably isn't for *Coronation Street* then,' Rebus said, pointing. The drivers laughed, just as a door opened and the soldier reappeared. He seemed nonplussed that Rebus and Siobhan were no longer where he'd left them. As he marched towards them, Rebus accepted his omelette from the chef and scooped up a mouthful. He was praising the food as the soldier halted in front of him.

'Want some?' Rebus offered, holding out his fork.

'It's an earful you'll be getting,' the soldier countered. Rebus turned towards Siobhan.

'Pretty good comeback,' she told him, taking her own plate from the chef.

'DS Clarke is an expert,' Rebus informed the soldier. 'We'll just finish our grub, then nip into one of the Mercs to watch *Columbo* ...'

'I'm keeping hold of your warrant cards,' the soldier said. 'For verification purposes.'

'Looks like we're stuck here then.'

'Which channel's *Columbo* on?' one of the drivers asked. 'I like that programme.'

'It'll be in the TV pages,' a colleague offered.

The soldier's head jerked upwards, chin jutting as he watched a helicopter approaching. It was low and deafening. The soldier stepped out from under the canopy to get a better view.

'You have got to be kidding,' Rebus said as the man stiffly saluted the underside of the machine.

'Does it every time,' one of the drivers yelled. Another asked if it might be Bush arriving. Watches were checked. The chef was covering his ingredients, in case flying debris from the down draught landed in them.

'He's due around now,' someone surmised.

'I brought Boki in from Prestwick,' another added, going on to explain that this was the name of the President's sniffer dog.

The helicopter had disappeared over a line of trees. They could hear it coming in to land.

'What do the wives do,' Siobhan asked, 'while the menfolk are arm-wrestling?'

'We can take them on a scenic tour ...'

'Or shopping.'

'Or museums and galleries.'

'Whatever they want, that's what they get. Even if it means shutting roads or clearing the public out of a shop. But they're also ferrying in some arty types from Edinburgh – writers and painters – to pass the time.'

'And Bono, of course,' another driver added. 'Him and Geldof are doing their glad-handing bit later today.'

'Speaking of which ...' Siobhan glanced at the time display on her mobile. 'I've got the offer of a Final Push ticket.'

'Who from?' Rebus asked, knowing she'd had no luck in the public draw.

'One of the guards in Niddrie. Think we'll be home in time?'

He just shrugged. 'Oh,' he said, 'something I meant to tell you ...'

'What?'

'I've co-opted Ellen Wylie on to the team.'

Siobhan's look became a glare.

'She knows more about BeastWatch than we do,' Rebus ploughed on, failing to make eye contact.

'Yes,' Siobhan said, 'a damned sight *too* much.'

'Meaning what?'

'Meaning she's too close to it, John. Think what a defence lawyer would do to her in court!' Siobhan was failing to keep her voice down. 'You didn't think to ask me? I'm the one whose head's on the block if this all falls apart!'

'She's just doing admin,' Rebus said, knowing himself how pathetic this sounded. He was saved by the soldier, striding back towards them.

'I need you to state your business,' the man announced crisply.

'Well, I'm in the CID business,' Rebus replied, 'as is my colleague here. We've been told to meet someone ... and this is where it's happening.'

'Which person? Whose orders?'

Rebus tapped the side of his nose. 'Hush-hush,' he said in an undertone. The drivers had returned to their own conversation, debating which stars they might be chauffeuring to the Scottish Open on Saturday.

'Not me,' one of them boasted. 'I'm doing the run between Glasgow and T in the Park ...'

'You're based in Edinburgh, Inspector,' the soldier was saying. 'This is way out of your jurisdiction.'

'We're investigating a murder,' Rebus hit back.

'Three murders, actually,' Siobhan corrected him.

'And that means no boundaries,' Rebus concluded.

'Except,' the soldier countered, rising on to his toes, 'you've been ordered to put your inquiry on ice.' He seemed to like the effect his words had on Siobhan in particular.

'Okay, so you made a phone call,' Rebus told him, not about to be impressed.

'Your Chief Constable wasn't very happy.' The soldier was smiling with his eyes. 'And neither was he ...' Rebus followed the direction of his gaze. A Land Rover was bumping its way towards them. The passenger-side window was wide open, Steelforth's head leaning out from it as though he was straining at some leash.

'Oh, crap,' Siobhan muttered.

'Chin up,' Rebus advised her, 'shoulders back.' He was rewarded with another withering look.

The car had screeched to a halt, Steelforth spilling out. 'Do you know,' he was yelling, 'how many months of training and preparation, weeks of deep cover surveillance ... do you know how much of that you've just blown to smithereens?'

'Not sure I follow you,' Rebus answered blithely, handing his empty plate back to the chef.

'I think he means Santal,' Siobhan said.

Steelforth glared at her. 'Of course I do!'

'She's one of yours?' Rebus asked, then he nodded to himself. 'Stands to reason. Send her to the campsite at Niddrie, get her taking photos of all those protesters. Compiling a nice little portfolio for future use ... So valuable to you, in fact, that you couldn't even spare her for her own brother's funeral.'

'*Her* decision, Rebus,' Steelforth snapped.

'Two o'clock *Columbo* started,' one of the drivers said.

Steelforth was not to be deflected. 'A surveillance operation like that, often they hardly get off the ground before the cover's blown. *Months* she'd been in place.'

Rebus picked up on that use of the past tense, and Steelforth confirmed it with a nod.

'How many people,' he asked, 'do you think saw you with her today? How many clocked you as CID? Either they'll start to mistrust her, or they'll feed her rubbish in the hope that we'll bite.'

'If she'd trusted us in the first place—' Siobhan was cut off by a harsh burst of laughter from Steelforth.

'*Trusted* you?' He laughed again, leaning forward with the effort. 'My God, that's a good one.'

'Should have been here earlier,' Siobhan told him. 'Our soldier friend's comeback was better.'

'And by the way,' Rebus said, 'I wanted to thank you for putting me in a cell overnight.'

'I can't help it if officers decide to use their own initiative – or if your own boss won't answer a phone call.'

'They were real cops then?' Rebus asked. Steelforth rested his hands on his waist, elbows jutting. He stared at the ground, then back up at Rebus and Siobhan.

'You'll be put on suspension, of course.'

'We don't work for you.'

'This week, *everyone* works for me.' He turned his attention to Siobhan. 'And you won't be seeing DS Webster again.'

'She has evidence ...'

'Evidence of what? That your mother got hit by a baton during a riot? It's up to *her* if she wants to make a complaint – have you even asked her?'

'I ...' Siobhan hesitated.

'No, you just tore off on this little crusade. DS Webster's being sent back home – your fault, not mine.'

'Speaking of evidence,' Rebus said, 'whatever happened to those CCTV tapes?'

Steelforth frowned. 'Tapes?' he echoed.

'The operations room at Edinburgh Castle ... cameras trained on the ramparts ...'

'We've been through this a dozen times,' Steelforth growled. 'Nobody saw *anything*.'

'So it's okay for me to watch the tapes?'

'If you can find any, be my guest.'

'They've been wiped?' Rebus guessed. Steelforth didn't bother replying. 'This suspension of ours,' Rebus went on, 'you forgot to add "pending an inquiry". I'm guessing that's because there won't be one.'

Steelforth shrugged. 'Up to the pair of you.'

'Dependent on our conduct? Like not pushing for the CCTV to be made available?'

Steelforth shrugged again. 'You can survive this – but just barely. I can make you look like heroes or villains ...' The radio clipped to Steelforth's belt crackled into life. Report from one of the watch-towers: security fence breached. Steelforth held the radio to his mouth and ordered a Chinook's worth of reinforcements, then strode back towards the Land Rover. One of the chauffeurs intercepted him.

'Wanted to introduce myself, Commander. Name's Steve and I'll be driving you to the Open—'

Steelforth snarled some sort of oath, stopping Steve dead. The other drivers started joking that he wouldn't be getting much of a tip this weekend. Steelforth's Land Rover meantime was already revving its engine.

'Not even a farewell kiss?' Rebus called out, offering a wave of his hand. Siobhan stared at him.

'You've got retirement to look forward to – some of us were hoping for a career.'

'You see what he's like, Shiv: moment this is all over, we'll have fallen off his radar.' Rebus kept waving as the vehicle roared away. The soldier was standing in front of them, holding out their warrant cards.

'Off you go now,' he snapped.

'Where exactly?' Siobhan asked.

'Or, more to the point, how?' Rebus added.

One of the drivers cleared his throat and stretched out an arm, drawing attention to the array of luxury cars. 'I just got a text – one of the suits has to get back to Glasgow. I could drop you off somewhere ...'

Siobhan and Rebus shared a look. Siobhan then smiled at the driver and nodded towards the cars.

'Do we get to choose?' she asked.

They ended up sitting in the back of a six-litre Audi A8, four hundred miles on its clock, most of them added since first thing that morning. Pungent aroma of new leather and the bright gleam of chrome. Siobhan asked if the TV was working. Rebus gave her a look.

'Just wondering if London got the Olympics,' she explained.

Their IDs were scrutinised at three separate checkpoints between the field and the hotel grounds.

'We don't go near the hotel itself,' the driver said. 'I'll pick up the suit from the meet 'n' greet next to the media centre.' Both were situated near the hotel's main car park. Rebus saw that no one was playing the golf course. Pitch-and-putt and croquet lawns – both empty, except for dapper, slow-paced security men.

'Hard to believe there's anything happening,' Siobhan commented. Her voice was just above a whisper; something about the place. Rebus felt it too. You didn't want to draw attention to yourself.

'Just be a sec,' the driver said, stopping the car. He pulled on his chauffeur's peaked cap as he exited. Rebus decided to get out too. He couldn't see any rooftop marksmen, but decided they were probably there nevertheless. They had parked to one side of the main baronial building, near a vast conservatory which Rebus guessed was probably the restaurant.

'Weekend here would do me grand,' he confided to Siobhan as she emerged from the back seat.

'Cost you a grand too, no doubt,' she countered. Inside

the media centre – a tented structure with solid sides – reporters could be glimpsed hammering copy into their laptops. Rebus had lit a cigarette. He heard a sound and turned to see a bicycle round the corner of the hotel. Its rider was bent low, aiming for speed, another bike tucked in directly behind. The leading cyclist passed within thirty feet, caught sight of them, and offered a wave. Rebus gave a flick of his cigarette in acknowledgement. But lifting his fingers from the handlebars had unbalanced the rider. His front wheel wobbled, slewing across the gravel. The other cyclist tried to avoid him, but ended up going over his own handlebars. Men in dark suits arrived as if from nowhere, making a rapid huddle around the two sprawled figures.

'Did we just do that?' Siobhan asked quietly. Rebus said nothing, just dumped the cigarette and eased himself back into the car. Siobhan followed his example, and they watched through the windscreen as the first cyclist was helped to his feet, rubbing his grazed knuckles. The other rider was still on the ground, but no one seemed to be paying him much heed. A question of protocol, Rebus guessed.

The needs of President George W. Bush must always come first.

'Did we just do that?' Siobhan repeated, her voice trembling a little.

The Audi driver had emerged from the meet 'n' greet, followed by a man in a grey suit. The man carried two bulging briefcases. Like the driver, he paused for a moment to watch the commotion. The chauffeur held open the passenger-side door and the civil servant got in without so much as a nod of greeting in the direction of the back seat. The chauffeur got behind the steering wheel, his cap grazing the Audi's roof, and asked them what was going on.

'Wheels within wheels,' Rebus offered. At last, the civil

servant decided to acknowledge that he was – possibly to his chagrin – not the only passenger.

'I'm Dobbs,' he said. 'FCO.'

Meaning Foreign and Commonwealth Office. Rebus reached out a hand.

'Call me John,' he invited. 'I'm a friend of Richard Pennen's.'

Siobhan looked to be taking none of this in. Her attention, as the car drew away, was on the scene unfolding behind them. Two men in green paramedics' uniforms were being prevented from reaching the US President by his insistent security detail. Hotel staff had emerged to watch, as had a couple of the reporters from the media centre.

'Happy birthday, Mr President,' Siobhan sang huskily.

'Pleased to meet you,' Dobbs was telling Rebus.

'Richard been here yet?' Rebus asked casually.

The civil servant frowned. 'Not sure he's on the list.' He seemed worried that he might have been kept out of the loop.

'Told me he was,' Rebus lied blithely. 'Thought the Foreign Sec had a role for him ...'

'Quite possibly,' Dobbs stated, trying to sound more confident than he looked.

'George Bush just fell off his bike,' Siobhan commented. It was as if the words needed to be spoken before they could become fact.

'Oh yes?' Dobbs said, not really listening. He was opening one of the briefcases, ready to immerse himself in some reading. Rebus realised the man had suffered enough small-talk, his mind geared to higher things: statistics and budgets and trade figures. He decided on one last try.

'Were you at the Castle?'

'No,' Dobbs drawled. 'Were you?'

'I was, as a matter of fact. Hellish about Ben Webster, wasn't it?'

'Ghastly. Best PPS we had.'

Siobhan seemed suddenly to realise what was going on. Rebus offered her a wink.

'Richard's not too sure he jumped,' Rebus commented.

'Accident, you mean?' Dobbs replied.

'Pushed,' Rebus stated. The civil servant lowered his sheaf of papers, turned his head towards the back seat.

'*Pushed?*' He watched Rebus slowly nod. 'Who the hell would do that?'

Rebus offered a shrug. 'Maybe he made enemies. Some politicians do.'

'Almost as many as your chum Pennen,' Dobbs countered.

'How do you mean?' Rebus tried to sound slighted on his friend's behalf.

'That company of his used to belong to the taxpayer. Now he's making a packet out of R and D *we* paid for.'

'Serves us right for selling it to him,' Siobhan chipped in.

'Maybe the government were badly advised,' Rebus teased the civil servant.

'Government knew bloody well what it was doing.'

'Then why sell to Pennen?' Siobhan asked, genuinely curious now. Dobbs was shuffling through his papers again. The driver was on the phone to someone, asking which routes were open to them.

'R and D departments are costly,' Dobbs was saying. 'When the MoD needs to make cuts, it always looks bad if it's regiments taking the brunt. Ditch a few boffins, the media doesn't so much as blink.'

'I'm still not sure I get it,' Siobhan admitted.

'Thing about a private company,' Dobbs went on, 'is that they can sell to pretty much anyone they like – fewer constraints than the MoD, FCO or Department of Industry. Result? Faster profits.'

'Profits made,' Rebus added, 'from selling to dodgy

300

dictators and spit-poor nations already up to their eyes in debt.'

'I thought he was your ...?' Dobbs flinched as he realised he was not necessarily amongst friends. 'Who did you say you were again?'

'John,' Rebus reminded him. 'And this is my colleague.'

'But you don't work for Pennen Industries?'

'Never implied that we did,' Rebus insisted. 'We're Lothian and Borders Police, Mr Dobbs. And I want to thank you for your frank answers to our questions.' Rebus stared over the seat towards the civil servant's lap. 'You seem to be crushing all your lovely papers. Is that to save on a shredder?'

Ellen Wylie was busy manning the phones when they got back to Gayfield Square. Siobhan had called her parents, discovering that they'd given up on the trip to Auchterarder, and had kept clear of the angry demo in Princes Street. There had been trouble stretching from The Mound to the Old Town – disgruntled protesters, prevented from leaving the city, clashing with riot police. As Rebus and Siobhan walked into the CID suite, Wylie gave them a look. Rebus reckoned she was on the verge of a demo herself – left alone all day in the station. But then a figure emerged from Derek Starr's private office – not Starr himself, but Chief Constable James Corbyn. His hands were clasped behind his back, showing impatience. Rebus stared at Wylie, who shrugged a response, indicating that Corbyn had stopped her from texting a warning.

'Pair of you, in here,' Corbyn snapped, retreating back into Starr's airless domain. 'Close the door after you,' he added. He was seating himself: no other chairs in the room, so Rebus and Siobhan stayed standing.

'I'm glad you could make time, sir,' Rebus stated, getting

his retaliation in first. 'I wanted to ask you about the night Ben Webster died.'

Corbyn was caught off-guard. 'What about it?'

'You were at the dinner, sir ... something you should probably have declared from the start.'

'We're not here to talk about *me*, DI Rebus. We're here so that I can formally suspend the pair of you from active duty with immediate effect.'

Rebus nodded slowly, as if this were a given. 'All the same, sir, now you *are* here, best if we get your statement. Looks like we're hiding something otherwise. Papers are flocking around like vultures. Hardly in the interests of public relations for the Chief Constable to be—'

Corbyn rose to his feet. 'Maybe you weren't listening, Inspector. You're no longer taking part in any inquiry. I want the pair of you off the premises in the next five minutes. You'll go home and sit by the phone, waiting for news of my investigation into your conduct. Is that clear?'

'I need a few minutes to update my notes, sir. Need to make our conversation a matter of record.'

Corbyn stabbed a finger towards Rebus. 'I've heard all about you, Rebus.' His gaze shifted to Siobhan. 'Might explain why you were so reluctant to give me your colleague's name when I put you in charge.'

'You never actually asked, sir, if you don't mind me saying,' Siobhan retorted.

'But you knew damned well trouble couldn't be far off.' His attention was firmly back on Rebus. 'Not with Rebus here in the vicinity.'

'With respect, sir—' Siobhan started to argue.

Corbyn slammed his fist against the desk. 'I told you to put the whole thing on ice! Instead of which it makes the front pages, and then you proceed to pitch up at Gleneagles! When I tell you you're off the case, that's all you need to know. End of game. Sayonara. Finito.'

'Picked up a few words at the dinner, eh, sir?' Rebus responded with a wink.

Corbyn's eyes bulged from his head. Just their luck if he were to collapse with an aneurysm. But instead he stalked from the room, almost sending Siobhan and a bookcase toppling as he passed them. Rebus exhaled noisily, ran a hand through his hair and scratched his nose.

'So what do you want to do now?' he asked.

Siobhan just looked at him. 'Pack my things?' she guessed.

'Packing certainly comes into it,' Rebus replied. 'We pack all the case-files off to my flat, set up camp there.'

'John ...'

'You're right,' he said, choosing to misinterpret her tone. 'They'll be noticed if they go missing. So we need to copy them instead.'

This time he got a smile.

'I'll do it if you want,' he added. 'I know you've got a hot date.'

'In the pouring rain.'

'Only excuse Travis need to play that bloody song of theirs.' He emerged from Starr's office. 'Did you catch any of that, Ellen?'

She was putting the phone down. 'I couldn't warn you,' she began.

'Don't apologise. I suppose Corbyn knows who you are now?' He perched on the corner of her desk.

'Didn't seem that interested. He got my name and rank, never bothered to ask if I was a regular here.'

'Perfect,' Rebus told her. 'Means you can keep being our ears and eyes.'

'Hang on a second,' Siobhan interrupted. 'That's not your call to make.'

'Yes, ma'am.'

Siobhan ignored him, focusing on Ellen Wylie. 'This is *my* show, Ellen. Understood?'

'Don't worry, Siobhan, I can tell when I'm not wanted.'

'I'm not saying you're not wanted, but I need to know you're on our side.'

Wylie prickled visibly. 'As opposed to whose?'

'Ladies, ladies,' Rebus said, stepping between them like an old-fashioned wrestling referee. His eyes were on Siobhan. 'An extra pair of hands wouldn't go amiss, boss, you have to admit that.'

She smiled eventually – 'boss' had done the trick. But her gaze stayed fixed on Wylie. 'Even so,' she said, 'we can't ask you to spy for us. It's one thing for John and me to get into bother, another to land you in the mire.'

'I don't mind,' Wylie said. 'Nice dungarees, by the way.'

Siobhan's smile reappeared. 'I suppose I should change before the show.'

Rebus exhaled noisily: flashpoint avoided. 'So what's been happening here?' he asked Wylie.

'Trying to alert all the offenders listed on BeastWatch. I've asked the various police authorities to tell them to be on their guard.'

'And did they sound enthusiastic?'

'Not exactly. Between times, I've had several dozen reporters following up on the front page.' She had the newspaper beside her, and tapped Mairie's headline. 'Amazed she gets the time,' she commented.

'How's that?' Rebus wondered.

Wylie opened the paper at a double-page spread. Byline: Mairie Henderson. An interview with Councillor Gareth Tench. Big photo of him in the midst of the Niddrie camp-site.

'I was there when they did that,' Siobhan said.

'I know him,' Wylie couldn't help countering. Rebus fixed her with a look.

'Explain.'

She gave a shrug, wary of his sudden interest. 'I just do.'

'Ellen,' he warned, drawing her name out.

She sighed. 'He's been seeing Denise.'

'Your sister Denise?' Siobhan asked.

Wylie nodded. 'It was me who hooked them up ... more or less.'

'They're an item?' Rebus had wrapped his arms around himself like a strait-jacket.

'They've been out a few times. He's been ...' She sought the right words. 'He's been good for her, brought her out of herself.'

'With the help of a drop of wine?' Rebus guessed. 'But how did you come to meet him?'

'BeastWatch,' she said quietly, eyes refusing to connect with his.

'Say again?'

'He saw that piece I wrote. Sent me an email full of praise ...'

Rebus had jumped to his feet, unfolding his arms as he searched the desk for a sheet of paper – the list Bain had given of BeastWatch subscribers.

'Which one is he?' he demanded, handing her the names.

'That one,' she said.

'Ozyman?' Rebus checked, watching her nod. 'Hell kind of name is that? He's not from Down Under, is he?'

'Ozymandias, maybe,' Siobhan offered.

'Ozzy Osbourne's more my line,' Rebus admitted. Siobhan leaned over a keyboard and stuck the name into a search engine. A couple of clicks and a biography appeared on the screen.

'King of kings,' Siobhan explained. 'Put up a huge statue of himself.' Two more clicks and Rebus was looking at a poem by Shelley.

'"Look on my works, ye Mighty",' he recited, '"and

despair!"' He turned towards Wylie. 'Not that he's big-headed or anything ...'

'Can't dispute it,' she conceded. 'All I said was, he's been good for Denise.'

'We need to talk to him,' Rebus said, his eyes running down the list of names, wondering how many more lived in Edinburgh. 'And you, Ellen, should have said something before now.'

'I didn't know you had a list,' she said defensively.

'He got to you through the website – stands to reason we'd want to question him. Christ knows, we've few enough leads to go on.'

'Or too many,' Siobhan countered. 'Victims in three different regions, clues left in another ... It's all so scattered.'

'I thought you were heading home to get ready?'

She nodded, looked around the office. 'You're really going to take it all with you?'

'Why not? I can copy the paperwork, Ellen here won't mind staying late to help.' He gave her a meaningful look. 'Will you, Ellen?'

'That's my punishment, is it?'

'I can appreciate you'd want Denise kept out of it,' Rebus told her, 'but you should still have given us Tench.'

'Just remember, John,' Siobhan interrupted, 'the councillor saved me from a beating that night in Niddrie.'

Rebus nodded. Could have added that he'd witnessed another side to Gareth Tench, but didn't bother.

'Enjoy your concert,' he said instead.

Siobhan's attention was back on Ellen Wylie. 'My team, Ellen. If I think you're hiding anything else ...'

'Message received.'

Siobhan started to nod slowly, then thought of something. 'Did BeastWatch subscribers ever have get-togethers?'

'Not that I know of.'

'But they can contact each other?'

'Obviously.'

'Did you know who Gareth Tench was before you met him?'

'First email he sent, he said he was based in Edinburgh, signed off with his real name.'

'And you told him you were CID?'

Wylie nodded.

'What's your thinking?' Rebus asked Siobhan.

'I'm not sure yet.' Siobhan started to get her things together. Rebus and Wylie watched her. Finally, with a wave over her shoulder, she was gone.

Ellen Wylie folded the newspaper and dumped it in a waste-paper bin. Rebus had filled the kettle and switched it on.

'I can tell you exactly what she's thinking,' Wylie told him.

'Then you're cleverer than me.'

'She knows that murderers don't always work alone. She also knows sometimes they need validation.'

'Over my head, Ellen.'

'I don't think so, John. If I know you, you're thinking much the same. Somebody decides to start killing perverts, they might want to tell someone about it – either beforehand, almost asking permission, or afterwards, to get it off their chest.'

'Okay,' Rebus said, busy with the mugs.

'Hard to work in a team if you're one of the suspects ...'

'I really do appreciate you helping out, Ellen,' he said, pausing before adding: 'So long as that's what you're doing.'

She sprang from the chair, placing her hands on her hips, elbows jutting. Rebus had been told once why humans did that – to make them seem bigger, more threatening, less vulnerable ...

307

'You think,' she was saying, 'I've been here half the day just to protect Denise?'

'No ... but I do think people will go a long way to protect family.'

'Like Siobhan and her mum, you mean?'

'Let's not pretend we wouldn't do the same.'

'John ... I'm here because *you* asked me.'

'And I've said I'm grateful, but here's the thing, Ellen – Siobhan and me have just been kicked into touch. We need someone to look out for us; someone we can trust.' He spooned coffee into the two chipped mugs. Sniffed the milk and decided it would do. He was giving her time to think.

'All right,' she said at last.

'No more secrets?' he asked. She shook her head. 'Nothing I should know?' Shook it again. 'You want to be there when I interview Tench?'

Her eyebrows lifted slightly. 'How do you plan to do that? You're on suspension, remember?'

Rebus made a face and tapped his head. 'Short-term memory-loss,' he told her. 'It comes with the territory.'

After the coffee, they got busy: Rebus filled the copier with a fresh ream of paper; Wylie asked what he wanted copying from the computer's various databases. The phone rang half a dozen times, but they ignored it.

'Incidentally,' Wylie chimed in at one point, 'did you hear? London got the Olympics.'

'Whoop-dee-doo.'

'It was great actually: everyone dancing around Trafalgar Square. Means Paris lost out.'

'Wonder how Chirac's taking it.' Rebus checked his watch. 'He'll be sitting down to dinner with the Queen right around now.'

'With TB doing his Cheshire cat impression, no doubt.'

Rebus smiled. Yes, and Gleneagles serving up the best of Caledonian fare for the French President. He thought back to that afternoon ... standing a few hundred yards from all those powerful men. Bush toppling from his bike, a painful reminder that they were every bit as fallible as anyone else. 'What does the G stand for?' he asked. Wylie just looked at him. 'In G8,' he amplified.

'Government?' she guessed, giving a shrug. There was a tapping against the open door: one of the duty uniforms from the front desk.

'Someone to see you downstairs, sir.' He glanced pointedly in the direction of the nearest phone.

'We've not been picking up,' Rebus explained. 'Who is it?'

'Woman called Webster ... She was hoping for DS Clarke, but said you'd do at a pinch.'

18

Backstage at the Final Push.

Rumours that some sort of rocket had been fired from the railway tracks nearby, falling short of its target.

'Filled with purple dye,' Bobby Greig had told Siobhan. He was in mufti: faded jeans and a battered denim jacket. Looked damp but happy as the rain drizzled down. Siobhan had changed into black cords and a pale green T-shirt, topped off with a biker jacket bought second-hand from an Oxfam shop. Greig had smiled at her. 'How come,' he'd said, 'whatever you wear, you still look like CID?'

She hadn't bothered replying. She kept fingering the laminated pass which was strung around her neck. It showed an outline of Africa and the legend 'Backstage Access'. Sounded grand, but Greig soon explained her place in the food chain. His own pass was 'Access All Areas', but beyond this were two further levels – VIP and VVIP. She'd already seen Midge Ure and Claudia Schiffer, both of them VVIPs. Greig had introduced her to the concert promoters, Steve Daws and Emma Diprose, the pair of them glamorous despite the weather.

'Amazing line-up,' Siobhan had told them.

'Thank you,' Daws had said. Then Diprose had asked if Siobhan had a favourite, but she'd shaken her head.

Throughout, Greig hadn't bothered mentioning to them that she was a cop.

There had been ticketless fans outside Murrayfield, begging to buy, and a few touts whose prices were deterring all but the wealthiest and most desperate. With her pass,

Siobhan had been able to wander around the base of the stage and on to the playing-pitch itself, where she joined sixty thousand drenched fans. But the hungry looks they gave in the direction of her little plastic rectangle made her uncomfortable, and she soon retreated behind the security fence. Greig was stuffing his face with the free food, while holding a half-empty bottle of continental lager. The Proclaimers had opened the show with a singalong of '500 Miles'. Word was, Eddie Izzard would be playing piano on Midge Ure's version of 'Vienna'. Texas, Snow Patrol and Travis were due up later, with Bono helping out the Corrs and a closing set by James Brown.

But the frenetic backstage activity was making Siobhan feel old. She didn't know who half the performers were. They looked important, moving to and fro with their various entourages, but their faces didn't mean anything to her. It struck her that her parents might be leaving on Friday, giving her just one more day with them. She'd called them earlier: they'd gone back to her flat, buying provisions on the way, and might go out for dinner. Just the two of them, her dad had said, making it look like this was what he wanted.

Or maybe so she wouldn't feel guilty at being elsewhere.

She was trying to relax, to get in the mood, but work kept intruding. Rebus, she knew, would still be hard at it. He wouldn't rest till his demons had been quelled. Yet each victory was fleeting, and each fight drained him a little more. Now that the sun was setting, the stadium was dotted with the flashes from phone-cameras. Luminous glowsticks were being waved in the air. Greig found an umbrella from somewhere and handed it to her as the rain got heavier.

'Had any more bother in Niddrie?' she asked him.

He shook his head. 'They've made their point,' he said. 'Besides which, they probably think there's a better chance of a rammy if they head into town.' He tossed his empty beer bottle into a recycling bin. 'Did you see it today?'

'I was in Auchterarder,' she said.

He looked impressed. 'Bits I watched on TV made it look like a war zone.'

'Wasn't *quite* that bad. How about here?'

'Bit of a demo when the buses were stopped from going. Nothing like Monday, though.' He nodded over her shoulder. 'Annie Lennox,' he pointed out. And so it was, not ten feet away, giving them a smile as she headed to her changing room. 'You played a belter at Hyde Park!' Greig called out to her. She just kept smiling, her mind on the performance ahead.

Greig went to fetch more beers. Most of the people Siobhan saw were just hanging about, looking bored. Technical crews who wouldn't be busy again until it was time to pack everything away and dismantle the stage. Personal assistants and record company staff – the latter wearing a uniform of black suits with matching V-neck sweaters, sunglasses on and phones clamped to their ears. Caterers and promoters and hangers-on. She knew she was one of the latter. No one had asked what role she was playing because no one thought she was a player.

The terraces, that's where I belong, she thought.

Either there or the CID room.

She felt so very different from the teenager who'd hitched her way to Greenham Common, singing 'We Shall Overcome' as she locked hands with the other women ringing the air base. Already, Saturday's Make Poverty History march seemed like history itself. And yet ... Bono and Geldof had managed to breach the G8 security, putting their case to the various leaders. They'd made damned sure those men knew what was at stake, and that millions expected great things of them. Tomorrow, decisions might be taken. Tomorrow would be crucial.

Her mobile was in her hand, and she was on the verge

of calling Rebus. But she knew he would laugh, tell her to switch it off and enjoy herself. She suddenly doubted that, despite the ticket pinned by a magnet to the fridge in her kitchen, she would go to T in the Park. Doubted the killings would be solved by then, especially now she was officially off the case. *Her* case. Except now Rebus had brought in Ellen Wylie ... it rankled that he hadn't thought to ask. Rankled, too, that he'd been right: they needed help. But now it turned out Wylie knew Gareth Tench and Tench knew Wylie's sister ...

Bobby Greig had returned with her beer. 'So what do you think?' he asked.

'I think they're all remarkably small,' she commented. He nodded his agreement.

'Pop stars,' he explained, 'must've been the school runts. This is how they get their revenge. You'll notice their heads are big enough, though ...' He saw that he had lost her attention.

'What's he doing here?' Siobhan asked.

Greig recognised the figure, gave a wave. Councillor Gareth Tench waved back. He was talking to Daws and Diprose, but broke off – a pat on the shoulder for the former; peck on either cheek for the latter – and came towards them.

'He's the council's Culture Convener,' Greig stated. He held out a hand for Tench to squeeze.

'How are you, lad?' Tench enquired.

'Just fine.'

'Keeping out of trouble?' This question was directed at Siobhan. She took the proffered hand and returned its firm grasp.

'Trying to.'

Tench turned back to Greig. 'Remind me again, where do I know you from?'

'The campsite. Name's Bobby Greig.'

Tench shook his head at his own incompetence. 'Of

course, of course. Well, isn't this great?' He clapped his hands together and looked around. 'Whole bloody world's got its eyes on Edinburgh.'

'Or on the concert at any rate,' Siobhan couldn't help qualifying.

Tench just rolled his eyes. 'There's no pleasing some folk. Tell me, did Bobby here sneak you in for free?'

Siobhan felt obliged to nod.

'And you're still complaining?' He gave a chuckle. 'Remember to give a donation before you leave, eh? Might look like a kickback otherwise.'

'That's a bit unfair,' Greig started to protest, but Tench waved the complaint aside. 'And how's that colleague of yours?' he was asking Siobhan.

'You mean DI Rebus?'

'That's the one. Seems a bit too pally with the criminal fraternity, if you ask me.'

'How do you mean?'

'Well, you work together ... I'm sure he confides in you. The other night?' As if jogging her memory. 'Craigmillar Faith Centre? I was making a speech when your man Rebus pitched up with a monster called Cafferty.' He paused. 'I'm assuming you know him?'

'I know him,' Siobhan confirmed.

'Seems strange to me that the forces of law and order would need to ...' He seemed to be searching for the right word. '*Fraternise*,' he decided. Then he paused, eyes boring into Siobhan's. 'I'm presuming DI Rebus wouldn't have kept any of this from you ... I mean, I'm not telling you anything you don't already know?'

Siobhan felt like a fish worried by an insistent hook.

'We all have our private lives, Mr Tench,' was the only reply she could muster. Tench seemed disappointed. 'And what about yourself?' she continued. 'Hoping to persuade a few bands into playing the Jack Kane Centre?'

He rubbed his hands again. 'If the opportunity presents ...'

His voice drifted away as he saw a face he recognised. Siobhan knew it too: Marti Pellow from Wet Wet Wet. The name reminded her to raise her umbrella. The rain tom-tommed off it as Tench moved away towards his target.

'What was all that about?' Greig asked. She just shook her head. 'Why do I get the feeling you'd rather be elsewhere?'

'Sorry,' she said.

Greig was watching Tench and the singer. 'Works fast, doesn't he? Not shy either ... I think that's why people listen. You ever heard him when he's giving a speech? The hairs on your arms start to rise.'

Siobhan nodded slowly. She was thinking about Rebus and Cafferty. It didn't surprise her that Rebus hadn't said anything. She looked at her phone again. She had an excuse now to call him, but still she held back.

I'm owed a private life, an evening off.

Otherwise, she'd become just like Rebus – obsessed and sidelined; thrawn and mistrusted. He'd been stuck at inspector rank for the best part of two decades. She wanted more. Wanted to do the job well, but be able to switch off now and again. Wanted a life outside her job, rather than a job which became her life. Rebus had lost family and friends, pushing them aside in favour of corpses and con men, killers, petty thieves, rapists, thugs, racketeers and racists. When he went out drinking, he did so on his own, standing quietly at the bar, facing the row of optics. He had no hobbies, didn't follow any sports, never took a holiday. If he had a week or two off, she could usually find him at the Oxford Bar, pretending to read the paper in a corner, or staring dully at the daytime telly.

She wanted more.

This time, she made the call. It was picked up and she broke into a smile. 'Dad?' she said. 'You still in the restaurant? Tell them to squeeze in an extra place-setting for dessert ...'

Stacey Webster was herself again.

Dressed much as she had been the time Rebus had met her outside the mortuary. Her T-shirt had long sleeves.

'That to hide the tattoos?' he asked.

'They're temporary,' she told him. 'They'll fade in time.'

'Most things do.' He saw the suitcase. It was standing on end, carry-handle retracted. 'Back to London?'

'Sleeper,' she nodded.

'Look, I'm sorry if we ...' Rebus looked around the reception area, as though reluctant to make eye contact.

'It happens,' she said. 'Maybe my cover wasn't breached, but Commander Steelforth doesn't like to risk his officers.' She seemed awkward and uncertain, brain stuck in the no-man's-land between two very separate identities.

'Time for a drink?' he asked.

'I came to see Siobhan.' She slid a hand into her pocket. 'Is her mum okay?'

'Recuperating,' Rebus said. 'Staying at Siobhan's.'

'Santal never got the chance to say goodbye.' She was holding her hand out towards Rebus. A clear plastic wallet, within which sat a silver disk. 'CD-ROM,' she said. 'Film copied from my camera, that day on Princes Street.'

Rebus nodded slowly. 'I'll see she gets it.'

'The Commander would kill me if ...'

'Our secret,' Rebus assured her, tucking the disk into his breast-pocket. 'Now let's get you that drink.'

Plenty of pubs available to them on Leith Walk. But the first they walked past looked busy, the Murrayfield concert blaring from the TV. Further downhill they found what they wanted – a quiet, traditional place with a jukebox soundtrack and a one-armed bandit. Stacey had left her suitcase behind the desk at Gayfield Square. She told him she wanted to offload some Scottish banknotes

– her excuse for getting the round. They settled at a corner table.

'Ever used the sleeper before?' Rebus asked.

'That's why I'm drinking vodka tonic – only way to sleep on that damned train.'

'Is Santal gone for good?'

'Depends.'

'Steelforth said you were undercover for months.'

'Months,' she agreed.

'Can't have been easy in London ... always the chance someone would recognise you.'

'I walked past Ben once.'

'As Santal?'

'He never knew.' She sat back. 'That's why I let Santal get close to Siobhan. Her parents had told me she was CID.'

'You wanted to see if your cover would hold?'

Rebus watched her nod, thinking now that he understood something. Stacey would have been devastated by her brother's death, but to Santal it would have mattered very little. Problem was, all that grief was still caged – something he knew a bit about.

'London wasn't really my main base, though,' Stacey was saying. 'A lot of the groups have moved out – too easy for us to monitor them there. Manchester, Bradford, Leeds ... that's where I spent most of my time.'

'You think you made a difference?'

She gave this some thought. 'We hope we do, don't we?'

He nodded his agreement, sipped at his own pint, then put it down. 'I'm still looking into Ben's death.'

'I know.'

'The Commander told you?' He watched her nod. 'He's been putting obstacles in my way.'

'He probably sees it as his job, Inspector. It's nothing personal.'

'If I didn't know better, I'd say he was trying to protect a man called Richard Pennen.'

'Pennen Industries?'

It was Rebus's turn to nod. 'Pennen was picking up your brother's hotel tab.'

'Strange,' she said. 'There wasn't much love lost.'

'Oh?'

She stared at him. 'Ben had visited plenty of war zones. He knew the horrors inflicted by the arms trade.'

'The line I keep being fed is that Pennen sells technology rather than guns.'

She snorted. 'Only a matter of time. Ben wanted to make things as awkward as possible. You should look back at *Hansard* – speeches he made in the House, asking all sorts of difficult questions.'

'Yet Pennen paid for his room ...'

'And Ben would have loved that. He'd take a room from a dictator, then spend the whole trip slamming them.' She paused and swirled her drink, then turned her eyes back towards him. 'You thought it was bribery, didn't you? Pennen buying Ben off?' His silence answered her question. 'My brother was a good man, Inspector.' At last tears were welling in her eyes. 'And I couldn't even go to his bloody funeral.'

'He'd have understood,' Rebus offered. 'My own ...' Had to stop and clear his throat. 'My own brother died last week. We cremated him on Friday.'

'I'm sorry.'

He lifted the glass to his mouth. 'He was in his fifties. Doctors say it was a stroke.'

'You were close?'

'Phone calls mostly.' He paused again. 'I put him in jail once for dealing drugs.' Looked at her to gauge her reaction.

'Is that what's bothering you?' she asked.

'What?'

'That you never told him ...' She struggled to get the words out, face twisting as the tears started falling. 'Never told him you were sorry.' She got up from the table, fled to the toilets – one hundred per cent Stacey Webster now. He thought maybe he should follow her, or at least send the barmaid in after her. But he just sat there instead, swilling the glass until fresh foam appeared on the surface of the beer, thinking about families. Ellen Wylie and her sister, the Jensens and their daughter Vicky, Stacey Webster and her brother Ben ...

'Mickey,' he said in a whisper. Naming the dead so they'd know they weren't forgotten.

Ben Webster.

Cyril Colliar.

Edward Isley.

Trevor Guest.

'Michael Rebus,' he said out loud, making a little toast with his glass. Then he got up and bought refills – IPA, vodka and tonic. Stood by the bar as he waited for his change. Two regulars were discussing Team Britain's chances at the 2012 Olympics.

'How come London always gets everything?' one of them complained.

'Funny they didn't want the G8,' his companion added.

'Knew what was bloody coming.'

Rebus had to think for a moment. Wednesday today ... it all wrapped up on Friday. Just one more full day and then the city could start getting back to normal. Steelforth and Pennen and all the other intruders would head south.

There wasn't much love lost ...

She'd meant between her brother and Richard Pennen ... the MP trying to stymie Pennen's expansion plans. Rebus had had Ben Webster all wrong, seeing him as a lackey. And Steelforth ... not letting Rebus near the hotel room. Not because he didn't want any fuss, didn't want the various bigwigs bothered with questions and theories. But to protect Richard Pennen.

Wasn't much love lost.

Making Richard Pennen a suspect; or at the very least giving him a motive. Any one of the guards at the Castle could have heaved the MP over the ramparts. There would have been bodyguards mixing with the guests ... Secret Service, too – at least one detail apiece to protect the Foreign Secretary and Defence Secretary. Steelforth was SO12, next best thing to the spooks at MI5 and MI6. But if you wanted rid of someone, why choose that method? It was too public, too showy. Rebus knew from experience: the successful murders were where there *was* no murder. Smothered during sleep, drugged and then left in a moving vehicle, or simply made to disappear.

'Christ, John,' he scolded himself. 'It'll be little green men next.' Blame the circumstances: easy to imagine any manner of conspiracy happening around you in G8 week. He set the drinks down at the table, a little concerned now that Stacey had yet to emerge from the toilets. It struck him that his back had been turned while he'd waited at the bar. Gave it five more minutes, then asked the barmaid to check. She came out of the ladies' shaking her head.

'Three quid wasted,' she told him, gesturing towards Stacey's drink. 'And too young for you anyway, if you don't mind me saying.'

Back at Gayfield Square, she'd taken her suitcase but left him a note.

Good luck, but remember – Ben was my brother, not yours. Make sure you do your own grieving too.

Hours yet until the sleeper left. He could head to Waverley, but decided against it; wasn't sure there was much more left to be said. Maybe she even had a point. By investigating Ben's death, he was keeping Mickey's memory close. Suddenly there was a question he wished he'd asked her:

What do you *think happened to your brother?*

Well, he had her business card somewhere, the one she'd given him outside the mortuary. He'd call her tomorrow maybe, see if she'd been able to sleep on the train to London. He'd told her he was still investigating the death, and all she'd said was 'I know'. No questions; no theories of her own. Warned off by Steelforth? A good soldier always obeyed orders. But she must have been thinking about it, weighing the options.

A fall.

A leap.

A push.

'Tomorrow,' he told himself, heading back to the CID room, a long night of clandestine photocopying ahead.

Thursday 7 July

19

The buzzer woke him.

He stumbled through to the hall and pushed the button on the intercom.

'What?' he rasped.

'I thought I worked here.' Tinny and distorted but still recognisable: Siobhan's voice.

'What time is it?' Rebus coughed.

'Eight.'

'*Eight?*'

'The start of another working day.'

'We're suspended, remember?'

'Are you still in your jim-jams?'

'I don't wear them.'

'Meaning I need to wait out here?'

'I'll leave the door open.' He buzzed her in, collected his clothes from the chair by the bed, and locked himself in the bathroom. He could hear her tapping on the door of the flat, pushing it open.

'Two minutes!' he called out, stepping into the bath and under the nozzle of the shower.

By the time he emerged, she had seated herself at the dining table and was sorting through last night's photocopies.

'Don't get too comfortable,' he said. He was halfway through knotting his tie. Remembering that he wouldn't be going into work, he tugged it free instead and threw it towards the sofa. 'We need supplies,' he told her.

'And I need a favour.'

'Such as?'

'A couple of hours at lunchtime – I want to take my parents out.'

He nodded his agreement. 'How's your mum doing?'

'She seems okay. They've decided to give Gleneagles a miss, even though climate change is on today's agenda.'

'They're heading home tomorrow?'

'Probably.'

'How was the show last night?' She didn't answer straight away. 'I caught the last bit on TV – thought I might have seen you bopping down the front.'

'I'd left by then.'

'Oh?'

She just shrugged. 'So what are these provisions?'

'Breakfast.'

'I've had mine.'

'Then you can watch me while I demolish a bacon roll. There's a café on Marchmont Road. And while I'm tucking in, you can call Councillor Tench, fix up a pow-wow.'

'He was at the show last night.'

Rebus looked at her. 'Gets about a bit, doesn't he?'

She'd wandered over to the hi-fi. There were LPs on a shelf, and she picked one up.

'That was made before you were born,' Rebus told her. Leonard Cohen, *Songs of Love and Hate*.

'Listen to this,' she said, reading the back of the sleeve. '"They locked up a man who wanted to rule the world. The fools, they locked up the wrong man." Wonder what that means?'

'Case of mistaken identity?' Rebus offered.

'I think it's to do with ambition,' she countered. 'Gareth Tench said he saw you ...'

'He did.'

'With Cafferty.'

Rebus nodded. 'Big Ger says the councillor's got plans to put him out of the game.'

She put the record back and turned to face him. 'That's a good thing, isn't it?'

'Depends what we get instead. Cafferty's view is that Tench himself would take over.'

'You believe him?'

Rebus seemed to be considering the question. 'Know what I need before I answer that?'

'Proof?' she guessed.

He shook his head. 'Coffee.'

Eight forty-five.

Rebus was on his second mug. All that was left of his roll was a side-plate spotted with grease. The café had a good selection of papers, Siobhan reading about the Final Push, Rebus showing her photos from yesterday's shenanigans at Gleneagles.

'That kid,' he said, pointing at one, 'didn't we see him?'

She nodded. 'But not with blood gushing from his head.'

Rebus turned the paper back towards him. 'They love it really, you know. Bit of blood always looks good to the media.'

'And makes us look like the villains of the piece?'

'Speaking of which ...' He lifted the CD-ROM from his pocket. 'A going-away present from Stacey Webster – or Santal, if you prefer.'

Siobhan took it from him, holding it between her fingers as Rebus explained the circumstances. When he'd finished, he took Stacey's business card from his wallet and tried her number. There was no answer. As he tucked the phone back into his jacket, he could smell the faintest trace of Molly Clark's perfume. He'd decided Siobhan didn't need to know about her; wasn't sure how she would react. He was still thinking it over when Gareth Tench walked in. Tench shook hands with both of them. Rebus thanked him for coming and gestured for him to sit.

'What can I get you?'

Tench shook his head. Rebus could see a car parked outside, the minders standing next to it.

'Good idea that,' he told the councillor, nodding towards the window. 'I don't know why more Marchmont residents don't use bodyguards.'

Tench just smiled. 'Not at work today?' he commented.

'Bit more informal,' Rebus explained. 'Can't have our elected politicians slumming it in cop-shop interview rooms.'

'I appreciate that.' Tench had made himself comfortable, but showed no sign of removing his three-quarter-length coat. 'So what can I do for you, Inspector?'

But it was Siobhan who spoke first. 'As you know, Mr Tench, we're investigating a series of murders. Certain clues were left at a site in Auchterarder.'

Tench's eyes narrowed. His focus was still on Rebus, but it was clear he'd expected some other conversation – Cafferty, maybe, or Niddrie.

'I don't see—' he started.

'All three victims,' Siobhan went on, 'were listed on a website called BeastWatch.' She paused. 'You know it, of course.'

'I do?'

'That's our information.' She unfolded a sheet of paper and showed it to him. 'Ozyman ... that's you, isn't it?'

He thought for a moment before answering. Siobhan folded the sheet and put it back in her pocket. Rebus winked at Tench, conveying a simple message: *She's good. So don't try mucking us around ...*

'It's me,' Tench finally conceded. 'What of it?'

Siobhan shrugged. 'Why are you interested in BeastWatch, Mr Tench?'

'Are you saying I'm a suspect?'

Rebus gave a cold laugh. 'That's a bit of a leap to make, sir.'

Tench glowered at him. 'Never know what Cafferty might try and hatch – with a little help from his friends.'

'I think we're straying from the point,' Siobhan interrupted. 'We need to interview anyone who had access to that site, sir. It's procedure, that's all.'

'I still don't know how you got from my screen-name to me.'

'You forget, Mr Tench,' Rebus said blithely, 'we've got the world's best intelligence officers here this week. Not much they can't do.' Tench looked ready to add some remark, but Rebus didn't give him the chance. 'Interesting choice: Ozymandias. Poem by Shelley, right? Some king gets a bit above himself, has this huge statue built. But over time it crumbles away, sitting there out in the desert.' He paused. 'Like I say, interesting choice.'

'Why so?'

Rebus folded his arms. 'Well, this king must have had some ego – that's the point of the poem. No matter how high and mighty you are, nothing lasts. And if you're a tyrant, your fall's all the greater.' He leaned forward a little across the table. 'Person who chose that name wasn't stupid ... had to know it wasn't about power as such ...'

'... but power's corrupting influence?' Tench smiled and nodded slowly.

'DI Rebus is a fast learner,' Siobhan added. 'Yesterday he was wondering if you might be Australian.'

Tench's smile broadened. His eyes remained fixed on Rebus. 'We did that poem at school,' he said. 'Had this really enthusiastic English teacher. He made us memorise it.' Tench offered a shrug. 'I just like the name, Inspector. Don't read any more into it.' His gaze shifted to Siobhan and back. 'Peril of the profession, I suppose – always looking for motive. Tell me ... what's your killer's motive? Have you considered that?'

'We think he's a vigilante,' Siobhan stated.

'Picking them off one by one from that website?' Tench didn't look convinced.

'You've still to tell us,' Rebus said quietly, 'your own motive for being so interested in BeastWatch.' He unfolded his arms and laid his palms on the tabletop, either side of his coffee mug.

'My ward's a dumping-ground, Rebus – don't say you haven't noticed. Agencies bring us their hard-to-house, the dealers and flotsam, sex offenders, junkies, toe-rags of all descriptions. Sites like BeastWatch give me a chance of fighting back. They mean I can argue my corner when some fresh problem's about to land on my doorstep.'

'And has it happened?' Siobhan asked.

'We had a guy released three months back, sex maniac ... I made sure he steered clear.'

'Making it someone else's problem,' Siobhan commented.

'Always been the way I've worked. Someone like Cafferty comes along, same thinking prevails.'

'Cafferty's been here a long time,' Rebus pointed out.

'You mean despite your lot, or because of them?' When Rebus didn't answer, Tench's smile became a sneer. 'No way he'd have lasted as long as he has without some help.' He leaned back and rolled his shoulders. 'Are we finished here?'

'How well do you know the Jensens?' Siobhan asked.

'Who?'

'The couple who run the site.'

'Never met them,' Tench stated.

'Really?' Siobhan sounded amazed. 'They live right here in Edinburgh.'

'And so do half a million just like them. I try to get about, DS Clarke, but I'm not made of elastic.'

'What are you made of, Councillor?' Rebus asked.

'Anger,' Tench offered, 'determination, a thirst for what's right and just.' He took a deep breath, but then released it noisily. 'We could be here all day,' he apologised with another smile. Then, rising to his feet: 'Bobby looked heartbroken when you walked out on him, DS Clarke. You want to be careful: passion's a snarling beast in some men.' He made a little bow as he headed for the door.

'We'll talk again,' Siobhan warned him. Rebus was watching through the window as one of the minders opened the back door of the car and Tench crammed his oversized frame inside.

'Councillors often have a well-fed look,' he commented. 'You ever notice that?'

Siobhan was rubbing a hand across her forehead. 'We could have handled that better.'

'You ducked out of the Final Push?'

'Wasn't really getting into it.'

'Anything to do with our esteemed councillor?' She shook her head. '"Destroyer and preserver",' Rebus muttered to himself.

'What?'

'It's another line from Shelley.'

'So which of them is Gareth Tench?'

The car was drawing away from the kerb. 'Maybe both,' Rebus offered. Then he gave a huge yawn. 'Any chance today will give us some respite?'

She looked at him. 'You could stop for lunch, come and meet my parents.'

'Pariah status has been lifted?' he guessed, raising an eyebrow.

'John ...' she warned.

'You don't want them to yourself?'

She shrugged. 'Maybe I've been a bit greedy.'

Rebus had taken a couple of paintings down from one wall of his living room. Details of the three victims were now pinned there instead. He was seated at the dining-table while Siobhan lay stretched out along the sofa. Both

331

were busy reading, asking occasional questions or pitching a notion.

'Don't suppose you've had a chance to listen to the Ellen Wylie tape?' Rebus asked at one point. 'Not that it really matters ...'

'Plenty more subscribers we could talk to.'

'Need to know who they are first: think Brains could do that without Corbyn or Steelforth getting a whiff?'

'Tench talked about motive ... could we be missing something?'

'Some connection between all three?'

'Come to that, why's he stopped at three?'

'Usual explanations: he's gone elsewhere, or we've arrested him for something else, or he knows we're on to him.'

'But we're *not* on to him.'

'Media say otherwise.'

'Why the Clootie Well in the first place? Because we were bound to go there?'

'Can't rule out a local connection.'

'What if this has nothing to do with BeastWatch?'

'Then we're wasting precious time.'

'Could he be sending a message to the G8? Maybe he's here right now, holding a banner somewhere.'

'Photo might be on that CD-ROM ...'

'And we'd never know.'

'If those clues were left to taunt us, how come he hasn't followed up? Shouldn't he be trying to make more of a game of it?'

'Maybe he doesn't need to follow up.'

'Meaning what?'

'He could be closer than we think ...'

'Thanks for that.'

'Do you want a cup of tea?'

'Go on then.'

'Actually, it's your turn – I paid for the coffees.'

'There's got to be a pattern, you know. We *are* missing something.'

Siobhan's phone bleeped: text message. She studied it. 'Turn on the TV,' she said.

'Which show are you missing?'

But she'd swung her legs off the sofa and punched the button herself. Found the remote and flipped channels. NEWS FLASH across the bottom of the screen. BLASTS IN LONDON.

'Eric sent the text,' she said quietly. Rebus came and stood next to her. There didn't seem to be much information. A series of blasts or explosions ... the London Underground ... casualties, several dozen.

'Suspected power surge,' the broadcaster was saying. He didn't sound convinced.

'Power surge, my bollocks,' Rebus growled.

Major railway stations closed. Hospitals on alert. The public advised not to try entering the city. Siobhan slumped back on to the sofa, elbows on knees, head in hands.

'Blindsided,' she said quietly.

'Might not just be London,' Rebus replied, but he knew it probably was. Morning rush-hour ... all those commuters, and Transport Police sent packing to Scotland for the G8. All those officers seconded from the Met. He squeezed shut his eyes, thinking: lucky it wasn't yesterday, thousands of revellers in Trafalgar Square, cheering the Olympic result; or Saturday night in Hyde Park ... two hundred thousand.

The National Grid had just confirmed that there were no apparent problems with its systems.

Aldgate.

King's Cross.

Edgware Road.

And fresh speculation that a bus had also been 'wrecked'. The broadcaster's face was pale. An emergency number was running along the foot of the screen.

'What do we do?' Siobhan asked quietly, as the TV showed live pictures from one of the scenes – medics running pell-mell, smoke billowing, casualties sitting kerbside. Glass and sirens and the alarms from parked cars and nearby offices.

'Do?' Rebus echoed. He was saved from answering by Siobhan's phone. She put it to her ear.

'Mum?' she said. 'Yes, we're watching it right now.' She paused, listening. 'I'm sure they're fine ... Yes, you could call the number. Might take a while to get through, though.' Another pause to listen. 'What? Today? They might have locked down King's Cross ...' She'd half turned from Rebus. He decided to leave the room, let her say whatever needed saying. In the kitchen he ran the tap, filled the kettle. Listened to the water running: such a basic sound, he almost never heard it. It was just there.

Normal.

Everyday.

And when he turned off the tap, there was a faint gurgle. Funny how he couldn't remember having caught it before. When he turned, Siobhan was standing there.

'Mum wants to go home,' she said, 'make sure the neighbours are okay.'

'I don't even know where they live.'

'Forest Hill,' she told him. 'South of the Thames.'

'No lunch then?'

She shook her head. He handed her a strip of kitchen-roll and she blew her nose.

'Puts things in perspective, something like this,' she said.

'Not really. It's been in the air all week. There were times I could almost taste it.'

'That's three tea bags,' she said.

'What?'

'You've just put three tea bags in that mug.' She handed him the tea pot. 'This what you were thinking of?'

'Maybe,' he conceded. In his mind he was seeing a statue in the desert, smashed to smithereens ...

Siobhan had gone home. She would help her parents, maybe take them to the train if that was still the plan. Rebus watched TV. The red double-decker had been ripped apart, its roof lying in the road in front of it. And yet there were survivors. A small miracle, it seemed to him. His instinct was to open the bottle and pour, but so far he'd resisted. Eye-witnesses were telling their stories. The Prime Minister was on his way south, leaving the Foreign Secretary in charge at Gleneagles. Blair had made a statement before leaving, flanked by his G8 colleagues. You could just make out the sticking plasters on President Bush's knuckles. Back on the news, people were talking about crawling over body parts to get out of the trains. Crawling through smoke and blood. Some had used their camera phones to capture the horror. Rebus wondered what instinct had kicked in to make them do that, turning them into war correspondents.

The bottle was on the mantelpiece. The tea was cold in his hand. Three bad men had been chosen for death by a person or persons unknown. Ben Webster had fallen to his doom. Big Ger Cafferty and Gareth Tench were squaring up for violence. *Puts things in perspective* – Siobhan's words. Rebus wasn't so sure. Because now more than ever he wanted answers to questions, wanted faces and names. He couldn't do anything about London or suicide bombers or casual carnage on the scale in front of him. All he could do was lock up a few bad people now and then. Results which didn't seem to change the bigger picture. Another image came to mind: Mickey as a kid, maybe Kirkcaldy beach or some holiday in St Andrews or Blackpool. Frantically scooping up lines of damp sand, creating a barrier against the creeping sea. Working as if his life depended on it. And big brother John, too, using the small plastic shovel to pile the sand on, Mickey patting it down. Twenty, thirty feet long, maybe six inches high ... But the first flecks of foam would be arriving before they had a chance, and they'd have to watch their edifice melt, becoming one with its surroundings. Squealing in defeat, stamping their feet and waving their tiny fists at the lapping water and the treacherous shore and the unmoved sky.

And God.

God above all else.

The bottle seemed to be swelling in size, or maybe it was that *he* was growing smaller. He thought of some lines in a Jackie Leven song: *but my boat is so small, and your sea is so immense*. Immense, yes, but why did it have to be so full of bloody sharks?

When the phone started ringing, he considered not answering. Considered for all of ten seconds. It was Ellen Wylie.

'Any news?' he asked. Then he barked out a short laugh and squeezed the bridge of his nose. 'Apart from the obvious, I mean.'

'State of shock here,' she told him. 'Nobody's about to twig that you copied all that stuff and took it home. I doubt anyone's going to look twice at anything until this week's over. I thought I might head back to Torphichen, see how my team are doing.'

'Good idea.'

'London contingent are being sent home. Could be we'll need all available hands.'

'I won't be holding my breath.'

'Actually, even the anarchists seem to be stunned. Word from Gleneagles is, it's all gone quiet. A lot of them just want to go home.'

Rebus had risen from his chair. He was standing by the mantelpiece. 'Time like this, you want to be near your loved ones.'

'John, are you all right?'

'Just dandy, Ellen.' He drew a finger down the bottle's length. It was Dewar's, pale gold in colour. 'You get yourself back to Torphichen.'

'Do you want me to drop by later?'

'I don't think we'll have accomplished much.'

'Tomorrow, then?'

'Sounds good. Talk to you then.' He cut the connection, leaned both hands against the edge of the mantelpiece.

Could have sworn the bottle was staring back at him.

20

There were buses heading south, and Siobhan's parents had decided to catch one of them.

'We'd have been leaving tomorrow anyway,' her father had said, giving her a hug.

'You never did get to Gleneagles,' she'd told him. He'd pecked her on the cheek, right on the line of her jaw, and for a few seconds she'd been a kid again. Always the same spot, be it Christmas or a birthday, good grades at school, or just because he was feeling happy.

Another embrace from her mother, and whispered words: 'It doesn't matter.' Meaning the damage to her face; meaning finding the culprit. And then, pulling free of the hug but still holding her at arm's length: 'Come see us soon.'

'Promise,' Siobhan had said.

The flat seemed empty without them. She realised that she lived most of her time there in silence. Well, not silence – there was always music or the radio or TV. But not many visitors, nobody whistling as they walked down the hall, or humming as they washed up.

Nobody but her.

She'd tried calling Rebus, but he wasn't answering. The TV was on; she couldn't bring herself to switch it off. Thirty dead ... forty dead ... maybe fifty. The Mayor of London had made a good speech. Al-Qaeda had claimed responsibility. The Queen was 'deeply shocked'. London's commuters were starting the long march home from work. Commentators were asking why the terror alert had been downgraded from 'severe general' to 'substantial'. She wanted to ask them: what difference would it have made?

She went to the fridge. Her mother had been busy at the local shops: duck fillets, lamb chops, a slab of cheese, organic fruit juice. Siobhan tried the freezer compartment and hauled out a frosted tub of Mackie's vanilla ice cream. Got herself a spoon and went back through to the living room. For want of anything else to do, she booted up her computer. Fifty-three emails. A quick glance told her she could delete the vast bulk of them. Then she remembered something, reached into her pocket. The CD-ROM. She slotted it into her hard drive. A few clicks of the mouse and she was studying a screen's worth of thumbnails. Stacey Webster had taken a few of the young mother and her pink-clad baby. Siobhan had to smile. The woman was obviously using her child as a prop, enacting the same nappy-changing scenario in different locations, always directly in front of police lines. A great photo op, and a potential flashpoint. There was even an image of the various press cameramen, Mungo included. But Stacey had been concentrating on the demonstrators, putting together a nice little dossier for her masters at SO12. Some of the cops would be from the Met. They'd be on their way south now, to help in the aftermath, to check on loved ones, maybe eventually to attend the funerals of colleagues. If her mother's attacker turned out to be from London ... she didn't know what she'd do.

Her mother's words: *It doesn't matter ...*

She shook the notion away. It was fifty or sixty pictures in before Siobhan spotted her mum and dad – Teddy Clarke trying to drag his wife away from the front line. A complete mêlée around them. Batons raised, mouths open in a roar or a grimace. Rubbish bins hurled. Dirt and uprooted flowers flying.

And then a stick connecting with the front of her

mother's face. Siobhan almost flinched, but forced herself to look. The stick looked like something picked up off the ground. Not a baton. And swung from the protesters' side of the trouble. The person holding it, he retreated fast. And suddenly Siobhan knew. It was just like she'd been told by Mungo the photographer: you hit out at the cops, and when they retaliate you make sure innocent civilians are in the firing-line. Maximum PR, make the cops look like thugs. Her mother staggered as contact was made. Her face was blurred with movement, but the pain was evident. Siobhan rubbed her thumb over the screen, as if to take away the hurt. Followed the stick back to its owner's bare arm. His shoulder was in shot, but not his head. She went back a few frames, then forward a few past the actual blow.

There.

He'd placed a hand behind his back, hiding the stick, but it was still there. And Stacey had caught him full-face, caught the glee in his eyes, the crooked grin. A few more frames and he was up on his toes, chanting. Baseball cap low down on his forehead, but unmistakable.

The kid from Niddrie, the leader of the pack. Heading down to Princes Street like many of his kind – just for the pure hell of it.

Last seen by Siobhan emerging from the sheriff court, where Councillor Gareth Tench waited. Tench's words: *a couple of my constituents got caught up in all that trouble ...* Tench returning the culprit's salute as he walked free from court ... Siobhan's hand was trembling slightly as she tried Rebus again. Still no answer. She got up and walked around the flat, in and out of every room. The towels in the bathroom had been neatly folded and left in a pile. There was an empty soup carton in the swing-bin in the kitchen. It had been rinsed out so that it wouldn't smell. Her mother's little touches ... She stood in front of her bedroom's full-length mirror, trying to see any resemblance. She thought she looked more like her father. They'd be on the A1 by now, making steady progress south. She hadn't told them the truth about Santal, probably never would. Back at the computer, she went through all the other photos, then started again from the beginning, this time on the lookout for just the one figure, one skinny little troublemaker in his baseball cap, T-shirt, jeans and trainers. Tried printing some of them off, but got a warning that her ink levels were low. There was a computer shop on Leith Walk. She grabbed her keys and purse.

The bottle was empty and there was no more in the house. Rebus had found a half-bottle of Polish vodka in the freezer, but its contents had been reduced to a single measure. Couldn't be bothered walking to the shops, so he made himself a mug of tea instead and sat down at the dining-table, skimming through the case-notes. Ellen Wylie had been impressed by Ben Webster's CV, and so was Rebus. He went through it again. The world's trouble-spots: some people were drawn to them – adventurers, newsmen, mercenaries. Rebus had been told a while back that Mairie Henderson's boyfriend was a cameraman and had travelled to Sierra Leone, Afghanistan, Iraq ... But Rebus got the feeling Ben Webster hadn't gone to any of these places from the vicarious need for a thrill, or even because he'd felt them particularly 'worthy' causes. He'd gone because that was his job.

'It is our most basic duty as human beings,' he'd said in one of his parliamentary speeches, 'to aid sustainable development wherever and whenever possible in the poorest and harshest regions of the world.' It was a point he'd hammered home elsewhere – to various committees, on public platforms, and in media interviews.

My brother was a good man ...

Rebus didn't doubt it. Nor could he think of any reason why someone would have pushed him from those ramparts on to the rocks below. Hard-working as he was, Ben Webster still hadn't posed much of a threat to Pennen Industries. Rebus was coming back round to the suicide option. Maybe Webster had been made depressed by all those conflicts and famines and catastrophes. Maybe he'd known in advance that little progress would be made at the G8, his hopes of a better world stalled once again. Leaping into the void to bring attention to the situation? Rebus couldn't really see that. Webster had sat down to dinner with powerful and influential men, diplomats and politicians from several nations. Why not voice his concerns to *them*? Make a fuss, kick up a stink. Shout and scream ...

That scream flying into the night sky as he launched himself into the dark.

'No,' Rebus said to himself, shaking his head. It felt to him as though the jigsaw was complete enough for him to make out the image, but with some of the pieces wrongly placed.

'No,' he repeated, going back to his reading.

A good man ...

After a further twenty minutes, he found an interview from one of the Sunday supplements of twelve months back. Webster was being questioned about his early days as an MP. He'd had a mentor of sorts, another Scottish MP and Labour high-flyer called Colin Anderson.

Rebus's own Member of Parliament.

'Didn't see you at the funeral, Colin,' Rebus said quietly, underlining a couple of sentences.

Webster is quick to credit Anderson for the help he gave the tyro MP: 'He made sure I avoided the obvious prat-falls, and I can't thank him enough for that.' But the sure-footed Webster is more reticent by far when questioned about the allegation that it was Anderson who propelled him into his current role as Parliamentary Private Secretary, placing him where he could be of future assistance to the Minister for Trade in any leadership contest ...

'Well, well,' Rebus said, blowing across the surface of his cup, even though the liquid within was tepid at best.

'I'd completely forgotten,' Rebus said, dragging a spare chair over to the table, 'that my own Member of Parliament was Minister for Trade. I know you're busy, so I'll keep this short.'

He was in a restaurant on Edinburgh's south side. Early evening, but the place was busy. The staff were making up a place-setting for him, trying to hand him a menu. The Right Honourable Colin Anderson MP was seated across from his wife at a table meant for two.

'Who the hell are you?' he asked.

Rebus was handing the menu back to the waiter. 'I'm not eating,' he explained. Then, to the MP: 'My name's John Rebus. I'm a detective inspector. Did your secretary not say?'

'Can I see some identification?' Anderson was asking.

'Not really her fault,' Rebus was telling him. 'I exaggerated a little, said it was an emergency.' He'd opened his warrant card for inspection. While the MP studied it, Rebus smiled in his wife's direction.

'Should I ...?' She motioned to rise from the table.

'Nothing top secret,' Rebus assured her. Anderson was handing back Rebus's ID.

'If you don't mind me saying, Inspector, this isn't exactly convenient.'

'I thought your secretary would have told you.'

Anderson lifted his mobile from the table. 'No signal,' he stated.

'You should do something about that,' Rebus commented. 'Lots of the city still like that ...'

'Have you been drinking, Inspector?'

'Only when off-duty, sir.' Rebus fussed in his pocket until he'd found the packet.

'There's no smoking in here,' Anderson warned him.

Rebus looked at the cigarette pack as though it had crawled unnoticed into his hand. He apologised and put it away again. 'Didn't see you at the funeral, sir,' he told the MP.

'Which funeral?'

'Ben Webster. You were a good friend to him in his early days.'

'I was otherwise engaged.' The MP made a show of checking his watch.

'Ben's sister told me that once her brother was dead, Labour would soon forget about him.'

'I think that's unreasonable. Ben was a friend of mine, Inspector, and I *did* want to attend the funeral ...'

'But you've been busy,' Rebus said, all understanding. 'And here you are, trying to catch a quick, quiet meal with your wife, and I come barging in unannounced.'

'It happens to be my wife's birthday. We managed – God knows how – to keep a window free.'

'And I've gone and smudged it.' Rebus turned to the wife. 'Many happy returns.'

The waiter was placing a wine glass in front of Rebus. 'Maybe some water instead?' Anderson suggested. Rebus nodded.

'Have you been busy with the G8?' the MP's wife asked, leaning forward.

'Busy *despite* the G8,' Rebus corrected her. He saw husband and wife exchange a glance, knew what they were thinking. A hungover cop, wired from all the demos and the chaos and now the bombings. Damaged goods, to be handled with care.

'Can this really not wait till morning, Inspector?' Anderson asked quietly.

'I'm looking into Ben Webster's death,' Rebus explained. His voice sounded nasal, even to his own ears, and there was a creeping mist at the edges of his vision. 'Can't seem to find a reason for him to take his own life.'

'More likely an accident, surely,' the MP's wife offered.

'Or he was given a hand,' Rebus stated.

'What?' Anderson had stopped arranging the cutlery in front of him.

'Richard Pennen wants to link overseas aid to arms sales, doesn't he? How's it going to work – he donates a chunk of money in exchange for looser controls?'

'Don't be absurd.' The MP allowed his voice to betray his irritation.

'Were you at the Castle that night?'

'I was busy at Westminster.'

'Any chance that Webster had words with Pennen? Maybe at your behest?'

'What sort of words?'

'Cutting back the arms trade … turning all those guns into plough-shares.'

'Look, you can't just go around defaming Richard Pennen. If there's any evidence, I'd like to see it.'

'Me too,' Rebus agreed.

'Meaning there's none? And you're basing this witch-hunt on what exactly, Inspector?'

'On the fact that Special Branch want me to butt out, or at the very least toe the line.'

'While you'd prefer to cross that same line?'

'Only way of getting anywhere.'

'Ben Webster was an outstanding Member of Parliament and a rising star in his party …'

'And he'd have supported you to the hilt in any leader-ship contest,' Rebus couldn't help adding.

'Now you're just being bloody scurrilous!' Anderson snarled.

'Was he the sort to get up the nose of big business?' Rebus asked. 'The sort who couldn't be bribed or bought off?' His head was feeling even muzzier.

'You seem exhausted, Officer,' the MP's wife said, voice sympathetic. 'Are you sure this really can't wait?'

Rebus was shaking his head, aware of its sheer mass. Felt like he might crash through the floor, his body was so heavy.

'Darling,' the MP's wife was telling her husband, 'here's Rosie.'

A flustered-looking young woman was squeezing her way between the tables. The staff looked worried that they might be asked to sit four at a table intended for two.

'I left message after message after message,' Rosie was saying, 'and then thought maybe you weren't getting them.'

'No signal,' Anderson growled, tapping his phone. 'This is the Inspector.'

Rebus had risen to his feet, offering Anderson's secretary his chair. She shook her head, avoiding eye contact.

'The Inspector,' she was telling the MP, 'is currently under suspension, pending an inquiry into his conduct.' Now her eyes met Rebus's. 'I made a couple of calls.'

One of Anderson's substantial eyebrows had lifted.

'I did say I was off-duty,' Rebus reminded him.

'I'm not sure it was *quite* as cut-and-dried as that. Ah ... the starters.' Two waiters were hovering: one with smoked salmon, the other with a bowl of orange-coloured soup. 'You'll be leaving now, Inspector.' It was statement rather than request.

'Ben Webster deserves a bit of consideration, don't you think?'

The MP ignored this, unfolding his napkin. But his secretary had no such qualms.

'Get out!' she snarled.

Rebus nodded slowly, and half-turned before remembering something. 'Pavements round my way are in a shocking state,' he told his MP. 'Maybe you could spare the time to visit your constituency once in a while ...'

*

'Jump in,' the voice ordered. Rebus turned and saw that Siobhan had parked in front of his tenement.

'Car looks good,' he told her.

'Just as well, the money your friendly mechanic charged.'

'I was just headed upstairs ...'

'Change of plan. I need you to come with me.' She paused. 'You okay?'

'Had a couple of drinks earlier. Did something I probably shouldn't.'

'Now there's a novelty.' But she still managed to look aghast when he told her about his trip to the restaurant.

'Another bollocking in store, no doubt,' were his closing words.

'You don't say.' Siobhan closed her own door as Rebus got into the passenger seat.

'What about you?' he asked.

She told him about her parents and the contents of Stacey Webster's camera. Reached into the back seat and handed him the evidence.

'So now we go talk to the councillor?' Rebus guessed.

'That was the plan. Why are you smiling?'

He pretended to be studying the pictures. 'Your mum says she's not bothered who whacked her. Nobody seems worried about Ben Webster's death. And yet here we both are.' He lifted his face towards her and gave a tired smile.

'It's what we do,' she replied quietly.

'My point exactly. No matter what anyone thinks or says. I just worry that you've learned all the wrong lessons from me.'

'Credit me with a bit of sense,' she chided him, putting the car into gear.

Councillor Gareth Tench lived in a sizeable Victorian villa on Duddingston Park. It was a main road, but its houses were set back far enough to give them some privacy. Not five minutes' drive from Niddrie, yet it was another world: respectable, middle-class, quiet. There was a golf course to the rear of the properties, and Portobello beach was within striking distance. Siobhan had taken a route along Niddrie Mains Road, so they could see that the campsite was disappearing fast.

'Want to drop in on your boyfriend?' Rebus teased.

'Maybe you should stay in the car,' she retorted. 'Let me talk to Tench.'

'I'm as sober as a judge,' Rebus argued. 'Well ... getting there anyway.' They'd stopped at a garage on Ratcliffe Terrace so he could buy Irn-Bru and paracetamol.

'Inventor deserves the Nobel Prize,' Rebus had stated, without specifying which product he was referring to.

There were two cars parked in Tench's forecourt. The whole front garden had been paved to make room for them. Lights blazed in the living room.

'Good cop, bad cop?' Rebus suggested as Siobhan rang the doorbell. She rewarded him with the beginnings of a smile. The door was opened by a woman.

'Mrs Tench?' Siobhan asked, holding up her warrant card. 'Any chance of a word with your husband?'

Then Tench's voice from inside the house: 'Who is it, Louisa?'

'Police, Gareth,' she bellowed back, retreating a little by way of invitation. They didn't need asking twice, and were in the living room by the time Tench trudged downstairs. The fittings weren't to Rebus's taste: sashed velvet drapes; brass lamps fixed to the walls either side of the fireplace; two oversized sofas taking up much of the floor space. Oversized and brassy seemed to describe Louisa Tench, too. She wore dangling earrings and a clatter of bracelets. The tan had come from a bottle or salon, as had the piled auburn hair. A little too much blue eye-shadow and pink lipstick. He counted five carriage clocks in the room and decided that nothing here had been chosen by the councillor.

'Evening, sir,' Siobhan said as Tench walked into the room. He rolled his eyes heavenward in reply.

'Don't they ever let up, Lord? Should I sue for harassment?'

'Before you do that, Mr Tench,' Siobhan went on calmly, 'maybe you could look at these photos.' She handed them to him. 'You recognise your constituent, of course?'

'He's the same one you hooked up with outside the court,' Rebus added helpfully. 'And by the way ... Denise says hello.'

Tench glanced fearfully towards his wife. She was back in her chair, staring at the TV with its sound muted. 'What about these photos, then?' he said, louder than was strictly necessary.

'You'll notice that he's attacking that woman with a wooden stick,' Siobhan continued. Rebus was watching carefully – and listening, too. 'In this next photo, he's trying to melt back into the crowd. But you'll agree that he'd just attacked an innocent bystander.'

Tench looked sceptical, eyes flitting between one photo and the other. 'Digital, aren't they?' he pointed out. 'Easy enough to manipulate.'

'It's not the photos that are being manipulated here, Mr Tench,' Rebus thought it his duty to state.

'What's that supposed to mean?'

'We want his name,' Siobhan said. 'We can get it tomorrow morning from the court, but we'd prefer to get it from you.'

He narrowed his eyes. 'Why's that, then?'

'Because we'd ...' Siobhan paused. 'Because *I'd* like to know what the connection is. Twice at the campsite you just happened along to save the day ...' she stabbed a finger at one photo, 'from *him*. Next thing you're waiting for him when he comes out of police custody. And now this.'

'He's just another kid from the wrong part of town,'

Tench said, keeping his voice down but emphasising each word. 'Wrong parents, wrong school, wrong choices at every fork in the road. But he lives on *my* patch and that means I look out for him, same as I would do for any other poor bloody kid in his position. If that's a crime, DS Clarke, then I'm ready to go into the dock and argue my case.' A fleck of saliva escaped his mouth and hit Siobhan on the cheek. She brushed it away with the tip of a finger.

'His name,' she repeated.

'He's already *been* charged.'

Louisa Tench was still in her chair, one leg crossed over the other, her eyes on the muted television.

'Gareth,' she said, '*Emmerdale*.'

'Don't want your wife missing her soap, do you, Mr Tench?' Rebus added. The opening titles were already onscreen. She had the remote in her hand, finger poised above the volume button. Three pairs of eyes boring into Gareth Tench, and Rebus mouthing the name *Denise* again.

'Carberry,' Tench said. 'Keith Carberry.'

Music burst suddenly from the TV. Tench slid his hands into his pockets, stalked out of the room. Rebus and Siobhan waited a few moments, then said their goodbyes to the woman who was tucking her legs beneath her on the chair. She ignored them, lost in a world of her own. The front door was ajar, Tench waiting for them outside, arms folded, feet apart.

'A smear campaign's not going to do anyone any good,' he told them.

'Just doing our job, sir.'

'I grew up near a farm, DS Clarke,' he said. 'I know bullshit when I smell it.'

Siobhan looked him up and down. 'And I know a clown when I see one, even out of costume.' She walked towards the pavement, Rebus pausing in front of Tench, leaning forward towards his ear.

'The woman your boy smacked is her mother. That means this never ends, understood? Not until we get a result we're happy with.' Leaned back again and nodded, reinforcing the message. 'Wife doesn't know about Denise, then?' he added.

'That's how you connected me to Ozyman,' Tench guessed. 'Ellen Wylie told you.'

'Not very clever of you, Councillor, playing away from home. This is more a village than a city, bound to come out sooner or—'

'Christ, Rebus, it wasn't like that!' Tench hissed.

'Not for me to say, sir.'

'And now I suppose you'll go tell your employer? Well, let him do what he likes – I'm not about to bow down to his kind ... or yours.' Tench gave a look of defiance. Rebus stood his ground a moment longer, then smiled and followed Siobhan back to the car.

'Special dispensation?' he asked, once he'd fastened his seat-belt. She looked across, saw that he was waving a cigarette packet.

'Keep the window open,' she ordered.

Rebus lit the cigarette and blew smoke into the evening sky. They'd only gone forty yards when a car pulled out in front of them, then braked, blocking half the road.

'Hell's this?' Rebus hissed.

'Bentley,' Siobhan told him. Sure enough, as the brake-lights dimmed, Cafferty emerged from the driver's side, walking purposefully towards them, leaning down so his head was framed by Rebus's open window.

'You're a ways from home,' Rebus advised him.

'So are you. A wee visit to Gareth Tench, eh? I hope he's not trying to buy you off.'

'He thinks you're paying us five hundred a week,' Rebus drawled. 'Made a counter-offer of two grand.' He blew smoke into Cafferty's face.

'I've just bought a pub in Portobello,' Cafferty said,

wafting his hands in front of him. 'Come and have a drink.'

'Last thing I need,' Rebus told him.

'A soft drink, then.'

'What is it you want?' Siobhan said. Her hands still gripped the steering wheel.

'Is it just me,' Cafferty asked Rebus, 'or is she toughening up?' Suddenly he reached a hand through the window, snatching one of the photos from Rebus's lap. Took a couple of steps back into the roadway, holding it close to his face. Siobhan was out of the car in an instant, marching towards him.

'I'm not in the mood for this, Cafferty.'

'Ah,' he was saying, 'I *did* hear something about your mother ... And I recognise *this* little bastard.'

Siobhan stopped dead, hand caught in mid-grab for the photo.

'Name's Kevin or Keith,' Cafferty went on.

'Keith Carberry,' she told him. Rebus was getting out of the car now. He could see that Cafferty had snared her.

'Nothing to do with you,' Rebus warned him.

'Of course not,' Cafferty agreed. 'I can understand it's personal. Just wondered if I could help, that's all.'

'Help how?' Siobhan asked.

'Don't listen to him,' Rebus warned. But Cafferty's gaze had her transfixed.

'Any way I can,' he said quietly. 'Keith works for Tench, doesn't he? Wouldn't it be better to bring down both of them, rather than just the messenger?'

'Tench wasn't in Princes Street Gardens.'

'And young Keith doesn't have the sense he was born with,' Cafferty countered. 'Tends to make lads like him *suggestible*.'

'Christ, Siobhan,' Rebus pleaded, gripping her by the arm. 'He wants Tench taken down. Doesn't matter to him

352

how it happens.' He wagged a finger at Cafferty. 'She's not part of this.'

'I was only offering …' Cafferty held up his hands in surrender.

'What's with the stakeout anyway? Got a baseball bat and a shovel in the Bentley?'

Cafferty ignored him, gave Siobhan back the photograph. 'Pound to a penny Keith's playing pool at that place in Restalrig. Only one way to find out …'

Her eyes were on the photo. When Cafferty said her name, she blinked a couple of times and focused on him instead. Then she shook her head.

'Later,' she said.

He gave a shrug. 'Whenever you like.'

'You won't be there,' she declared.

He tried to look hurt. 'Hardly fair, after everything I've told you.'

'You won't *be* there,' she repeated. Cafferty turned his attention to Rebus.

'Did I say she was toughening up? Might have been an understatement.'

'Might have been,' Rebus agreed.

21

He'd been steeping in a bath for twenty minutes when the intercom buzzed. Decided to ignore it, then heard his mobile ringing. Whoever it was left a message – the phone beeped afterwards to let him know. When Siobhan had dropped him, he'd warned her to go straight home, get some rest.

'Shit,' he said, realising that she might be in trouble. Got out of the bath and wrapped a towel around himself, leaving wet footprints as he padded into the living room. But the message wasn't from Siobhan. It was Ellen Wylie. She was outside in her car.

'Never been so popular with the ladies,' he muttered, punching the recall button. 'Give me five minutes,' he told her. Then he went and changed back into his clothes. The intercom sounded again. He let her in, and waited at the door, listening to the sandpaper sound of her shoes as she climbed the two flights of stone steps.

'Ellen, always a pleasure,' he said.

'I'm sorry, John. We were all down the pub, and I just couldn't stop thinking about it.'

'The bombings?'

She shook her head. 'Your case,' she clarified. They were in the living room by now. She walked across to where the paperwork lay; saw the wall and moved towards it, scanning the pictures pinned there. 'I've spent half the day reading about all these monsters ... reading what their victims' families think of them, and then having to alert those same bastards that there might be someone out for revenge.'

'It was still the right thing to do, Ellen. Time like this, we need to feel we're doing *something*.'

'Say they were bombers instead of rapists ...'

'What's the point in that?' he asked, waiting until she'd given an answering shrug. Then: 'Anything to drink?'

'Maybe some tea ...' She half-turned towards him. 'This is okay, isn't it? Me barging in like this?'

'Glad of the company,' he lied, heading for the kitchen.

When he came back with the two mugs, she was seated at the dining table, poring over the first pile of paperwork. 'How's Denise?' he asked.

'She's fine.'

'Tell me, Ellen ...' He paused until he was sure she was giving him her attention. 'Did you know Tench is married?'

'Separated,' she corrected him.

Rebus pursed his lips. 'Not by much,' he added. 'They live in the same house.'

She didn't blink. 'Why are all men bastards, John? Present company excepted, naturally.'

'Makes me wonder about him,' Rebus went on. 'Why is he so interested in Denise?'

'She's not *that* bad a catch.'

Rebus conceded the point with a twitch of the mouth. 'All the same, I suspect the councillor is attracted to victims. Some men are, aren't they?'

'What are you getting at?'

'I'm not sure really ... just trying to work out what makes him tick.'

'Why?'

Rebus snorted. 'Another bloody good question.'

'You think he's a suspect?'

'How many do we have?'

She offered a shrug. 'Eric Bain has managed to pull some names and details from the subscription list. My guess is, they'll turn out to be the families of victims, or professionals working in the field.'

'Which camp does Tench fall into?'

'Neither. Does *that* make him a suspect?'

Rebus was standing next to her, staring down at the case-notes. 'We need a profile of the killer. All we know so far is that he doesn't confront the victims.'

'Yet he left Trevor Guest in a hell of a state – cuts, scratches, bruises. Also left us Guest's cash card, meaning we had his name straight away.'

'You're calling that an anomaly?'

She nodded. 'But then you could just as easily say Cyril Colliar is the anomaly, being the only Scot.'

Rebus stared at a photograph of Trevor Guest's face. 'Guest spent time up here,' he said. 'Hackman told me as much.'

'Do we know where?'

Rebus shook his head slowly. 'Must be in the files some-where.'

'Any chance that the third victim had some Scottish connection?'

'I suppose it's possible.'

'Maybe that's the key. Instead of concentrating on BeastWatch, we should be thinking more about the three victims.'

'You sound ready to get started.'

She looked at him. 'I'm too wired to sleep. How about you? I could always take some stuff away with me?'

Rebus shook his head again. 'You're fine where you are.' He picked up a handful of reports and headed over to his chair, switching on a floor-lamp behind him before settling down. 'Won't Denise worry where you are?'

'I'll text her, say I'm working late.'

'Best not to mention where … don't want any gossip.'

She smiled. 'No,' she agreed, 'we certainly wouldn't want that. Speaking of which, should we let Siobhan know?'

'Know what?'

'She's in charge of the case, isn't she?'

'I keep forgetting,' Rebus replied casually, going back to his reading.

It was almost midnight when he woke up. Ellen was tip-toeing back from the kitchen with a fresh mug of tea.

'Sorry,' she apologised.

'I dozed off,' he said.

'Well over an hour ago.' She was blowing across the surface of the liquid.

'Did I miss anything?'

'Nothing to report. Why don't you go to bed?'

'Leaving you grafting on your own?' He stretched his arms out, feeling his spine crackle. 'I'll be fine.'

'You look exhausted.'

'So everyone keeps telling me.' He'd risen to his feet and was walking towards the table. 'How far have you got?'

'Can't find any connection between Edward Isley and Scotland – no family, no jobs, and no holidays. I began to wonder if we were going at it from the wrong end.'

'How do you mean?'

'Maybe it was Colliar who had connections with the north of England.'

'Good point.'

'But that doesn't seem to be panning out either.'

'Maybe you need to take a break.'

She hoisted the mug. 'What does this look like?'

'I meant something more substantial.'

She was rolling her shoulders. 'Haven't got a jacuzzi or a masseur on the premises by any chance?' She saw the look on his face. 'I'm joking,' she reassured him. 'Something tells me you're not an expert at back-rubs. Besides ...' But she broke off, lifting the mug to her face.

'Besides what?' he asked.

She lowered the mug again. 'Well, you and Siobhan ...'

'... are colleagues,' he stated. 'Colleagues *and* friends. Nothing more than that, despite the rumour-mill.'

'Stories *have* gone around,' she admitted.

'And that's what they are – stories. Meaning fiction.'

'Wouldn't be the first time, though, would it? I mean, you and DCS Templer.'

'Gill Templer was years back, Ellen.'

'I'm not saying she wasn't.' She stared into space. 'This job we do ... how many do you know manage to keep a relationship together?'

'There are a few. Shug Davidson's been married twenty years.'

She conceded the point. 'But you, me, Siobhan ... dozens more I could name ...'

'Comes with the territory, Ellen.'

'All these other lives we get to know ...' She wafted a hand over the case-files. 'And we're rubbish at finding one for ourselves.' She looked at him. 'There's really nothing between you and Siobhan?'

He shook his head. 'So don't go thinking you can some-how drive a wedge between us.'

She tried to look outraged by the suggestion, but strug-gled for words.

'You're flirting,' he told her. 'Only reason I can think of for that is so you can wind Siobhan up.'

'Jesus Christ.' She slammed the mug down on the table, splashing the paperwork spread out there. 'Of all the arro-gant, misguided, thick-headed ...' She was rising from her chair.

'Look, if I'm wrong I apologise. It's the middle of the night, maybe we both need some shut-eye ...'

'A thank-you would be nice,' she demanded.

'For what?'

'For slogging while you were snoring! For helping you out when it could cost me a bollocking! For *everything*!'

Rebus stood, seemingly dazed, for another moment

before opening his mouth and uttering the two words she wanted to hear.

'Thank you.'

'And fuck you too, John,' she retorted, picking up her coat and bag. He stood back to give her room as she walked out, listened to the door slam behind her. Took a handkerchief from his pocket and dabbed the tea-stained paperwork.

'No real damage,' he said to himself. 'No real damage ...'

'Thanks for this,' Morris Gerald Cafferty said, holding open the passenger-side door. Siobhan paused for a moment, then decided to get in.

'We're just talking,' she warned him.

'Absolutely.' He closed her door gently and walked around to the driver's side. 'It's been a hell of a day, hasn't it?' he said. 'There was a bomb scare on Princes Street ...'

'We don't move from here,' she decreed, ignoring him.

He closed his own door and half turned towards her. 'We could have talked upstairs.'

She shook her head. 'No way you're crossing *that* threshold.'

Cafferty accepted the slur on his character. He peered out at her tenement. 'Thought you'd be living somewhere better by now.'

'Suits me fine,' she snapped back. 'Though I wouldn't mind knowing how you found me.'

He gave a warm smile. 'I have friends,' he told her. 'One phone call, job done.'

'Yet you can't manage the same trick with Gareth Tench? One call to a professional and he's never heard of again ...'

'I don't want him dead.' He sought the right phrase. 'Just brought low.'

'As in humiliated? Cowed? Scared?'

'I think it's time people saw him for what he is.' He leaned over a little closer. '*You* know what he is now. But in focusing on Keith Carberry, you'll be missing a clear shot at goal.' He gave another smile. 'I speak as one football fan to another, even if we're on opposite sides in our choices.'

'We're on opposite sides in *everything*, Cafferty – never think otherwise.'

He bowed his head slightly. 'You even sound like him, you know.'

'Who?'

'Rebus, of course. You both share the same chippy attitude – think you know better than anyone … think you *are* better than anyone.'

'Wow, a counselling session.'

'See? There you go again. It's almost as if Rebus is working the strings.' He chuckled. 'Time you became your own woman, Siobhan. And it has to happen before Rebus gets the gold watch … meaning soon.' He paused. 'No time like the present.'

'Advice from you is the last thing I need.'

'I'm not offering advice – I'm offering to *help*. Between us we can bring Tench down.'

'You made John the same offer, didn't you? That night at the church hall? I'm betting he said no.'

'He wanted to say yes.'

'But he didn't.'

'Rebus and me have been enemies too long, Siobhan. We've almost forgotten what started it. But you and me, we've not got that history.'

'You're a gangster, Mr Cafferty. Any help from you, I *become* like you.'

'No,' he said, shaking his head, 'what you do is, you put away the people responsible for that attack on your mother. If all you've got to work from is that photo, you're not going to get further than Keith Carberry.'

'And you're offering so much more?' she guessed. 'Like one of those shysters on the shopping channels?'

'Now that's cruel,' he chided her.

'Cruel but fair,' she corrected him. She was staring out through the windscreen. A taxi was dropping a drunk-looking couple at their door. As it moved away, they hugged and kissed, almost losing their balance on the pavement. 'What about a scandal?' she suggested. 'Something that would put the councillor on the front of the tabloids?'

'Anything in mind?'

'Tench plays away from home,' she told him. 'Wife sitting in front of the TV while he visits his girlfriends.'

'How do you know this?'

'There's a colleague of mine, Ellen Wylie ... her sister's ...' But if news broke, it wouldn't just be Tench on the front pages ... it would be Denise too. 'No,' she said, shaking her head. 'Forget that.' Stupid, stupid, stupid ...

'Why?'

'Because we'd be hurting a woman whose skin's more fragile than most.'

'Then consider it forgotten.'

She turned to face him. 'So tell me, what *would* you do if you were me? How would you get to Gareth Tench?'

'Through young Keith, of course,' he said, as if it were the most obvious thing in the starlit world.

Mairie was relishing the chase.

This wasn't features; wasn't some puff-piece for a chum of the editor, or interview-as-marketing-tool for an over-hyped film or book. It was an investigation. It was why she'd gone into journalism in the first place.

Even the dead ends were thrilling, and so far she'd taken plenty of wrong turns. But now she'd been put in touch with a journalist down in London – another freelancer. The two of them had danced around one another during their first telephone conversation. Her London connection was attached to a TV project, a documentary about Iraq. *My Baghdad Launderette*, it was going to be called. At first, he wouldn't tell her why. But then she'd mentioned her Kenyan contact, and the man in London had melted a little.

And she'd allowed herself a smile: if there was any dancing to be done, *she'd* be the one doing the leading.

Baghdad Launderette because of all the money washing around Iraq in general, and its capital in particular. Billions – maybe tens of billions of US-backed dollars – had gone into reconstruction. And much of it could not be accounted for. Suitcases of cash used for the bribing of local officials. Palms greased to ensure that elections would go ahead no matter what. American companies moving into the emerging market 'with extreme prejudice', according to her new friend. Money sloshing around, the various sides in the conflict needing to feel safe in these uncertain times ...

Needing to be armed.

Shiites and Sunnis and Kurds. Yes, water and electricity were necessities, but so were efficient guns and rocket-launchers. For defence only, of course, because reconstruction could only come when people felt protected.

'I thought arms were being taken out of the equation,' Mairie had commented.

'Only to be put back in again as soon as nobody's looking.'

'And you're linking Pennen to all of this?' Mairie had eventually asked, scribbling notes to herself furiously, the phone clenched between cheek and shoulder.

'Just the tiniest portion. He's a footnote, a little PS at the end of the missive. And it's not even him per se really, is it? It's the company he runs.'

'And the company he keeps,' she couldn't help adding. 'In Kenya he's been making sure his bread's buttered on both sides.'

'Funding the government *and* the opposition? Yes, I'd heard about that. As far as I know, it's no big deal.'

But the diplomat Kamweze had given her a little more. Cars for government ministers; road-building in districts run by opposition leaders; new houses for the most important tribal leaders. All of it described as 'aid', while arms powered by Pennen technology added to the national debt.

'In Iraq,' the London journalist went on, 'Pennen Industries seems to fund rather a grey area of reconstruction – namely, private defence contractors. Armed and subsidised by Pennen. It may be the first war in history run largely by the private sector.'

'So what do these defence contractors do?'

'Act as bodyguards for people coming into the country to do business. Plus man the barricades, protect the Green Zone, ensure local dignitaries can turn their car key in the ignition without having to fear a *Godfather* moment ...'

'I get the picture. They're mercenaries, right?'

'Not at all – perfectly legit.'

'But sponsored by Pennen cash?'

'To a degree ...'

Eventually she'd ended the call with promises on both sides to stay in touch, her London friend stressing that as long as she steered clear of the Iraq story, they might be able to help one another. Mairie had typed up her notes while they were fresh, then had bounced through to the living room where Allan was slumped in front of *Die Hard 3* – watching all his old favourites again now that he had his home cinema to play with. She'd given him a hug and poured them both a glass of wine.

'What's the occasion?' he'd asked, pecking her on the cheek.

'Allan,' she said, 'you've been to Iraq ... tell me about it.'

Later that night, she'd slipped out of bed. Her phone

was beeping, telling her she had a text. It was from the Westminster correspondent of the *Herald* newspaper. They'd sat next to one another at an awards dinner two years back, sinking the Mouton Cadet and laughing at the short-lists in every single category. Mairie had kept in touch with him, actually quite fancied him though he was married – happily married, as far as she knew ... She sat on the carpeted stairs, dressed in just a T-shirt, chin on her knees, reading his text.

U shd hv said u had interest in Pennen. Call me 4 more!

She'd done more than call him. She'd driven to Glasgow in the middle of the night and made him meet her at a twenty-four-hour café. The place was full of student drunks, bleary rather than loud. Her friend was called Cameron Bruce – it was a joke with them – 'the name that works just as well from both directions'. He arrived wearing a sweatshirt and jogging-pants, his hair tousled.

'Morning,' he said, glancing meaningfully at his watch.

'You've only got yourself to blame,' she chided him. 'You can't go teasing a girl at close to midnight.'

'It has been known,' he replied. The twinkle in his eye told her she'd need to check the current status of that happy marriage. She thanked God she hadn't arranged to meet him at a hotel.

'Spit it out then,' she said.

'Coffee's not that bad actually,' he replied, lifting his mug.

'I didn't drive halfway across Scotland for bad jokes, Cammy.'

'Then why did you?'

So she sat back and told him about her interest in Richard Pennen. She left bits out, of course – Cammy was the competition, after all, despite being a friend. He was wise enough to know there were gaps in her story – every time she paused or appeared to change her mind about something, he gave a little smile of recognition. At one point she had to break off while the staff dealt with an unruly new client. It was all done professionally and at speed, and the man found himself back on the pavement. Gave the door a few kicks and the window a few thumps, but then slouched away.

They ordered more coffees, and rounds of buttered toast. And then Cameron Bruce told her what he knew.

Or, rather, what he suspected – all of it based on stories doing the rounds. 'And therefore to be taken with the usual cellar of salt.'

She nodded her understanding.

'Party funding,' he stated. Mairie's reaction: feigned sudden sleep. Bruce laughed and told her it was actually quite interesting.

'You don't say?'

Richard Pennen, it transpired, was a major personal donor to the Labour Party. Nothing wrong with that, not even when his own company stood to benefit from government contracts.

'Happens with Capita,' Bruce commented, 'and plenty of others.'

'You're saying you dragged me all the way here to tell me Pennen's doing something completely legal and above board?' Mairie sounded less than overwhelmed.

'I'm not so sure about that. See, Mr Pennen is playing on both sides of the net.'

'Giving money to the Tories as well as Labour?'

'In a manner of speaking, yes. Pennen Industries has sponsored several Tory shindigs and bigwigs.'

'But that's the company rather than Pennen himself? So he's probably not breaking any laws.'

Bruce just smiled. 'Mairie, you don't have to break the law to get into trouble in politics.'

She glared at him. 'There's something else, isn't there?'

'Might be,' he said, biting into another half-slice of toast.

SIDE FOUR

The Final Push

Friday 8 July

22

The front pages were carnage. Large colour photos of the red London double-decker. Survivors speckled with blood and soot, eyes vacant. One woman with a huge white compress held to her face. Edinburgh had a post-traumatic feel to it. The bus on Princes Street, the one with the suspect package, had been towed away, once a controlled explosion had been carried out. Same procedure with a shopping bag left in one of the nearby stores. Some shards of glass on the road, and a few flowerbeds still ruptured by the Wednesday riot. But it all seemed such a long time ago. People were back at work, boards removed from windows, barriers lifted on to flat-bed lorries. The protesters were melting away from Gleneagles, too. Tony Blair had flown back from London in time for the closing ceremony. There would be speeches and signings, but people seemed unsure how to feel about any of it. The London bombs had given the perfect excuse for trade talks to be curtailed. There would be extra aid for Africa, but not as much as the campaigners had wanted. Before poverty could be tackled, the politicians had a more immediate war to wage.

Rebus folded the newspaper closed and tossed it on to the small table next to his chair. He was in a corridor on the top floor of Lothian and Borders Police HQ, Fettes Avenue. The summons had come just as he was stirring from bed. The Chief Constable's secretary had been insistent, when Rebus had tried querying the time-frame.

'At once,' she'd stipulated. Which was why Rebus had

stopped off just long enough for a coffee, bun and paper. He still had the last chunk of dough-ring in his hand when James Corbyn's door opened. Rebus stood, thinking he would be going inside, but Corbyn seemed content that their conversation would take place right there in the corridor.

'I thought you'd been given fair warning, DI Rebus – you were off the case.'

'Yes, sir,' Rebus agreed.

'Well then?'

'Well, sir, I knew I wasn't allowed to work the Auchterarder case, but thought I'd tie up a few loose ends regarding Ben Webster.'

'You were suspended from duty.'

Rebus looked dumbfounded. 'Not just the one case?'

'You know damned well what a suspension means.'

'Sorry, sir – age creeping up.'

'It is indeed,' Corbyn purred. 'You're already on the maximum pension. Makes me wonder why you stick around.'

'Nothing better to do, sir.' Rebus paused. 'Incidentally, sir, is it a crime for a constituent to ask his MP a question?'

'He's Minister for Trade, Rebus. That means he has the PM's ear. The G8 finishes today, and we don't want a black mark against us at this stage.'

'Well, I've no reason to bother the Minister again.'

'Bloody right you haven't – or anyone else for that matter. This is your last chance. At the moment, you might escape with an official reprimand, but if your name comes sailing on to my desk one more time ...' Corbyn held up a finger for effect.

'Message received, sir.' Rebus's phone started ringing. He lifted it from his pocket and checked the number: no one he knew. Put the little silver box to his ear.

'Hello?'

'Rebus? It's Stan Hackman. Meant to call you yesterday, but with everything that happened ...'

Rebus could feel Corbyn's eyes on him. 'Sweetheart,' he crooned into the phone, 'I'm going to call you back, promise.' He made a kissing sound and killed the call. 'Girlfriend,' he explained to Corbyn.

'She's a brave woman,' the Chief Constable said, opening the door to his office.

Meeting over.

'Keith?'

Siobhan was seated in her car, window down. Keith Carberry was walking towards the door of the pool-hall. The place opened at eight, and Siobhan had been there since quarter to, just to be on the safe side, watching sluggish workers trudging to the bus stop. She motioned him towards the car with her hand. He looked to left and right, fearing some sort of ambush. There was a thin black carrying-case under his arm – his personal cue. Siobhan reckoned it would come in handy as a weapon should occasion demand.

'Yeah?' he said.

'Remember me?'

'I can smell the bacon from here.' The hood of his navy top had been pulled over his pale baseball cap. Same outfit he'd been wearing in the photos. 'Knew I'd be seeing you again – you were gagging for it that night.' He reinforced the message by adjusting his crotch with a cupped hand.

'How was your day in court?'

'Lovely.'

'Charged with breach of the peace,' she recited. 'Bailed on condition you steer clear of Princes Street and sign in daily at Craigmillar Police Station.'

'You stalking me? I've heard of women who get obsessed like that.' He laughed and straightened up. 'We done here?'

'Just getting started.'

'Fine.' He turned away. 'See you inside then.'

She called out his name again but he ignored her. Yanked open the door and went into the pool-hall. Siobhan wound her window up, got out and locked the car. Followed him into Lonnie's Pool Academy – 'Best Tables in Restalrig'.

It was dimly-lit and fuggy, as though never quite cleaned properly at the end of each day. There were already two tables in play. Carberry was sticking coins into a drinks machine, pulling out a can of cola. Siobhan couldn't see any staff, which meant they were probably playing. Balls clattered and dropped into pockets. Swearing seemed to be mandatory between shots.

'Jammy bastard.'

'Fuck off. Six in the top corner, watch this, ya choob.'

'Fanny alert.'

Four pairs of eyes looked up at Siobhan. Only Carberry ignored her, drinking his drink. There was a radio playing in the background, its signal distorted.

'Help you, sweetheart?' one of the players asked.

'Looking to play a few games,' she said, handing him a five-pound note. 'Any chance of some change?'

He was still in his teens, but obviously ran the early shift. Took the note from her and keyed open the till behind the food counter, counted out ten fifty-pence pieces.

'Cheap tables,' she told him.

'Crap tables,' one of the players corrected her.

'Fuckin' shut it, Jimmy,' the teenager said. But Jimmy was just getting into his stride.

'Hey, sweetheart, ever see that film *The Accused*? If you feel a Jodie Foster moment coming on, we can make sure the door's bolted.'

'Try anything, *you'll* be the one doing the bolting,' Siobhan snapped back.

'Just ignore him,' the teenager advised her. 'I'll give you a game if you want.'

'It's me she wants to take on,' Keith Carberry called out, stifling a burp as he crushed the empty can in his fist.

'Maybe after,' Siobhan told the teenager, making her way to Carberry's table. She crouched to slot home the coin. 'Rack them up,' she said. Carberry got busy with the triangle while she chose a cue. The tips were ragged, and there was no sign of chalk. Carberry had opened his case, screwed his two-piece cue together. Drew a fresh cube of blue from his pocket and got to work. The chalk went back into his pocket and he winked at her.

'Want some, you'll have to reach in and get it. Going to toss me for break?'

There were guffaws at this, but Siobhan was already leaning down over the cue ball. The rust-coloured baize was snagged in places, despite which she made pretty good contact, splitting open the pack, a stripe finding the middle pocket. Potted two more before she missed an angle.

'She's better than you are, Keith,' one of the other players chipped in.

Carberry ignored him and potted three in a row. Tried doubling the fourth the length of the table. Missed by half an inch. Siobhan played safe, and he decided to get out of the snooker by coming off three cushions. Fouled it.

'Two shots,' Siobhan reminded him. She needed both to pot her next ball, then succeeded with a double of her own, bringing a whoop from one of the other tables. The games had paused so they could watch. The last two pots were straightforward, leaving only the black. She ran it along the bottom cushion, but it stopped in the jaws of the pocket. Carberry cleaned up.

'Want another tanning?' he asked with a smirk.

'Think I'll get a drink first.' She walked over to the machine and got a Fanta. Carberry followed her. The other games were back in play; seemed to Siobhan she'd won some level of acceptance.

'You've not told them who I am,' she stated quietly. 'Thanks for that.'

'What is it you're after?'

'I'm after *you*, Keith.' She handed him a folded piece of paper. It was a printout of the photo from Princes Street Gardens. He took it from her and studied it, then tried handing it back.

'So?' he said.

'The woman you hit ... take another look at her.' She swigged from her can. 'Notice any family resemblance?'

He stared at her. 'You're joking.'

She shook her head. 'You put my mother in hospital, Keith. Didn't matter to you who it was, or how badly they were injured. You went down there for a rammy, and you were going to get one.'

'And I've been to court for it.'

'I looked at the notes, Keith. Prosecutor doesn't know about this.' Siobhan tapped the photo. 'All he's got on you is witness testimony from the cop who pulled you out of the crowd. Saw you tossing the stick away. What do you reckon you'll get? Fifty-pound fine?'

'Payable at a pound a week off my giro.'

'But if I give them this photo – and all the others I've got – suddenly it's looking more like jail, isn't it?'

'Nothing I can't handle,' he said with confidence.

She nodded. 'Because you've been inside more than once. But there's time,' she paused, 'and then there's *time*.'

'Eh?'

'A word from me, and suddenly the screws aren't so friendly. There are wings they can put you on where only the bad men go: sex offenders, psychopaths, lifers with nothing to lose. Your record says you've done Young Offender, open prisons with day release ... See, the reason you say you can handle it is that you haven't had to *try*.'

'All this because your mum got in the way of a swing?'

'All this,' she corrected him, 'because I *can*. Tell you something, though – your pal Tench knew about this last night ... funny he didn't think to warn you.'

The teenager in charge of the hall was getting a text message. He called across to them: 'Hey, lovebirds – boss wants a word.'

Carberry tore his eyes away from Siobhan. 'What?'

'Boss.' The teenager was pointing to a door marked Private. Above it, screwed to the wall, sat a CCTV camera.

'I think we better oblige,' Siobhan said, 'don't you?' She led him towards the door and tugged it open. Hallway behind it, and stairs leading up. The roof-space had become an office: desk, chairs, filing cabinet. Broken cues and an empty water-cooler. Light coming in through two dusty Veluxes in the ceiling.

And Big Ger Cafferty waiting for them.

'You must be Keith,' he said, holding out a hand. Carberry shook it, his eyes flitting between the gangster and Siobhan. 'Maybe you know who I am?' Carberry hesitated, then nodded. 'Of course you do.' Cafferty gestured for the young man to sit. Siobhan stayed on her feet.

'You own this place?' Carberry asked with the slightest of tremors.

'Have done for years.'

'What about Lonnie?'

'Dead before you were born, son.' Cafferty brushed a hand over one of his trouser legs, as if he'd found some chalk dust there. 'Now, Keith ... I hear good things about you – but seems to me you've been led astray. Got to get back on the straight and narrow before it's too late. Mum worries about you ... Dad's lost the plot now he can't thump you without getting double-rations back. Older brother already in Shotts for thieving cars.' Cafferty gave a slow shake of his head. 'It's like your life's mapped out, nothing you can do but go along with it.' He paused.

'But we can change that, Keith, if you're willing to let us help.'

Carberry looked confused. 'Am I getting a whipping or what?'

Cafferty shrugged. 'We can arrange that too, of course – nothing DS Clarke here would like better than to see you cry like a baby. Only fair, when you think what you did to her mum.' Another pause. 'But then there's the alternative.'

Siobhan shifted a little, part of her wanting to haul Carberry out of there, getting both of them away from Cafferty's hypnotic voice. The gangster seemed to sense this, and shifted his gaze to her for a moment, awaiting her decision.

'What alternative?' Keith Carberry was asking. Cafferty didn't answer. His eyes were still locked on Siobhan.

'Gareth Tench,' she explained to the young man. 'We want him.'

'And you, Keith,' Cafferty added, 'are going to deliver.'

'Deliver?'

Siobhan noticed that Carberry's legs were all but refusing to hold him up. He was terrified of Cafferty; terrified of her too, most probably.

You wanted this, she told herself.

'Tench is using you, Keith,' Cafferty was saying, his voice as soft as a bedtime lullaby. 'He's not your friend, never has been.'

'Never said he was,' the youth felt compelled to argue.

'Good lad.' Cafferty was rising slowly to his feet, almost as wide as the desk he now stood behind. 'Just keep telling yourself that,' he advised. 'It'll make everything so much easier when the time comes.'

'Time?' Carberry echoed.

'To turn him over to *us*.'

'Sorry about earlier,' Rebus told Stan Hackman.

'What was I interrupting?'

'A bollocking from my Chief Constable.'

Hackman laughed. 'You're a man after my own heart, Johnny boy. But why did I have to become your sweetheart?' He held up a hand. 'No, let me guess. You didn't want him to know it was business ... meaning you're not supposed to *have* any business – am I right?'

'I've been suspended,' Rebus confirmed. Hackman clapped his hands together and laughed again. They were sitting in a pub called The Crags. It had just gone opening time, and they were the only customers. It was the nearest watering-hole to Pollock Halls and catered to students with its array of video and board games, a sound system, and cheap burgers.

'Glad someone finds my life such a source of fun,' Rebus muttered.

'So how many anarchists did you thump?'

Rebus shook his head. 'I just kept sticking my nose in where it wasn't wanted.'

'Like I say, John – a man after my own heart. By the way, I haven't thanked you properly for introducing me to the Nook.'

'Glad to be of service.'

'Did you end up bedding the lap-dancer?'

'No.'

'Tell you what, she was the best of a mediocre bunch. I didn't even bother with the VIP booth.' His eyes glazed over for a moment, lost to memories, then he blinked and shook himself back to the present. 'So now that you've been red-carded, what do I do? Offer you the info I've gleaned, or stick it in the "pending" pile?'

Rebus took a sip from his glass – fresh orange. Hackman had already seen off half his lager. 'We're just two combatants having a chat,' Rebus told him.

'That we are.' The Englishman nodded thoughtfully. 'And sharing a final drink before the off.'

'You're shipping out?'

'Later today,' he confirmed. 'I won't say it hasn't been fun.'

'Come back another time,' Rebus offered, 'I'll show you the rest of the sights.'

'Well, that just about finalises the deal.' Hackman slid a little further forward on his chair. 'Remember I told you Trevor Guest spent some time up here? Well, I asked one of the lads back at base to dust off the archives.' He reached into his pocket for a notebook, and opened it at a page of jottings. 'Trevor was in the Borders for a bit, but he spent more time right here in Edinburgh.' He jabbed the tabletop with a fingertip. 'Had a room in Craigmillar and helped out at a day centre – they can't have been doing background checks back then.'

'A day centre for adults?'

'Old people. He wheeled them from shithouse to dinner table. At least, that's what he told us.'

'He had a criminal record by then?'

'Couple of burglaries ... Class A possession ... roughed up a girlfriend but she wouldn't take it to court. Means two of your victims have a local connection.'

'Yes,' Rebus agreed. 'How far back are we talking?'

'Four, five years.'

'Can you give me a minute, Stan?' He got up and walked into the car park, took out his mobile and called Mairie Henderson.

'It's John,' he told her.

'About bloody time. Why's everything gone quiet on the Clootie Well case? My editor's nagging me stupid.'

'I've just discovered that the second victim spent some time in Edinburgh. Worked in a day centre in Craigmillar. I'm wondering if he got himself into any bother while he was here.'

'Don't the police have computers to tell them things like that?'

'I prefer to use good old-fashioned contacts.'

'I can do a search of the database ... maybe ask our court guy if he knows anything. Joe Cowrie's been doing the job for decades – and he remembers every bloody case.'

'Just as well – this may go back five years. Call me with whatever you get.'

'You think the killer could be right here under our noses?'

'I wouldn't go telling your editor ... might have to dash his hopes at a later date.'

Rebus ended the call and went back inside. Hackman had settled down with a fresh pint. He nodded towards Rebus's glass.

'I wouldn't insult you by offering to buy another of those.'

'I'm fine,' Rebus assured him. 'Thanks for taking a bit of trouble with this.' He tapped the open notebook.

'Anything for a fellow officer in his hour of need.' Hackman toasted him with the glass.

'Speaking of which, what's the mood like at Pollock?'

Hackman's face hardened. 'Last night was grim. Lot of the Met lads were on their phones non-stop. Others had already shipped out. I know we all hate the place, but when I saw those Londoners on the telly, determined to keep going no matter what ...'

Rebus nodded agreement.

'Bit like yourself, eh, John?' Hackman laughed again. 'I can see it in your face – you're not about to give up, just because they're out to nail you.'

Rebus took a moment to consider his response, then asked Hackman if he happened to have an address for the day centre in Craigmillar ...

It wasn't much more than a five-minute drive from The Crags.

On the way, Rebus took a call from Mairie, who was

drawing blanks on Trevor Guest's time in Edinburgh. If Joe Cowrie didn't remember him, he hadn't ended up in court. Rebus thanked her anyway and promised she still had first refusal on anything he dug up. Hackman had gone back to Pollock to begin packing. They'd parted with a handshake and a reminder from Hackman about Rebus's promised tour of 'the fleshpots beyond the Nook'.

'You have my word,' Rebus had told him, neither man really believing it would ever happen.

The day centre was next door to an industrial estate. Rebus could smell diesel fumes and something like burning rubber. Gulls were on the scrounge, cackling overhead. The centre itself was an extended bungalow with a sun-trap added. Through the windows, he could see old people listening to accordion music.

'Ten years from now, John,' he muttered to himself. 'And that's if you're lucky.'

The very efficient secretary was called Mrs Eadie – no first name offered. But although Trevor had only worked a couple of hours a week, and then only for a month or so, she still had his paperwork in the filing cabinet. No, she couldn't show it to him – right to privacy and so on. If he applied for permission, well, that might be another story.

Rebus nodded his understanding. The building's thermostat was set to death-ray, and sweat was pouring down his back. The office was tiny and airless, with a sickly background aroma of talcum powder.

'This guy,' he told Mrs Eadie, 'he'd had some trouble with the police. How come you didn't know that when you hired him?'

'We knew he'd had problems, Inspector. Gareth told us as much.'

Rebus stared at her. 'Councillor Tench? Tench brought Trevor Guest here?'

'Never easy to get strong young men to work in a place like this,' Mrs Eadie explained. 'The councillor's always been a good friend to us.'

'Finding you volunteers, you mean?'

She nodded. 'We owe him a debt of gratitude.'

'I'm sure he'll be round to collect it one of these days.'

Five minutes later, as Rebus emerged into the fresh air, he could hear that the accordion had been replaced by a recording of Moira Anderson. There and then he made a vow to top himself rather than sit with a shawl across his lap being spoon-fed boiled eggs to the strains of 'Charlie Is My Darling'.

Siobhan sat in her car outside Rebus's tenement. She'd already been upstairs: he wasn't home. Probably just as well – she was still shaking. Felt jittery inside and didn't think she could blame the caffeine. When she checked herself in the rearview mirror, her face was paler than usual. She gave her cheeks a few pats, trying to cheat some of the colour back. She had the radio on, but had given up on the news stations: all the voices sounded either too brittle and urgent, or syrupy and colluding. She'd settled instead for Classic FM. Recognised the tune but couldn't name it. Couldn't even be bothered trying.

Keith Carberry had walked out of Lonnie's Pool Academy like a man whose lawyers had just secured his release from Death Row. If there was a world outside, he wanted a taste of it. The manager had had to remind him to pick up his cue on the way out. Siobhan had watched the whole thing on CCTV. The screen had been greasy, blurring the figures. Cafferty had wired the place for sound, too, voices crackling from a battered-looking speaker some feet away from the monitor.

'Where's the fire, Keith?'

'Get lost, Jim-Bob.'

'What about your light-sabre?'

Carberry pausing just long enough to replace the cue in its case.

'I think,' Cafferty had said quietly, 'we can safely say we've got him.'

'For what it's worth,' Siobhan had added.

'Got to be patient,' Cafferty advised. 'A lesson well worth the learning, DS Clarke ...'

Now, in her car, she pondered her options. The simplest would be to hand the evidence over to the Procurator Fiscal, get Keith Carberry in court again on the more serious charge. That way, Tench would go untouched, but so what? Even supposing the councillor had set up those attacks on the Niddrie campsite, he really had come to her rescue in the gardens behind the flats – Carberry hadn't been toying with her. His blood was up, adrenalin pumping ...

The threat had been for real.

He'd wanted to taste her fear, see her panic.

Not always controllable. Tench just managing to rescue the situation.

She owed him that much ...

On the other hand, Carberry for her mother didn't sound like a fair deal. Didn't taste like justice. She wanted *more*. Beyond an apology or a show of remorse, beyond a custodial sentence of weeks or months.

When her phone rang she had to ease her fingers from around the steering wheel. The screen said it was Eric Bain. She whispered an oath before answering.

'What can I do for you, Eric?' she asked, just a little too brightly.

'How's it all going, Siobhan?'

'Slowly,' she admitted with a laugh, pinching the bridge of her nose. No hysterics, girl, she warned herself.

'Well, I'm not sure about this, but I might have someone you should talk to.'

'Oh yes?'

'She works at the university. I helped her out months back with a computer simulation ...'

'Good for you.'

There was a moment's silence on the line. 'Sure you're all right?'

'I'm fine, Eric. How's everything with you? How's Molly?'

'Molly's great ... I, uh, was telling you about this lecturer?'

'Of course you were. You think I should go see her.'

'Well, maybe just call her up first. I mean, it might turn out to be a dead end.'

'It usually does, Eric.'

'Thanks for nothing.'

Siobhan closed her eyes and sighed loudly into the phone. 'Sorry, Eric, sorry. Shouldn't be taking it out on you.'

'Taking what out on me?'

'A week's worth of crap.'

He laughed. 'Apology accepted. I'll call again later, when you've had a chance to—'

'Just hang on a sec, will you?' She reached across to the passenger seat, extracting her notebook from her bag. 'Give me her number and I'll talk to her.'

He recited the number and she jotted it down, adding the name as best she could, neither of them being totally sure how it was spelled.

'So what is it you think she might have for me?' Siobhan asked.

'A few crackpot theories.'

'Sounds great.'

'Can't do any harm to listen,' Bain advised.

But by now, Siobhan knew differently. Knew that listening could have repercussions.

Bad ones at that.

*

Rebus hadn't been to the City Chambers in a while. The building was situated on the High Street, opposite St Giles Cathedral. Cars were supposedly banned from the roadway between the two, but like most locals Rebus ignored the signs and parked kerbside. He seemed to remember hearing that the council's HQ had been built as some sort of merchants' meeting place, but the local traders had shunned it and carried on as before. Rather than concede defeat, the politicians had moved in and made it their own. Soon, however, they'd be on the move – a car park next to Waverley Station had been earmarked for development. No way of telling as yet how far over budget it would run. If it turned out anything like the Parliament, the bars of Edinburgh would soon have a fresh topic to inflame the drinkers' indignation.

The City Chambers had been built on top of a plague street called Mary King's Close. Years back, Rebus had investigated a murder in the dank underground labyrinth – Cafferty's own son the victim. The place had been tidied up now and was a tourist haunt in the summer. One of the staff was busy on the pavement, handing out flyers. She wore a housemaid's cap and layered petticoats and tried to offer Rebus a discount voucher. He shook his head. The papers said local attractions were feeling the bite of the G8 – all week tourists had been steering clear of the city.

'Hi-ho, silver lining,' Rebus muttered, starting to whistle the song's first verse. The receptionist at the front desk asked him if it was Kylie, then smiled to let him know she was teasing.

'Gareth Tench, please,' Rebus said.

'I doubt he'll be here,' she warned. 'Friday, you know ... A lot of our councillors do ward business on a Friday.'

'Giving them an excuse to knock off early?' Rebus guessed.

'I don't know *what* you're implying.' But her smile was back, meaning she knew damned well. Rebus liked her.

Checked for a wedding ring and found one. Changed his whistling to 'Another One Bites the Dust'.

She was looking down a list on the clipboard in front of her. 'Seems you're in luck,' she announced. 'Urban Regeneration Committee Sub-Group ...' She glanced at the clock behind her. 'Meeting's due to break up in five minutes. I'll tell the secretary you're here, Mr ...?'

. 'Detective Inspector Rebus.' He offered a smile of his own. 'John, if you prefer.'

'Take a seat, John.'

He gave a little bow of his head in thanks. The other receptionist was having a lot less luck, trying to fend off an elderly couple who wanted to talk to someone about the bins in their street.

'Aye fu' wi' they fly-tippers.'

'We've got the car numbers an' aw'thing, but naebody's been near ...'

Rebus took a seat, and decided against any of the reading material: council propaganda disguised as newsletters. They appeared regularly through Rebus's letterbox, helping him contribute to the recycling effort. His mobile sounded, and he flipped it open. Mairie Henderson's number.

'What can I do for you, Mairie?' he asked.

'I forgot to tell you this morning ... I'm getting somewhere with Richard Pennen.'

'Tell me more.' He moved outside into the quadrangle again. The Lord Provost's Rover was parked by the glass-panelled doors. He stopped next to it and lit a cigarette.

'Business correspondent on one of the London broadsheets put me on to a freelancer who sells stuff to the likes of *Private Eye*. He in turn set me up with a TV producer who's been keeping an eye on Pennen ever since the company split off from the MoD.'

'Okay, so you've earned your bawbees this week.'

'Well, maybe I'll just head to Harvey Nicks and start spending them.'

387

'All right, I'm shutting up now.'

'Pennen has links to an American company called TriMerino. They've got people on the ground in Iraq just now. During the war, a lot of equipment got trashed, including weaponry. TriMerino are in the business of re-arming the good guys ...'

'Whoever they are.'

'... making sure the Iraqi police and any new armed forces can hold their own. They see it as – wait for this – a humanitarian mission.'

'Meaning they're looking for aid money?'

'Billions are being poured into Iraq – quite a bit's already gone missing, but that's another story. The murky world of foreign aid: that's the TV producer's pitch.'

'And he's lassoing Richard Pennen?'

'Hoping to.'

'And how does this tie in to my dead politician? Any sign that Ben Webster had control of Iraqi aid money?'

'Not yet,' she conceded. Rebus noticed that some of his ash had landed on the Rover's gleaming bonnet.

'I get the feeling you're holding something back.'

'Nothing to do with your deceased MP.'

'Going to share with Uncle John?'

'Might not come to anything.' She paused. 'I can still make a story, though. I'm the first print journalist the producer's told the whole story to.'

'Good for you.'

'You could try that again with a bit more enthusiasm.'

'Sorry, Mairie ... mind's on other things. If you can tighten the screws on Pennen, so much the better.'

'But it doesn't necessarily help you?'

'You've been doing me a lot of favours – only right you get *something* out of it.'

'My feelings exactly.' She paused again. 'Any progress your end? I'm betting you visited the day centre where Trevor Guest worked?'

'Didn't get much.'

'Anything worth sharing?'

'Not yet.'

'That sounds like evasion.'

Rebus moved aside as some people started to emerge from the building – a liveried driver, followed by another man in uniform carrying a small case. And behind them, the Lord Provost. She seemed to notice the flecks of ash on her vehicle, gave Rebus a scowl and disappeared into the back of the car. The two men got into the front, Rebus guessing that the case held her chain of office.

'Thanks for letting me know about Pennen,' he told Mairie. 'Keep in touch.'

'It's your turn to phone *me*,' she reminded him. 'Now we're back on speaking terms, I don't want one-way traffic.'

He ended the call, stubbed out his cigarette, and headed back indoors, where his receptionist had joined in the debate about wheelie-bins.

'It's Environmental Health you need to speak to,' she was stressing.

'Nae good, hen, that lot never listen.'

'Summat's got to be done!' his wife shouted. 'Folk are fed up being treated like numbers!'

'All right,' the first receptionist said, caving in with a sigh. 'I'll see if someone's available to talk to you. Take a ticket from over there.' She nodded towards the dispenser. The old man pulled a sliver of paper from it and stared at what he'd been given.

A number.

Rebus's receptionist beckoned him over, leaned forward to whisper that the councillor was on his way down. She glanced towards the couple, letting him know she didn't want them to share the information.

'I'm assuming it's official business?' she asked, fishing for some inside gen. Rebus leaned even closer to her ear, smelling perfume rising from her nape.

'I'm wanting my drains cleaned,' he confided. She looked shocked for a moment, then gave a lopsided grin, hoping he was joking.

Moments later, Tench himself emerged grimly into the reception area. He was clasping a briefcase to his chest, as though it could afford some useful protection.

'This is a bollock-hair away from serious harassment,' he hissed. Rebus nodded as if in agreement, then stretched out an arm in the direction of the waiting couple.

'This is Councillor Tench,' he informed them. 'He's the helpful sort.' They were already on their feet and shuffling towards the glowering Tench.

'I'll be waiting outside when you're done,' Rebus told him.

He'd smoked another cigarette by the time Tench emerged. Through the window, Rebus could see that the couple had taken their seats again, looking satisfied for the moment, as though some further meeting had been arranged.

'You're a bastard, Rebus,' Tench growled. 'Give me one of those fags.'

'I didn't know you indulged.'

Tench lifted a cigarette from the pack. 'Only when I'm stressed ... but this smoking ban's on the horizon so I reckon I should claim my share while I can.' With the cigarette lit, he inhaled deeply, letting the smoke pour down his nostrils. 'Only real pleasure some people have, you know. Remember John Reid talking about single mums on sink estates?'

Rebus remembered it well. But Reid, the Defence Secretary, had given up the smokes, so wasn't much of an apologist for the habit.

'Sorry I did that,' Rebus offered, nodding in the direction of the window.

'They've got a point,' Tench conceded. 'Someone's

coming to talk to them ... wasn't too happy about me calling him, mind. I think his tee shot had just clipped the ninth green. Chip and run for a birdie ...'

He smiled, and Rebus smiled with him. They smoked in silence for a moment. The atmosphere could almost have been called companionable. But then Tench had to spoil it.

'Why do you side with Cafferty? He's a badder bugger than I could ever be.'

'I'm not disputing it.'

'Well then?'

'I don't side with him,' Rebus stated.

'Not what it looks like.'

'Then you're refusing to see the whole picture.'

'I'm good at what I do, Rebus. If you don't believe me, talk to the people I represent.'

'I'm sure you're terrific at what you do, Mr Tench. And sitting on the Regeneration Committee must tip a wheen of cash into your ward, making your constituents cheerful, healthy and well behaved.'

'Slums have been replaced by new housing, local industry offered incentives to stay put ...'

'Nursing homes given upgrades?' Rebus added.

'Absolutely.'

'And staffed by your own recommendations ... Trevor Guest being a case in point.'

'Who?'

'While back you placed him in a day centre. He was from Newcastle originally.'

Tench was nodding slowly. 'He'd had a few problems with drink and drugs. Happens to some of us, doesn't it, Inspector?' Tench gave Rebus a meaningful look. 'I was looking to integrate him into the community.'

'Didn't work. He headed back south to be murdered.'

'Murdered?'

'One of the three whose effects we found in Auchterarder.

391

Another was Cyril Colliar. Funnily enough, *he* used to work for Big Ger Cafferty.'

'You're at it again – trying to pin something on me!' Tench made jabbing motions with the cigarette.

'Just want to ask about the victim. How you met him, why you felt the need to help.'

'It's what I *do* – I keep telling you that!'

'Cafferty thinks you're muscling in.'

Tench rolled his eyes. 'We've been through all this. All I want is for *him* to be consigned to the scrap-heap.'

'And if we won't do it, you will?'

'I'll do my damnedest – I've already said as much.' He rubbed his palms across his face, as though washing. 'Has the penny not dropped yet, Rebus? Always supposing you're not in his pocket, hasn't it occurred to you that he might be using you to get to me? Big drugs problem in my ward – something I've vowed to control. With me out of the way, Cafferty has free rein.'

'You're in charge of the gangs down there.'

'I'm not!'

'I've seen the way it works. Your little runt of a hoodie runs amok, gives you the chance to state your case for more cash from the authorities. You've turned havoc into a nice little earner.'

Tench stared at him, then gave a loud exhalation. He looked to left and right. 'Between us?' But Rebus wasn't about to comply. 'All right, maybe there's an element of truth in what you say. Money for regeneration: that's the bottom line. I'm happy to show you the books – you'll see that every last cent and penny is accounted for.'

'What's Carberry listed under on the balance sheet?'

'You don't *control* someone like Keith Carberry. A bit of channelling sometimes ...' Tench offered a shrug. 'What happened in Princes Street had nothing to do with me.'

Rebus's cigarette was down to its filter. He flicked it away. 'And Trevor Guest?'

'Was a damaged man who came to me for help. He said he wanted to give something back.'

'For what?'

Tench shook his head slowly, stubbing his cigarette underfoot, and began to look thoughtful. 'I got the feeling something had happened ... put the fear of death into him.'

'What sort of thing?'

A shrug. 'The drugs maybe ... dark night of the soul. He'd had a bit of bother with the police, but seemed to me there was more to it than that.'

'He went to jail eventually. Aggravated burglary, assault, attempted sexual assault ... Your Good Samaritan act didn't exactly win him over.'

'I hope it's never been an act,' Tench said quietly, eyes focused on the street beneath him.

'You're putting on an act right now,' Rebus told him. 'I think you do it because you're good at it. Same sort of act that got Ellen Wylie's sister out of her knickers – bit of wine and sympathy at your end, and no mention of the missus back home in front of the telly.'

Tench made a pained face, but all Rebus did was give a cold chuckle.

'I'm curious,' he went on. 'You looked at the BeastWatch site – it's how you snared Ellen and her sister. So you had to've seen your old pal Trevor's picture there. Seems odd to me that you never said.'

'And put myself further in the frame you've been try-ing to nail together around me?' Tench shook his head slowly.

'I'll need something in your own words about Trevor Guest – everything you've told me, and anything else you can add. You can drop it off at Gayfield Square – this afternoon will do. Hope that's not going to eat into your golf time.'

Tench looked at him. 'How do you know I play?'

'Way you spoke earlier – like you knew what you were talking about.' Rebus leaned towards him. 'You're easy enough to read, Councillor. Compared to some I've known, you're Janet and fucking John.'

The line was adequate, and Rebus left Tench with it. Back at the car, a warden was hovering. Rebus pointed out the POLICE notice on his dashboard.

'At *our* discretion,' the warden reminded him.

Rebus blew the man a kiss and got behind the steering wheel. As he pulled away, he checked in his rearview, and saw that someone was watching from outside the cathedral. Same outfit he'd been wearing that day at court: Keith Carberry. Rebus slowed the car but kept moving. Carberry's attention shifted, and Rebus stopped the Saab, kept watching in the rear view. Expected Carberry to cross the street, go say a few words to his employer, but he stayed where he was, hands tucked into the front of his hooded jacket, some sort of narrow black carry-case held beneath one arm. Content to stand in the midst of what tourists there were.

Paying them no heed.

Staring across the roadway.

Towards the City Chambers.

The City Chambers ... and Gareth Tench.

23

'What have you been up to?' Rebus asked.

She'd been waiting for him on Arden Street. He'd said maybe he should give her a key, if they were going to keep using his flat as an office.

'Not much,' Siobhan replied, taking off her jacket. 'How about you?'

They went into the kitchen and he boiled the kettle, telling her about Trevor Guest and Councillor Tench. She asked a few questions, watching him spoon coffee into two mugs.

'Gives us our Edinburgh connection,' she agreed.

'Of a kind.'

'You sound doubtful.'

He shook his head. 'You said so yourself ... so did Ellen. Trevor Guest could be the key. Started off looking different from the others with all those wounds ...' He broke off.

'What is it?'

But he shook his head again, stirred a spoon in his mug. 'Tench thinks something happened to him. Guest had been taking drugs, hitting the bottle pretty hard ... Then he scurries north and ends up in Craigmillar ... meets the councillor ... works with old people for a few weeks.'

'Nothing in the case-notes to suggest he did anything like that before or since.'

'Funny thing to do when you're a thief and you probably need a bit of cash.'

'Unless he was planning to fleece them in some way.

Did the day centre mention anything about money going missing?'

Rebus shook his head, but took out his phone and called Mrs Eadie to ask. By the time she'd answered in the negative, Siobhan was seated at the dining table in the living room, delving into the files again.

'What about his time in Edinburgh?' she asked.

'I got Mairie to check.' She looked at him. 'Didn't want anyone else getting wind that we're still active.'

'So what did Mairie say?'

'Her answer wasn't definitive.'

'Time to call Ellen?'

He knew she was right, and made that call too, but warned Ellen Wylie to be careful.

'Start searching the computer and you'll be leaving a calling-card.'

'I'm a big girl, John.'

'Maybe so, but the Chief Constable's keeping a beady eye.'

'It'll be fine.'

He wished her luck and slid the phone back into his pocket. 'You all right?' he asked Siobhan.

'Why?'

'Seemed to be in a dream. Have you spoken to your parents?'

'Not since they left.'

'Best thing you can do is hand those photos to the Procurator Fiscal, make sure of a conviction.'

She nodded, but didn't look convinced. 'That's what you'd do, right?' she asked. 'If someone had lashed out at your nearest and dearest?'

'There's not much room on the ledge, Shiv.'

She stared at him. 'What ledge?'

'The one I always seem to be perched on. You know you don't want to be standing too close.'

'What's that supposed to mean?'

'It means hand over the photos, leave the rest to judge and jury.'

Her eyes were still boring into his. 'You're probably right.'

'No alternative,' he added. 'None you'd ever want to consider.'

'That's true.'

'Or you could always ask me to kick the crap out of Mr Baseball Cap.'

'Aren't you a bit long in the tooth for that?' she asked with the hint of a smile.

'Probably,' he acknowledged. 'Might not stop me trying, though.'

'Well, there's no need. I only wanted the truth.' She considered for a moment. 'I mean, when I thought it was one of us ...'

'Way this week's gone, it might well have been,' he said quietly, pulling out a chair and seating himself across from her.

'But I couldn't have stood it, John. That's what I'm getting at.'

He made a show of turning some of the paperwork towards him. 'You'd have chucked it in?'

'It was an option.'

'But now it's all right again?' He was hoping for some reassurance. She gave a slow nod, picking up some paperwork of her own. 'Why hasn't he struck again?'

It took Rebus's brain a moment to shift gears. He'd been on the verge of telling her about seeing Keith Carberry outside the City Chambers. 'I've no idea,' he eventually conceded.

'I mean, they speed up, right? Once they get a taste for it?'

'That's the theory.'

'And they don't just stop?'

'Maybe some do. Whatever it is inside them ... maybe

it gets earthed somehow.' He shrugged. 'I don't pretend to be an expert.'

'Me neither. That's why we're meeting someone who claims she is.'

'What?'

Siobhan was checking her watch. 'In an hour from now. Which just gives us time to decide what questions we need to ask ...'

The University of Edinburgh Department of Psychology was based in George Square. Two sides of the original Georgian development had been flattened and replaced with a series of concrete boxes, but the Psychology department was based in an older building sandwiched between two such blocks. Dr Roisin Gilreagh had a room on the top floor, with views over the gardens.

'Nice and quiet this time of year,' Siobhan commented. 'The students being gone, I mean.'

'Except that in August the gardens play host to various Fringe shows,' Dr Gilreagh countered.

'Offering a whole new human laboratory,' Rebus added. The room was small and awash with sunlight. Dr Gilreagh was in her mid-thirties, with thick curly blonde hair falling past her shoulders, and pinched cheeks which Rebus took to be clues as to her Irish ancestry, despite the resolutely local accent. When she smiled at Rebus's comment, her sharp nose and chin seemed to become even more jagged.

'I was telling DI Rebus on the way here,' Siobhan interrupted, 'that you're considered a bit of an expert in the field.'

'I wouldn't go that far,' Dr Gilreagh felt obliged to argue. 'But there are interesting times ahead in the field of offender profiling. Crichton Street car park is being turned into our new Centre for Informatics, part of which will be dedicated to behaviour analysis. Add in Neuroscience and Psychiatry and you begin to see that there are potentials ...' She beamed at both her visitors.

'But you work for none of those particular departments?' Rebus couldn't help pointing out.

'True, true,' she was happy to acknowledge. She kept twitching in her seat, as though stillness were a crime. Motes of dust danced across the sunbeams in front of her face.

'Could we maybe draw the blind?' he suggested, squinting a little for effect. She leapt to her feet and apologised as she pulled the roller-blind down. It was pale yellow and made from something like tent canvas, doing little to relieve the room's glare. Rebus gave Siobhan a look, as if to suggest that Dr Gilreagh was kept locked in the attic for a reason.

'Tell DI Rebus about your research,' Siobhan said encouragingly.

'Well.' Dr Gilreagh clapped her hands together, straightened her back, gave a little wriggle and took a deep breath. 'Behavioural patterning in offenders is nothing new, but I've been concentrating on victims. It's by delving into the behaviour of the victim that we begin to see why offenders act the way they do, whether on impulse or through a more deterministic approach.'

'Almost goes without saying,' Rebus offered with a smile.

'Term-time being over, and thus having room for some smaller personal projects, I was intrigued by the little "shrine" – I suppose the description is fitting – in Auchterarder. The newspaper reports were sometimes sketchy, but I decided to take a look anyway ... and then, as if it were meant to be, Detective Sergeant Clarke asked for a meeting.' She took another deep breath. 'I mean, my findings aren't really ready to ... no, what I mean is, I've only scratched the surface as yet.'

'We can get the case-notes to you,' Siobhan assured her,

'if that would help. But in the meantime, we'd be grateful for any thoughts you might have.'

Dr Gilreagh clapped her hands together again, stirring the cloud of dust particles in front of her.

'Well,' she said, 'interested as I am in victimology ...' Rebus tried to catch Siobhan's eye, but she wouldn't let him. '... I have to admit that the locus stirred my curiosity. It's a statement, isn't it? I'm guessing you've considered the possibility that the killer lives locally, or has some longstanding knowledge of the immediate area?' She waited till Siobhan had nodded. 'And you will also have speculated that the murderer knows of the Clootie Well because its existence is recorded in various guidebooks and also extensively on the World Wide Web?'

Siobhan sneaked a glance at Rebus. 'Actually, we hadn't really followed that particular path,' she admitted.

'It's mentioned on a number of sites,' Dr Gilreagh assured her. 'New Age and pagan directories ... myths and legends ... world mysteries. Allied to which, anyone with a knowledge of the sister site on the Black Isle might have come across the one in Perthshire.'

'I'm not sure this gets us anywhere we haven't already been,' Rebus said. Siobhan looked at him again.

'People who accessed the BeastWatch site,' she stated. 'What if they also accessed sites referring to the Clootie Well?'

'And how would we find out?'

'The Inspector raises a fair question,' Dr Gilreagh admitted, 'though of course you may have computer experts of your own ... But in the interim, one has to concede that the locus must have some significance for the perpetrator.' She waited until Rebus had nodded. 'In which case, might it also have significance for the victims?'

'In what way?' Rebus asked, eyes narrowing.

'Countryside ... deep woods ... but close to human dwellings. Is this the sort of terrain the victims inhabited?'

Rebus snorted. 'Hardly likely – Cyril Colliar was an Edinburgh bouncer fresh out of the nick. Can't see him with a knapsack and bar of Kendal Mint Cake.'

'But Edward Isley travelled up and down the M6,' Siobhan countered, 'and that's the Lake District, isn't it? Plus, Trevor Guest spent time in the Borders ...'

'... as well as Newcastle and Edinburgh.' Rebus turned to the psychologist. 'All three served time ... *that's* your link right there.'

'Doesn't mean there aren't others,' Siobhan warned.

'Or that you're not being led astray,' Dr Gilreagh said with a kindly smile.

'Led astray?' Siobhan echoed.

'Either by patterns which don't exist, or by patterns the killer is placing in full view.'

'To toy with us?' Siobhan guessed.

'It's a possibility. There is such a huge sense of *playfulness* ...' She broke off, her face falling into a frown. 'You'll have to forgive me if that sounds frivolous, but it's the only word I can think of. This is a killer determined to be seen, as shown by the display he left at the Clootie Well. And yet immediately his work is discovered he withdraws, perhaps behind a smokescreen.'

Rebus leaned forward, elbows on knees. 'You're saying all three victims are a smokescreen?'

She gave a little wriggle of her shoulders, which he interpreted as a shrug.

'A smokescreen for what?' he persevered.

She wriggled again. Rebus threw an exasperated look towards Siobhan.

'The display,' Gilreagh said at last, 'is slightly wrong. A piece cut from a jacket ... a sports shirt ... a pair of cord trousers ... inconsistent, you see. A serial killer's trophies would normally be more similar – *only* shirts, or *only* patches. It's an untidy collection and ultimately *not quite right*.'

'This is all very interesting, Dr Gilreagh,' Siobhan said quietly. 'But does it get us any further?'

'I'm not a detective,' the psychologist stressed. 'But coming back to the rural motif and the display, which may be a classic magician's feint ... I'd wonder again about why those particular victims were chosen.' She began nodding to herself. 'You see, sometimes victims choose themselves almost, in that they fulfil the killer's basic needs. Sometimes all that means is a lone woman in a vulnerable situation. But most often there are other considerations.' She focused her attention on Siobhan. 'When we spoke on the phone, DS Clarke, you mentioned anomalies. Those can be signifiers in themselves.' She paused meaningfully. 'But scrutiny of the case-notes might help me towards a more thorough determination.' She was looking at Rebus now. 'I can hardly blame you for your scepticism, Inspector, but contrary to all your available visual evidence, I'm not in the least bit batty.'

'I'm sure you're not, Dr Gilreagh.'

She clapped her hands together again, and this time leapt to her feet to indicate that their time was up.

'Meantime,' she said, 'rurality and anomalies, rurality and anomalies.' She held up two fingers to stress the points, then added a third. 'And, perhaps above all else, wanting you to see things that aren't really there.'

'Is rurality even a word?' Rebus asked.

Siobhan turned the ignition. 'It is now.'

'And you're still going to give her the notes?'

'Worth a punt.'

'Because we're that desperate?'

'Unless you've got a better idea.' But he had no answer for that, and wound down the window so he could smoke. They passed the old car park.

'Informatics,' Rebus muttered. Siobhan signalled right, making towards The Meadows and Arden Street.

'The anomaly is Trevor Guest,' she ventured, once a few more minutes had elapsed. 'We've said that from the start.'

'So?'

'So we know he spent time in the Borders – doesn't get much more rural than that.'

'Hell of a long way from either Auchterarder or Black Isle,' Rebus stated.

'But something happened to him in the Borders.'

'We've only got Tench's word for that.'

'Fair point,' she conceded. All the same, Rebus got out Hackman's number and gave him a call.

'Ready for the off?' he asked.

'Are you missing me already?' Hackman replied, recognising Rebus's voice.

'One question I meant to ask. Where in the Borders did Trevor Guest spend time?'

'Do I hear the sound of a hand grasping at straws?'

'You do,' Rebus conceded.

'Well, I'm not sure I can be much of a lifeguard. I seem to think Guest mentioned the Borders during one of our sessions with him.'

'We've not seen all the transcripts yet,' Rebus reminded him.

'Lads in the Toon being their usual efficient selves? Got an email address on you, John?' Rebus recited it. 'Check your computer in about an hour's time. But be warned – POETS day, meaning the CID cupboard might be a bit on the Mother Hubbard side.'

'Appreciate anything you can get for us, Stan. Happy trails.' Rebus clicked the phone shut. 'POETS day,' he reminded Siobhan.

'Piss Off Early, Tomorrow's Saturday,' she recited.

'Speaking of which – you still going to T in the Park tomorrow?'

'Not sure.'

'You fought hard enough for the ticket.'

'Might wait till evening. I can still catch New Order.'

'After a hard Saturday's grafting?'

'You were thinking of a walk along the seafront at Portobello?'

'Depends on Newcastle, doesn't it? Been a while since I took a day trip to the Borders ...'

She double-parked and climbed the two flights with him. The plan was to have a quick recce of the case-notes, decide what might be useful to Dr Gilreagh, and head to a copy-shop with them. Ended up with a pile an inch thick.

'Good luck,' Rebus said as she headed out of the door. He could hear a horn blaring downstairs – a motorist she'd managed to block. He pulled the window open to let in some air, then collapsed into his chair. He felt dog-tired. His eyes stung and his neck and shoulders ached. He thought again of the massage Ellen Wylie had wanted him to offer. Had she really meant anything by it? Didn't matter – he was just relieved now nothing had happened. His waist strained against his trouser belt. He undid his tie and opened the top two buttons of his shirt. Felt the benefit, so worked the belt loose too.

'Shellsuit's what you need, fatso,' he chided himself. Shellsuit *and* slippers. And a home help. In fact, everything short of 'Charlie Is My Darling'.

'And just a touch more self-pity.'

He rubbed a hand over one knee. Kept waking in the night with a sort of cramp there. Rheumatics, arthritis, wear and tear – he knew there was no point troubling his GP. He'd been there before with the blood pressure: less salt and sugar, cut down the fat, take some exercise. Kick the booze and ciggies into touch.

Rebus's response had been shaped as a question: 'Ever felt you could just write it on a board, stick it on your chair and bugger off home for the afternoon?'

Producing one of the weariest smiles he'd ever seen on a young man's coupon.

The phone rang and he told it to get stuffed. Anyone wanted him that much, they'd try the mobile. Sure enough, it rang thirty seconds later. He took his time picking it up: Ellen Wylie.

'Yes, Ellen?' he asked. Didn't feel she needed to know he'd just been thinking of her.

'Only the one wee spot of bother for Trevor Guest during his stay in our fine city.'

'Enlighten me.' He leaned his head against the back of the chair, letting his eyes close.

'Got into a fight on Ratcliffe Terrace. You know it?'

'Where the taxi drivers buy their petrol. I was there last night.'

'There's a pub across the street called Swany's.'

'I've been in a few times.'

'Now there's a surprise. Well, Guest went there at least the once. A drinker seemed to take against him, and it ended up outside. One of our cars happened to be in the garage forecourt – stocking up on provisions, no doubt. Both combatants were taken into custody for the night.'

'That was it?'

'Never went to court. Witnesses saw the other man swing the first punch. We asked Guest if he wanted to press charges, and he declined.'

'I don't suppose you know what they were fighting about?'

'I could try asking the arresting officers.'

'I don't suppose it matters. What was the other guy's name?'

'Duncan Barclay.' She paused. 'He wasn't local, though ... gave an address in Coldstream. Is that in the Highlands?'

'Wrong end of the country, Ellen.' Rebus had opened his eyes, was easing himself upright. 'It's bang in the middle

405

of the Borders.' He asked her to wait while he readied some paper and a pen, then picked up the phone again.

'Okay, give me what you've got,' he told her.

24

The driving-range was floodlit. Not that it was completely dark yet, but the brilliance of the illumination made it look like a film set. Mairie had hired a three wood and a basket containing fifty balls. The first two stalls were taken. Plenty of gaps after that. Automatic tees – meant you didn't have to go to the trouble of bending down to replace the ball after each shot. The range was broken up into fifty-yard sections. Nobody was hitting two hundred and fifty. Out on the grass, a machine resembling a miniaturised combine-harvester was scooping up the balls, its driver protected by a mesh screen. Mairie saw that the very last stall was in use. The golfer there was being given tuition. He addressed the tee, took a swing, and watched his ball hit the ground no more than seventy yards away.

'Better,' the tutor lied. 'But try to focus on not bending that knee.'

'I'm scooping again?' his pupil guessed.

Mairie placed her metal basket on the ground, next stall over. Decided to take a few practice swings, loosen up her shoulders. Tutor and pupil seemed to resent her presence.

'Excuse me?' the tutor said. Mairie looked at him. He was smiling at her over the partition. 'We actually booked that bay.'

'But you're not using it,' Mairie informed him.

'Point is, we paid for it.'

'A matter of privacy,' the other man butted in, sounding irritated. Then he recognised Mairie.

'Oh, for pity's sake ...'

His tutor turned to him. 'You know her, Mr Pennen?'

'She's a bloody reporter,' Richard Pennen said. Then, to Mairie: 'Whatever it is you want, I've got nothing to say.'

'Fine by me,' Mairie answered, readying for her first shot. The ball sailed into the air, making a clean, straight line to the two hundred-yard flag.

'Pretty good,' the tutor told her.

'My dad taught me,' she explained. 'You're a professional, aren't you?' she asked. 'I think I've seen you on the circuit.' He nodded his agreement.

'Not at the Open?'

'Didn't qualify,' he admitted, cheeks reddening.

'If the two of you have finished,' Richard Pennen interrupted.

Mairie just shrugged and prepared for another shot. Pennen seemed to be doing likewise, but then gave up.

'Look,' he said, 'what the hell *do* you want?'

Mairie said nothing until she'd watched her ball sail into the sky, dropping just short of two hundred and a little to the left.

'Bit of fine tuning needed,' she told herself. Then, to Pennen: 'Just thought I should offer fair warning.'

'Fair warning of what exactly?'

'Probably won't make the paper till Monday,' she mused. 'Time enough for you to prepare some sort of response.'

'Are you baiting me, Miss ...?'

'Henderson,' she told him. 'Mairie Henderson – that's the by-line you'll read on Monday.'

'And what will the headline be? "Pennen Industries Secures Scottish Jobs at G8"?'

'That one might make the business pages,' she decided. 'But mine will be page one. Up to the editor how he phrases it.' She pretended to think. 'How about "Loans Scandal Envelops Government and Opposition"?'

Pennen gave a harsh laugh. He was swinging his club

one-handed, to and fro. 'That's your big scoop, is it?'

'I dare say there's plenty of other stuff to come out in the wash: your efforts in Iraq, your back-handers in Kenya and elsewhere ... But for now I think I'll stick with the loans. See, a little birdie tells me that you've been bank-rolling both Labour *and* the Tories. Donations are a matter of record, but loans can be kept hush-hush. Thing is, I very much doubt either party knows you're backing the other. Makes sense to me: Pennen split off from the MoD because of decisions made under the last Tory government; Labour decided the sell-off could go ahead unhindered – favours owed to both.'

'There's nothing illegal about commercial loans, Miss Henderson, secret or not.' Pennen was still swinging the club.

'Doesn't stop it from being a scandal, once the papers get hold of it,' Mairie retorted. 'And like I say, who knows what else will come bubbling to the surface?'

Pennen brought the club-head down with force against the partition. 'Do you know how hard I've worked this week, arranging contracts worth tens of millions to UK industry? And what have *you* been doing, apart from some useless muck-raking?'

'We all have our place in the food-chain, Mr Pennen.' She smiled. 'Won't be "Mr" for much longer, will it? Money you've been shelling out, that peerage can't be far off. Mind you, once Blair finds out you're bankrolling his enemies ...'

'Any trouble here, sir?'

Mairie turned to see three police uniforms. The one who'd spoken was looking at Pennen; the other two had eyes for her and her alone.

Unfriendly eyes.

'I think this woman was just leaving,' Pennen mut-tered.

Mairie made a show of peering over the partition. 'Got a

magic-lamp there or something? Any time I've ever called the cops, they've taken half an hour.'

'Routine patrol,' the group's leader stated.

Mairie looked him up and down: no markings on his uniform. The face tanned, hair cropped, jaw set.

'One question,' she said. 'Do any of you know the penalty for impersonating a police officer?'

The leader scowled and made to grab her. Mairie wriggled free and ran from the safety of the driving area on to the grass surface itself. Fled towards the exit, dodging shots from the first two bays, the players yelling in outrage. She reached the door just before her pursuers. The woman at the till asked where her three wood was. Mairie didn't answer. Pushed open another door and found herself in the car park. Ran to her car, stabbing the remote. No time to look around. Into the driver's seat and all four doors locked. Key in the ignition. A fist thumping at her window. The lead uniform trying the handle, then shuffling around to the front of the car. Mairie gave him a look which said she didn't care. Gunned the accelerator.

'Watch out, Jacko! The bint's crazy!'

Jacko had to dive sideways; that or be killed. In the wing-mirror, she could see him picking himself up. A car had drawn up alongside him. No markings on it either. Mairie screamed out on to the main carriageway – airport to her left, city to the right. The road back into Edinburgh gave her more options, more chances to lose them.

Jacko: she'd remember that name. 'Bint' one of the others had called her. It was a term she'd only heard from the mouths of soldiers. Ex-military ... with tans picked up in hot climes.

Iraq.

Private security disguised as constabulary.

She looked in the rearview: no sign of them. Didn't mean they weren't there. A8 to the bypass, breaking the speed limit all the way, flashing her lights to let the drivers in front know she was coming ...

Where to next, though? It would be easy for them to get her address; absurdly easy for a man like Richard Pennen. Allan was on a job, wouldn't be back in town until Monday. Nothing to stop her driving to the *Scotsman* and working on her article. Her laptop was in the boot, all the information inside it. Notes and quotes and her rough drafts. She could stay in the office all night if need be, topped up by coffee and snacks, cocooned from the outside world.

Writing Richard Pennen's destruction.

It was Ellen Wylie who gave Rebus the news. He in turn called Siobhan, who picked him up in her car twenty minutes later. They drove to Niddrie in silence through the dusk. The Jack Kane Centre's camp-ground had been dismantled. No tents, no showers or toilets. Half the fencing had been removed, and the security guards were gone, replaced for the moment by uniformed officers, ambulancemen, and the same two mortuary assistants who had collected Ben Webster's shattered remains from the foot of Castle Rock. Siobhan parked alongside the line of vehicles. Rebus recognised some of the detectives – they were from St Leonard's and Craigmillar. They nodded a greeting towards the new arrivals.

'Not exactly your patch,' one of them commented.

'Let's just say we've an interest in the deceased,' Rebus replied. Siobhan was by his side. She leaned towards him so as not to be overheard.

'News hasn't leaked that we're on suspension.'

Rebus just nodded. They were nearing a circle of crouched Scene of Crime officers. The duty doctor had pronounced death and was signing his name to some forms on a clip-board. Flash photographs were being taken, torches scouring the grass for clues. Onlookers were being kept at a distance by a dozen uniforms while the area was taped off. Kids on bikes, mums with their toddlers in buggies. Nothing quite drew a crowd like a crime scene.

Siobhan was getting her bearings. 'This is pretty much where my parents' tent was pitched,' she told Rebus.

'I'm assuming they're not the ones who left the mess.' He flicked an empty plastic bottle into the air with his toe. Plenty of other debris strewn across the park: discarded banners and leaflets, fast-food cartons, a scarf and a single glove, a baby's rattle and a rolled-up nappy ... Some of it was being bagged by the SOCOs, to be checked for blood or fingerprints.

'Love to see them get the DNA from that,' Rebus said, nodding towards a used condom. 'You think maybe your mum and dad ...?'

Siobhan gave him a look. 'I'm not going any closer.'

He shrugged, and left her behind. Councillor Gareth Tench was growing cold on the ground. He lay on his front, legs bent as if he'd collapsed in a heap. His head was turned to one side, eyes not quite shut. There was a dark stain on the back of his jacket.

'I'm guessing stabbed,' Rebus told the doctor.

'Three times,' the man confirmed. 'In the back. Wounds don't look all that deep to me.'

'Doesn't take much,' Rebus stated. 'What sort of knife?'

'Hard to tell as yet.' The doctor peered over his half-moon glasses. 'Blade about an inch wide, maybe a little less.'

'Anything missing?'

'He's got some cash on him ... credit cards and such like. Made identification that bit easier.' The doctor gave a tired smile and turned his clipboard towards Rebus. 'If you could countersign here, Inspector ...'

But Rebus held his hands up. 'Not my case, Doc.' The doctor looked towards Siobhan, but Rebus shook his head slowly and walked off to join her.

'Three stab wounds,' he informed her.

She was staring at Tench's face, and seemed to be trembling a little.

'Feeling the chill?' he asked.

'It's really him,' she said quietly.

'You thought he was indestructible?'

'Not quite.' She couldn't tear her eyes away from the body.

'I suppose we should tell someone.' He looked around for a likely candidate.

'Tell them what?'

'That we've been giving Tench a bit of grief. Bound to come out sooner or—'

She had snatched his hand and was dragging him towards the sports centre's grey concrete wall.

'What's up?'

But she wasn't about to answer, not until she felt they were far enough away. Even then, she stood so close to him that they could have been readying to waltz. Her face was hidden in shadow.

'Siobhan?' he prompted her.

'You must know who did this,' she said.

'Who?'

'Keith Carberry,' she hissed. Then, when he didn't respond, she raised her face to the heavens and screwed shut her eyes. Rebus noticed that her hands had become clenched fists, her whole body tensed.

'What is it?' he asked quietly. 'Siobhan, what the hell have you done?'

Eventually she opened her eyes, blinking back tears and getting her breathing under control. 'I saw Carberry this morning. We told him ...' She paused. '*I* told him I wanted Gareth Tench.' She glanced back in the direction of the corpse. 'Must be his way of delivering ...'

Rebus waited for her to meet his eyes. 'I saw him this afternoon,' he said. 'He was keeping watch on Tench at the City Chambers.' He slid his hands into his pockets. 'You said "we", Siobhan ...'

'Did I?'

'Where did you talk to him?'

'The pool hall.'

'Same one Cafferty told us about?' He watched as she nodded. 'Cafferty was there, too, wasn't he?' Her look was the only answer he needed. He pulled his hands from his pockets and slapped one of them against the wall. 'For Christ's sake!' he spat. 'You and Cafferty?' She just nodded again. 'When he gets his claws into you, Shiv, they don't come out. All these years you've known me, you must've seen that.'

'What do I do now?'

He thought for a moment. 'If you keep your mouth shut, Cafferty knows he's got you.'

'But if I own up ...'

'I don't know,' he confessed. 'Bounced back into uniform, maybe.'

'Might as well type out my resignation right now.'

'What did Cafferty say to Carberry?'

'Just that he was to hand us the councillor.'

'Who's the "us", Cafferty or the law?'

She gave a shrug.

'And how was he going to deliver?'

'Hell, John, I don't know. You've said yourself, he was shadowing Tench.'

Rebus looked towards the murder scene. 'Bit of a leap from there to stabbing him in the back three times.'

'Maybe not in Keith Carberry's mind.'

Rebus thought about this for a moment. 'We keep it quiet for now,' he decided. 'Who else saw you with Cafferty?'

'Just Carberry. There were people in the pool hall, but upstairs it was just the three of us.'

'And you knew Cafferty would be there?' He watched

her nod. 'Because you'd set the whole thing up with him?' Another nod. 'Without thinking to tell me.' He struggled to keep the anger out of his voice.

'Cafferty came to my flat last night,' Siobhan confessed.

'Jesus ...'

'He owns the pool hall ... that's how he knew Carberry goes there.'

'You've got to stay away from him, Shiv.'

'I know.'

'Damage is done, but we can try some running repairs.'

'Can we?'

He stared at her. 'By "we", I meant "I".'

'Because John Rebus can fix anything?' Her face had hardened a little. 'I can take my own medicine, John. You don't always get to do the knight-in-shining-armour thing.'

He placed his hands on his hips. 'Are we finished mixing our metaphors?'

'You know why I listened to Cafferty? Why I went to that pool hall knowing he'd be there?' Her voice was shaking with emotion. 'He was offering me something I knew I wouldn't get from the law. You've seen it here this week – how the rich and powerful operate ... how they get away with anything they like. Keith Carberry went down to Princes Street that day because he thought it was what his boss wanted. He thought he had Gareth Tench's blessing to cause as much mayhem as he liked.'

Rebus waited to see if there would be more, then touched his hands to her shoulders. 'Cafferty,' he said quietly, 'wanted Gareth Tench put out to pasture, and he was happy to use you as a means to that end.'

'He told me he didn't want him dead.'

'And he told *me* he did. I had quite a descriptive little rant from him on that subject.'

'We didn't tell Keith Carberry to kill him,' she stated.

'Siobhan,' Rebus reminded her, 'you said it yourself

just a minute ago: Keith does pretty much what he thinks people want him to do – powerful people, people who've got some measure of control over him. People like Tench ... and Cafferty ... and you.' He pointed a finger at her.

'So I'm to blame?' she asked, eyes narrowing.

'We can all make a mistake, Siobhan.'

'Well, thanks for that.' She turned on her heels and started striding back across the playing field. Rebus looked down at his feet and gave a sigh, then reached into his pocket for cigarettes and lighter.

The lighter was empty. He shook it, tipped it up, blew on it, rubbed it for luck ... not so much as a spark. He sauntered back towards the line of police vehicles, asked one of the uniforms if he had a light. His colleague was able to oblige, and Rebus decided he might as well beg another favour.

'I need a lift,' he said, watching Siobhan's tail-lights receding into the night. Couldn't believe Cafferty had got his claws into her. No ... he could believe it all too readily. Siobhan had wanted to prove something to her parents – not just that she'd made a success of her job, but that it meant something in the greater scheme. She'd wanted them to know there were always answers, always solutions. Cafferty had promised her both.

But at a price – *his* price.

Siobhan had stopped thinking like a cop, turning back into a daughter again. Rebus thought of how he had let his own family drift away from him, first his wife and daughter, and then his brother. Pushing them away because the job seemed to demand it, demanded his unconditional attention. No room for anyone else ... Too late now to do anything about it.

But not too late for Siobhan.

'You still want that lift?' one of the uniforms was asking. Rebus nodded and got in.

*

His first stop: Craigmillar Police Station. He got himself a cup of coffee and waited for the team to reconvene. Stood to reason they'd set up the murder room here. Sure enough, the cars started to arrive. Rebus didn't know the faces, but introduced himself. The detective angled his head.

'It's DS McManus you want.'

McManus was just coming through the door. He was younger even than Siobhan – maybe not yet thirty. Boyish features, tall and skinny. Looked to Rebus as though he might have grown up locally. Rebus offered a handshake and introduced himself again.

'I was beginning to think you were a myth,' McManus said with a smile. 'I hear tell you were based here a while back.'

'True.'

'Worked with Bain and Maclay.'

'For my sins.'

'Well, they're both long gone, so you needn't worry.' They were walking down the long hallway behind the reception desk. 'What can I do for you, Rebus?'

'Just something I thought you ought to know.'

'Oh aye?'

'I'd had a few run-ins recently with the deceased.'

McManus glanced at him. 'That right?'

'I've been working the Cyril Collar case.'

'Still just the two additional victims?'

Rebus nodded. 'Tench had links to one of them – guy worked at a day-care centre not far from here. Tench got him the position.'

'Fair enough.'

'You'll be interviewing the widow ... she'll probably say CID paid a visit.'

'And that was you?'

'Myself and a colleague, yes.'

They'd taken a left turn into an adjoining corridor,

Rebus following McManus into the CID office, where the team was gathering.

'Anything else you think I should know?'

Rebus tried to look as though he were racking his brains. Finally, he shook his head. 'That's about it,' he said.

'Was Tench a suspect?'

'Not really.' Rebus paused. 'We were a bit concerned by his relationship with a young tearaway called Keith Carberry.'

'I know Keith,' McManus said.

'He was in court, charged with affray in Princes Street. When he came out, Councillor Tench was waiting for him. They seemed pretty pally. Then surveillance cameras showed Carberry whacking some innocent bystander. Looked like he might be in deeper trouble than first thought. I happened to be at the City Chambers this lunchtime, talking with Councillor Tench. When I left, I saw Carberry watching from across the street ...' Rebus ended the speech with a shrug, as if to indicate that he'd no idea what any of this might mean. McManus was studying him.

'Carberry saw the pair of you together?' Rebus nodded. 'And that was lunchtime?'

'I got the feeling he was tailing the councillor.'

'You didn't stop to ask?'

'I was in my car by then ... only caught a glimpse of him in the rearview.'

McManus was gnawing on his bottom lip. 'Need a quick result on this,' he said, almost to himself. 'Tench was hellish popular, did this area a power of good. There are going to be some very angry people.'

'No doubt,' Rebus confirmed. 'Did you know the councillor?'

'Friend of my uncle's ... they go back to schooldays.'

'You're from round here,' Rebus stated.

'Grew up in the shadow of Craigmillar Castle.'

'So you'd known Councillor Tench for some time?'

'Years and years.'

Rebus tried to make his next question sound casual. 'Ever hear rumours about him?'

'What sort of rumours?'

'I don't know ... the usual stuff, I suppose – extramarital flings, money going astray from the coffers ...'

'Guy's not even cold yet,' McManus complained.

'Just wondering,' Rebus apologised. 'I'm not trying to imply anything.'

McManus was looking towards his team – seven of them, including two women. They were trying to look as though they weren't eavesdropping. McManus stepped away from Rebus and stood in front of them.

'We go to his house, inform the family. Need someone to make the formal ID.' He half turned his head towards Rebus. 'After that, we bring in Keith Carberry. Few questions we need to ask him.'

'Such as "Where's the knife, Keith?",' one of the team offered.

McManus allowed the joke. 'I know we've had Bush and Blair and Bono up here this past week, but in Craigmillar Gareth Tench counts as royalty. So we need to be proactive. More boxes we can tick tonight, happier I'll be.'

There were a few groans, but they lacked force. Seemed to Rebus that McManus was well liked. His officers would go the extra hour for him.

'Any overtime?' one of them asked.

'G8 wasn't enough for you, Ben?' McManus retorted. Rebus stayed put for a moment, ready to say something like 'thanks' or 'good luck', but McManus's attention was on this fresh new case. He'd already started doling out tasks.

'Ray, Barbara ... see if there's any CCTV footage from around the Jack Kane Centre. Billy, Tom ... you're going to light some bangers under our esteemed pathologists

– ditto those lazy sods at Forensics. Jimmy, you and Kate go pick up Keith Carberry. Sweat him in the cells till I get back. Ben, you're with me, little trip to the councillor's house in Duddingston Park. Any questions?'

No questions.

Rebus headed back down the corridor, hoping Siobhan could be kept out of it. No way of telling. McManus owed Rebus no favours. Carberry might spill his guts, which would be awkward, but nothing they couldn't handle. Rebus was already forming the story in his head.

DS Clarke had information that Keith played pool in Restalrig. When she got there, the owner, Morris Gerald Cafferty, also happened to be present ...

He doubted McManus would swallow it. They could always deny any meeting had taken place, but there'd been witnesses. Besides, the denial would only work if Cafferty played along ... and the only reason he'd do that would be to tighten the noose around Siobhan. She would owe Cafferty her whole future, and so would Rebus. Which was why, out in reception, he asked for another lift, this time to Merchiston.

The uniforms in the patrol car were chatty, but didn't question where he was headed. Maybe they thought CID could afford to own homes in this quiet, tree-lined enclave. The detached Victorian houses sat behind high walls and fences. The street lighting seemed subdued, so as not to keep the inhabitants awake. The wide streets were almost empty – no parking problems here: each house boasted a driveway for half a dozen cars. Rebus got the patrol car to stop on Ettrick Road – didn't want to be too obvious. They seemed content to hang about and watch him enter whichever house was his final destination. But he waved them away, busying himself with lighting a cigarette. One of the uniforms had gifted him half a dozen matches. Rebus struck one against a wall, and watched the patrol car signal right at the end of the street. At the foot of Ettrick

Road he took a right – still no sign of the patrol car and no place they could be hiding. No sign of life anywhere: no traffic or pedestrians, no sounds from behind the thick stone walls. Huge windows muffled by wooden shutters. Bowling green and tennis courts deserted. He took another right and walked halfway up this new street. Holly hedge in front of one house. Its porch was lit, flanked by stone pillars. Rebus pushed open the gate. Yanked on the bell-pull. Wondered if maybe he should go around to the back. Last time he was here, there was a hot tub there. But then the heavy wooden door gave a shudder as it was opened from within. A young man was standing there. His body had been sculpted in the gym, and he wore a tight black T-shirt to underline the fact.

'Need to go easy on those steroids,' Rebus warned him. 'Is your lord and master home?'

'Does it look like he'd want whatever you're selling?'

'I'm selling salvation, son – everybody needs a taste of that, even you.' Over the man's shoulder, Rebus could see a pair of female legs descending the staircase. Bare feet, the legs slim and tanned and ending at a white towelling robe. She stopped halfway and leaned down so she could see who was at the door. Rebus gave her a little wave. She'd been brought up well – waved back, even though she'd no idea who he was. Then she turned and started padding back upstairs.

'You got a warrant?' the bodyguard was saying.

'The penny drops,' Rebus exclaimed. 'But me and your boss go back a ways.' He pointed a finger in the direction of one of the entrance hall's many doors. 'That's the living room, and that's where I'll wait for him.' Rebus made to pass the man, but an open palm against his chest stopped him.

'He's busy,' the bodyguard said.

'Shagging one of his employees,' Rebus agreed. 'Which means I may have to hang around for all of two minutes

– always supposing he doesn't have a coronary halfway through.' He stared at the hand which was pressed like a lead weight against him. 'You sure you want this?' Rebus met the bodyguard's stare. 'Every time we meet from now on,' he said quietly, 'this is what I'll be remembering ... and believe me, son, whatever failings people may tell you I have, I've got a whole fistful of gold medals in carrying a grudge.'

'And the wooden spoon when it comes to timing,' a voice roared from the top of the stairs. Rebus watched Big Ger Cafferty descend, tying his own voluminous bathrobe around him. What hair he still possessed was rising in tufts from his head and his cheeks were red from exertion. 'What the bloody hell brings you here?' he growled.

'It's a bit lame as an alibi,' Rebus commented. 'Bodyguard, plus some girlfriend you probably pay by the hour ...'

'What do I need an alibi for?'

'You know damned well. Clothes in the washing-machine, are they? Blood can be hard to get out.'

'You're making no sense.'

But Rebus could tell that Cafferty had bitten down on the hook; time to reel him in. 'Gareth Tench is dead,' he stated. 'Stabbed in the back – which is probably just your style. Want to discuss it in front of Arnie here, or should we step into the parlour?'

Cafferty's face gave nothing away. The eyes were small dark voids, the mouth set in a thin, straight line. He placed his hands in the pockets of his robe and gave a little flick of the head, a signal the bodyguard seemed to read. The hand dropped, and Rebus followed Cafferty into the huge drawing room. There was a chandelier hanging from the ceiling, and a baby grand piano taking up space next to the bay window, huge loudspeakers either side of it and a state-of-the-art hi-fi on a rack by the wall. The paintings were brash and modern, violent splashes of colour. Above the fireplace hung a framed copy of the jacket from

Cafferty's book. He was busying himself at the drinks cabinet. It meant his back was kept turned to Rebus.

'Whisky?' he asked.

'Why not?' Rebus replied.

'Stabbed, you say?'

'Three times. Outside the Jack Kane Centre.'

'Home turf,' Cafferty commented. 'A mugging gone wrong?'

'I think you know better.'

Cafferty turned round and handed Rebus a glass. It was quality stuff, dark and peaty. Rebus didn't bother offering a toast, just washed it around his mouth before swallowing.

'You wanted him dead,' Rebus went on, watching Cafferty take the smallest sip of his own drink. 'I listened to you rant and rave on the subject.'

'I was a bit emotional,' Cafferty conceded.

'In which state I'd put nothing whatsoever past you.'

Cafferty was staring at one of the paintings. Thick blotches of white oil, melting into oozing greys and reds. 'I won't lie to you, Rebus – I'm not sorry he's dead. Makes my life that bit less complicated. But I didn't have him killed.'

'I think you did.'

Cafferty gave the slightest twitch of one eyebrow. 'And what does Siobhan say to all this?'

'She's the reason I'm here.'

Now Cafferty smiled. 'Thought as much,' he said. 'She told you about our little chat with Keith Carberry?'

'After which, I happened to catch him stalking Tench.'

'That was his prerogative.'

'You didn't make him?'

'Ask Siobhan – she was there.'

'Her name's Detective Sergeant Clarke, Cafferty, and she doesn't know you the way I do.'

'Have you arrested Carberry?' Cafferty turned his attention back from the painting.

Rebus gave a slow nod. 'And my money says he'll talk. So if you *did* have a little word in his ear ...'

'I didn't tell him to do anything. If he says I did, he's lying – and I've got the detective sergeant as my witness.'

'She stays out of this, Cafferty,' Rebus warned.

'Or what?'

Rebus just shook his head. 'She stays out,' he repeated.

'I like her, Rebus. When they finally drag you kicking and screaming to the Twilight Benevolent Home, I think you'll be leaving her in good hands.'

'You don't go near her. You never speak to her.' Rebus's voice had dropped to a near-whisper.

Cafferty gave a huge grin and emptied the crystal tumbler into his mouth. Smacked his lips and exhaled loudly. 'It's the boy you should be worried about. Your money says he'll talk. If he does, he could well end up dropping DS Clarke right in it.' He made sure he had Rebus's full attention. 'We could, of course, make sure he doesn't get a chance to talk ...'

'I wish Tench was still alive,' Rebus muttered. 'Because now I *know* I'd help him take you down.'

'But you're changeable, Rebus ... like a summer's day in Edinburgh. Next week you'll be blowing me kisses.' Cafferty puckered his lips for effect. 'You're already suspended from duty. Are you sure you can afford any more enemies? How long has it been since they started to outnumber your friends?'

Rebus looked around the room. 'I don't see you hosting too many parties.'

'That's because you're never invited – the book launch excepted.' Cafferty nodded towards the fireplace. Rebus looked again at the framed artwork from Cafferty's book. *Changeling: The Maverick Life of the Man They Call 'Mr Big'.*

'I've never heard you called Mr Big,' Rebus commented.

Cafferty shrugged. 'Mairie's idea, not mine. I must give her a call ... I think she's been avoiding me. That wouldn't be anything to do with your good self, I suppose?'

Rebus ignored him. 'With Tench out of the way, you'll be moving into Niddrie and Craigmillar.'

'Will I?'

'With Carberry and his ilk as your foot-soldiers.'

Cafferty gave a chuckle. 'Mind if I make some notes? I wouldn't want to forget any of this.'

'When you talked to Carberry this morning, you were letting him know the outcome you wanted – the only outcome that would save his neck.'

'You're assuming young Keith was the only person I spoke to.' Cafferty was dribbling more whisky into his glass.

'Who else?'

'Maybe Siobhan herself flew off the handle. I assume the murder team will want to talk to her?' Cafferty's tongue was protruding slightly from his mouth.

'Who else have you talked to about Gareth Tench?'

Cafferty swilled the liquid around his glass. 'You're supposed to be the detective around here. I can't go fighting *all* your battles for you.'

'Judgement day's coming, Cafferty. For you and me both.' Rebus paused. 'You know that, right?'

The gangster shook his head slowly. 'I see us in a couple of deckchairs, somewhere hot but with ice-cold drinks. Reminiscing about the sparring we used to do, back in the days when the good guys thought they knew the bad guys. One thing this week should have shown all of us – only takes a few moments for everything to change. Protests crumble, poverty goes on the back-burner ... some alliances are strengthened, others weaken. All that effort sidelined, the voices silenced. In the time it takes to snap your fingers.' He did just this, as if to reinforce his point. 'Makes all *your* hard work seem a little bit petty and unimportant, wouldn't you say? And Gareth Tench … a year from now, think anyone's going to remember him?' He drained his glass for the second time. 'Now I really have to get back upstairs. Not that I don't always enjoy our little get-togethers, you understand.' Cafferty placed his empty glass on the coffee table and gestured for Rebus to do the same. As they left the room, he switched off the lights, said something about doing his bit for the planet.

The bodyguard was in the hall, hands clasped in front of him.

'Ever worked as a bouncer?' Rebus asked. 'One of your colleagues – name of Colliar – he ended up on a stainless-steel slab. Just one of many perks associated with your dodgy employer.'

Cafferty was already climbing the staircase. It gratified Rebus that he was having to use the banister to haul himself up each step. But then … *he* did much the same thing these days in his tenement.

The bodyguard held the door open. Rebus brushed past him none too gently – not even a ripple of movement from the younger man. The door slammed after him. He stood on the path a moment, walked back to the gate and let it clank shut. Scratched another match and lit a cigarette. Headed up the street, but paused beneath one of the underpowered lamp-posts. Took out his phone and tried Siobhan's number, but she didn't pick up. He walked to the top of the road and back down again. While he was standing there, an emaciated fox trotted out of a driveway and into the one next door. He'd started seeing them a lot in the city. They never seemed to panic or be shy. The look they gave their human neighbours was close to disdain or disappointment. Hunts had been banned from chasing them across country; people in the towns left scraps out for them. Hard to think of them as predators – but it was in their nature.

Predators being treated like pets.

Mavericks.

It was another thirty minutes before he began to hear the approaching taxi, its toiling diesel engine as distinctive as birdsong. Rebus climbed into the back and closed the door, but told the driver they were waiting for one more.

'Remind me,' he added, 'is it cash or contract?'

'Contract.'

'MGC Holdings, right?'

'The Nook,' the driver corrected him.

'Dropping off at ...?'

The driver now turned in his seat. 'What's the game, pal?'

'No game.'

'It's a woman's name on the pick-up sheet – and if you're toting a fanny you should get on the blower to one of those extreme make-over programmes.'

'Thanks for the advice.' Rebus tucked himself into the furthest corner of the cab as Cafferty's door opened and closed. Heels clacking down the footpath, and then the cab's door was opened, perfume wafting in.

'In you get,' Rebus said, before the woman could complain. 'I just need a lift home.'

She hesitated, but climbed in eventually and settled herself as far from Rebus as was possible. The red button was lit, meaning the driver would be able to listen in. Rebus found the right switch and turned it off.

'You work at the Nook?' he asked quietly. 'Didn't realise Cafferty'd got his mitts on it.'

'What's it to you?' the woman snapped back.

'Just making conversation. Friend of Molly's?'

'Never heard of her.'

'I was going to ask how she was. I'm the guy who dragged the diplomat off her the other night.'

The woman studied him. 'Molly's fine,' she said at last. Then: 'How did you know you wouldn't be waiting till dawn?'

'Human psychology,' he offered with a shrug. 'Cafferty's never struck me as the kind who'd let a woman stay the night.'

'Clever you.' There was just the hint of a smile. Hard to make out her features in the taxi's shadowy interior. Clean hair, the sheen of lipstick, the smell of her perfume. Jewellery and high heels and a three-quarter-length coat, falling open to show a much shorter dress beneath. Plenty of mascara, the eyelashes exaggerated.

He decided on another nudge: 'So Molly's all right?'

'As far as I know.'

'What's Cafferty like to work for?'

'He's okay.' She turned to stare out at the passing scene, the street lighting showing him half her face. 'He told me about you ...'

'I'm CID.'

She nodded. 'When he heard your voice downstairs, it was like someone had changed his batteries.'

'I do have that effect on people. Are we headed to the Nook?'

'I live in the Grassmarket.'

'Handy for work,' he commented.

'What is it you want?'

'You mean apart from a lift at Cafferty's expense?' Rebus gave a shrug. 'Maybe I just want to know why anyone would want to get close to him. See, I'm beginning to think he carries a virus – everyone he touches gets hurt in some way.'

'You've known him a lot longer than I have,' she replied.

'That's true.'

'Meaning you must be immune?'

He shook his head. 'Not immune, no.'

'He's not hurt me yet.'

'That's good ... but the damage isn't always immediate.' They were turning into Lady Lawson Street. The driver signalled to make a right. Another minute and they'd be in Grassmarket.

'Finished your Good Samaritan routine?' she asked, turning to face Rebus.

'It's your life ...'

'That's right.' She leaned forward towards the driver's panel. 'Pull over next to the lights.'

He did as ordered. Started filling in the contract slip, but Rebus told him there was one last drop-off to make. She was climbing out of the cab. He waited for her to say something, but she slammed the door, crossed the road and headed down a darkened close. The driver kept the engine running until a beam of light showed him she'd opened her stairwell door.

'Always like to make sure,' he explained to Rebus. 'Cannae be too careful these days. Where to, chief?'

'Quick U-turn,' Rebus answered. 'Drop me at the Nook.' It was a two-minute ride, at the end of which Rebus told the driver to add twenty quid to the chitty as a tip. Signed his name to it and handed it back.

'Sure about this, chief?' the driver asked.

'Easy when it's someone else's cash,' Rebus told him, getting out.

The doormen at the Nook recognised him, which didn't mean they were happy to renew the acquaintance.

'Busy night, lads?' Rebus asked.

'Paydays always are. Been a good week for overtime, too.'

Rebus got the bouncer's meaning the moment he walked in. A large group of drunken cops seemed to have monopolised three of the lap-dancers. Their table groaned with champagne flutes and beer glasses. Not that they looked out of place – a stag party on the far side of the room was enjoying the competition. Rebus didn't know the cops, but their accents were Scottish – a last night on the town for this motley crew before they headed home to their wives

429

and girlfriends in Glasgow, Inverness, Aberdeen ...

Two women were gyrating on the small central stage. Another was parading along the top of the bar for the benefit of the lone drinkers seated there. She squatted to allow a five-pound note to be tucked into her G-string, earning the donor a peck on the pockmarked cheek. There was just the one stool left, and Rebus took it. Two dancers emerged from behind a curtain and started working the room. Hard to say if they'd been giving private dances or taking a cigarette break. One started to approach Rebus, her smile evaporating as he shook his head. The barman asked him what he was drinking.

'I'm not,' he said. 'Just need to borrow your lighter.' A pair of high heels had stopped in front of him. Their owner wriggled her way down until she was at eye level with him. Rebus broke off lighting his cigarette long enough to tell her he needed a word.

'I've a break coming in five minutes,' Molly Clark said. She turned towards the barman. 'Ronnie, give my friend here a drink.'

'Fine,' Ronnie answered, 'but it's coming out of your wages.'

She ignored him, stretching herself upright again and treading gingerly towards the other end of the bar.

'Whisky, thanks, Ronnie,' Rebus said, pocketing the lighter unnoticed, 'and I prefer to add my own water.'

Even so, Rebus could have sworn the stuff poured from the bottle had already seen its share of adulteration. He wagged a finger at the barman.

'You want to tell Trading Standards you've been here, that's your business,' Ronnie shot back.

Rebus pushed the drink aside and turned on his stool, as though interested in the dancers, when actually he was watching the posse of cops. What was it, he wondered, that marked them out? A few had moustaches; all had neat haircuts. Most still wore a tie, though their suit jackets

430

were draped over their chairs. Various ages and builds, yet he couldn't help feeling there was something *uniform* about them. They acted like a small, separate tribe, slightly at odds with the rest of the world. Moreover, all week they'd been in charge of the capital – saw themselves as conquerors ... invincible ... all-powerful.

Look on my works ...

Had Gareth Tench really seen himself that way too? Rebus thought it was more complex. Tench had known he would fail, but was determined to give it a try all the same. Rebus had considered the outside chance that the councillor had been their killer, his 'works' the little gallery of horror in Auchterarder. Determined to rid the world of its monsters – Cafferty included. Killing Cyril Collar had put Cafferty briefly in the frame. A lazy investigation might have ended there, with Cafferty the chief suspect. Tench had also known Trevor Guest ... helped the guy out then was incensed to come across his details on a website. Decided he'd been betrayed ...

Leaving only Fast Eddie Isley. Nothing to connect Tench to *him*, and Isley had been the first victim, the one who set the whole train in motion. And now Tench was dead, and they were going to blame it on Keith Carberry.

Who else have you talked to about Gareth Tench?

You're supposed to be the detective around here ...

Or a poor excuse for one. Rebus reached for his drink again, just to give himself something to do. The dancers on the stage looked bored. They wanted to be down on the floor, where pay packets were being emptied into peek-a-boo bras and minuscule thongs. Rebus didn't doubt there'd be a rota – they'd get their chance. More men were coming inside – executive types. One of them was grinding to the room's pounding soundtrack. He was a stone overweight and the moves didn't suit him. But no one was about to ridicule him: that was the whole point of somewhere like the Nook. It was all about the shedding of inhibitions. Rebus couldn't help thinking back to the 1970s, when most Edinburgh bars had offered a lunchtime stripper. The drinkers would hide their faces behind their pint glasses whenever the dancer looked in their direction. All that reticence had melted away in the course of the intervening decades. The businessmen were yelping encouragement as one of the lap-dancers at the police table started doing her stuff, while her victim sat with legs parted, hands on knees, grinning and sweaty-faced.

Molly was standing next to Rebus. He hadn't noticed her ending her routine. 'Give me two minutes to throw a coat on, and I'll see you outside.'

He nodded distractedly.

'Penny for them,' she said, suddenly curious.

'Just thinking about how sex has changed down the years. We used to be such a shy wee nation.'

'And now?'

The dancer was gyrating her hips mere inches from her victim's nose.

'Now,' Rebus mused, 'it's ... well ...'

'In your face?' she offered.

He nodded his agreement, and placed the empty glass back on the bar.

She offered him a cigarette from her own packet. She'd wrapped a long black woollen coat around her, and was leaning against one of the Nook's walls, just far enough from the doormen for eavesdropping to be a problem.

'You don't smoke in the flat,' Rebus commented.

'Eric's allergic.'

'It was Eric I wanted to speak to you about, actually.' Rebus was making a show of examining his cigarette's glowing tip.

'What about him?' She shuffled her feet and Rebus noticed she'd exchanged the stilettos for trainers.

432

'When we talked before, you said he knows how you go about earning a wage.'

'And?'

Rebus shrugged. 'I don't really want him getting hurt, which is why I think maybe you should leave him.'

'Leave him?'

'So I don't have to tell him that you've been milking him for inside info, and passing everything he tells you back to your boss. See, I've just been talking to Cafferty, and it suddenly clicked. He's known stuff he shouldn't, stuff he's been getting from the inside ... and who knows more than someone like Brains?'

She snorted. 'You call him Brains ... why don't you start crediting him with some?'

'How do you mean?'

'You think I'm the big bad hooker, wheedling stuff out of the poor sap.' She rubbed a finger across her top lip.

'I'd go a bit further actually – seems to me you're only living with Eric because Cafferty tells you to ... probably feeds that coke habit of yours to make it all worthwhile. First time we met, I thought it was just nerves.'

She didn't bother denying it.

'Soon as Eric stops being useful,' Rebus went on, 'you'll drop him like a stone. My advice is to do that right now.'

'Like I said, Rebus, Eric's no idiot. He's known all along what the score is.'

Rebus narrowed his eyes. 'In the flat, you said you stopped him taking job offers – how will he feel when he finds out that was because he'd be no use to your boss in the private sector?'

'He tells me stuff because he *wants* to,' she went on, 'and he knows damned fine where it'll end up.'

'Classic honey trap,' Rebus muttered.

'Once you get a taste ...' she said teasingly.

'You're still going to walk away from him,' he demanded.

433

'Or what?' Her eyes burned into him. 'You'll go tell him something he already knows?'

'Sooner or later, Cafferty's walking the plank – you really want to be there with him?'

'I'm a good swimmer.'

'It's not water you'll end up in, Molly. Time inside will play havoc with those looks, I guarantee it. See, slipping confidential gen to a criminal is just about as serious as it gets.'

'You shop me, Rebus, Eric gets shopped too. So much for protecting him.'

'Price has to be paid.' Rebus flicked away the remains of the cigarette. 'First thing tomorrow, I'll be talking to him. Your bags had better be packed.'

'What if Mr Cafferty doesn't agree?'

'He will. Once your cover's blown, CID could be feeding you any amount of manure dressed as caviar. Cafferty takes one bite, and we've got him.'

Her eyes were still fixed on his. 'So why aren't you doing that?'

'Sting operation means telling the brass ... and that really would be the end of Eric's career. You walk away now, I get Eric back. Too many lives shat on by your boss, Molly. I just want a few of them sluiced down.' He reached into his pocket for his cigarettes, opened the pack and offered her one. 'So what do you say?'

'Time's up,' one of the doormen called, pressing a finger to his earpiece. 'Clients three deep in there ...'

She looked at Rebus. 'Time's up,' she echoed, turning towards the backstage door. Rebus watched her go, lit himself another cigarette, and decided the walk home across The Meadows would do him good.

His phone was ringing as he unlocked the door. He picked it up from the chair.

'Rebus,' he said.

'It's me,' Ellen Wylie said. 'What the hell's been happening?'

'What do you mean?'

'I've had Siobhan on the phone. I don't know what you've been saying to her, but she's in a hell of a state.'

'She thinks she should take some of the blame for Gareth Tench.'

'I tried telling her she's crazy.'

'That'll have helped.' Rebus started turning on the lights. He wanted them all on – not just the living room, but the hall and the kitchen, the bathroom and his bedroom.

'She sounded pretty pissed off with you.'

'You don't need to sound so happy about it.'

'I spent twenty minutes calming her down!' Wylie yelled. 'Don't you dare start accusing me of enjoying any of this!'

'Sorry, Ellen.' Rebus meant it, too. He sat on the edge of the bath, shoulders slumped, phone tucked in against his chin.

'We're all tired, John, that's the trouble.'

'I think my troubles go just that little bit deeper, Ellen.'

'So go beat yourself up about it – wouldn't be the first time.'

He puffed air from his cheeks. 'What's the bottom line with Siobhan?'

'Maybe give her a day to calm down. I told her she should drive up to T in the Park, let off some steam.'

'Not a bad idea.' Except that his own weekend plans included the Borders ... looked like he'd be heading south unaccompanied. No way he could invite Ellen – didn't want it getting back to Siobhan.

'At least we can rule Tench out as a suspect,' Wylie was saying.

'Maybe.'

'Siobhan said you'd be arresting some kid from Niddrie?'

'Probably already in custody.'

'So it has nothing to do with the Clootie Well or BeastWatch?'

'Coincidence, that's all.'

'So what happens now?'

'Your notion of a weekend break sounds good. Everybody's back to work on Monday ... we can organise a proper murder inquiry.'

'You won't be needing me then?'

'There's a place for you if you want it, Ellen. You've got a whole forty-eight hours to think it over.'

'Thanks, John.'

'But do me a favour ... give Siobhan a call tomorrow. Let her know I'm worried.'

'Worried *and* sorry?'

'I'll leave the wording to you. Night, Ellen.'

He ended the call and studied his face in the bathroom mirror. He was surprised not to see scourge marks and raw flesh. Looked much the same as ever: sallow and needing a shave, hair unkempt, bags under his eyes. He gave his cheeks a few slaps and headed through to the kitchen, made himself a cup of instant coffee – black; the milk had decided it was sour – and ended up seated at the table in the living room. The same faces stared down at him from his walls:

Cyril Colliar.

Trevor Guest.

Edward Isley.

He knew that on TV the main topic would still be the London bombs. Experts would be debating What Could Have Been Done and What To Do Next. All other news would have been pushed aside. Yet he still had his three unsolved murders ... which were actually Siobhan's now that he thought of it. Chief Constable had put *her* in charge. Then there was Ben Webster, receding into obscurity with each turn of the news cycle.

Nobody'd blame you for coasting ...

Nobody but the dead.

He rested his head on his folded arms. Saw the well-fed Cafferty descending that million-pound staircase. Saw Siobhan falling for his tricks. Saw Cyril Collier doing his dirty work and Keith Carberry doing his dirty work and Molly and Eric Bain doing his dirty work. Cafferty coming downstairs, perfumed from the shower, smelling sweeter than any nosegay.

Cafferty the mobster knew Steelforth's name.

Cafferty the author had met Richard Pennen.

Who else ...?

Who else have you talked to ...?

Cafferty with his tongue protruding. *Maybe Siobhan herself ...*

No, not Siobhan. Rebus had seen the way she acted at the murder scene – she hadn't known a thing.

Which didn't mean she hadn't wanted it to happen. Hadn't wished it into existence by letting her eyes meet Cafferty's for just that second too long.

Rebus heard a plane climbing into the sky from the west. There weren't many late flights out of Edinburgh. He wondered if maybe it was Tony Blair or some of his minions. Thank you, Scotland, and good night. The summit would have enjoyed the best the country had to offer – scenery, whisky, ambience, food. The morsels turning to ash as that red London bus exploded. And meantime three bad men had died ... and one good man – Ben Webster ... and one Rebus wasn't sure about even now. Gareth Tench might have been acting from the best of motives, but with his conscience hammered into submission by circumstance.

Or he could have been on the cusp of wrenching away Cafferty's tarnished crown.

Rebus doubted he would ever know for sure. He stared at the phone lying in front of him on the dining table.

Seven digits and he'd be connected to Siobhan's flat. Seven tiny points of pressure on the keypad. How could something be so difficult?

'What makes you think she's not better off without you?' he found himself asking the silver lozenge. It replied with a bleep, and his head twitched upwards. He snatched at it, but all it was trying to tell him was that its battery was low.

'No lower than mine,' he muttered, rising slowly to his feet to seek out the charger. He'd just plugged it in when it rang: Mairie Henderson.

'Evening, Mairie,' Rebus said.

'John? Where are you?'

'At home. What's the problem?'

'Can I email you something? It's the story I'm writing on Richard Pennen.'

'You need my proof-reading skills?'

'I just want ...'

'What's happened, Mairie?'

'I had a run-in with three of Pennen's goons. They were wearing uniforms, but they were no more cops than I am.'

Rebus eased himself down on to the arm of his chair. 'One of them called Jacko?'

'How did you know?'

'I've met them too. What happened?'

She told him, adding her suspicion that they might have spent time in Iraq.

'And now you're scared?' Rebus guessed. 'That's why you want to make sure there are copies of your piece?'

'I'm sending out a few.'

'But not to other journalists, right?'

'Don't want to put temptation in their way.'

'No copyright on scandal,' Rebus agreed. 'Do you want to take things any further?'

'How do you mean?'

'You were right first time – impersonating a cop *is* a serious matter.'

'Once I've filed my copy, I'll be fine.'

'You sure?'

'I'm sure, but thanks for asking.'

'If you need me, Mairie, you've got my number.'

'Thanks, John. Good night.'

She ended the call and left him staring at his phone. The 'charge' symbol came on again, the battery taking its little sips of electricity. Rebus walked to the dining table and switched on his laptop. Plugged the cable into the phone socket and managed to get himself online. It never ceased to amaze him when it actually worked. Mairie's email was waiting for him. He clicked 'download' and added her story to one of his folders, hoping he'd be able to find it again. There was another email, this time from Stan Hackman.

Better late than never, it read. *Here I am back in the Toon and about to hit a few night-spots. Just time to let you know about our Trev. Interview notes say he moved to Coldstream for a time – don't say why or for how long. Hope this helps. Your pal, Stan.*

Coldstream – same place as the man he'd had the fight with outside Swany's on Ratcliffe Terrace.

'Clickety-click,' Rebus said to himself, deciding he was owed a drink.

Saturday 9 July

25

Only a week since Rebus had walked down to The Meadows and found all those people there, dressed in white.

A long time in politics, so the saying went. Every moment of every day, life moved on. The hordes of people making the pilgrimage north today would be headed for the outskirts of Kinross and T in the Park. Sports fans would venture further west, to Loch Lomond and the final rounds of the Scottish Open Golf Championship. Rebus reckoned his own route south would take under two hours, but there were a couple of detours first – Slateford Road to start with. He sat in the idling car, staring up at the windows of the converted warehouse. Thought he could tell Eric Bain's flat. The curtains were open. Rebus was playing the Elbow CD again, the singer comparing the leaders of the free world to kids chucking stones. He was about to get out of the car when he saw Bain himself shambling into view, returning from the corner shop. He hadn't shaved or combed his hair. His shirt wasn't tucked in. He carried a carton of milk and a dazed expression. In most people, Rebus might have put it down to tiredness. He wound down his window and sounded the horn. Bain took a second or two to recognise him and crossed the road towards the car.

'Thought that was you,' Rebus stated. Bain said nothing, just nodded, mind elsewhere. 'She's left you then?' This seemed to focus Bain's thoughts.

'Left a message saying someone would come by to pick up her stuff.'

Rebus nodded. 'Get in, Eric. We need to have a little chat.'

But Bain stood his ground. 'How did you know?'

'Talk to anyone, Eric, they'll tell you I'm the last one who should be giving relationship advice.' Rebus paused. 'On the other hand, we can't have you passing inside information to Big Ger Cafferty.'

Bain stared at him. 'You ...?'

'I had a word with Molly last night. If she's scarpered, that means she'd rather keep working at the Nook than stay shacked up with you.'

'I don't ... I'm not sure I ...' Bain's eyes widened as though lit by a jolt of caffeine. The milk carton fell from his grasp. His hands reached in through the window and found Rebus's throat. His teeth were bared with the effort. Rebus pushed himself back towards the passenger seat, one hand scrabbling at Bain's fingers, the other finding the window button. Up went the glass, trapping Bain. Rebus slid all the way over to the passenger side and exited the car. Walked around to where Bain was extracting his arms from the door frame. As Bain turned, Rebus kneed him in the crotch, sending him down on to his knees in the widening pool of milk. Rebus swung a punch at Bain's chin and landed him on his back. Straddled him, holding his shirt by its open collar.

'*Your* fault, Eric, not mine. One whiff of fanny and you start spilling your guts. And according to your "girlfriend", you were delighted to oblige, even after you'd sussed it wasn't just natural curiosity on her part. Made you feel important, did it? That's the reason most grasses start gabbing.'

Bain wasn't putting up any sort of a struggle, apart from a jerking of his shoulders – and even this fell far short of resistance. In point of fact, he was sobbing, face spattered with droplets of milk, like a kid whose favourite plaything had just been lost. Rebus rose to his feet, straightening his own clothes.

'Get up,' he ordered. But Bain seemed content to lie there, so Rebus hauled him to his feet. 'Look at me, Eric,' he said, drawing out a handkerchief and passing it over. 'Here, wipe your face.'

Bain did as he was told. There was a bubble of snot swelling from one of his nostrils.

'Now listen,' Rebus ordered. 'The deal I made with her was that if she left, we'd let it go at that. Meaning I don't go telling Fettes about any of this – and you get to keep your job.' Rebus angled his face until Bain met his eyes. 'Do you understand?'

'Plenty more jobs.'

'In IT? Sure, and they all want an employee who can't keep secrets from strippers ...'

'I loved her, Rebus.'

'Maybe so, but she was playing you like Clapton with a six-string ... What're you smiling at?'

'I'm named after him ... my dad's a fan.'

'Is that a fact?'

Bain looked up at the sky, his breathing slowing a little. 'I really thought she—'

'Cafferty was using you, Eric – end of story. But here's the thing ...' Rebus made sure he had eye contact. 'You can't go near her, you don't go to the Nook pining for her. She's sending someone for her stuff because she knows that's how it works.' Rebus emphasised his point by chopping the air karate-style with his hand.

'You saw her that day in the flat, Rebus ... She must've liked me at least a little bit.'

'Keep thinking that if you like ... just don't go asking her. If I hear you're trying to contact her, don't think I won't tell Corbyn.'

Bain mumbled something Rebus didn't catch. He asked him to repeat it. Bain's eyes drilled into him.

'It wasn't about Cafferty at the start.'

'Whatever you say, Eric. But it *was* about him eventually ... trust me on that.'

Bain was silent for a few moments. He stared down at the pavement. 'I need more milk.'

'Best get yourself cleaned up first. Look, I'm heading out of town. You're going to spend all day turning this over – what if I give you a bell tomorrow, you can let me know the score?'

Bain nodded slowly, tried handing Rebus back his handkerchief.

'You can keep that,' he was advised. 'Got a friend you can talk to?'

'On the net,' Bain said.

'Whatever works.' Rebus patted his shoulder. 'Are you okay now? I need to get going.'

'I'll manage.'

'Good boy.' Rebus took a deep breath. 'I'm not going to apologise for what I did, Eric ... but I'm sorry you had to get hurt.'

Bain nodded again. 'It's me who should ...'

But Rebus silenced him with a shake of the head. 'All in the past now. Just got to pick yourself up and move on.'

'No use crying over spilt milk?' Bain offered with an attempt at a smile.

'Been trying my damnedest not to say it these past ten minutes,' Rebus admitted. 'Go stick your head under the shower, wash it all away.'

'Might not be that easy,' Bain said quietly.

Rebus nodded agreement. 'But all the same ... it's a start.'

Siobhan had spent a good forty minutes soaking in the bath. Normally she only had time for a shower in the morning, but today she was determined to pamper herself.

446

About a third of a bottle of Space NK bath foam, and a big glass of fresh orange juice. BBC 6 Music on her digital radio and her mobile phone switched off. The ticket to T in the Park was on the sofa in the living room, next to a makeshift list of things she would need – bottled water and snacks, her cagoule, suntan lotion (well, you never could tell). Last night she'd been on the verge of calling Bobby Greig and offering him her ticket. But why should she? If she didn't go, she'd just end up slouched on the sofa with the TV playing. Ellen Wylie had called first thing, told her she'd been talking to Rebus.

'He's sorry,' Ellen had reported.

'Sorry for what?'

'For anything and everything.'

'Nice of him to tell you instead of me.'

'My fault,' Ellen had admitted. 'I said he should leave you in peace for a day or so.'

'Thanks. How's Denise?'

'Still in bed. So what's the plan for today? Bopping yourself into a sweat at Kinross, or would you rather we go somewhere and drown all our sorrows?'

'I'll bear that offer in mind. But I think you're right – Kinross might be just what I need.'

Not that she'd be staying the night. Although her ticket was valid for both days, she'd had quite enough of the outdoors life. She wondered if the dope dealer from Stirling would be there, plying his trade. Maybe this time she would decide to indulge, break yet another rule. She knew plenty of officers who did a bit of blaw; had heard rumours of some who even did coke at weekends. All kinds of ways to unwind. She considered the options, and decided she'd better pack a couple of condoms, just in case she *did* end up in someone's tent. She knew two women PCs who were heading to the festival. They were hoping to rendezvous with her by text message. A wild pair they were, with a crush on the front men with the Killers and

Keane. They were already in Kinross – wanted to be sure of a place front-of-stage.

'You better text us when you get there,' they'd warned Siobhan. 'Leave it too long, we might be in a sorry state.'

Sorry ...

For anything and everything.

But what had he to feel sorry about? Had he sat in the Bentley GT and listened to Cafferty's plan? Had he climbed those stairs with Keith Carberry and stood with him as Cafferty held court? She screwed shut her eyes and ducked her head beneath the surface of the bath water.

I'm to blame, she thought. The words kept bouncing around the inside of her skull. Gareth Tench ... so vividly alive, voice booming ... Charismatic like all the best showmen – just 'happening along' to chase Carberry and his mates away, proving to the outside world that he was the only man for the job. A bravura con trick, finessing grant aid for his constituents. Larger than life and seemingly indefatigable ... and now lying cold and naked in one of the drawers at the city mortuary, turned into a series of incisions and statistics.

Someone had told her once: an inch-long blade was all it took. A single slender inch of tempered steel could knock the whole world out of kilter.

She heaved herself up into daylight, spluttering and wiping the hair and suds from her face. She'd thought she could hear a phone ringing, but there was nothing, just a floorboard creaking in the flat upstairs. Rebus had told her to stay away from Cafferty, and he was right. If she lost it in front of Cafferty, *she'd* be the loser.

But then she was already the loser, wasn't she?

'And so much fun to be around,' she muttered to herself, rising to a crouch and stretching out a hand towards the nearest towel.

It didn't take her long to pack – same bag she'd taken

with her to Stirling. And even though she wouldn't be staying the night, she dropped in her toothbrush and toothpaste anyway. Maybe once she was in the car, she'd just keep on driving. If she ran out of land, she could always take a ferry to Orkney. That was the thing about a car – it gave the illusion of freedom. The adverts always played on that sense of adventure and discovery, but in her case 'flight' would be more accurate.

'Not doing that,' she explained to the bathroom mirror, hairbrush in hand. She'd said as much to Rebus, told him she could take her own medicine.

Not that Cafferty was medicine – more like poison.

She knew the route she *should* take: go see James Corbyn and tell him how badly she'd messed up, then end up back in uniform as a result.

'I'm a good copper,' she told the mirror, trying to imagine how she would explain it to her dad ... her dad who'd become so proud of her. And to her mother, who'd told her it didn't matter.

Didn't matter who'd hit her.

And just why had it mattered so much to Siobhan? Not really because of the anger at thinking it might be another cop, but because she could use it to prove she *was* good at her job.

'A good cop,' she repeated quietly. And then, wiping steam from the mirror: 'Despite all the evidence to the contrary.'

Second and final detour: Craigmillar police station. McManus was already at work.

'Conscientious,' Rebus said, walking into the CID office. There was no else about as yet. McManus was dressed casually – sports shirt and denims.

'What does that make you?' McManus asked, wetting a finger so he could turn the page of the report he was reading.

'PM results?' Rebus guessed.

McManus nodded. 'I'm just back.'

'Déjà vu all over again,' Rebus commented. 'I was in your shoes last Saturday – Ben Webster.'

'No wonder Professor Gates looked miffed – two Saturdays in a row ...'

By now Rebus was standing next to McManus's desk. 'Any conclusions?'

'Serrated knife, seven-eighths of an inch in width. Gates reckons you'd find them in most kitchens.'

'He's right. Is Keith Carberry still on the premises?'

'You know the drill, Rebus: after six hours, we charge or chuck out.'

'Meaning you've not charged him?'

McManus looked up from the report. 'He denies any involvement. Even has an alibi – he was playing pool at the time, seven or eight witnesses.'

'All of them doubtless good friends of his ...'

McManus just shrugged. 'Plenty of knives in his mum's kitchen, but no sign any of them's missing. We've lifted the lot for analysis.'

'And Carberry's clothes?'

'Went through those too. No traces of blood.'

'Meaning they've been disposed of, same as the knife.'

McManus leaned back in his chair. 'Whose investigation is this, Rebus?'

Rebus held up his hands in surrender. 'Just thinking aloud. Who was it interviewed Carberry?'

'I did it myself.'

'You think he's guilty?'

'He seemed genuinely shocked when we told him about Tench. But just behind those nasty blue eyes of his, I thought I could see something else.'

'What?'

'He was scared.'

'Because he'd been found out?'

McManus shook his head. 'Scared to say anything.'

Rebus turned away, not wanting McManus to see anything behind *his* eyes. Say Carberry didn't do it ... was Cafferty himself suddenly in the frame again? The young man scared because that was his thinking too ... and if Cafferty had struck at Tench, would Keith himself be next?

'Did you ask him about tailing the councillor?'

'Admitted waiting for him. Said he wanted to thank him.'

'For what?' Rebus turned to face McManus again.

'Moral support after he was bailed for affray.'

Rebus gave a snort. 'You believe that?'

'Not necessarily, but it wasn't grounds to hold him indefinitely.' McManus paused. 'Thing is ... when we told him he could go, he was reluctant – tried not to show it, but he was. Looked to left and right as he walked out of the door, as though expecting something. Fairly hared away too.' McManus paused again. 'Do you see what I'm getting at, Rebus?'

Rebus nodded. 'Hare rather than fox.'

'Along those lines, yes ... Makes me wonder if there's something you're not telling me.'

'I'd still have him down as a suspect.'

'Agreed.' McManus rose from his chair, fixed Rebus with a look. 'But is he the only one we should be speaking to?'

'Councillors make enemies,' Rebus stated.

'According to the widow, Tench counted you among them.'

'She's mistaken.'

McManus ignored this, and concentrated on folding his arms instead. 'She also thinks the family home was being watched – not by Keith Carberry, though. Description she gave was a silver-haired man in a big posh car. Does that sound to you like Big Ger Cafferty?'

Rebus shrugged a reply.

'Another little story I hear ...' McManus was approaching Rebus. 'Concerns you and a man answering that same description at a meeting in a church hall, just a few days back. The councillor had a few words with this third man. Care to enlighten me?'

He was close enough for Rebus to feel his breath on his cheek. 'Case like this,' he speculated, 'you'll always get stories.'

McManus just smiled. 'I've never *had* a case like this, Rebus. Gareth Tench was loved and admired – plenty of friends of his out there, angry at their loss and wanting answers. Some of them packing all sorts of clout ... clout they've promised to share with me.'

'That's nice for you.'

'An offer I'd find it very hard to refuse,' McManus went on. 'Meaning this might be the only chance I'll be able to give.' He took a step back. 'So, DI Rebus, having apprised you of the situation ... is there anything at all you want to tell me?'

There was no way to land Cafferty in it without embroiling Siobhan. Before he could do anything, he had to be sure she'd be safe.

'Don't think so,' he said, folding his own arms. McManus nodded towards the gesture.

'Sure sign you've got something to hide.'

'Really?' Rebus slid his hands into his pockets. 'How about you then?' He turned and headed for the door, leaving McManus to wonder just when it was exactly that he'd decided to fold his own arms ...

Nice day for a drive, even if he spent half the journey behind a lorry. South to Dalkeith and from there to Coldstream. At Dun Law, he passed a wind farm, turbines either side of the road – it was as close as he'd ever come to them. Sheep and cattle grazing, and plenty of road-kill: pheasants and hares. Birds of prey hovering overhead, or peering intently from fence-posts. Fifty miles and he hit Coldstream, passed through the town and over a bridge, finding himself suddenly in England. A road sign told him he was only sixty miles north of Newcastle. He turned at a hotel car park and headed back across the border, parking kerbside. There was a police station, cleverly disguised as just another gabled house with a blue wooden door. The sign told him it was only open weekdays, nine till twelve. Coldstream's main drag was dominated by bars and small shops. Day-trippers took up most of the space on the narrow pavements. A single-decker bus from Lesmahagow was decanting its chatty cargo at the Ram's Head. Rebus beat them inside and demanded a half of best. Looking around, he saw that the tables had been block-booked for lunch. There were filled rolls behind the bar and he asked for cheese and pickle.

'We've soup too,' the barmaid informed him. 'Cock-a-leekie.'

'Tinned?'

She gave a tut. 'Would I poison you with that muck?'

'Go on then,' he said with a smile. She called his order out to the kitchen and he gave his spine a stretch, rolling his shoulders and neck.

'Where are you off to?' she asked on her return.

'I'm already there,' he replied, but before he could get a conversation going, the coach party started swarming in. She called out again to the kitchen and a waitress emerged, notepad in hand.

The chef himself, ruddy-faced and wide of girth, delivered Rebus's soup. He rolled his eyes as he calculated the average age of the new arrivals.

'Guess how many will want steak pie,' he said.

'All of them,' Rebus decided.

'And the goat cheese and filo starter?'

'Not a hope,' Rebus confirmed, unwrapping his spoon from its paper serviette.

There was golf on TV. Looked breezy up at Loch Lomond. Rebus searched in vain for salt and pepper, then found that the soup needed neither. A man in a short-sleeved white shirt came and stood next to him. He was mopping his face with a vast handkerchief. What hair he possessed was slicked back from his forehead.

'Warm one,' he announced.

'Are those your lot?' Rebus said, indicating the scrum at the tables.

'I'm theirs, more like,' the man stated. 'Never seen so many back-seat drivers ...' He shook his head and begged the barmaid for a pint of orange juice and lemonade with plenty of ice. She winked as she placed it in front of him – no payment necessary. Rebus knew the score: by bringing his coach parties here, the driver was on freebies for life. The man seemed to read his mind.

'Way the world turns,' he confessed.

Rebus just nodded. Who was to say the G8 didn't operate in much the same way? He asked the driver what Lesmahagow was like.

'Sort of place that makes a day out to Coldstream an attractive proposition.' He risked a glance towards his party. There was some sort of dispute over the seating plan. 'I swear to God, the UN would have trouble with this lot.' He gulped his drink. 'You weren't in Edinburgh last week, were you?'

'I work there.'

The driver feigned a wince. 'I had twenty-seven Chinese tourists. Arrived by train from London on the Saturday morning. Could I get anywhere near the station to pick them up? Could I buggery. And guess where they were staying? The Sheraton on Lothian Road. More security there than Barlinnie. On the Tuesday, we were halfway to Rosslyn Chapel when I realised we'd taken one of the Japanese delegates with us by mistake.' The driver started chuckling, and Rebus joined him. Christ, it felt good.

'So you're just down for the day?' the man asked. Rebus nodded. 'Some nice walks, if the fancy takes you ... but you don't seem the type.'

'You're a good judge of character.'

'Comes with the job.' He gave a slight jerk of his head. 'See that lot back there? I could tell you right now which ones will tip at day's end, and even how much they'll give.'

Rebus tried to look impressed. 'Buy you another?' The man's pint glass was empty.

'Better not. I'll just need a pitstop halfway through the afternoon, and that means most of them will follow suit. Might take half an hour to get them on board again.' The driver offered his hand for Rebus to shake. 'Nice talking to you, though.'

'You too,' Rebus said, returning the firm grip. He watched the driver head for the door. A couple of elderly women cooed and waved, but he pretended not to have noticed. Rebus decided another half of best was in order. The chance encounter had cheered him, because it was a taste of another life, a world running almost parallel to the one he inhabited.

The ordinary. The everyday. Conversation for its own sake. No search for motives or secrets.

Normality.

The barmaid was placing a fresh glass in front of him. 'You look a bit better,' she stated. 'When you came in, I wasn't sure what to make of you. Looked as likely to throw a punch as blow a kiss.'

'Therapy,' he explained, lifting the glass. The waitress had finally worked out what each customer wanted, and was fleeing to the kitchen before minds could be changed again.

'So what brings you to Coldstream?' the barmaid continued to probe.

'I'm CID, Lothian and Borders. Doing background on a

455

murder victim, name of Trevor Guest. He was a Geordie, but lived round here a few years back.'

'I can't say I know the name.'

'Might have been using another one.' Rebus held up a photo of Guest, taken around the time of his trial. She peered at it – needed spectacles but didn't like the thought of them. Then she shook her head.

'Sorry, dear,' she apologised.

'Anyone else I could show it to? Maybe the chef ...?'

She took the photograph from him and disappeared behind the partition, towards the clanking sound of pots and bowls being moved. She was back less than a minute later, handed the photo back to him.

'To be fair,' she said, 'Rab's only been in town since last autumn. You say this guy was a Geordie? Why would he come here?'

'Newcastle might've been getting too hot for him,' Rebus explained. 'He didn't always stay the right side of the law.' Seemed glaringly obvious to him now – much more likely that whatever had changed Guest, it had happened in Newcastle itself. If fleeing, you might want to dodge the A1 – too obvious. You could branch off at Morpeth on to a road which led you straight here. 'I suppose,' he said, 'it's too much to ask you to cast your mind back four or five years. No spate of housebreakings locally?'

She shook her head. Some of the bus party had made it as far as the bar. They carried with them a jotted order list.

'Three halves of lager, one lager and lime – Arthur, go check if that's a half or a whole – a ginger ale, advocaat and lemonade – ask if she wants ice in the advocaat, Arthur! No, hang on, it's two halves of lager and a lager shandy ...'

Rebus drained his drink and mouthed to the barmaid that he'd be back. He meant it, too – if not this trip, then some other time. Trevor Guest might have dragged him here, but it would be the Ram's Head that brought him back. It was only when he was outside that he remembered he'd not asked about Duncan Barclay. He walked past a couple of shops and stopped at the newsagent's, went inside and showed the photo of Trevor Guest. A shake of his head from the proprietor, who went on to say that he'd lived in the town all his life. Rebus then tried him with the name Duncan Barclay. This time he got a nod.

'Moved away a few years back, though. A lot of the young folk do.'

'Any idea where?'

Another shake of the head. Rebus thanked him and moved on. There was a grocer's, but he drew a blank there – the young female assistant only worked Saturdays, told him he might have more luck on Monday morning. Same story down the rest of that side of the street. Antique shop, hairdresser's, tea room, charity shop ... Only one other person knew of Duncan Barclay.

'Still see him around.'

'He's not moved far then?' Rebus asked.

'Kelso, I think ...'

Next town along. Rebus paused for a moment in the afternoon sunshine and wondered why his blood was coursing. Answer: he was working. Old-fashioned, dogged police work – almost as good as a holiday. But then he noticed that his final destination was another pub, and this one didn't look half as welcoming.

It was a far more basic affair than the Ram's Head. A floor of faded red linoleum, pocked with cigarette burns. A frayed dartboard frequented by two equally frayed-looking drinkers. Three flat-capped pensioners hammering out a game of dominoes at a corner table. All of it shrouded in a cigarette haze. The colour on the TV seemed to be bleeding, and even at this distance Rebus could tell that beyond the door to the toilets the urinal needed sluicing. He felt his spirits dip, but realised this was probably more Trevor Guest's sort of place. Problem was, that very fact meant his queries were less likely to yield a helpful smile. The barman had a nose like a chewed tomato – a real boozer's face, etched with scars and nicks, each one hinting at a story for late at night. Rebus knew his own face contained a few explicit chapters of its own. He hardened his whole demeanour as he approached the bar.

'Pint of heavy.' No way he could ask for a half in a place like this. He already had his cigarettes out. 'Ever see Duncan these days?' he asked the barman.

'Who?'

'Duncan Barclay.'

'Don't seem to know the name. In trouble, is he?'

'Not especially.' One question in and already he'd been rumbled. 'I'm a detective inspector,' he declared.

'You don't say?'

'Couple of questions I need to ask Duncan.'

'Doesn't live here.'

'Moved to Kelso, right?' The barman just shrugged. 'So which boozer does he now call home?' The barman had yet to make eye contact. 'Look at me,' Rebus persisted, 'and tell me I'm in the mood for this shit. Go on, do it!'

The sound of chairs scraping against floor as the old-timers got to their feet. Rebus half turned towards them.

'Still game, eh?' he said with a grin. 'But I'm looking into three murders.' The grin vanished as he held up three fingers. 'Any of you want to become part of that investigation, just keep standing ...' He paused long enough for them to lower themselves back into their seats. 'Clever boys,' he said. Then, to the barman: 'Whereabouts in Kelso will I find him?'

'You could ask Debbie,' the barman muttered. 'She aye had a wee crush on him.'

'And where would I find Debbie?'

'Saturdays, she works in the grocery.'

Rebus pretended this was fine. He took out the creased and print-smeared photograph of Trevor Guest.

'Years back,' the barman admitted. 'Buggered off back south, I heard.'

'You heard wrong – he headed for Edinburgh. Got a name for him?'

'Wanted to be called "Clever Trevor" – never quite saw why.'

Probably after the Ian Dury song, Rebus mused. 'He drank in here?'

'Not for long – barred him for taking a swing.'

'He lived in the town, though?'

The barman shook his head slowly. 'Kelso, I think,' he said. Then he started nodding. 'Definitely Kelso.'

Meaning Guest had lied to the cops in Newcastle. Rebus was starting to get a bad feeling. He left the pub without bothering to pay. Reckoned he'd played it just about right. Took him a few minutes outside to let the tension ebb. Tracked back to the grocer's, and the Saturday girl – Debbie. She could see straight away that he knew. Opened her mouth and began another version, but he waved a hand in front of her and she stuttered to a halt. Then he leaned across the counter, knuckles pressed down on it.

'So what can you tell me about Duncan Barclay?' he asked. 'We can either do it here, or in a cop-shop in Edinburgh – your decision.'

She had the good grace to start blushing. In fact, her colour became so heightened, he thought maybe she would burst like a balloon.

'He lives in a cottage down Carlingnose Lane.'

'In Kelso?'

She managed a slow nod. Put a hand to her forehead as though she felt dizzy. 'But as long as there's still light in the sky, he's usually out in the woods.'

'The woods?'

'Behind the cottage.'

Woods ... What had the psychologist said? Woods might be important.

459

'How long have you known him, Debbie?'

'Three ... maybe four years.'

'He's older than you?'

'Twenty-two,' she confirmed.

'And you're ... what? Sixteen, seventeen?'

'Nineteen next birthday.'

'The two of you are an item?'

Bad choice of question: her colour deepened further. Rebus had known paler blackcurrants. 'We're just friends ... I don't even see him that much these days.'

'What does he do?'

'Wood-carvings – fruit bowls and stuff. Sells them in the galleries in Edinburgh.'

'Artistic type, eh? Good with his hands?'

'He's brilliant.'

'Nice sharp tools?'

She started to answer, but then stopped. 'He hasn't done anything!' she cried.

'Have I said he has?' Rebus tried to sound peeved. 'What makes you think that?'

'He doesn't trust *you*!'

'Me?' Now Rebus sounded confused.

'All of you!'

'Been in trouble before, has he?'

She shook her head slowly. 'You don't understand,' she said quietly. Her eyes were growing moist. 'He *said* you wouldn't ...'

'Debbie?'

She burst out crying, and pulled open the hatch, emerging from behind the counter. She had her arms stretched out, and he did the same.

But she darted beneath them. And by the time he'd turned, she was at the door, hauling it open so its chimes rattled a complaint.

'Debbie!' he called. But when he got to the pavement, she was halfway down the street. He cursed under his breath, and realised that a woman toting an empty wicker basket was standing next to him. He reached back behind the door and turned the sign from OPEN to CLOSED. 'Half-day on Saturday,' he told her.

'Since when?' she spluttered in outraged tones.

'Okay,' he conceded, 'then let's say it's self-serve ... just leave your money on the counter.' He pushed past her and headed for his car.

Siobhan felt like the spectre at the feast: the crowd jostling her as it bounced on its toes. Off-key singalongs. Flags of all nations obscuring her view. Sweary, sweaty neds and nedettes dancing reels with college Henrys and Henriettas, cheap beer and cider spuming from shared cans. Pizza crusts slippery underfoot. And the bands performing on a stage quarter of a mile away. Constant queues for the toilets. She allowed herself a small smile as she remembered her backstage pass at the Final Push. She'd dutifully texted her two friends, but so far without reply. Everybody looked so happy and boisterous, and she could feel none of it. All she could think about were:

Cafferty.

Gareth Tench.

Keith Carberry.

Cyril Colliar.

Trevor Guest.

Edward Isley.

She'd been entrusted by her own Chief Constable with a major case. A result would have been a big step towards promotion. But she'd been side-swiped by the assault on her mother. Finding the attacker had become all-consuming, throwing her too close to Cafferty. She knew she had to focus, had to get involved again. Monday morning, the investigation proper would be up and running – probably under DCI Macrae and DI Derek Starr – a team organised, as much manpower as was necessary.

And she'd been suspended. Only thing she could do was track down Corbyn and apologise ... persuade him to let her back in. He would want her to swear she wouldn't let Rebus anywhere near, all ties severed. The thought gave her pause. Sixty–forty chance she'd agree if asked.

A new band had taken the main stage, and someone had turned the volume up. She checked her phone for texts.

One missed call.

She studied the caller's number: Eric Bain.

'Last bloody thing I need,' she told herself. He'd left a message, but she wasn't about to listen to it. Stuck the phone back in her pocket and pulled a fresh bottle of water from her bag. Sweet smell of dope wafting over her, but no sign of the dealer from Camp Horizon. The young men on the stage were working hard, but there was too much treble to their sound. Siobhan moved further away. Couples were lying on the ground, snogging, or staring up at the sky with dreamy smiles on their faces. She realised she was still walking – lacked the will to stop herself – heading for the field where she'd parked her car. New Order were hours away, and she knew she wouldn't be coming back for them. What was waiting for her in Edinburgh? Maybe she would phone Rebus and tell him she was starting to forgive. Maybe she'd just find herself a wine bar and a chilled bottle of Chardonnay, sit there with notebook and pen, rehearsing the speech she'd give the Chief Constable on Monday morning.

If I let you back on the team, there's no room for your partner in crime ... understood, DS Clarke?

Understood, sir. And I really do appreciate this.

And you agree to my terms? Well, DS Clarke? A simple yes will suffice.

Except that there was nothing simple about it.

Back on to the M90, heading south this time. Twenty

minutes and she was at the Forth Road Bridge. No more vehicle searches; everything the way it had been before the G8. On the outskirts of Edinburgh, Siobhan realised she was near Cramond. She decided she would drop in on Ellen Wylie, thank her in person for listening to the previous night's rant. She turned left down Whitehouse Road, parked outside the house. There was no answer. Called Ellen's mobile.

'It's Shiv,' she said when Ellen answered. 'I was going to bum a coffee off you.'

'We're out walking.'

'I can hear the weir ... are you just behind the house?'

There was silence on the line. Then: 'Later would be better.'

'Well, I'm right here.'

'I thought maybe a drink in town ... just you and me.'

'Sounds good.' But a frown had crept across Siobhan's face. Wylie seemed almost to sense this.

'Look,' she said, 'maybe a quick cup of coffee then. See you in five ...'

Rather than wait, Siobhan walked to the end of the terrace and down a short path to the River Almond. Ellen and Denise had been as far as the ruined mill, but were heading back. Ellen waved, but Denise didn't seem so keen. She was gripping her sister's arm. *Just you and me ...*

Denise Wylie was shorter and thinner than her sister. Teenage fears about her weight had left her with a starved look. Her skin was grey, the hair mousy-brown and lifeless. She refused to meet Siobhan's eyes.

'Hiya, Denise,' Siobhan said anyway, receiving a grunt in reply. Ellen, on the other hand, seemed almost unnaturally buoyed, talking twenty to the dozen as they made their way back to the house.

'Go through to the garden,' she insisted, 'and I'll stick the kettle on – or a glass of grog if you'd prefer, but you're driving, aren't you? Show wasn't up to much then? Or did you not go in the end? I'm way past the age of going to watch pop groups, though I'd change my mind for Coldplay – even then I'd want to be sitting. Standing all day in a field? Isn't that what scarecrows and tattie-pickers do? Are you away upstairs, Denise? Will I bring you a cup up?' She emerged from the kitchen to place a plate of shortbread on the table. 'You all right there, Shiv? Water's boiling, can't remember what you take in it ...'

'Just milk.' Siobhan peered up at the bedroom window. 'Is Denise all right?'

At that moment, Wylie's sister appeared behind the glass, eyes widening as she caught Siobhan staring at her. She yanked the curtains shut. Despite the clammy day, the window itself was closed too.

'She'll be fine,' Wylie said, dismissing the question with a flick of her hand.

'And what about you?'

Wylie gave a fluttering laugh. 'What about me?'

'Pair of you look like you've raided the medicine cabinet but found different bottles.'

Another short, sharp laugh and Wylie retreated to the kitchen. Siobhan rose slowly from the hardwood chair and followed her, pausing at the threshold.

'Have you told her?' she asked quietly.

'About what?' Wylie opened the fridge and found the milk, but then started searching for a jug.

'Gareth Tench – does she know he's dead?' The words almost caught in Siobhan's throat.

Tench plays away from home ...

There's a colleague of mine, Ellen Wylie ... her sister's ...

Skin's more fragile than most ...

'Oh, Christ, Ellen,' she said now, reaching out a hand to grip the door-jamb.

'What's the matter?'

'You know, don't you?' Siobhan's voice was hardly above a whisper.

'You're not making sense,' Wylie stated, fretting now with the tray, lifting saucers on and then off again.

'Look me in the eye and tell me you don't know what I'm talking about.'

'I've absolutely no idea what you're—'

'I asked you to look me in the eye.'

Ellen Wylie made the effort, her mouth a thin, determined line.

'You sounded so weird on the phone,' Siobhan told her. 'And now all this jabbering while Denise shoots upstairs.'

'I think you should go.'

'You might want to reconsider, Ellen. But before you do, I want to apologise.'

'Apologise?'

Siobhan nodded, keeping her eyes on Wylie. 'It was me who told Cafferty. Wouldn't have been hard for him to get an address. Were you here?' She watched Wylie bow her head. 'He came here, didn't he?' she persisted. 'Came here and told Denise about Tench still being married. She was still seeing him?'

Wylie was shaking her head slowly. Tears splashed from her cheeks on to the tiled floor.

'Ellen ... I'm so sorry.' There it was on the work surface near the sink – a wooden rack of knives, one slit empty. Kitchen spotless, no sign of washing-up anywhere.

'You can't have her,' Ellen Wylie sobbed, still shaking her head.

'Did you find out this morning? After she got up? It's bound to come out, Ellen,' Siobhan argued. 'Keep denying it, it'll destroy both of you.' Siobhan remembered Tench's own words: *passion's a snarling beast in some men.* Yes, and in some women, too ...

'You can't have her,' Ellen Wylie repeated. But the words had taken on a resigned, lifeless sound.

465

'She'll get help.' Siobhan had taken a couple of steps into the small boxy room. She pressed her hand to Ellen Wylie's arm. 'Talk to her, tell her it'll be all right. You'll be there for her.'

Wylie rubbed the back of her forearm across her face, smearing the tears. 'You've no evidence,' she mumbled: lines she'd walked herself through. A scripted denial, prepared for the eventuality.

'Do we need any?' Siobhan asked. 'Maybe I should ask Denise ...'

'No, please.' Another shake of the head, and eyes which burned into Siobhan's.

'What are the chances no one saw her, Ellen? Think she won't pop up somewhere on CCTV? Think the clothes she wore won't turn up? The knife she ditched? If it were my case, I'd send a couple of frogmen to the riverbank. Maybe that's why you went there – looking to retrieve it and make a better job of disposal ...'

'Oh God,' Wylie said, voice cracking. Siobhan gave her a hug, feeling the body beginning to tremble – delayed shock.

'You need to be strong for her, Ellen. Just for a little while longer, you need to hang on ...' Siobhan's thoughts churned as she rubbed a hand across Wylie's back. If Denise was capable of killing Gareth Tench, what else might she have done? She felt Ellen Wylie tense and pull away from her. The two women's eyes met.

'I know what you're thinking,' Wylie said quietly.

'Do you?'

'But Denise never so much as looked at BeastWatch. *I* was the one who was interested, not her.'

'You're also the one trying to hide Gareth Tench's killer, Ellen. Maybe it's *you* we should be looking at, eh?' Siobhan's voice had hardened; so too had Wylie's face, but after a moment it cracked into a sour smile.

'Is that the best you can do, Siobhan? Maybe you're

466

not as hot as people seem to think. Chief Constable might have put you in charge, but we both know it's John Rebus's show ... though I don't suppose that'll stop you taking the credit – always supposing you get a result. So go ahead and charge me if you want.' She held out her wrists as if awaiting handcuffs, then, when Siobhan did nothing, began a slow, humourless laugh. 'Not as hot as people think,' she echoed.

Not as hot as people think ...

26

Rebus lost no time on the road to Kelso. It was only eight miles away. No sign of Debbie in any of the cars he saw. Didn't mean she hadn't contacted Barclay already by phone. The countryside would have been impressive if he'd given it any heed. He sped past the sign welcoming safe drivers to the town, and braked hard when he spotted his first pedestrian. She was dressed head to foot in tweed and walking a small, bug-eyed dog. Looked like she was on her way into the Lidl supermarket.

'Carlingnose Lane,' Rebus told her. 'Know where it is?'

'I'm afraid I don't.' She was still apologising as Rebus drove off. He tried again in the town centre. Received half a dozen different possibilities from the first three locals he asked. Near Floors Castle ... up by the rugby ground ... the golf course ... the Edinburgh road.

Eventually, he found that Floors Castle was on the road marked Edinburgh. Its high perimeter wall seemed to stretch for hundreds of yards. Rebus saw signs to the golf course, then spotted a park with sets of rugby posts. But the housing all around him looked too new, until a couple of schoolgirls walking a dog put him right.

Behind the new houses.

The Saab complained as he slammed it back into first. Engine was making a funny sound; he'd only just noticed it. Carlingnose Lane comprised a single row of tumble-down cottages. The first couple had been modernised and given a lick of paint. The track ended at the final cottage, its whitewashed walls turning yellow. A homemade sign proclaimed LOCAL CRAFTS FOR SALE. Bits of discarded tree lay strewn across the small front garden. Rebus stopped the car at a five-bar gate, beyond which a trail led across a meadow and into some woods. He tried Barclay's door and peered in through the small window. Living room with kitchenette off, and untidy with it. Part of the back wall had been removed and French doors fitted, meaning Rebus could see that the back garden was every bit as deserted and unkempt as the front. He looked up and saw that a pylon fed an electricity cable to the house. No aerial, though, and no sign of a TV inside.

And no phone line. Next door had one – arcing towards it from a wooden telegraph pole in the meadow.

'Doesn't mean he's not got a mobile,' Rebus muttered to himself – in fact, probably made it more likely. Barclay had to keep in touch with those Edinburgh galleries somehow. To the side of the cottage sat a venerable Land Rover. Didn't look like it was used much, bonnet cool to the touch. But the key dangled from the ignition, meaning one of two things – no fear of car thieves, or ready for a quick getaway. Rebus opened the driver's-side door and removed the key, tucking it into his top pocket. He stood by the meadow and lit a cigarette. If Debbie had managed to warn Barclay, he'd either hoofed it on foot, or had access to another vehicle … or he was on his way back.

He took out his own phone. Signal strength of a single bar. Angling the phone, the words NO SIGNAL came up. He climbed the gate and tried again.

NO SIGNAL.

Decided that what was left of the afternoon merited a walk into the woods. The air was warm; birdsong and distant traffic. A plane high overhead, its undercarriage glinting. I'm on my way, Rebus thought, to meet a man, in the middle of nowhere, with no phone worth the name. A man who once got into a fight. A man who knows the police are coming and doesn't like them …

'Just great, John,' he said out loud, his breathing a little ragged as he climbed towards the treeline. Couldn't even say what kinds of trees they were. Brown ones with leaves – which ruled out conifers but not much else. He hoped to hear sounds of an axe or maybe a chainsaw. No ... scrub that – didn't want Barclay holding any form of sharpened tool. Wondered if maybe he should call out. Cleared his throat but didn't get any further. Now he was higher up, maybe his phone would ...

NO SIGNAL.

Lovely views, though. Pausing to catch his breath, he just hoped he would live to remember them. Why was Duncan Barclay nervous of seeing the police? Rebus would be sure to ask, if he ever found him. He'd entered the forest now, the ground yielding underfoot, a thick mulchy carpet. He had the feeling he was on a path of some kind, invisible to the untutored eye but there all the same – a route between saplings and shorn trunks, avoiding the low scrub. The place reminded him a lot of the Clootie Well. He kept glancing to left and right, stopping every few steps for another listen.

All alone.

And then another track appeared – this one wide enough for a vehicle. Rebus crouched down. The pattern of tyres looked crusted – a few days old at the very least. He gave a little snort.

'Not exactly Tonto,' he muttered, straightening up and brushing dried mud from his fingers.

'Not exactly,' a man's voice echoed. Rebus looked around and spotted its owner eventually. He was seated on a fallen tree, one leg crossed over the other. A few yards off the track, and dressed in olive-green outer-wear.

'Good camouflage,' Rebus said. 'Are you Duncan?'

Duncan Barclay gave a little bow of his head. Rebus got closer and noted the sandy hair and freckled face. Maybe six feet tall, but wiry. The eyes were the same pale colour as their owner's jacket.

'You're a policeman,' Barclay stated. Rebus wasn't about to deny it.

'Did Debbie warn you?'

Barclay stretched out his arms. 'No means ... I'm a Luddite in that regard as several others.'

Rebus nodded. 'I noticed at the cottage – no TV or phone line.'

'And no cottages either, soon enough – developer's got his eye on them. Then it'll be the field, and after that the woods ... I thought you'd be coming.' He paused at Rebus's look. 'Not you personally ... But someone like you.'

'Because ...?'

'Trevor Guest,' the young man stated. 'I didn't know he was dead till I read it in the paper. But when they said the case was being handled in Edinburgh ... well, I thought there might still be something about me in the files.'

Rebus nodded and lifted out his cigarettes. 'Mind if I ...?'

'I'd rather you didn't – and so would the trees.'

'They're your friends?' Rebus asked, putting the packet away again. Then: 'So you only found out about Trevor Guest ...?'

'When it was in the papers.' Barclay paused to consider. 'Was it Wednesday? I didn't actually buy a paper, you understand – I've no time for them. But I saw the headline on the front of the *Scotsman*. Went and got himself done in by some sort of serial killer.'

'Some sort of killer, yes.' Rebus took a step back as Barclay suddenly bounded to his feet, but all the young man did was gesture with a crooked finger and then start walking.

'Follow me and I'll show you,' he said.

'Show me what?'

'The whole reason you're here.'

Rebus held back, but eventually relented, catching up with Barclay. 'Is it far, Duncan?' he asked.

Barclay shook his head. He walked with long, purposeful strides.

'You spend a lot of time in the woods?'

'As much as I can.'

'Other woods too? Not just these ones, I mean.'

'I find bits and pieces all over.'

'Bits and ...?'

'Branches, uprooted trunks ...'

'And the Clootie Well?'

Barclay turned his head towards Rebus. 'What about it?'

'Ever been there?'

'Don't think so.' Barclay stopped so suddenly, Rebus almost went past him. The young man's eyes had widened. He slapped a hand to his forehead. Rebus could see the bruised fingernails and traces of scar tissue – evidence of an artisan's life.

'Holy Christ!' Barclay gasped. 'I can *see* what you're thinking!'

'And what's that, Duncan?'

'You think maybe I did it! *Me!*'

'Really?'

'Holy Mother of Christ ...' Barclay gave a shake of the head and started walking again, almost faster than before so that Rebus struggled to keep up.

'Just wondering why you and Trevor Guest had that fight,' he asked between lungfuls of oxygen. 'Background info, that's all I'm here for.'

'But you *do* think I did it!'

'Well, did you?'

'No.'

'Nothing to worry about then.' Rebus looked around, not really sure of his bearings. He could retrace the vehicle track, but would he know where to branch off to reach the meadow and civilisation?

'I can't believe you think that.' Barclay gave another shake of his head. 'I conjure new life from dead wood. The living world means *everything* to me.'

'Trevor Guest isn't coming back as a fruit bowl any time soon.'

'Trevor Guest was an animal.' As abruptly as before, Barclay stopped again.

'Aren't animals part of the living world?' Rebus asked breathlessly.

'You *know* I don't mean it like that.' He was sweeping the area with his eyes. 'They said as much in the *Scotsman* ... he was locked up for burglary, rape ...'

'Sexual assault, actually.'

Barclay continued regardless. 'He was locked away because they'd finally caught up with him – the truth had come out. But he'd been an animal long before that.' He was heading into the woods again, Rebus trailing after him, trying to get images of *Blair Witch* out of his head. The landscape was sloping down a gradient, growing steeper. Rebus realised they were now the *other* side of the track from civilisation. He started looking around for a weapon of some kind; bent down and picked up a tree-branch, gave it a shake and it crumbled in his hand, its innards rotted away.

'What is it you're going to show me?' he asked.

'One more minute.' Barclay held up a single digit for effect. 'Hey, I don't even know who you are.'

'Name's Rebus. I'm a detective inspector.'

'I talked to you guys, you know ... back when it happened. Tried to get you to look at Trevor Guest, but I don't think you did. I was in my teens – already marked out as "the weird kid". Coldstream's like one big tribe, Inspector. When you don't fit in, it's not easy to pretend you do.'

'I'm sure that's true.' A comment rather than the question Rebus really wanted to ask – *What the hell are you talking about?*

'It's better now. People see the things I make, they can appreciate that there's a glimmer of talent there.'

'When did you move to Kelso?'

'This is my third year.'

'Must like it, then.'

Barclay looked at Rebus, then gave a quick smile. 'Making conversation, eh? Because you're nervous?'

'I don't like games,' Rebus stated.

'I'll tell you who does, though – whoever left those trophies at the Clootie Well.'

'That's something we agree on.' Rebus almost lost his footing, felt something tear in his ankle as he went over on it.

'Careful,' Barclay said, without stopping.

'Thanks,' Rebus replied, hobbling after him. But the young man stopped again almost immediately. There was a chain-link fence in front of them, and further down the hill a modern bungalow.

'Great views,' Barclay offered. 'Nice and quiet. You have to drive all the way down there ...' he traced the route with a finger, 'to reach the main road.' He turned his whole body towards Rebus. 'This is where she died. I'd seen her in town, chatted to her. We were all in shock when it happened.' His look intensified as he saw Rebus was still in the dark. *Mr and Mrs Webster*,' he hissed. 'I mean, *he* died later, but that's where his wife was murdered.' He stabbed a finger at the bungalow. 'In *there*.'

Rebus's mouth felt dry. 'Ben Webster's mother?' Yes, of course – holiday home in the Borders. He remembered the photos from the file Mairie had compiled. 'You're saying Trevor Guest killed her?'

'He'd moved here only a few months before; moved out again sharpish afterwards. A few of his drinking pals said it was because he already had a history with the police in Newcastle. He used to hassle me in the street, tell me I was a teenager with long hair so I had to know where he could get drugs.' He paused for a moment. 'Then I was up in Edinburgh that night, drinking with a mate, and I saw him. I'd already told the cops I thought he did it ... Seemed to me the whole case was shoddy.' He stared hard at Rebus. 'You never followed it up!'

'You saw him in the pub ...?' Rebus's head was reeling, the blood pounding in his ears.

'I lashed out, I admit it. Felt bloody wonderful. And then when I saw that he'd been killed ... well, I felt better still – and vindicated, too. Said as much in the paper – he'd been in jail for burglary and rape.'

'Sexual assault,' Rebus said weakly. The anomaly ... one of several.

'And that's what he'd done here – broken in, killed Mrs Webster, and ransacked the place.'

Then fled to Edinburgh, suddenly penitent and of a mind to help those older and weaker than himself. Gareth Tench had been right – something *had* happened to Trevor Guest. Something life-changing ...

If Rebus were to believe Duncan Barclay's story.

'He didn't assault her,' Rebus argued.

'Say again?'

Rebus cleared his throat, spat out some gluey saliva. 'Mrs Webster wasn't raped or assaulted.'

'No, because she was too old – the kid he did in Newcastle was in her teens.' Yes, and hadn't Hackman confirmed it – *liked them a bit on the young side.*

'You've given it a lot of thought,' Rebus seemed to concede.

'But you wouldn't *believe* me!'

'Well, I'm sorry about that.' Rebus leaned against a tree and ran a hand through his hair. His fingers came away coated in sweat.

'And I can't be a suspect,' Barclay went on, 'because I didn't know the other two men. *Three* killings,' he stressed, 'not just one.'

'That's right ... not just one.' A killer who likes games. Rebus thought back to Dr Gilreagh – *rurality and anomalies*.

'I could tell he was trouble,' Barclay was saying, 'from the first time I clapped eyes on him in Coldstream.'

'I could use one of those right now,' Rebus interrupted. A nice cool current of water to duck his head under.

Trevor Guest as the killer of Ben Webster's mother.

The father dies of a broken heart ... meaning Guest has destroyed the whole family.

Goes to jail for another offence, but when he gets out ...

And soon after, Ben Webster MP takes a nose-dive over the parapets of Edinburgh Castle.

Ben Webster?

'Duncan!' A yell in the distance, somewhere uphill.

'Debbie?' Barclay called back. 'Down here!' He started clambering up the slope, Rebus toiling in his wake. By the time he reached the vehicle track, Barclay was enveloping Debbie in a hug.

'I wanted to tell you,' she was explaining, her words muffled by his jacket, 'and I couldn't get a lift, and I knew he'd be looking for me, and I got here as soon as—' She broke off as she caught sight of Rebus. Gave a little squeal and pulled back from Barclay.

'It's all right,' he told her. 'Me and the Inspector have just been talking, that's all.' He looked over his shoulder at Rebus. 'And what's more, I actually think he's been listening.'

Rebus nodded his agreement with this, and slid his hands into his pockets. 'But I'll need you in Edinburgh all the same,' he announced. 'Everything you've just said could do with being a matter of record, don't you think?'

Barclay smiled a tired smile. 'After all this time, it'll be my pleasure.'

Debbie bounced on her toes, one arm sliding around

Duncan Barclay's waist. 'I want to come too. Don't leave me here.'

'Thing is,' Barclay said with a sly glance at Rebus, 'the Inspector here has me down as a suspect ... which would make you my accomplice.'

She looked shocked. 'Duncan wouldn't hurt a soul!' she squealed, gripping him more tightly than ever.

'Or a woodlouse, I dare say,' Rebus added.

'These woods have looked after me,' Barclay said quietly, eyes fixed on Rebus. 'That's why the stick you picked up fell apart in your hand.' He gave a huge wink. Then, to Debbie: 'You sure about this? Our first date, a police station in Edinburgh?' She replied by going up on to her tiptoes again and planting a kiss on his lips. The trees started rustling in a sudden gentle breeze.

'Back to the car, children,' Rebus commanded. He'd taken half a dozen tentative steps along the track when Barclay indicated that he was headed in completely the wrong direction.

Siobhan realised she was headed the wrong way.

Well, not the wrong way exactly – depended which destination she had in mind, and that was the problem: she couldn't think of one. Home, probably, but what would she do there? As she was already on Silverknowes Road, she pushed on until Marine Drive, then pulled over at the side of the road. Other cars were already parked there. It was a popular spot at weekends, with views across the Firth of Forth. Dogs were being exercised, sandwiches eaten. A helicopter rose loudly into the air, taking its passengers on one of the regular sightseeing tours, reminding her of the chopper at Gleneagles. One year, Siobhan had bought Rebus a voucher for the tour as a birthday present. As far as she knew, he'd never used it.

She knew he'd want to hear about Denise and Gareth Tench. Ellen Wylie had promised to call Craigmillar and get them to come and take a statement, which hadn't stopped Siobhan requesting the self-same thing as soon as she'd left the house. She'd had half a mind to get them to pull both women in, kept hearing Wylie's laughter ... more than a touch of hysteria to it. Maybe natural under the circumstances, but all the same ... She lifted her phone now, took a deep breath and punched in Rebus's number. The woman who answered was just a recording: *Your call cannot be taken ... please try again later*.

She stared at the liquid crystal display and remembered that Eric Bain had left a message.

'In for a penny,' she muttered to herself, pushing more buttons.

'Siobhan, it's Eric.' The recorded voice sounded slurred. 'Molly's walked out and ... Christ, I don't know why I'm ...' The sound of coughing. 'Juss wann you to ... matryin to say?' Another dry cough, as though he was on the verge of being sick. Siobhan stared out at the scenery, not really seeing it. 'Oh, hell and ... taken ... taken too many ...'

She cursed under her breath and turned the ignition, slammed the car into gear. Headlights switched to full beam and her hand pressed to the horn at every red light. Managed to steer and call for an ambulance at the same time. Reckoned she'd still have the beating of it. Twelve minutes and she was pulling to a stop outside his block – no damage other than a scrape to her bodywork and a dinged wing-mirror. Meaning another trip to Rebus's friendly repair shop.

Outside Bain's flat, she didn't even have to knock – the door had been left ajar. She ran in, found him slumped on the floor in the living room, head resting against a chair. Empty Smirnoff bottle, empty paracetamol bottle. She snatched his wrist – it was warm, his breathing shallow but steady. A sheen of sweat on his face, and a stain at the crotch where he'd wet himself. She shouted his name a few times, slapping his cheeks, prising open his eyes.

'Come on, Eric, wakey-wakey!' Shaking his body. 'Time to get up, Eric! Come on, you lazy sod!' He was too heavy for her; no way she could haul him to his feet unaided. She checked that his mouth was clear – nothing impeding the airways. Shook him again. 'How many did you take, Eric? How many tablets?'

The door left ajar was a good sign – meant he wanted to be found. And he'd called her too ... called *her*.

'You always were a drama queen, Eric,' she told him, pushing the slick hair back from his forehead. The room was messy. 'What if Molly comes back and sees how untidy you've made everything? Better get up right now.' His eyes were fluttering, a groan coming from deep within him. Noises at the door: paramedics in their green uniforms, one of them toting a carry-box.

'What's he taken?'

'Paracetamol.'

'How long ago?'

'Couple of hours.'

'What's his name?'

'Eric.'

She got up and moved back a little, giving them room. They were checking his pupils, taking out the instruments they'd need.

'Can you hear me, Eric?' one of them asked. 'Any chance you can give me a nod? Maybe just move your fingers for me? Eric? My name's Colin and I'm going to be looking after you. Eric? Just nod your head if you're hearing me. Eric ...?'

Siobhan stood there with arms folded. When Eric spasmed and then started to puke, one of the paramedics asked her to look around the rest of the flat: 'See what else he might have ingested.'

As she left the room, she wondered if maybe he was just trying to spare her the sight. Nothing in the kitchen – it was spotless, apart from a litre of milk which needed putting in the fridge ... and next to it the screw-cap from the Smirnoff. She crossed to the bathroom. The door of the medicine cabinet stood open. Some unopened sachets of flu remedy had ended up in the sink. She put them back. There was a fresh bottle of aspirin, its seal intact. So maybe the paracetamol bottle had been opened previously, meaning he might not have taken as many as she'd thought.

Bedroom: Molly's things were still there, but strewn across the floor, as though Eric had planned some act of retribution upon them. A snapshot of the pair of them had been removed from its frame, but was otherwise undamaged, as though he'd been unable to go through with it.

She reported back to the paramedics. Eric had stopped vomiting, but the room reeked of the stuff.

'So that's seventy centilitres of neat vodka,' the one called Colin said, 'and maybe thirty tabs as a chaser.'

'Most of which has just come back to say hello,' his colleague added.

'So he'll be all right?' she asked.

'Depends on the internal damage. You said two hours?'

'He called me two ... nearly three hours ago.' They looked at her. 'I didn't get the message until ... well, seconds before I called it in.'

'How pissed was he when he called?'

'His speech was slurred.'

'No kidding.' Colin locked eyes with his partner. 'How do we get him downstairs?'

'Strapped to a stretcher.'

'Stairwell has a few tight corners.'

'So give me an alternative.'

'I'll call for back-up.' Colin rose to his feet.

'I could take his legs,' Siobhan offered. 'Those corners won't seem nearly so tight if there's no stretcher to manoeuvre.'

'Fair point.' The paramedics shared another look.

Siobhan's phone started ringing. She went to turn it off, but caller ID had flashed up the letters JR. She stepped out into the hall and answered the call.

'You're not going to believe it,' she blurted out, realising as she did so that Rebus was telling her the exact same thing.

27

He had decided on St Leonard's – reckoned there was less chance of being spotted there. No one on the front desk had seemed to know he was under suspension; they hadn't even asked why he wanted the use of an interview room, and had let him borrow a constable to act as witness to the recording he was about to make.

Duncan Barclay and Debbie Glenister sat next to one another throughout, nursing cans of cola and feasting on chocolate from the vending-machine. Rebus had broken open a fresh pack of cassette tapes, slotting two into the machine. Barclay had asked why two.

'One for you and one for us,' Rebus had answered.

The questioning had been straightforward, the constable sitting bemused throughout, Rebus having failed to explain any of the background to him. Afterwards, Rebus had asked the officer if he could arrange transport for the visitors.

'Back to Kelso?' he'd guessed, sounding daunted. But Debbie had squeezed Barclay's arm and said maybe they could be dropped somewhere along Princes Street instead. Barclay had hesitated, but finally agreed. As they were preparing to leave, Rebus had slipped him forty pounds. 'Drinks here can be that bit more expensive,' he'd explained. 'And it's a loan rather than a handout. I want one of your best fruit bowls next time you're in town.'

So Barclay had nodded and accepted the notes.

'All these questions, Inspector,' he'd said. 'Have they helped you at all?'

'More than you might think, Mr Barclay,' Rebus had said, shaking the young man's hand before retreating to one of the empty upstairs offices. This was where he'd been based before the flit to Gayfield Square. Eight years of crimes solved and shelved ... It surprised him that no mark had been left. There was no visible trace of him here, or of all those convoluted cases – the ones he remembered best. The walls were bare, most of the desks unused and lacking even chairs to sit on. Before St Leonard's, he'd worked at the station on Great London Road ... and the High Street before that. Thirty years he'd been a cop, and thought he'd seen just about everything.

Until this.

There was a large white marker-board on one wall. He wiped it clean with some paper towels from the gents'. The ink was hard to shift, meaning it had been there for weeks – background to Operation Sorbus. Officers would have heaved their backsides on to the desks and sat there swigging coffee while their boss filled them in on what was to come.

Now safely erased.

Rebus searched in the drawers of the nearest desks until he found a marker. He began to write on the board, starting at the top and working down, with lines branching off to the sides. Some words he double-underlined; others he encircled; a few he stuck question marks after. When he was finished, he stood back and surveyed his mind-map of the Clootie Well killings. It was Siobhan who'd taught him about such maps. She seldom worked a case without them, though usually they stayed in her drawer or briefcase. She would bring them out to remind herself of something – some avenue not yet explored or connection meriting further inspection. It took a while for her to own up to their existence. Why? Because she'd thought he would laugh at her. But in a case as apparently complex as this, a mind-map was the perfect tool, because when you started to look at it, the complexity vanished, leaving just a central core.

Trevor Guest.

The anomaly, his body attacked with unusual viciousness. Dr Gilreagh had warned them to look out for feints, and she'd been right. The whole case had been almost nothing *but* a magician's misdirection. Rebus slid his backside on to one of the desks. It gave only the mildest creak of complaint. His legs made little paddling motions as they hung above the floor. His palms were pressed against the surface of the desk either side of him. He leaned forward slightly, gazing at the writing on the wall ... the arrows and underlinings and question marks. He started to see ways to resolve those few questions. He started to see the whole picture, the one the killer had been trying to disguise.

And then he walked out of the office and the station, into the fresh air and across the road. Headed to the nearest shop and realised he didn't really want anything. Bought cigarettes and a lighter and some chewing-gum. Added the afternoon edition of the *Evening News*. Decided to call Siobhan at the hospital to ask how much longer she would be.

'I'm *here*,' she told him. Meaning St Leonard's. 'Where the hell are you?'

'I must just have missed you.' The shopkeeper called out as he pulled open the door to leave. Rebus twitched his mouth in apology and reached into his pocket to pay the man. Where the hell was his ...? Must've given Barclay his last two twenties. He pulled out some loose change instead, poured it on to the counter.

'Not enough for cigarettes,' the elderly Asian complained. Rebus shrugged and handed them back.

'Where are you?' Siobhan was asking into his ear.

'Buying chewing-gum.'

And a lighter, he could have added.

But no cigarettes.

They sat down with mugs of instant coffee, silent for the first minute or so. Then Rebus thought to ask about Bain.

'Ironically,' she said, 'given the amount of painkillers he'd scarfed, the first thing he complained of was a thumping headache.'

'My fault in a way,' Rebus told her, explaining first of all about his morning conversation with Bain, and then about his chat the night before with Molly.

'So we have a falling-out over Tench's corpse,' Siobhan said, 'and you head straight to a lap-dancing club?'

Rebus shrugged, deciding he had been right to leave out the visit to Cafferty's home.

'Well,' Siobhan went on with a sigh, 'while we're playing the self-blame game ...' And she filled him in on Bain and T in the Park and Denise Wylie, at the end of which there was another lengthy silence. Rebus was on his fifth piece of chewing-gum – didn't really go with coffee, but he needed some outlet for the current that was pounding through him.

'You really think Ellen's turned her sister in?' he asked eventually.

'What else could she do?'

He gave a shrug, then watched as Siobhan picked up a handset and made a call to Craigmillar.

'Guy you want is DS McManus,' he informed her. She looked at him as if to say: how the hell do you know that? He decided it was time to get up and find a bin in which to deposit the wad of flavourless gum. When she finished the call, Siobhan joined him in front of the marker-board.

'Pair of them are there right now. McManus is going easy on Denise. Reckons she could play the mental cruelty card.' She paused. 'When was it exactly that you spoke to him?'

Rebus deflected the question by pointing to the board.

'See what I've done here, Shiv? Taken a leaf out of your book, so to speak.' He tapped the middle of the board with his knuckles. 'And it all boils down to Trevor Guest.'

'Theoretically?' she added.

'Evidence comes later.' He started to trace the time-line of the killings with a finger. 'Say Trevor Guest *did* kill Ben Webster's mother. In fact, we don't *need* to say that at all. It's enough that Guest's killer *believed* he did. The killer sticks Guest's name into a search engine and comes up with BeastWatch. That's what gives the killer the idea. Make it *look* like there's a serial killer at large. The police are banjaxed as a result, looking in all the wrong places for the motive. Killer knows about the G8, so decides to leave a few clues right there under our noses, knowing they'll be found. Killer was never a BeastWatch subscriber, so knows they've got nothing to fear. We'll be run ragged tracking down all the people who were, and warning all the other sex attackers ... and with the G8 and everything, chances are the investigation will end up tying itself in knots too tight ever to be unravelled. Remember what Gilreagh said – the "display" was slightly wrong. She was right, because it was only ever Guest the killer wanted ... only ever Guest.' He prodded the name again. 'The man who'd torn the Webster family apart. Rurality and anomalies, Siobhan ... and being led up the garden path.'

'But how could the killer have known that?' Siobhan felt obliged to ask.

'By having access to the original inquiry, maybe going through it all with a fine-tooth comb. Going to the Borders and asking around, listening in on the local gossip.'

She was standing next to him, staring at the board. 'You're saying Cyril Collar and Eddie Isley died as a diversion?'

'Worked, too. If we'd been running a full-scale inquiry, we might have missed the Kelso connection.' Rebus gave a short, harsh laugh. 'I seem to remember I gave a snort when Gilreagh started talking about the countryside and deep woods near human dwellings.' *Is this the sort of terrain the victims inhabited?* 'Spot on, Doc,' he said in an undertone.

Siobhan ran her finger along Ben Webster's name. 'So why did he kill himself?'

'How do you mean?'

'Well, do you think it was the guilt finally catching up with him? He's killed three men when only one was necessary. He's under a lot of pressure because of the G8. We've just identified the patch from Cyril Colliar's jacket ... He starts to panic that we *will* catch him – is that how you see it?'

'I'm not even sure he knew about the patch,' Rebus said quietly. 'And how would he have gone about procuring heroin for those lethal injections?'

'Why are you asking me?' Siobhan gave a short laugh.

'Because you're the one who's accusing an innocent man. No access to hard drugs ... no easy access to police files.' Rebus traced the line from Ben Webster to his sister. 'Stacey, on the other hand ...'

'*Stacey?*'

'Is an undercover cop. Probably means she knows a few dealers. She's spent the past few months infiltrating anarchist groups; told me herself they tend to base themselves outside London these days – Leeds and Manchester and Bradford. Guest died in Newcastle, Isley in Carlisle – both a manageable drive from the Midlands. As a cop, she'd be able to access any information she liked.'

'Stacey's the killer?'

'Using your wonderful system ...' Rebus slapped his hand against the board again, 'it's the obvious conclusion.'

Siobhan was shaking her head slowly. 'But she was ... I mean, we *talked* to her.'

'She's good,' Rebus conceded. 'She's very good. And now she's back in London.'

'We've no proof ... not a shred of evidence.'

'True, up to a point. But when you listen to Duncan Barclay's tape, you'll hear him say she was in Kelso last year, asking around. She even spoke to him. He mentioned Trevor Guest to her. Trevor with his housebreaker's credentials. Trevor who was in the area, same time Mrs Webster was killed.' Rebus gave a shrug, to let her know he had no trouble accepting any of this. 'All three were attacked from behind, Siobhan, whacked hard so they couldn't retaliate – just the way a woman would do it.' He paused. 'Then there's her name. Gilreagh said there could be something significant about trees.'

'Stacey's not the name of a tree.'

He shook his head. 'But Santal is. It means sandalwood. I always thought sandalwood was just a perfume. Turns out it's a tree ...' He shook his head in wonder at Stacey Webster's intricate construction. 'And she left Guest's cash card,' he concluded, 'because she wanted to be sure we'd have his name ... leading us by the nose. A bloody smokescreen, just like Gilreagh said.'

Siobhan was studying the board again, probing the schematic for flaws. 'So what happened to Ben?' she asked at last.

'I can tell you what I think ...'

'Go on then.' She folded her arms.

'Guards at the Castle thought there was an intruder. My guess is, it was Stacey. She knew her brother was there, and was bursting to tell him. We'd found the patch – she'd probably heard about that from Steelforth. Reckoned it was time to share news of her exploits with her brother. As far as she was concerned, Guest's death meant closure. And by Christ, she'd made sure he paid for his crimes – mutilating his body. She relishes the challenge of sneaking past the guards. Maybe she's sent him a message, so he comes out to meet her. She tells him everything ...'

'And he tops himself?'

Rebus scratched the back of his head. 'I think she's the only one who can tell us. In fact, if we play it right, Ben's going to be crucial in getting a confession. Think how hellish she must be feeling – that's her whole family gone now, and the one thing she thought would bring her and Ben closer together has actually destroyed him. And it's all her fault.'

'She did a pretty good job of hiding it.'

'Behind all those masks she wears,' Rebus agreed. 'All these warring sides to her personality ...'

'Steady,' Siobhan warned. 'You're starting to sound like Gilreagh.'

He burst out laughing, but stopped just as abruptly and scratched at his head again, eventually running the hand through his hair. 'Do you think it holds up?'

Siobhan puffed out her cheeks and exhaled loudly. 'I need to give it a bit more thought,' she conceded. 'I mean ... scrawled on a board like this, I can see it makes a kind of sense. I just don't see how we'll prove any of it.'

'We start with what happened to Ben.'

'Fine, but if she denies it, we're left with nothing. You've just said so yourself, John, she wears all these masks. Nothing to stop her slipping one on when we start asking about her brother.'

'One way to find out,' Rebus said. He was holding Stacey Webster's business card, the one with her mobile number.

'Think for a minute,' Siobhan counselled. 'Soon as you call her, you're giving her advance warning.'

'Then we go to London.'

'And hope Steelforth lets us talk to her?'

Rebus considered for a moment. 'Yes,' he said quietly, 'Steelforth ... Funny how quickly he knocked her back to London, isn't it? Almost as if he knew we were getting close.'

'You think he *knew*?'

'There was CCTV at the Castle. He told me there was nothing to see, but now I'm wondering.'

'There's no way he's going to let us go public,' Siobhan argued. 'One of his officers turns out to be a killer, and might even have done away with her own brother. Not exactly the PR he's looking for.'

'Which is why he might be willing to do a deal.'

'And what exactly have we got to offer?'

'Control,' Rebus stated. 'We step back and let him do it his way. If he turns us down, we go to Mairie Henderson.'

Siobhan spent the best part of a minute considering the options. Then she saw Rebus's eyes widen.

'And we don't even have to go to London,' he told her.

'Why not?'

'Because Steelforth's not in London.'

'Then where is he?'

'Under our bloody noses,' Rebus explained, starting to wipe the board clean.

By which he meant: an hour's rapid drive to the west.

They spent the whole trip going through Rebus's theory. Trevor Guest hightailing it out of Newcastle – maybe owing money on some deal. Quick route to the handily anonymous border country. Scratches around, but can't find a fix, and hasn't any money. His one area of expertise: burglary. But Mrs Webster is home, and he ends up killing her. Panics and flees to Edinburgh, where he assuages his guilt by working with the elderly, with people like the woman he murdered. Not sexually assaulted – he liked them a lot younger.

Meanwhile, Stacey Webster is destroyed by her mother's murder, heartbroken when the death destroys her father too. Using her detectives' skills to track down the likely culprit, only he's already behind bars. But due out soon. Giving her time to plan her revenge. She's found Guest on BeastWatch, alongside others like him. She picks her targets geographically – easy reach of her undercover assignments. Her counterculture existence gives her access to heroin. Does she get Guest to confess before she murders him? It doesn't really matter: by then she's already killed Eddie Isley. Adds one more, to reinforce the notion that a serial killer is at large, then stops. Sated and at peace. Far as she's concerned, she's been cleaning scum off the streets. SO12's G8 planning has led her to the Clootie Well, and she knows it's the perfect spot. *Someone* will happen upon it. And they'll spot the clues. To be certain, she ensures they have one name straight away ... the only name that matters.

No way she's going to be found.

The perfect crime.

Nearly ...

'I have to admit,' Siobhan said, 'it sounds plausible.'

'That's because it's what happened. Thing about the truth, Siobhan: it almost always makes sense.'

They made good time along the M8, and got on to the A82. The village of Luss was just off the main road on the western shore of Loch Lomond.

'They used to film *Take the High Road* here,' Rebus informed his passenger.

'One of the few soaps I've never watched.'

Cars were crawling past them on the other side of the road.

'Looks like play's finished for today,' Siobhan commented. 'Might have to come back tomorrow.'

But Rebus wasn't about to concede defeat. Loch Lomond Golf Club was a members-only facility, and the arrival of the Open had brought with it extra security. There were guards on the main gate, and they checked both Rebus's and Siobhan's ID carefully, before phoning on ahead, during which time a mirror on a long stick was played along the length of the car's undercarriage.

'After Thursday, we're taking no chances,' the guard

explained, handing back their warrant cards. 'Ask at the clubhouse for Commander Steelforth.'

'Thanks,' Rebus said. 'By the way ... who's winning?'

'It's a tie – Tim Clark and Maarten Lafeber, fifteen under. Tim shot six under today. Monty's nicely placed though – ten under. Be a cracker tomorrow.'

Rebus thanked the guard again and put the Saab into gear. 'Did you catch any of that?' he asked Siobhan.

'I know "Monty" means Colin Montgomerie ...'

'Then you're every bit as well informed about the royal and ancient game as I am.'

'You've never tried?'

He shook his head. 'It's those pastel jumpers ... I could never see myself wearing one.'

As they parked and climbed out, half a dozen spectators walked past, discussing the day's events. One wore a pink V-neck, the others yellow or pale orange or sky blue.

'See what I mean?' Rebus said. Siobhan nodded her agreement.

The clubhouse was Scots baronial and called Rossdhu. There was a silver Merc parked up alongside, the chauffeur snoozing in the front seat. Rebus remembered him from Gleneagles – Steelforth's designated driver.

'Cheers, Big Man,' he said, raising his eyes to the heavens.

A short, bespectacled gent with a highly developed moustache and sense of his own importance was striding out of the building towards them. All manner of laminated passes and ID cards were strung around his neck, clacking together as he moved. He barked out a word which sounded like 'sekty' but which Rebus chose to translate as secretary. The bony hand which shook Rebus's was trying too hard. But at least he *got* a handshake; Siobhan might as well have been a shrub.

'We need to speak to Commander David Steelforth,' Rebus explained. 'I doubt he's the type to rub shoulders with the unwashed masses.'

'Steelforth?' The Secretary took off his glasses and rubbed them against the sleeve of his crimson jumper. 'Could he be corporate?'

'That's his driver,' Rebus said, nodding towards the Merc.

Siobhan chipped in: 'Pennen Industries?'

The Secretary slipped his glasses back on, and directed his reply at Rebus. 'Oh yes, Mr Pennen has a hospitality tent.' He glanced at his wristwatch. 'Probably winding down by now.'

'Mind if we check?'

The Secretary's face twitched and he told them to wait, before disappearing back into the building. Rebus looked at Siobhan, awaiting some comment.

'Officious twerp,' she obliged.

'You won't be wanting an application form?'

'Have you *seen* any women since we got here?'

Rebus looked around before admitting she had a point. He turned at the sound of an electric motor. It was a golf cart, emerging from behind Rossdhu House and driven by the Secretary.

'Hop on,' he told them.

'Can't we walk?' Rebus asked.

The Secretary shook his head and repeated the instruction. There were two rear-facing cushioned seats at the back of the cart.

'Lucky you're small-boned,' Rebus told Siobhan. The Secretary was ordering them to hold on tight. The machine clunked into action at a rate just above walking speed.

'Whee,' Siobhan said, managing to look underwhelmed.

'Reckon the Chief Constable's a golf fan?' Rebus asked.

'Probably.'

'The luck we've had this week, we'll be passing him any moment.'

But they didn't. The course itself was home to only a

few last stragglers. The stands were vacant, and the sun was setting.

'Amazing,' Siobhan was forced to admit, as she stared across Loch Lomond to the mountains beyond.

'Takes me back to my youth,' Rebus told her.

'Did you come here on holiday?'

He shook his head. 'But the neighbours did, and they always sent a postcard.' Swivelling round as best he could, he saw they were approaching a village of tents with its own cordon and security. White marquees, piped music and the sounds of loud conversation. The Secretary slowed the cart to a stop and nodded towards one of the larger tents. It had clear plastic windows and liveried serving staff. Champagne was being poured, oysters offered from silver salvers.

'Thanks for the lift,' Rebus said.

'Shall I wait?'

Rebus shook his head. 'We'll find our own way, sir. Thanks again.'

'Lothian and Borders,' Rebus stated to the guards, opening his warrant card.

'Your Chief Constable's in the champagne tent,' one of the guards replied helpfully. Rebus gave Siobhan a look. That kind of week ... He picked up a glass of fizz and worked his way through the throng. Thought he recognised some of the faces from Prestonfield – G8 delegates; people Richard Pennen wanted to do business with. The Kenyan diplomat, Joseph Kamweze, met Rebus's gaze but turned away quickly, pushing deeper into the crowd.

'Quite the United Nations,' Siobhan commented. Eyes were appraising her: not too many women on show. But the ones who were ... well, 'on show' summed it up: cascading hair, short, tight dresses and fixed smiles. They would describe themselves as 'models' rather than 'escorts', hired by the day to add glamour and sunbed tan to proceedings.

'Should have smartened yourself up,' Rebus scolded Siobhan. 'Bit of make-up never goes amiss.'

'Listen to Karl Lagerfeld,' she retorted.

Rebus tapped her shoulder. 'Our host.' He gave a nod in the direction of Richard Pennen. Same immaculate hair, glinting cufflinks, heavy gold wristwatch. But something had changed. The face seemed less bronzed, the posture less confident. When Pennen laughed at something his companion was saying, he threw his head back a little too far, mouth open too wide. Faking it, obviously. His companion seemed to think so too, and studied Pennen, wondering what to make of him. Pennen's flunkeys – one per shoulder as at Prestonfield – also looked nervous at their boss's inability to play the game as before. Rebus thought for a moment of walking right up to him and asking how things were, just for the pleasure of getting a reaction. But Siobhan had placed a hand on his arm, directing his attention elsewhere:

David Steelforth, emerging from the champagne tent, deep in conversation with Chief Constable James Corbyn.

'Bugger,' Rebus said. Then, after a deep breath: 'In for a pound ...'

He could feel Siobhan hesitate, and turned towards her. 'Maybe you should go walkabout for a few minutes.'

But she'd come to her decision, and actually led the way towards the two men.

'Sorry to interrupt,' she was saying as Rebus caught up.

'What the hell are you two doing here?' Corbyn spluttered.

'Never one to dodge free bubbly,' Rebus explained, raising his glass. 'Expect that's your reasoning too, sir.'

Corbyn's face had reddened mightily. 'I was *invited*.'

'Us too, sir,' Siobhan said, 'in a manner of speaking.'

'How's that?' Steelforth asked, looking amused.

'Murder inquiry, sir,' Rebus said. 'Tends to act as a VIP pass.'

'VVIP,' Siobhan corrected him.

'You're saying Ben Webster was murdered?' Steelforth asked, eyes on Rebus.

'Not quite,' Rebus answered. 'But we've an inkling *why* he died. And it seems to connect to the Clootie Well.' He shifted his gaze to Corbyn. 'We can fill you in later, sir, but right now it's Commander Steelforth we need to talk to.'

'I'm sure it can wait,' Corbyn snapped.

Rebus turned back to Steelforth, who offered another smile, this time for Corbyn's benefit.

'I think I'd better listen to what the Inspector and his colleague have to say.'

'Very well,' the Chief Constable relented. 'Fire away.'

Rebus paused, exchanging a glance with Siobhan. Steelforth was quick to catch on. He made a show of handing his untouched glass to Corbyn.

'I'll be right back, Chief Constable. I'm sure your officers will explain everything to you in due course ...'

'They'd better,' Corbyn stressed, eyes boring into Siobhan. Steelforth patted his arm reassuringly and walked away, Rebus and Siobhan close behind. When all three reached the low white picket fence, they stopped. Steelforth faced away from the crowd, towards the course, where groundsmen were hard at work replacing divots and raking bunkers. He slid his hands into his pockets.

'What is it you think you know?' he asked nonchalantly.

'I think *you* know,' Rebus answered. 'When I mentioned the link between Webster and the Clootie Well, you didn't blink. Makes me think you already suspected something. Stacey Webster's your officer, after all. You probably like to keep tabs on her ... maybe started wondering why she was making sorties north to places like Newcastle and Carlisle. Also makes me wonder what you saw on the CCTV film that night at the Castle.'

'Spit it out,' Steelforth hissed.

Siobhan took over. 'We think Stacey Webster is our serial killer. She wanted Trevor Guest, but was prepared to kill two more men to hide the fact.'

'And when she went to tell her brother the news,' Rebus continued, 'well, he didn't take it well. Maybe he jumped; maybe he was appalled and threatened to go public ... she decided he had to be silenced.' He gave a shrug.

'Fanciful stuff,' Steelforth commented, still not looking at either of them. 'Being good detectives, you'll have put together a watertight case?'

'Should be easy enough, now we know what we're looking for,' Rebus told him. 'Of course, it'll be damaging for SO12 ...'

Steelforth gave a twitch of the mouth, turned a hundred and eighty degrees to watch the feasting. 'Until about an hour ago,' he drawled, 'I'd have told the pair of you to go fuck yourselves. Know why?'

'Pennen offered you a job,' Rebus said. Steelforth raised an eyebrow. 'Educated guess,' Rebus explained. 'It's *him* you've been protecting throughout. Must've been a reason for it.'

Steelforth nodded slowly. 'It so happens you're right.'

'But you've changed your mind?' Siobhan added.

'You just need to look at him. It's all crumbling to dust, isn't it?'

'Like a statue in the desert,' Siobhan commented, eyes on Rebus.

'Monday, I was tendering my resignation,' Steelforth said ruefully. 'Special Branch could have gone to hell.'

'Some might say it already has,' Rebus stated, 'when one of its operatives is allowed to slaughter left and right ...'

Steelforth was still staring at Richard Pennen. 'Funny the way it sometimes works ... it's the tiniest flaws that bring a structure down.'

'Like Al Capone,' Siobhan added helpfully. 'They only got him for tax evasion, didn't they?'

Steelforth ignored her, and turned his attention to Rebus instead. 'The CCTV wasn't conclusive,' he admitted.

'It showed Ben Webster meeting someone?'

'Ten minutes after he took a call on his mobile.'

'Do we need to check the phone company records, or shall we assume it was Stacey?'

'As I say, the CCTV wasn't conclusive.'

'So what *did* it show?'

Steelforth gave a shrug. 'Two people talking . . . a lot of arm waving . . . obviously arguing about something. Ended with one grabbing the other. Difficult to see though, and it was pretty dark . . .'

'And?'

'Then there was only one.' Steelforth locked eyes with Rebus. 'In that instant, I think he wanted it to happen.'

There was silence for a moment, broken by Siobhan. 'And you'd have swept it all under the carpet, so as not to make a fuss . . . just like you've dispatched Stacey Webster to London.'

'Yes, well . . . good luck discussing that with DS Webster.'

'What do you mean?'

He turned towards her. 'She's not been heard of since Wednesday. Seems she boarded the night train to Euston.'

Siobhan's eyes narrowed. 'The London bombings?'

'Be a miracle if we ID'd every victim.'

'Bollocks to that,' Rebus said, pressing his face close to Steelforth's. 'You're hiding her!'

Steelforth gave a laugh. 'You *do* see conspiracies everywhere, don't you, Rebus?'

'You knew what she'd done. Bombs were the perfect cover for her to vanish!'

Steelforth's face hardened. 'She's *gone*,' he said. 'So go ahead and compile any evidence you can find – somehow I doubt it'll get you anywhere.'

'It'll dump a trailer-load of dung on your head,' Rebus warned.

'Will it?' Steelforth's jaw jutted out, barely an inch from Rebus's face. 'Good for the land, though, isn't it, the occasional bit of manure? Now, if you'll excuse me, I'm going to get absolutely bladdered at Richard Pennen's expense.' He strode away from them, removing his hands from his pockets so he could take his glass back from Corbyn. The Chief Constable said something, and gestured towards the two Lothian and Borders detectives. Steelforth just shook his head, then leaned a little towards Corbyn and said something which caused the Chief Constable to arch his neck, presaging a loud – and entirely genuine – guffaw.

'What kind of result is that?' Siobhan asked, not for the first time. They were back in Edinburgh, seated in a bar on Broughton Street, just around the corner from her flat.

'Hand those photos from the Princes Street Gardens over,' Rebus told her, 'and your little skinhead friend might get the custodial sentence he deserves.'

She stared at him and gave a wild, humourless laugh. 'Is that it? Four men dead because of Stacey Webster, and we've got *that*?'

'We've got our health,' Rebus reminded her. 'And the whole bar listening in on us.'

Eyes turned away as she strafed the clientele. Four gin and tonics she'd had so far, to Rebus's pint and three Laphroaigs. They were seated in a booth. The bar was busy and had been relatively noisy until she'd started mentioning multiple murders, a suspicious death, a stabbing, sex offenders, George Bush, Special Branch, the Princes Street riots, and Bianca Jagger.

'We've still got to put the case together,' Rebus reminded her. She responded by blowing a raspberry.

'What good will that do?' she queried. 'Can't prove anything.'

'Plenty of circumstantial.'

This time she merely snorted and started counting on her fingers. 'Richard Pennen, SO12, the government, Cafferty, Gareth Tench, a serial killer, the G8 ... looked for a little while like they all connected. They *do* all connect when you start to think of it!' She was holding up seven fingers in front of his face. When he didn't respond, she lowered them and seemed to be studying him. 'How can you be so calm about it?'

'Who said I'm calm?'

'You're bottling it up then.'

'I've had a bit of practice.'

'Not me.' She shook her head extravagantly. 'Something like this happens, I want to shout it from the rooftops.'

'I'd say the first steps have already been taken.'

She was staring at her half-full glass. 'And Ben Webster's death had nothing to do with Richard Pennen?'

'Nothing,' Rebus conceded.

'But it's destroyed him too, hasn't it?'

He just nodded. She muttered something he didn't catch. He asked her to repeat it, so she did.

'No gods, no masters. I've been mulling it over since Monday. I mean, supposing it's true ... who do we look up to? Who's running the show?'

'I'm not sure I can answer that, Siobhan.'

She gave a twitch of the mouth, as though he had confirmed some sort of suspicion. Her phone sounded, alerting her to a message. She glanced at the screen, but did nothing about it.

'You're popular tonight,' Rebus pointed out. She gave a shake of the head in reply. 'If I had to guess, I'd say it's Cafferty.'

She glowered at him. 'So what if it is?'

'You might want to change your number.'

She nodded agreement. 'But only after I've sent him a nice long text telling him exactly what I think of him.' She looked around the table. 'Is it my shout?' she asked.

'I thought maybe some food ...'

'Didn't you have enough of Pennen's oysters?'

'Hardly a meal of substance.'

'There's a curry-house up the street.'

'I know.'

'Course you do, you've been here all your life.'

'Most of it,' he agreed.

'Never known a week like this one, though,' she challenged him.

'Never,' he conceded. 'Now drink up and we'll go get that curry.'

She nodded, her hands gripping her glass vice-like. 'My mum and dad were in that Indian on Wednesday night. I got there in time for coffee ...'

'You can always go see them in London.'

'Just wondering how much longer they'll be around.' Her eyes were glistening. 'Is this what it's like to be Scottish, John? A few drinks to make you maudlin?'

'We do seem cursed,' he admitted, 'to be always looking back.'

'And then you go and join CID, which only makes it worse. People die, and we look back into their lives ... and we can't change anything.' She tried lifting her glass, but its mass defeated her.

'We could go give Keith Carberry a kicking,' Rebus suggested.

She nodded slowly.

'Or Big Ger Cafferty, come to that ... or anyone else we felt like. There's two of us.' He leaned forward a little, trying for eye contact. 'Two against nature.'

She gave him a sly look. 'Song lyric?' she guessed.

'Album title: Steely Dan.'

'Tell you what I've always wondered.' She slouched against the back of the booth. 'How did they get their name?'

'I'll tell you when you're sober,' Rebus offered, draining his glass.

He could feel eyes following them as he helped her to her feet and out of the bar. There was a sharp breeze and a smattering of rain. 'Maybe we should go back to yours,' he suggested. 'We can phone out for food.'

'I'm not *that* drunk!'

'Fair enough, then.' They started the steep uphill climb, side by side, not saying anything. Saturday night, the town back to normal: souped-up teenagers in their souped-up cars; money looking for a place to spend itself; the diesel chug of cruising taxi-cabs. At some point, Siobhan snaked her arm through his, said something he didn't catch.

'It's not enough, is it?' she repeated. 'Just ... symbolic ... because there's nothing else you can do.'

'What are you talking about?' he asked with a smile.

'The naming of the dead,' she told him, resting her head against his shoulder.

Epilogue

Monday morning he was on the first train south. Left Waverley at six, due into King's Cross just after ten. At eight, he called Gayfield Square and told them he was sick, which wasn't so far from the truth. If they'd asked him the cause, he might have had some problems.

'Spending the overtime,' was all the duty sergeant said.

Rebus went to the restaurant car and ate his fill of breakfast. Back at his seat, he read the paper and tried to avoid his fellow passengers. There was a surly-looking youth across the table, nodding along to the guitar music leaking from his earphones. Businesswoman next to him, annoyed that she didn't have enough room to spread out the contents of her office. Nobody in the seat next to Rebus – not until York. He hadn't been on the train in years. Busy with tourists and their baggage, mewling infants, holidaymakers, workers heading back to their weekday jobs in London. After York came Doncaster and Peterborough. The pudgy man who'd settled down in his reserved seat next to Rebus had drifted off to sleep, after pointing out that really he'd booked the window seat, but didn't mind the aisle if Rebus didn't want to shift.

'Fine,' was all Rebus had said.

The newsagent's at Waverley had opened only a few minutes before the train was due to leave, but Rebus had managed to grab a *Scotsman*. Mairie's piece had made the front page. It wasn't the main story, and it was full of words like 'alleged' and 'perhaps' and 'potentially', but the headline still gladdened Rebus's heart:

ARMS BOSS IN PARLIAMENT LOANS MYSTERY.

Rebus knew an opening salvo when he saw one; Mairie would be holding back plenty of ammo for the future.

He'd brought no luggage with him; fully intended being on the last train back. There was the option to upgrade to a sleeper compartment, and it might even come to that – a chance to question the crew, see if any of them had worked the sleeper south from Edinburgh on Wednesday. Rebus had, it seemed, been the last person to see Stacey Webster – unless the GNER staff could oblige. If he'd followed her to Waverley that night, he could have satisfied himself that she'd actually taken the train. As it was, she could be anywhere – including tucked away somewhere until Steelforth could arrange a new identity for her.

Rebus doubted she'd have any trouble picking up a new life. It had dawned on him last night: all those multiple personalities of hers: cop, Santal, sister, killer. Bloody quadrophenic, just like the Who album said. On Sunday, Kenny, Mickey's son, had arrived at the flat in his BMW, telling Rebus there was something for him on the back seat. Rebus had gone to look – albums, tapes and CDs, 45s ... Mickey's entire collection.

'They were in the will,' Kenny had explained. 'Dad wanted you to have them.'

After they'd hauled the whole lot up two flights of stairs, and Kenny had rested long enough for a glass of water, Rebus had waved him goodbye and stared at the gift. Then he'd eased himself down on to the floor beside the boxes and started going through them: a mono *Sergeant Pepper*, *Let It Bleed* with the Ned Kelly poster, a lot of Kinks and Taste and Free ... some Van Der Graaf and Steve Hillage. There were even a couple of eight-track cartridges – *Killer* by Alice Cooper; a Beach Boys album. A treasure trove of memories. Rebus placed the sleeves beneath his nose – the very smell of them took him back in time. Warped Hollies singles, left too long on the turntable after a party

... a copy of 'Silver Machine' with Mickey's writing on it – 'This Belongs to Michael Rebus – Paws Off!!!'

And *Quadrophenia*, of course, its corners creased, the vinyl scarred but still playable.

Sitting on the train, Rebus remembered Stacey's last words to him: *Never told him you were sorry ...* Just before she'd bolted to the toilet. He'd thought she'd been talking about Mickey, but now realised she was meaning her and Ben, too. Sorry she'd killed three men? Sorry she'd gone and told her brother? Ben realising he would have to turn her in, feeling the thick stone rampart behind him, sensing the drop immediately behind it ... Rebus thought of Cafferty's memoirs – *Changeling*. Decided it was a title most people could use for their own autobiographies. People you knew, they might always look the same on the surface – a few grey hairs or a thickening around the middle – but you could never tell what was going on behind their eyes.

It was Doncaster before his phone rang, waking his softly snoring neighbour. The number was Siobhan's. Rebus ignored it, so she sent a text, which – newspaper finished and countryside boring – he eventually opened.

Where r u? Corbyn wants 2 talk 2 us. Need 2 tell him sth. Call me.

He knew he couldn't, not from the train – she'd guess where he was headed. To delay the inevitable, he waited half an hour and texted a reply.

In bed not well talk later

Hadn't mastered any of the punctuation. She texted straight back:

Hangover?

Loch lomond oysters, he responded.

Switched the phone off to save its battery, then closed his eyes, just as the conductor announced that London King's Cross would be the 'next and final station stop'.

'Next and final,' the loudspeaker repeated.

There had been an announcement earlier concerning tube station closures. The stern-faced businesswoman had consulted her map of the underground, holding it close to her so as not to share the information. On the outskirts of London, Rebus recognised a few of the local stations as the train trundled through them. The regular travellers began putting away their things, getting to their feet. The businesswoman's laptop went back into her shoulder-bag, along with her files and papers, diary and map. The pudgy man next to Rebus rose to his feet with a bow, as if they had shared some lengthy, heartfelt conversation. Rebus, in no real hurry, was one of the last to leave the train, and had to squeeze past the cleaning crew on his way out.

London was hotter, stickier than Edinburgh. His jacket felt too heavy. He exited the station on foot, no need for a taxi or tube train. Lit a cigarette and let the traffic noise and fumes wash over him. Blew a ring of smoke back at it all and took a sheet of paper from his pocket. It was a map, lifted from an A–Z and provided by Commander David Steelforth. Rebus had called him on Sunday afternoon, explained that they'd be taking things easy on the Clootie Well killings, and would consult him about their findings before handing the case over to the Procurator Fiscal – if it ever came to that.

'All right,' Steelforth had said, properly wary. Background noise: Edinburgh airport; the Commander heading home. Rebus on the other end of the line, having just fed him a sack of crap, and now asking for a favour.

Result: a name, an address, and a street-map.

Steelforth had even apologised for Pennen's goons. Their orders had been to watch him; harassment never part of the brief. 'Only found out about it afterwards,' Steelforth had said. 'You think you can control men like that ...'

Control ...

Rebus picturing Councillor Tench again, trying to

manage an entire community, unable to alter his own destiny.

Less than an hour's walk, Rebus had estimated. And not a bad day for it. One of the bombs had gone off on a tube train between King's Cross and Russell Square, another on a bus heading from Euston to Russell Square. All three were on the map he held in his hands. The sleeper would have arrived at Euston around seven that morning.

8.50 a.m. – the tube blast.

9.47 a.m. – the bus blast.

Rebus couldn't believe Stacey Webster had been near either of them. The train conductor had assured them they were lucky: past three days, the service had been terminating at Finsbury Park. Rebus could hardly have said that Finsbury Park would have done just as well …

Cafferty was alone in the pool hall. He didn't even look up when Siobhan walked in, not until he'd played his shot. It was an attempt at a double.

And it missed.

He walked around the table, chalking his cue. Blew away some excess powder from the tip.

'You've got all the moves,' Siobhan told him. He gave a grunt and lowered himself over the cue.

Missed again.

'And yet you're still lousy,' she added. 'Just about sums you up really.'

'Good morning to you too, Detective Sergeant Clarke. Is this a social call?'

'Does it *feel* like a social call?'

Cafferty glanced up at her. 'You've been ignoring my little messages.'

'Get used to it.'

'Doesn't change what happened.'

'And what exactly *did* happen?'

He seemed to consider the question for a moment. 'We

both got something we wanted?' he pretended to guess. 'Except now you're feeling guilty.' He rested the cue against the floor. 'We both got something we wanted,' he repeated.

'I didn't want Gareth Tench dead.'

'You wanted him punished.'

She took a couple of steps towards him. 'Don't try to pretend any of this was for my benefit.'

Cafferty made a tutting sound. 'You need to start enjoying these little victories, Siobhan. Life doesn't offer too many, in my experience.'

'I screwed up, Cafferty, but I'm a quick learner. You've had a bit of fun down the years with John Rebus, but from now on you've got another enemy breathing down your neck.'

Cafferty chuckled. 'And that's you, is it?' He leaned against the cue. 'But you have to admit, Siobhan, we made a pretty good team. Imagine how we could run the city between us – information exchanged, tip-offs and trades ... Me going about my business and you swiftly climbing that promotion ladder. Isn't that what we both want, when it comes down to it?'

'What I want,' Siobhan said quietly, 'is to have nothing to do with you until I'm standing in the witness box and you're in the dock.'

'Good luck with that,' Cafferty said with another low chuckle. He turned his attention back to the table. 'Want to thrash me at pool in the meantime? I was never any good at this bloody game ...'

But when he turned around, she was heading for the door.

'Siobhan!' he called to her. 'Remember the two of us? Upstairs in the office here? And the way that little toerag Carberry started squirming? I saw it in your eyes ...'

She'd pulled the door open, but couldn't resist the question. 'Saw what, Cafferty?'

'You were starting to like it.' He ran his tongue around his lips. 'I'd say you were definitely starting to like it.'

His laughter followed her out into the daylight.

Pentonville Road and then Upper Street ... further than he thought. He stopped at a café opposite Highbury and Islington tube, ate a sandwich and flicked through the first edition of the day's *Evening Standard*. Nobody in the café was speaking English, and when he placed his order they struggled with his accent. Good sandwich, though ...

He could feel blisters forming on the soles of both feet as he headed back outside again. Turning off St Paul's Road into Highbury Grove. Opposite some tennis courts he found the street he was looking for. Found the block he wanted. Found the flat number and its buzzer. No name next to it, but he pressed it anyway.

No reply.

Checked his watch, then pushed the other buzzers until someone answered.

'Yeah?' the voice crackled from the intercom.

'Parcel for number nine,' Rebus said.

'This is Flat Sixteen.'

'Thought maybe I could leave it with you.'

'Well you can't.'

'Outside their door, then?'

The voice swore, but the buzzer sounded and Rebus was in. Up the stairs to the door of Flat 9. It boasted a spy-hole. He pressed his ear to the wood. Took a step back and studied it. Solid door, with half a dozen locks and a steel plate around the rim.

'Who lives in a place like this?' Rebus asked himself quietly. 'David, it's over to you ...' The catchphrase from a TV show called *Through the Keyhole*. Difference was, Rebus knew exactly who lived here: information gleaned by – and from – David Steelforth. Rebus rapped at the door half-heartedly, then headed back downstairs again. Tore the lid from his cigarette packet and wedged it in the main door, so it couldn't lock. Then went outside and waited.

He was good at waiting.

There were a dozen residents' parking bays, each one protected by a vertical metal pole. The silver-coloured Porsche Cayenne came to a stop while its owner got out and undid the padlock on the pole, laying it flat so he could manoeuvre into the space. He was whistling contentedly as he walked around the car, giving its tyres a kick because that was what blokes did. He rubbed his sleeve over a spot of dirt and tossed his keys in the air, snatching them and returning them to his pocket. Another bunch of keys emerged, and he sought the one that would unlock the main door to the block. He seemed bemused that the door wasn't fully closed. Then his face smashed into it as he was propelled from behind, through the door and into the stairwell, Rebus not giving him any sort of a chance. Grabbed him by the hair and pummelled the face into the grey concrete wall, smearing blood across it. A knee in the back and Jacko was on the ground, dazed and semiconscious. A rabbit punch to the neck and another punch to the jaw. The first for me, Rebus thought, the second for Mairie Henderson.

Rebus stared closely at the man's face. Scar tissue, but well fed. He'd been ex-army for a while, growing fat courtesy of the private sector. The eyes glazed over and then slowly closed. Rebus waited a moment, in case it was a trick. Jacko's whole body had gone limp. Rebus made sure he still had a pulse and his airways weren't blocked. Then he yanked the man's hands behind his back and secured them with the plastic restraints he'd brought.

Secured them nice and tight.

Climbed to his feet, took the car keys from Jacko's pocket, and headed back outside, checking no one was watching. Over to the Porsche, where he scored one side of the bodywork with the ignition key before opening the driver's-side door. Slotted the key home and left the door open invitingly. Paused a moment to catch his breath, and then headed for the main road again. Any passing taxi or bus, he'd take it. Five o'clock train from King's Cross would see him back in Edinburgh before closing time. He had a GNER open return – could have flown to Ibiza for less. But it meant he could catch any train he liked.

He had unfinished business at home, too.

His luck was in: a black cab with its yellow roof-light shining. In the back, Rebus reached into his pocket. He'd told the cabbie Euston – knew it was a short walk from there to King's Cross. He took out a sheet of paper and a roll of Sellotape. Unfolded the sheet and studied it – crude but to the point. Two photos of Santal/Stacey: one from Siobhan's cameraman friend, the other from an old newspaper. Above them in thick black pen the single word MISSING, underlined twice. Below, Rebus's sixth and final attempt at a credible message:

My two friends, Santal and Stacey, missing since the bombs. Arrived at Euston that morning on night-train from Edinburgh. If you have seen them or have any news, please call me. Need to know they are safe and well.

No name at the bottom, just his mobile number. And half a dozen copies in his other pocket. He'd already flagged her up as a missing person with the Police National Computer: both identities; height, age and eye colour; a few background snippets. Next week, her description would go out to the homeless charities, the *Big Issue* sellers. When Eric Bain was out of hospital, Rebus would ask him about websites. Maybe they could even set up one of their own. If she was out there, she was traceable. No way Rebus would be giving up on this one.

Not for a good while yet.

Acknowledgements

There is no Clootie Well in Auchterarder. However, the one on the Black Isle is worth a visit, if you like your tourist attractions on the skin-crawling side.

There is also no Ram's Head in Coldstream, though a decent steak pie can be had at the Besom public house.

My thanks to Dave Henderson for the extended loan of his photographic archive, and to Jonathan Emmans for the introduction.

Rebus's joke about Basque separatists is 'borrowed' (with permission) from Peter Ross of the *Sunday Herald* news-paper.